SOUTH OF HAPPILY

G.A. ANDERSON

Black Rose Writing | Texas

The author grants the final approval for this literary material.

First printing

ISBN: 978-1-68513-104-3
PUBLISHED BY BLACK ROSE WRITING
www.blackrosewriting.com

Printed in the United States of America
Suggested Retail Price (SRP) $22.95

South of Happily is printed in Sabon

*As a planet-friendly publisher, Black Rose Writing does its best to eliminate unnecessary waste to reduce paper usage and energy costs, while never compromising the reading experience. As a result, the final word count vs. page count may not meet common expectations.

To my dad, Andrew Robert Reich.
This is how I keep you close.
Amig újra nem találkozunk

SOUTH OF HAPPILY

CHAPTER 1
CHEESE PUFF

The seagulls battle over a cheese puff on the sidewalk. They shriek, thrash their wings, and rip it to shreds. I step over the scattering of orange rubble left behind. Poor cheese puff, it reminds me of my marriage.

I'm three minutes early for my appointment with Jesse. Jessica Tanner, Attorney at Law. She was my best friend from freshman year of college until the day I married the blue-eyed Floridian. On that day, when the circle of loving family and friends should have expanded, mine shriveled. And with it went Jesse, who receded into the shadows of my former life.

The familiar grumble of her voice answers my knock, and I step into her cramped office. In front of the only window, slivers of sunlight stream around the edges of a dented vertical file and bathe the room in a dim yellow glow. Pop cans stuffed with bouquets of spent cigarettes decorate her desk.

"Been a while," she says, brushing pretzel crumbs off her silk shirt. "I've heard rumors about you here and there, and saw you hide from me at the grocery store." The chair creaks under her weight as she follows my movement into the room.

"I wasn't hiding," I tell her, though I was. Like an ostrich with its head in the sand, the rest of it exposed in its inability to negotiate a good friendship while having a bad marriage. And the rumors aren't here or there, they're everywhere, because Dufferin Beach is a small town, one communal body with gossip effectively moving through capillaries, arteries, all the connective tissue.

"It wasn't you, ducking out of the produce section?" she asks.

I shrug. "I dunno."

"Yes, it was." She pulls on the sleeves of her Ann Taylor suit, Big and Tall for her six-foot frame. "Nobody else squashes five pounds of hair into a fuzzy pink elastic band."

"Where was I standing?" I tug on my five pounds of hair.

"By the lemons. And your jeans had white handprints on them."

"It was flour. I didn't see you."

"Sure you didn't. So, what can I do for you? Need an exterminator for the walking-talking flea infestation you vowed to honor and obey?"

I lean away from her anger and think back to my wedding day when I should have felt happy and blessed like the brides gushing on Facebook and Say Yes to the Dress. All I remember is feeling like I'd eaten some bad shrimp. And my parents' faces; Dad smiling in that odd way that wasn't really a smile, and Mom crying in that odd way that was more of an anxiety attack.

"I screwed up, Jesse. I'm sorry."

She nods, pushes away the bag of pretzels and begins asking lawyer questions. Has he been unfaithful, abusive, drinking, drugging? She has no interest in marital reconciliation, no intention to mediate. She's the endgame.

"I'm not conflicted about this. I want out."

"Out is easy," she says. "It's the how and what you want that causes all the trouble. I assume you're not pregnant?"

I run my hand over my belly. Pretty flat with fewer curves now than the day I was born.

"No babies for the foreseeable future. I'd like my life back. And the house. And my maiden name."

"House, freedom, no baby. Easy enough. I'm expensive, Katy Kiss."

"I can pay your fee, even if you charge extra because you hate me now."

"I don't hate you. I hate the shit you do. We're not going to talk about it."

"Okay," I mumble. "Not talking about it."

"What about Dylan? I'm guessing money will be an issue based on his glowing reputation for job hopping."

"It's more quitting than hopping. And yeah, he'll want cash, which I'm not handing over unless it's on fire."

"I don't guarantee results," she says. "Is he still in the house? Have you talked to him about splitting up?"

"Hell no, I haven't said anything. And yes, he's still in the house."

"Have you talked to anyone about it, Katy?"

"I'm talking to you."

"Because we're so close?" She pauses long enough to make me uncomfortable. "Are things peaceful, or has it gotten weird?"

"Does peaceful mean no lurking behind a door with a baseball bat or pouring bleach into his beer?"

She lets out a quiet groan. "Has there been any violence, calls to a hitman? Are you still having sex with him?"

"Maybe." I twirl a wisp of hair that's sprung loose from my industrial strength ponytail holder.

"Maybe what, Katy? There's a hitman, or you're still sleeping with him?"

"There's no hitman."

"Beautiful. Does he know you're using him for break-up sex?"

"It's not break-up sex, Jess. It's *I don't want you to catch on that I'm divorcing you*, sex. Totally not the same thing."

She rubs her temples. "Tell me why you want a divorce."

"I want a divorce because my life sucks."

"Dig deeper. Convince me you're serious."

"Everything sucking isn't doing it for you?"

"Nope. I need more."

"More. Okay." I take a breath. "How about I'm tired of living with someone who doesn't love me, or even like me? At least one of those two things should be required between a husband and wife." I look away from her. "Marrying Dylan was not the best decision."

"No kidding. I wish you would have gone to therapy before you married him."

"I don't need therapy. I'm not nuts."

"I disagree, Kiss."

"You think I'm nuts?"

"Not clinically. You're lovable and entertaining, but you have some things."

"What things?"

She buries a hand into her dark brown hair and scratches her scalp. "You're a wrecking ball. Everything you do is a fix for the last thing you screwed up. It's not news, Katy. You bounce around your life like you've stuck your tongue into an electric socket."

"What a shocking statement." I grit my teeth and try not to smile.

"Indeed," she says. "I want you to see a therapist. Someone neutral."

"What do you mean by neutral?"

"I mean someone professionally trained to work with someone like you." She rolls a cigarette between her fingers and pulls a lighter from under a pile of papers. The flame is set to blow torch, high enough to block the right side of her face.

"Ever light your eyelashes on fire with that thing?"

"One time," she says. "When I wore mascara."

"Since when do you wear makeup? And seriously, I have to see a shrink?"

"Yup." She inhales. The tip of the cigarette burns bright orange.

"I'll be fine once we're divorced," I say, twisting the narrow wedding band on my finger.

"You weren't fine when you got married."

"It was a wobble in judgment."

"Wobble, my ass. See a shrink, it'll be good for you."

"Perhaps," I grumble. Mental health is important, and I could go for being enlightened or evolved; in possession of a well-adjusted brain with all the neurons twinkling like a freaking Lite Bright. But I have a short in my circuitry, and a stubborn streak, making me question how a professional's sage advice will stop me from screwing everything up. From always picking door number wrong.

"Perhaps," she repeats. "Do you understand what it means to minimize?"

I nod. Of course, I do. Avoid, evade, hedge — all productive tools, allowing me to arrive at this stellar moment in time.

"You willingly participated, Katy. You invited him into your life. That's not his issue, it's yours."

"You should have stopped me." I prepare to duck in case she tosses the stapler in my direction. "Or sat on me or put me in timeout."

"You don't think I tried? I'm a lawyer, not your mommy."

"That's not very diplomatic."

"Diplomacy is just lying strategically. Also, you're dismissing the benefits of therapy in the same breath as asking why I didn't stop you from doing something stupid. It's time to figure it out yourself." She takes another drag from her cigarette, blows smoke out through her nose. I watch the gray plume curl toward the ceiling. "Those are my rules, and you're following them if you want my help."

"You make it sound so intense, Jess."

She rolls her eyes, drops the half-smoked butt into a pop can. "It's your decision, Katy. Agree to the terms and I'll represent you."

"I am agreeable," I say and stand up. Her words are simple, concise; yet getting out of a wretched marriage is turning out to be more complicated than getting into one. She hands me a business card for a therapist as I head to the door.

"Call her today, not next week."

"Got it, Judge Jesse. Today."

"Don't call me that. And don't hang up before she answers."

"I won't."

"I am sorry things went to shit, Katy. Your life isn't turning out to be the two babies by twenty-five deal you always talked about."

I look up from the card. "It's like the saying, woman makes a plan, God giggles?"

"Absolutely not how that goes."

"Whatever," I tell her.

"Make the call, Kiss. Do not pretend you have the wrong number."

"I said fine, I'll do it."

"Promise me."

I promise again, disappointed because I fully intended to do all the things she just told me not to do.

CHAPTER 2
THE POINT

A slew of reasons to avoid the shrink race through my mind while I walk from Jesse's office to my work, the Hungarian restaurant my parents opened when they moved to Florida. *Pont Itt*, translated into English, means *right here*. Dad says this name is "vond-air-fool", wonderful. It's short, clever, with undertones of smart-ass. Much like him.

The locals call it The Point, and it's known for having the best European food in town, despite one or two friendly suggestions from the Health Department. Nothing serious, just a few things Americans obsess about, and the rest of the world somehow survives. Dad says germs are the building blocks of the immune system, and those not healthy enough to handle a little dirt and bacteria don't deserve to live anyway.

The dining room is small, crowded with tables, four booths, and a long mahogany bar in the back where customers drink, eat, and chat-up anyone within earshot.

This has been my second home, where I slept, swaddled in a bassinet, or bobbed in a pink bouncy chair at Mom or Dad's feet. It's where I hopped and clapped as a toddler, while they flipped paper-thin crepes into the air, bowing theatrically after the delicate pancakes landed back in the sizzling hot pan.

My first job was here, learning to wash dishes and mop floors under the watchful eyes of my parents. In high school, I waited tables, and in college they taught me how to order supplies and manage the staff. After graduation, Mom and Dad were still focused on my every move, and it wasn't until recently that I'd noticed a subtle shift in their behavior. A precursor of things to come.

And those things came when they announced plans to travel the world. My mother, lukewarm about leaving her home and daughter, dug deep to remain supportive of her husband. Dad was ecstatic. He said they'd worked hard for years, saved up money, and wanted an adventure before one of them dropped dead. They handed me the business with wishes of good luck and a request not to obliterate everything they'd accomplished.

With the challenge accepted, The Point has turned into my haven. A safe place to hide from the marriage I thought would transform me into a normal American girl, instead of Katy Kiss, daughter of those weird Hungarian immigrants.

But it's not safe today. Dylan's motorcycle is parked in the back of the building. My hand passes over the engine before I open the door. Cold. He's been here a while.

"Where the fuck have you been?" He greets me this way, twisting the cap off a beer. "Isn't it time to spoon feed your fancy customers?"

"I was having breakfast," I lie and hurry to the office, where a stack of his gaming magazines sits on my desk near the bottles he's already polished off. My fingers curl as I imagine hurling one at his head, listening to the thud of glass slamming against his skull. This is my space, and my tolerance for him is bleeding away.

"So, where the hell were you really?" he asks.

"I told you, I went out to grab breakfast. Why aren't you at work, Dylan?"

"Job fell through. They don't understand my vision."

"You quit?"

"They're old school. They won't make it past spring." He leans against the wall and winks at me.

"Why not try to help them?"

His expression morphs from arrogance to anger. "It's a dead-end job. Why would I go down with the ship?"

I hold his stare until my eyes sting.

"You want me to drown, Katy, with the ship? You want Dylan to drown?"

Automatically, I think of excuses on his behalf. Rationalizations I'll repeat to my co-workers or family about my husband's inability to keep a job for more than three months. Then I remember I'm divorcing him, and as of this morning, his employment status is no longer my burden to bear.

"Katy wants Dylan to work for losers?" he pushes.

"I'm not arguing. It's fine. Do whatever you want, just don't speak in the third person. It freaks me out."

"Request denied. Dylan speaks in any person he wants to. Third, fourth, seventh. It's not Katy's goddamn business."

"You're right, it's all good." He's so fucking stupid. Who knew being agreeable would be this easy when the consequences no longer apply? I flash a sugary smile. This is the last time I'm raising the white flag of appeasement so my husband can roll in my feigned compliance like a pig in shit.

He points the bottle at my head. "Katy needs to stay in line."

"Uh-huh." I fidget with the microscopic opal earrings he bought for my birthday. Which is in May, and the birthstone is emerald.

"Got a problem, wifey?"

I exhale, my smile falters.

"What is it, Katy?"

"I didn't say anything." I duck past him, head to the butcher block island, and pull three baking dishes from the rack.

He trails after me. "Is the Hungarian princess pouting?"

I turn the ovens on to three-fifty while he whispers in my ear. "Mommy and Daddy don't have your spoiled ass today, do they?"

"I need to get ready, Dylan."

"You do that. I gotta take a leak." He backs away from me, long legs, ripped arms and expensive clothes. He's so pretty on the outside, infested by a thousand red ants under the surface.

I pull a tub of flour from the cabinet and consider texting Jesse about my flea infestation mutating into an ant colony. Nasty bastards crawling all over my life.

"Is this what you call working hard?" He returns while I daydream about bugs. "What's so complicated here that you can't get home in time to take care of Dylan?"

I hold my breath. Stare into his blue eyes.

"Katy's too slow to think on her feet?" He smiles. His lips are chapped.

I look down at his hands. No wedding ring, only a woven leather bracelet I don't recognize.

He comes closer. "Were you this stupid when we were dating?"

I catch a whiff of the cologne I bought him at Christmas. Hateful motherfucker. Wish I didn't love the way it smells on him.

"Dylan's disappointed in Katy."

The air conditioning kicks on. I fidget, then notice his fly is unzipped. The corner of his starched white shirt peeks through the opening. "Your..."

"My what?" He interrupts.

"Nothing." I pivot around him and walk to the back of the kitchen; certain he'll stay on my ass like bad karma dragging along behind me. "Katy needs to work," I tell him. "And she needs Dylan to leave." I pull the door open and stand with my hands on my hips.

"No loss. I have better places to be. And Princess," he whispers, craning his neck toward me. "Never. Copy. Dylan." He drops the beer bottle onto the floor and leaves with his shirt still flapping through the gaping hole of his zipper.

I secure the deadbolt behind him. His existence is overwhelming. It hurts my body from the inside out. He's my personal parasite, and I've let almost everything good about me wither away to feed his insatiable appetite. My hands drop, and I stand hunched over like I'm a hundred years old. If not knowing where I was for breakfast pushes him into third person-psycho-mode, what will he turn into when he finds out I'm leaving him?

CHAPTER 3
THERAPY SUCKS

A few days later, I arrive for my first appointment with the shrink. Large waiting room, six empty chairs and a supersized picture of dead-eyed woodland creatures. This is not art. This is a big ass rectangle with a connect-the-dot drawing, and its only value lies in its enormity, and that it matches the faded blue carpet, which is as dull as the vase on the table sprouting dried stems and twigs.

I sit down in a leather armchair closest to the front door and force myself to look at the picture. It's tilted slightly to the left, and I wonder if this is a psychological pretest. Who gets up and straightens it, who's relaxed enough to let the damn thing hang off-center? Who runs away screaming? I search for a hidden camera as a door squeaks open.

A thin woman appears. She walks gingerly, like her feet are bound.

"Katy Decker?" She smiles. "I'm Eudora Jonas."

I stand and return the smile. This is not where I want to be. I'm not crazy. I don't eat soap or lick doorknobs.

"Shall we?" She motions for me to accompany her through a narrow hallway leading to her office. I walk quietly, breathe quietly. The less she notices me, the less she'll be able to judge me.

"Please." She extends her right hand and directs me to sit on a puffy beige couch.

The theme of dull, non-committal colors continues into this room, with a fake fern in the corner and a box of tissues located conveniently to my left. Are these for people with allergies, or does she think I'm going to bust open some emotional waterspout so I can live my life in self-actualized harmony? Not going to happen. I'm fine, I've got this. Anyway, misery is a pothole on the means to the end. And the end is where you learn the pothole is where all the action was.

She hands me a packet of papers and begins speaking. "Nice to meet you, Katy. On the phone, you mentioned a lawyer suggested therapy as you go through the divorce process."

"Yes."

"Is there anything specific we should address today, anything urgent?"

"No." I sit on my hands. This whole thing is stupid, and the less information I give her, the better off I'll be.

"Okay." She flashes a reassuring smile. "In the first session, I usually go over a few standard items, so you understand what we'll be doing."

She shifts in the chair, and I try to guess her age. Mid-thirties, with a frame so brittle that a piece of her might break off and crumble to the floor. Her face is angular, and the line of her nose is sharp enough to slice a can of green beans open.

I nod like I've been listening. Standard items are her items, which means we'll be avoiding my items. She explains rules regarding confidentiality, the cancellation policy and the importance of coming to scheduled appointments, then quotes statistics on how crucial it is to stay focused. I tune her out, fixating instead on the textbooks resting on a shelf over her shoulder. Organic Chemistry, Grief, Trauma, Anxiety, Anger, Depression. No wonder she looks so severe. All the softness would rub off anyone surrounded by all this despair.

I'm given documents about payments, privacy laws and sharing information. I'm barely conscious at this point. Her words fuse, mutate. Termination of therapy is important, or did she say trepidation or sedation? I pinch the inside of my palm in an effort to stay awake and sign the forms without looking at them or listening to most of what she's said. For all I know, I may have just agreed to give up a kidney.

She takes the papers and slips them into a new manilla folder. I'm trapped now, and soon to be missing a vital organ.

She asks, "Do you have questions before we begin?"

"I don't know. What do other people do?"

"Everyone's different. You should do whatever you like, Katy."

"I'm not sure what I like."

Her head tilts to the right. Does this mean she doesn't understand me, or does she think I don't understand her?

"Let's keep going. Has your lawyer mentioned any requirement for me to testify on your behalf?"

"Oh, I don't think it'll come to that. Jesse just wants me to talk to someone neutral."

Dr. Jonas makes a weird nasally sound, then asks what Jesse means.

"She wants me to get therapy with someone who's never met me. She says I'm strange, and kind of a wrecking ball." I want the words back as soon as they leave my mouth. Strange is too strong. I'm complicated, layered, like an onion. Some layers are healthy, others less palatable.

"You don't seem strange to me. You seem a bit uncomfortable."

"So do you!" I blurt out, wanting to ask why she looks like a stick bug instead of a human.

"Let's try to keep the focus on you, Katy."

"Uh-huh." I glance at the dull carpet, and all the other dull things in this room.

"Everyone has issues," she says. "And you should feel comfortable bringing those up in this space. So many of our negative feelings are side effects of self-awareness. The questioning of purpose, experience and consequence are both beneficial and detrimental, stressful to the human organism. It's best to work them out instead of holding them in."

What the hell? Is this the opening soliloquy for each new patient and why did she say organism? I wonder how often she slips up and accidentally says orgasm. A snort of laughter escapes me as I imagine the jumbled sentence.

"Allergies," I tell her, trying to regain control.

She asks me again if I have any questions.

"I guess not. My husband doesn't know I'm filing for divorce yet."

"You're early in the process, then?" She crosses her legs.

"Just starting." Hasn't she heard doing this can cause varicose veins? Should I say something, or is it too personal for a first appointment?

"Why don't you tell me about yourself?" She uncrosses her legs. Relief floods through me.

"I'm an only child."

"That can be a very special bond."

"Special good or special, we can't handle more kids if they're gonna be like you?"

Her brown eyes flicker. "Katy, you're not responsible for the number of children your parents had."

I stare at her. How has this thought never occurred to me? My parents treat me like a toddler. At what point would they have sought my council on procreation?

She bends toward me. I can see the lines on her neck. My head tilts up, my brain slithers to the back of my skull to hide from Dr. Eudora Jonas.

"How would you describe yourself to a stranger?" she asks.

I study a dusty air vent. Why is there so much talking? So far, I'm not loving this therapy shit.

"Katy?"

"I'm curious," I tell her, dropping my gaze. "And ask too many questions. I've been told it's irritating."

"Go on."

"I'm too sensitive and I hate confrontation."

She nods for me to continue.

"My sense of humor is all wrong. I'm not very tactful and sometimes I laugh at things other people think are serious."

"Everyone has those moments," she says. "They're not uncommon."

"I might be using up everyone else's moments."

She smiles and relaxes into her chair. Her bony knees push into the fabric of her pants. All angles, like fractured glass.

"You're pretty hard on yourself," she tells me.

"I am?"

"You are, and the behavior you describe doesn't sound like it has much to do with being an only child."

"What does it sound like?"

"It sounds like you feel guilty."

"Why would I feel guilty?" I peek at my phone. Three new texts. I've been here thirty-four minutes.

"Have you ever been in therapy before, Katy?"

"Does this have anything to do with my divorce?"

"Possibly. Feelings of guilt, issues with self-image. Those are all things which can affect a relationship."

"So, I have to come back?"

Dr. Jonas is quiet for a few seconds while she writes on a yellow lined sheet of paper. "Let's backtrack. How long have you been married?"

"Almost three years. Are you writing stuff about me?"

"I am. The information is confidential and used to organize our work. I do it for every client."

I nod. Was this note thing covered in those papers I signed? Can I take some fucking notes on her? I feel a twinge where I think my kidney might be.

"Describe the relationship to me."

"Do I have to?" I ask.

"Can you tell me his name?"

"Dylan. I was with him for almost a year before we got married."

"Okay. You felt satisfied during that year?"

"Not exactly. I'd rather not talk about it."

She makes the weird noise again. I'm unclear if it's affirmation or dismay. "Are you close to your parents? What are they like?"

"They're mostly normal, but opinionated and have this weird need to tell everyone we're Hungarian."

"Where do they live?"

"Here, in Dufferin Beach."

"How's your relationship with them?"

"Good. Fine." We're back to short answers. I can play this game if she's willing to give me some certificate of completion or whatever Jesse requires to get on with the divorce. I check the phone again. Thirty-nine minutes, holy crap.

"Any other family nearby?"

"No. I have people in Canada and Hungary."

Wrinkled, white-haired people, who in my youth, told stories of a mysterious past while Mom shushed them and covered my ears. My grandmother was the exception. She'd smile, pinch my cheeks, and say in broken English, "go finding your happily life."

"Where were you born?" Her question pulls me away from the memories.

"Here, in Florida."

"Interesting."

"Why is it interesting?" I ask.

"Because I don't meet many families from Hungary."

"Have you ever met anyone from Hungary?"

"I just met you." She holds her pencil tight.

"I'm American. My parents are from Hungary."

"Okay, you're American. I thought you didn't like confrontation."

"I don't," I tell her. Or do I? And why am I being a bitch right now?

She clears her throat. "Tell me about Dylan."

I look around the room. At the tissue box. "I think he hates me."

"I'm sorry to hear it."

"Not sure he ever actually loved me." My eyes sting. I'm not going to cry.

"What are your feelings for him?"

I chew on the pink skin around my thumb. "Nothing good for a long time. It's kind of confusing."

"Emotions often are," she says. "Unfortunately, we're running out of time for today."

"Can I leave?"

"Let's discuss how to move forward."

"Now?"

"It won't take long." She puts my file on her lap. "I'd suggest meeting weekly. It will help you become more comfortable with me and the idea of therapy. Sound all right, Katy?"

"Is that how it usually works?"

"Yes, that's how it usually works." She swipes at her phone screen and asks if mornings are good.

"I guess."

"Monday at ten?"

"For how long?" I ask.

"Until ten-fifty," she says, looking at me the same way my fifth-grade teacher did when I couldn't tell him when the War of 1812 was.

"I meant for how long, a month, six months?"

"I'm not sure, Katy."

"Okay." I rub my fingers together.

"I'm glad you came in, and I'm looking forward to spending time with you." She writes the time and date on a card. "Call if anything comes up, okay?"

I'll be fine, I promise, and launch myself off the couch, grabbing the appointment card from her hand like a relay baton. How hard can this whole splitting up thing be? I pull the door open, a little too slow, a little too late, and the edge slams into my cheek. The sound startles Dr. Jonas, her mouth forming into an O as I apologize approximately one and a half times before I disappear down the hallway.

CHAPTER 4
CLOSING TIME

I'm sitting at the bar at work, updating inventory and checking receipts when the bells on the front door jingle. It's three minutes to ten and I've suffered enough today, as evidenced by the ice pack applied to my bruised cheek. My face hurts, and I'm in no mood to wait for someone to peruse the menu or keep my hard-working staff from leaving on schedule. I swivel on the stool, prepared to deliver my polite, "have you never worked in a restaurant—get the fuck out," speech.

Jesse walks in for the first time in almost three years. Before I married Dylan, she'd show up this late because she's antisocial in a town where small talk is almost all the talk. Now the two remaining dinner guests are chatting her up about the weather. Her face twists in polite agony as she extricates herself from the conversation.

"What's the fascination with the weather? We're in Florida, and the temperature is always some variation of blazing hot." She takes a seat beside me and picks up a menu. "What the hell did you do to your face?"

"Had a thing with a door. Kitchen's closed unless you can handle leftovers." I put my pen down. "And wow, you're here."

"I have documents for you to sign. Are you sure it was a door? Do I need to worry?"

She unloads an accordion folder from a worn briefcase. Her phone tumbles to the ground. She cusses at it, like it was trying to escape. Well, maybe it was.

God, I've missed her. She may be cynical and hard to love, but she's also the most genuine person I've ever known. She's logical where I'm impetuous; measured in her decisions while I plunge onto a sinking ship, only to wonder where it all went wrong. Throughout college, I lightened her contempt for the universe while she kept me from floating away on every whim. At least until Dylan showed up.

"I'm sorry about how weird I've been, Jess. I don't know what I was thinking."

She sighs. "You were hoping for the shiny good thing, like you always do. It just didn't work out."

I pick the pen back up. "Not even close. We're back though, you and me."

"Only if we skip the weepy, crying, you're my best friend ever, part."

"Skip it entirely?"

"Yes, Katy. I'm here. I missed you too, blah, blah, blah, all that happy shit." She pulls documents from the folder and instructs me to sign by the green sticky-notes.

I sign my name for the second time today and wonder what other body parts are about to go missing. "All set. Now food?"

On cue, Russ pushes through the kitchen door. He's worked here since we were in high school, the only junior in my freshman algebra class. He needed a job, and because he was "super-cute", I begged my parents to hire him. Years later, he's still charming and the hardest worker we've ever had. The "super-cute", though, is fading prematurely. His square jaw is softer around the edges, and the bright whites of his blue eyes are beginning to show the yellow stain of alcohol induced liver damage.

"Am I seeing right?" Oblivious to her discomfort, he gives Jesse a bear hug. "It's been almost a year."

"Almost three." She corrects him.

"No kidding?"

"None whatsoever. How've you been?"

"You know darlin', a little here and there."

She gives me the side-eye and I can read her mind. *What's happened to Russ?*

"Do we have anything we can reheat for her?" I ask him.

"Some chicken paprikash with some kick-ass dumplings?"

"Sounds great," she says.

"Right on!" He winks at some unfocused object between us and walks away.

Jesse leafs through the documents. "Did he say right on?"

I sigh. "He misses the good old days."

"Days prior to his birth?"

I tell her about his degeneration over the past few years. He dabbles in women, drugs, and alcohol because he's convinced it's his family's curse. His grandfather drank himself to death at sixty, his father at forty. Russ is almost thirty, way past due.

We stop talking when he returns holding a large white plate with tiny red and blue painted flowers decorating the rim. It's loaded with orange-tinted chicken and dumplings. Cucumber salad is served in a bowl with the same floral pattern. Stepping behind the bar, he takes out a bottle of wine and pours three generous glasses. We tap them together, toasting our thus-far mediocre lives. With the bottle tucked under his arm, he retreats into the kitchen.

"Did you see Doctor Eudora?" Bits of chicken shoot out of her mouth.

"I did. What's with her name? Eudora? Is she really a doctor?"

"She has a PhD in neuropsychology. And you're passing judgment on weird names, Katy Kiss?"

I swirl the dark red wine in my glass. "Why would she agree to see me?"

"Professional courtesy."

"So, a favor?"

"Sure. How was the appointment?"

"It was dumb."

"Why was it dumb?"

"It's confidential. I signed papers promising not to discuss it."

She sucks meat off a drumstick. "No, you signed papers saying *she* wouldn't discuss it."

I watch her drop the bare bone onto the plate. "Talking about professional courtesy, did you help my parents with some legal crap before they left on vacation?"

Her expression transforms from feeding frenzy to deadpan. "Why would you ask me that?"

"Because I found an invoice with your name on it in the office."

She stares at me. "I can neither confirm nor deny."

"So, you wrote up a will for my mom and dad? The invoice says estate planning."

"Ask them."

"Ask them to explain a document they won't admit exists?"

She holds my stare while running her index finger through the remaining sauce on her plate and plops it into her mouth. "Yes. Ask them."

"What's in the will? Is it the usual stuff like the extra house key is under the rock Katy broke her tooth on when she was five, or is there something else?"

No response.

"Come on, Jess? Did they draw it up because they're traveling, or is something wrong with one of them?"

"To the best of my knowledge, your parents are in good health."

"Don't hand me a bunch of lawyer-talk. Am I adopted or something?"

"Look in the mirror, Kiss. You're a DNA replica of your parents."

"Then what is it? If it's because they're travelling they would have shown it to me."

"I can neither confirm nor deny," she repeats.

"But now I'm going to obsess."

She nods.

"What in the hell is so messed up that they need to be dead before I find out?"

"No comment."

"Fine," I say, and down the rest of my wine. "I'll ask them directly."

"Excellent idea."

"You're not gonna say anything?"

She stays quiet, puts her fork on the plate and cracks her knuckles.

"Fuck you, Tanner."

"Right back at you, baby. Client-attorney privilege."

I break the stare before she does. Not sure why I thought I could out-argue a lawyer. After a few moments of uncomfortable silence, I hop off the bar stool to check on the couple who asked about the weather. He and his wife have been coming here for years and have long since stopped asking for the bill. They assure me the food was perfect and hand over fifty dollars. After the obligatory hugs, they leave with full bellies and smiles on their faces.

"Keeping up appearances?" Jesse asks after I lock the door behind them. She sticks a finger into her mouth and pretends to gag.

"They're nice people, leave 'em alone." I glance above her head.

"What are you looking at?" she asks.

"Just wondering if Melissa's still here."

"Who's Melissa?"

"I hired her after my parents went on vacation. She's a sweetheart."

"Is she hot?" She wiggles her eyebrows.

"I guess," I tell her, and refocus on the inventory and nightly sales. The Point is making good money. Each week, I add up the numbers and proudly watch the bank account grow. Jesse drinks, chews loudly, and bangs her silverware on the china.

"So?" she says, watching me work.

"Yes, ma'am?"

"You're a shitty listener, Katy."

I push the calculator away. "I'm trying to get out of here on time."

"You're ignoring my question about Dr. Jonas."

"I did answer you."

"You sidestepped. What did I ask you?"

"You asked why your mama never taught you any table manners."

She grins, opens her mouth, and shows me remnants of food stuck to her teeth.

"Thank you," I grunt. "I'm doing everything you told me to do. I signed the papers, listened to the shrink's orgasm speech, and judged her decorating skills."

"Orgasm speech? Sounds entertaining." She picks up the bowl of cucumber salad, guzzles the sweet vinegar dressing, smacks her lips together and burps.

The kitchen door opens again; this time it's Quinn walking out with a laptop.

"Hey," he nods at Jesse. "I'm Quinn."

"Jesse Tanner. I've seen you around." Her eyes move down from his face.

"Quinn's a friend of Dylan's," I tell her. "He helps with computer stuff."

"I have computer stuff." She grins.

"Jesse." I wave my hand in front of her. "The Point is not an escort service."

Quinn clears his throat. "I updated a couple of passwords and deleted some old files."

"Thanks. Did you eat?"

"Yeah. Tasty as usual."

"Katy, can I have dessert?" Jesse, still gaping at Quinn, shoves me off my chair.

I grab her dishes and tell her to behave.

The remains of the cake are in the fridge. It's delicious, homemade with chocolate frosting, topped with roasted hazelnuts. I'm smothering it with whipped cream when I overhear Melissa telling Russ she'd rather not fool around with him. I pry her away and give her permission to swing a cast-iron pan at his head the next time he bothers her. Russ gets a lecture on sexual harassment and blunt force trauma.

"Cake," I announce, back in the dining room, and slide the dish over to Jesse.

"That'll do." She takes her first bite, then pushes the plate toward Quinn. "Wanna share?"

He declines the offer, listens to her chew and groan, then excuses himself for the evening.

"You've got crumbs on your face." I move a cloth napkin in her direction.

"He's hot." She wipes her chin up to her forehead. "Nice shoulders, damn."

"Have you not had sex in a while?" I ask.

"I have not. What's with his hair? First, I thought it was brown, then I saw those gold streaks. I bet they're highlights. That doesn't happen naturally."

She licks frosting directly off the dish. "He's into you, Katy."

"No, he's not. He's just Quinn."

"What do you mean just Quinn? I was making a move, and he kept talking about how exceptional you are. That's the word he used...exceptional."

"He's being polite."

"He said you're an amazing person."

I snort. "That's stupid."

"I agree."

"I guess he's good-looking." I nudge the dish closer to her. "Do you have to eat like that?"

"Ya, I do. Do they still hang out, Dylan and Quinn?"

I try to remember the last time they were together. When I met Dylan, Quinn was often by his side; partying, going out on the water, or watching football. After a while Quinn began defending me and pushing back on Dylan's insults. It made things more tense, as my husband's behavior had with my other friends, then it made him go away.

Jesse watches me. "They don't hang out anymore, do they?"

"Not at the house." I say, picking a stray hazelnut off the bar. Jesse eats like a six-year-old boy.

"He can't stand the way Dylan treats you."

"So, he feels pity for me, like he would a stray kitten. Did you tell him I'm getting a divorce?"

"That would be an ethical violation. And you were only gone for five minutes, so that's as far as it got. Unfortunately. He's pretty."

"Well, he's all yours, Jess, but the girls he hangs out with have one-tenth of your bandwidth."

"Everyone I know has one-tenth of my bandwidth."

"Also, his type of girl doesn't want to kill the men they've had sex with."

"Then they're suppressing what they feel. Everyone I've slept with deserved to die."

"Of course, they have, Jessica. Anyway, he's just being polite."

"I'm telling you what I think... as your divorce lawyer."

"Consider me told, Your Honor."

"Don't call me that." She picks up her briefcase, slides off the stool, and shuffles to the door. "I've had enough of this day. Please let me out."

After finishing up at the restaurant, I drive home, imagining how it would feel to be with someone whose happiness isn't a by-product of my sadness. By the time I roll into the driveway, there are tears in my eyes. Embarrassed, I wipe them away, and walk inside to spend another miserable night with a man who will tell me how much he'd prefer anyone else in the world over me.

CHAPTER 5
MELTING

Friday morning, while Dylan's still sleeping, I slip out the door and head to the beach. All my life, the ocean's been my backyard, my refuge. I appreciate regimented relaxation...for others, but yoga and meditation stress me out and bending my legs behind my ass or allowing my spine to commune with the earth, feels a lot like gateway porn.

I kick off my flip-flops, step into the cool sand and inhale the salty sea air. In front of me, the dawn's first rays of sunshine reflect off the waves. A cruise ship skims the horizon, a pair of jet skis pop in and out of the surf, and the cry of seagulls fills my ears with lovely white noise.

The last few days, though uneventful, have taken their toll. Dylan isn't looking for a new job because he's too busy complaining about the old one. He spends the day sleeping or at a bar "networking," after which he stumbles home at dawn to wake me up and lie about the important connections he's made. I watch his lips flap up and down, wishing he had a mute button.

At work, trying not to think about my divorce does nothing but make me obsess about it. The harder I try to stay on task, the more my brain turns into a tornado of non-productive thought, random signals playing pinball inside my skull.

Until I get to the shore, where foamy sea water coils around my ankles and dulls the stress I can't relieve any other way.

I press my hands to my cheeks and inhale. My heartbeat slows, my muscles unclench. My phone vibrates in my hip pocket. I try to ignore it, hoping the restaurant isn't burning down, or my house isn't sliding into a sinkhole. This is an impossibility, though, because I'm blessed with extreme anxiety and an overactive imagination. I look at the screen. It's my mother.

"Hey, Mom, what's up?"

"Is this how you answer now?"

I step back from the water and sit down on the hard sand. "Good morning valued parental unit."

"Is this funny for you, Katy?"

I groan and hold the phone away from my face, wondering if an extra six inches will buffer me from her dismay.

"Katy! Are you there? Hello?"

"Yes, I'm here. It's early."

"Then don't answering." Her grammar is deteriorating in lockstep with her mood. This is going to be fun.

"Is that an option?" I ask.

"Yes, it is your choice. I take my problem somewhere else."

"What problem, Mom? Is something wrong?" I suck in my breath wondering if this is about the mysterious will.

"Nothing is wrong, dear. What is wrong with you?"

So many things… "You called me, Mom."

"Yes. This is true. I am having, what you call it, angry issue, with the men."

"What men?"

"Well dear, most of them."

"Care to expand?"

"Nothing is to expand on, Katy."

"So, you called to tell me nothing's going on?"

"Yes."

"Are you lying to me?" I ask.

"Lying is very subjective."

She is so not a secret agent, or she's an awesome secret agent. Or she's a politician.

"What are you lying about, Mom?"

"Apuka."

"What about Dad? Did something happen?"

"No."

"Seriously, Mother?" I cross my legs, balance the phone on my shoulder, and dig into the wet sand.

"Yes, all right. I had the fight with your father and leave him to rot in jungle. He is behaving like boy who never has woman before."

"What jungle?" I ask, stretching my feet into the seawater. "What the hell do you mean, you left him?"

"Please do not get upset, Katy."

"I'm not upset. I'm curious. Dad looked at another woman and you're pissed?"

"Fui! You do not use this language with your mother!"

A sinkhole would have been easier.

"Sorry. Please tell me what happened."

"Well, we were on the jungle tour in Thailand."

"You're in Thailand?"

"No, I am certainly not."

"You just now said you were."

"Igen," she replies. Yes. "I was, now I am not. Why is this making the confusion for you? We finish the tour and go to the beach. Very nice beach, by the ways. Thailand is beautiful but too hot. They should all melt."

"What? Something melted?" My family is crazy. Dr. Jonas will be so pleased. "Tell me what happened with Dad."

"I am trying, but you keep with the interruptings. So, we are walking on beach and a young girl comes right up to him. She says something and does funny laugh, and then he does funny laugh. I was not one of my feet away and they do this!"

"Uh-huh," I tell her, scraping sand from under my nails.

"After, he looks at me and his face is a big guilty writing on it."

"Okay."

"So, we continue with our walk, and have the pleasant evening. Nice food, little fishy. You would not like it there. Then I go to sleep and when I wake up your father is gone."

"Gone where?"

"Two in the morning and he is missing in the actions!"

My stomach contracts. I bend forward and drop my head between my knees.

"I wait for him to come back. Imagine how long this takes?"

"Nu-uh." I mumble.

"Five, Katy. Five in the morning. I tell him I know where he was, and he does not deny it. She says she was with the girl."

"He," I whisper.

"What?"

"He was with the girl, not she."

Her tone is pinched, as always, when I correct her grammar. "He! Do you understand it better this way?"

"So, you left?"

"Yes, dear. I leave him to rot in jungle." This time, she speaks without emotion.

"I see."

"Are you curious of where I am?" she asks.

"Curiosity is only one of the emotions I'm feeling right now."

"France."

"Why didn't you come home, Mom?"

"I visit with Márton and Josephine. You know how I love Paris."

"Did you tell Dad where you are?"

"He said maybe it is best thing."

"I don't get it. Why would he do that? Are you okay?"

"I am very well. How is the restaurant? You are not pregnant, are you? You are sounding pregnant. I think this is appropriate time, Katy. People are expecting the nice Hungarian baby by now."

"People, or you and the family?" I ask, wondering what my mother thinks gestation sounds like. "And no, I'm not pregnant."

"Are you sure, dear? I think you might be. You seem nervous."

"I'm sure, Mom." I stand up and brush the sand off my palms. "So, where's Dad? Is he coming home?"

"How would I know this? He has a new phone. I give you number. Men after they have sex are very stupid."

I shut my eyes, trying to erase the picture she's just burned into my brain.

"How long are you staying in Paris?"

"I stay for this month. After, I am not sure. You do not need me anymore. Your father...fui. I will not speak of him. Now is good time for baby?"

"Uh-huh, no. Not a good time. All the people will have to wait."

"Oh... no baby?" She sounds hurt. "I give you his number. You can tell him I have French boyfriend who takes me to opera and not to see a big lizard in jungle."

The call continues, and she fills me in on her brother and his wife, Josephine, in decline from dementia. Márton is several years older than Mom and somewhat mysterious to me. He'd escaped Budapest after the Hungarian Revolution, and my parents' exit from the country was with his help. My mother's first love was Paris, so it's no surprise she'd retreat there to lick her wounds. By the end of the conversation, I've done most of the listening, with no opportunity to ask about the will or drop my bombshell on an already tense situation. I inhale more ocean air after I hang up and make my way back home.

CHAPTER 6
HIT AND RUN

Dufferin Beach, unlike other Florida towns, discourages tourism. We're situated south of Sarasota and north of Ft. Myers. The major attraction is the private university where students major in business, science, pre-law, and pre-married. As the school's tuition rises, the city similarly acclimates to absorb more of everyone's money. The crown jewel of Duff Beach is Ocean Avenue, lined with boutiques, bookstores and cafes selling exotic herbal teas and tiny overpriced coffees.

North of downtown, fast-food restaurants, and a Target Superstore give way to the university; a seaside compound with dorms fashioned after luxury apartments and a student union resembling a mash-up of brewery and bookstore.

Most of the year-round residents live south of town, including me and my parents, a few blocks away. My house is a two-bedroom bungalow with a red Spanish tile roof and a yard packed with palm trees, hibiscus and bougainvillea sprouting hot pink flowers on a thorny blood-letting vine.

The interior is cluttered with my family's secondhand furniture, Persian carpets, and brightly colored oil paintings. In the dining room, an ancient china cabinet tilts forward, threatening to let loose the semi-valuable trinkets of my hoarding ancestors.

In the kitchen, a bay window frames the sink, the ledge crowded with African violets and a basil plant in need of repotting. Last year I repainted the walls an eye-piercing, granny apple green, so bright, that in retrospect I wondered if I had a disease or a vitamin deficiency warping my color perception. My mother was appalled, and took to the internet, researching if the gallons of espresso she drank while pregnant could have had a latent effect on my vision. My father, who helped me paint, had no comment except for the bemused expression in his eyes.

After cleaning the sand off my sandals, I let myself into the house and head to the bedroom, furnished with the few belongings my husband brought to the marriage; an ugly wood-framed bed and a matching set of drawers.

Dylan's still out cold, straight on his back, arms folded across his chest. An empty Corona sits on the table next to him, a spent lime tossed to the side. He's almost out of the picture, so there's no need to be pissed off because he's sleeping through another day. I take a wrong step and trip over a random shoe he must have kicked off late last night. I catch myself, but the thump of my foot hitting the ground is enough to wake him.

"What?" He pushes up on his elbows.

"Nothing," I whisper.

"What the hell do you want?"

"I don't want anything. I'm getting ready for work." Unintentionally, I glance at the empty bottle.

"You got a problem with it?" He leans forward, sweeping thick blond hair from his eyes, flexing, checking out his triceps while he stretches.

With my patience already tested this morning, any desire to be the apologetic one is waning. "You might if that's a fresh beer." Typical. I have a big mouth and an underdeveloped backup plan.

"Goddamn it!" he yells in a sudden burst of anger. "I'm sick of your bitching and complaining." He jumps up and pulls on the same jeans for the second day in a row. I draw in my breath. Something about him is different. A piece of his personality has come untethered. He's no longer the charming boy I dated or the whiny asshole I've learned to live with. This man is crazed. He's the inbred spawn of the devil.

He takes one long stride to reach me, and I stand mesmerized. Fight-or-flight goes for the elusive third option; the inability to pick either of the first two. My brain locks up. I might as well be skipping down the basement stairs in a slasher movie.

"Katy." His voice is suddenly soft, with the same forced tenderness he uses after sex. "I want to tell you something important." He reaches up, grabs my shoulders, and gently pulls me close. I smell the lime on his breath. "You're a cunt," he hisses.

I try to turn away. His grip tightens, easily keeping me in place, lifting me so my toes are barely touching the ground. He squeezes harder, digging into my biceps with enough force to make my fingers go numb. I shut my eyes. He whispers it again and again. "Do you understand, cunt?" Day-old stubble grazes my cheek.

"Look at me," he growls. Not in a position to argue, I open one eye at a time and see the face of a complete stranger. Subtle variations of color radiate from his tightly dilated pupils, dark blue, thin streaks of green, a nascent wrinkle on his brow. His lips curl, enjoying the control.

This isn't what I agreed to during our marriage vows. No promises were made to abuse and disrespect. No permission was granted to annihilate my life. This is horseshit, and my anger flows through me like a jolt of electricity. My feet pedal in the air and slide across the carpet. Dylan looks down, shocked I would dare protest. I push off the ground, gathering leverage to kick his legs. His fingers loosen. One foot hits the floor again, and with improved traction, I go at him.

"What the fuck?" His voice rises to a screech.

Unable to stop, I thrash and slap with open fists. I swipe at his face, neck, and arms while he cowers to defend himself. My thumb clips his chin. I watch it bend in slow motion. He squeals and stumbles, taking cover with the powerful hands that just held me in a vise grip.

"You freak!" He dives on the bed, squirms over the blankets, and lands ungracefully on the other side.

"Is Dylan running away from his cunt wife?"

"Damn straight I am. You're fucking crazy!"

"I hate you!" The words spill out of me, more air than sound.

"I get it, now back off!"

He's out of my reach, bug-eyed, grasping for his shirt, tending to his golden locks. Amazing. His first order of business is to re-establish his image, to check his good looks. Too bad everything he carries on the surface is the inverse of what's inside. I tell him I hate him, and I truly do, but I've just begun hating myself a lot less.

"You surprised me is all. I was sleeping, and you woke me up. Can you chill out for a minute and lay off?"

I nod, trying to catch my breath, holding up my palms as a sign of peace.

"Don't follow me. Stay right there." He side-steps, back against the wall.

"Don't ever fucking touch me again," I whisper as he slithers away from me.

The front door opens and shuts. His motorcycle starts up. The gears engage, the tires crunch on the asphalt, then fade into the distance.

I creep around the house, locking the windows and doors. My arms ache. My right thumb feels like a nail has been driven through it and a mind-numbing weariness falls over me. I reach for the phone to call my parents, then stop. They're thousands of miles away. It's too much information at once. My mom in France, Dad with a stranger in Thailand, Dylan, the divorce. I hobble to the living room and drop onto the couch, landing hard enough to push it a few inches back. Curling into a fetal position, I pass out while the shit storm blows up all around me.

CHAPTER 7
TATTOO

My body is stiff when I wake up, my mind is cloudy. I rush in and out of a lukewarm shower, trip stepping into my jeans and wipeout on the bathroom floor. My sore thumb takes the brunt of the fall.

In the mirror, I see dark blue rings forming tattoos around my upper arms. Dylan's left his mark on me, and some pain. My mind goes back to the exhilaration I felt when we were engaged. I'd be married. Sprinkles and fairy dust would swirl in the air. My husband would adore me. Today, when I look at these bruises, inflicted by the same person, I feel the excitement of being free from the marriage instead of shame from its failure. These wounds will fade over the next few weeks, and if everything goes as planned, Dylan will fade soon after.

• • • • •

Russ's bicycle is propped against the back wall of the restaurant. He must have lost his car again, too drunk to remember where he last left it. Inside, he's charging around the kitchen with mixing bowls and a tub of sugar. He stops when he sees me, opens his mouth to speak.

"Don't ask." I hold up my hand, tell him it's all good and scurry to the office. Quinn's at my desk, working on the laptop.

"You're late." His voice sounds deeper than it did a few days ago.

I scold myself. Not the time to be thinking about another man. This is Jesse's fault. She planted the seed. How didn't I notice he's tall, dark, and handsome?

I twist sideways to slide the bag off my shoulder, wincing as it rolls down my arm, bangs into my thumb, and drops to the floor.

"Having a rough day?" He turns and studies me.

"Possibly."

He sighs, begins typing; long fingers playing the keyboard like a piano.

"You've heard from my loving husband, haven't you?"

"He said you woke him up, dragged him out of bed, and beat the living shit out of him."

"That's an interesting take on it."

"He didn't mention the part where he hurt you."

"I hurt him back."

"Who started it?" he asks.

"Technically, I did. But I can defend myself."

"From someone twice your size?"

"Would you rather I hide in a corner waiting for him to announce his undying love for me? We have a horrible marriage. Let's stop pretending you haven't noticed."

"You've never said it out loud."

"Well, I am now."

"True enough." He looks back at the computer, hits the enter key. "All set."

I'm too distracted to read his expression. It's late, I'm behind, and unprepared to announce my divorce.

He stands up, grabs his keys. "Should I be worried? Can we talk about it?"

"Why?" I ask, noticing the color of his eyes. Chocolate with specks of gold. I swallow, look down at my sneakers. What the hell is wrong with me? A couple of hours ago, I got into a physical fight with Dylan and now I'm having palpitations over eyeballs and wavy hair, and holy crap, it looks so soft.

He blinks. "You jumping into a boxing ring with your husband?"

"I'm fine. Don't worry about Dylan and me." I push my hands into my pockets at the same time he tries to hug me. The result is an awkward moment of anticipation where the flame flares up just before it flickers out.

I walk him to the door and promise to call if anything else happens. He acknowledges, gently brushes my shoulder, and leaves right as Diana, the second server I hired after my parents went on vacation, arrives. She stomps past us without a greeting.

Russ has questions, and I wait until she's out of earshot to answer. I don't need her in on the gossip and she already rubs me the wrong way, though not for any good reason. She stares at me, but never smiles when I catch her doing it. I'm sure Diana Johnson is connected to the Russian or Italian Mob, and she's here to take me down. If only I was so important, with my little life, working in my little restaurant, making an okay living in this little town.

• • • • •

After the dinner rush, I look up the country code to Thailand, and call my dad on the far side of the planet. "Savadika", a childish female voice announces before going into a sing-song recording. I hang up and try again with the same result. What has he gotten himself into, and how do I leave a message when I may not even be calling the right number? To hell with it. On the third attempt, I record an awkward voicemail he'll probably never get. I'm short-tempered for the rest of the night, distracted by the new hurdles in my life, and fearful I'll do what I've done so many times before. Trip all over myself and land flat on my face.

CHAPTER 8
RASPBERRY DONUT

My next therapy appointment rolls around too quickly, and I brace for another fifty minutes with Dr. Jonas. With the generic formalities of our intake session recorded and filed into a plain manilla folder, I fear a more severe psychological interrogation is looming.

I settle into the overstuffed seat and glance at the box of tissues. Because of Eudora Jonas's sharp features, it's impossible to tell if she's relaxed or aiming to rip a vein out of my neck. She begins the session by asking how my week is going. I tell her Dylan has once again quit his job, and I'm avoiding him by hiding out at the restaurant. We've come to a silent agreement wherein he doesn't appear to notice my absence as long as I don't appear to notice his unemployment.

"How was this decided?" she asks, yellow lined paper at the ready.

"We... created new boundaries."

She puts the tip of the pen between her teeth, which are small, though her gums are not. I contemplate giving her an anonymous gift of whitening strips for Christmas.

"We had a fight," I offer.

She stares at me; I look away.

"Can you tell me about it?"

I sigh. "He grabbed my arms because I woke him up, so I flipped out and started hitting him."

"Did the police get involved?"

"No."

"Did he hurt you?"

"Here." I show her the bruises. "And I bent my thumb back when I punched him." I wiggle my finger.

"We need to discuss a safety plan. Are you both still living at home?"

"Yes. Quite peacefully."

She shakes her head and scribbles something on the paper. My mind wanders. Do people make shit up to mess with their shrinks, and if so, would that be considered a separate clump of sickness? Because I've got no expertise in this area, I decide lying is probably cover for someone who isn't ready to be helped yet.

"It's not for too much longer." I interrupt her essay on the fucked-up life of Katy Kiss.

"You know that. Dylan doesn't. We need a plan in place before you leave today."

"Okay. Also, my mom walked out on my dad."

"I'm sorry. Was it unexpected?"

"Definitely. I'd rather not go into it yet."

"Whenever you're ready."

She nods for me to continue, so I tell her about the conversation I had with Jesse at her office. Why I got married in the first place and why, as Jess said, I bounce around my life like a live wire.

"We find each other for all sorts of reasons, Katy, not all of them healthy. I'm sure you've heard the saying about accepting the love you believe you deserve."

"Uh-huh."

"It's good to figure out how you got here, and why you believe you deserve this situation or experience. Your core values can dictate how you perceive your self-worth. As you might imagine, those beliefs are some of the most difficult to change."

She asks if there are any significant or traumatic occurrences from my childhood. I laugh and tell her my mother was so overprotective a mosquito couldn't have gotten near me. There is nothing at all to explain my actions as an adult.

"Did you go to college?"

"I went here in town and lived in the dorms for two years, then in an apartment with some friends. Jesse was one of my roommates."

"How did your parents handle you leaving the nest?"

"Mom cried a lot."

Eudora writes notes through our game of twenty questions.

"How about your dad?"

"He acted like it was no big deal. I think maybe it was."

"Why do you say that?"

"Because he bugged me more than Mom. He'd show up with food or a toolbox, saying he'd noticed something broken last time he was over."

"And how was that for you?"

"Fine. The free food was nice, and something was usually broken. Everybody liked my parents. Nobody minded."

"Katy, you just told me how it was for everyone else. How was it for you?"

"Oh. Annoying, I guess."

"They're slightly overprotective?" she asks.

"More than slightly."

"Their behavior stood out to you?"

"We've always been enmeshed in each other's lives."

"Did you ever ask them why they're so, let's use your word, enmeshed?"

"Not really our style. We don't discuss those things. Emotions...or, well, emotions."

I shrug and consider bringing up the will, then decide against it. I am the offspring of avoidant immigrants and I'll do as I was taught by keeping my mouth shut and suffering in silence.

"Let's talk about college some more," she says. "Any significant relationships during that time?"

"Is that important?"

She rubs smeared makeup from underneath her eyes. "It is now." She smiles, her thin lips rise at the corners.

"I had a friend. I guess you'd call him a friend with benefits."

"What was his name?"

"Why?"

She frowns. I have the right to ask. This is my therapy, not hers.

"It helps with my notes."

I groan. "Nick." I haven't said his name in years. *Nick-Nick-Nickety-Nick*. My cheeks burn at the thought of him.

"What do you remember most about your relationship with Nick?"

"Nothing."

"Nothing at all?"

"It wasn't a thing. We were just friends. Sometimes when we were bored or drunk, we'd have sex." I focus on my chewed-off fingernails and hope this doctor of neuro-blah-blah-psycho-babble can't read body language.

"Does it feel that way now?" Her pen moves at lightning speed while she speaks. I guess she can read body language. Wasn't she ever a college student, sleeping around and slashing people with her razor-sharp appendages?

"Katy?"

"Yeah?"

"How was the relationship?" she asks, leaning into the question.

"Fine."

"How would you have answered me at the time?"

I squeeze my pinkie. "I've got no clue how I would have answered you."

"Can you pick an emotion to describe your feelings for him?"

"Why?" I ask.

"Why not?"

"It's been so long; I try not to go there."

"Was he important to you?"

"Yes."

The questions keep coming. Why did the friendship end? Did I want more, or something better, and holy crap, who gives a shit anymore? It was years ago; an unpleasant, confusing episode I wouldn't want to repeat. Oh...wait a minute. Nick... Dylan? That can't be right.

She keeps talking about youth, life-lessons and building self-esteem while I look for a distraction. I find it in the hard, linear features of her face. How can someone who appears physically untouchable make a living trying to get close to everyone else?

"May I tell you how the situation looks from my point of view? Correct me if I'm wrong."

"Sure," I say, though I'm terribly fucking unsure.

"It sounds to me like you established the relationship with Nick based on friendship."

"Sure," I tell her. This is not exactly true, but she doesn't need to know that I slept with him the first time we met.

"Until the boundaries changed," she adds.

"You mean because we fooled around?"

"Yes, whether you discussed it or not, sex shifted the parameters."

"Awfully deep for a bunch of wasted college kids."

"Don't get lost in the technicalities, Katy."

She's right, but who cares? My blood sugar is plunging because I replaced a healthy breakfast with this torture.

"I'd say you, at some point, wanted a more committed relationship with him."

"Uh-huh." If I can't get a raspberry donut in the next ten minutes, I will for sure, literally, die of starvation.

She continues, "one you wanted, as opposed to your perception of what he wanted."

"That might have happened."

"You never spoke to him about it?"

"No."

"So why not ask for a commitment?"

I'm getting a headache. A hot band of pain compressing my brain from ear to ear. If I couldn't figure it out in college, I sure as hell won't get it now. I offer the first thing that pops into my mind. "I was afraid if I pushed him, I'd lose him."

"Fair enough," she says. "Still, the friendship continued, as did the confusion about the rules. Then you graduated, parted ways?"

"Something like that. We haven't spoken in years."

"Not at all?"

I shake my head. He's probably married to some perfect woman who's bore him a perfect set of twins. They have a fabulous dog, a Golden Retriever named Rex, who is also perfect, except in the Christmas picture where he does something adorable and the entire family laughs at exactly the right moment, and the picture, though ruined, is still entirely fucking perfect. Eudora's voice brings me back.

"What I did was take you step by step through the events in order to create a simple outline. If it's all right with you, next week we can compare the similarities with your marriage to Dylan. In finding some things in common, perhaps we'll find some patterns."

"Great," I say, not wanting to listen anymore, in simplified terms or complicated ones. This is exhausting. What does the past have to do with my failed marriage? Again, the connections float around my brain until I disconnect the dots and push them away.

Before I can jettison myself from her office, she stands up and heads to a gray filing cabinet. From a dark purple file, she hands me a leaflet titled, *Your Safety Plan.* We spend twenty minutes discussing how it works and how it applies to me. I map out who to call or where to go if I'm in danger.

Finally, she asks if there is anything else I need to address. I say no before she finishes her sentence. She confirms our next appointment and I scurry out of her office, this time without any visible damage to myself or the door frame.

CHAPTER 9
BANGKOK CALLING

The rest of the week moves past in a haze. I'm consumed by thoughts of my parents, Quinn, and the secrecy of the divorce. My overactive imagination propels me through each day, one moment ecstatic, the next moody, and impatient.

On Jesse's orders, I remove receipts, closing documents, and tax returns from the house. All of these required to demonstrate which participant of the marriage has done the falling down.

By the end of the weekend, I'm livid because my parents haven't checked in. Existing on a diet of Cap'n Crunch and espresso, I've developed a strong case of the shakes and a significantly diminished need for sleep.

Early Monday morning I sit in my office at work, staring at a wall, considering how many hours to wait between bowls of cereal. My cell phone vibrates. I jump several inches into the air.

"Hallo!" My father sounds happy and energetic, his Hungarian accent more pronounced than I remember.

"Hi, Dad."

"How are you, love?"

"Present, I guess. Here."

"This is not answer to my question."

"Why are you still in Thailand?"

"Because the country is lovely, and they hide all the old people inside."

"You're old." I say, eyeing my empty coffee cup.

"I am a foreigner with money. They hide the others, so all you see is beautiful young people."

"What if the old people are so beautiful they have you fooled?"

He's quiet for several seconds. "Or maybe they killing them."

"Yeah, Dad, you're making no sense at all."

"It is to show the best of your face in the forward."

"Best face forward? Are you saying that in public?"

"Who would understand me? Everybody smile and do the bow. They are teaching me how to do this. Bend little for nice people on street, bend very much for King. It's the most exercise I have in years."

"Are you planning on meeting the King?"

"You never know who you will meet, Katy."

I rotate my chair in half circles. "Why did you fool around on Mom?"

"You spoke to her? Are you in office? I hear the damn chair. Why you don't oil it?"

"Been kind of busy. And yeah, her account was colorful, to say the least."

He laughs, and now I miss him. Have been missing him, if I'm being honest.

"She tells you she catches me like the fly in Vaseline?"

"Yup," I say, trying to sit still. If I can't swivel, I can at least tap my feet.

"I'm sorry I hurt her, but I stay here for a while. It is peaceful, and it makes me happy."

"You weren't happy here?" I ask.

"Of course, but time for me to do something for myself. I take care of you and your mother for many of the years. I do everything the right way. Even I am nice to asshole husband of yours."

"I don't understand, Dad."

"I do what is fun for me, for little while. I am getting older. All my life, I am there when you need me, no?"

I hear the unmistakable sound of him inhaling smoke.

"Oh my God, did you start smoking again?"

He doesn't answer right away. "How did you know?"

"I can hear it!"

"Really, you have the excellent ears."

"You worked so hard to quit. Why would you give it all up?"

"I stop after I get home, no problem. Now, please get the ticket and come see me. I have lovely apartment. You can meet Lia."

"Who's Lia?" I ask.

He's hanging out with some woman in Thailand because it's less of a burden than his family in Florida? Frustrated, I shove a pile of papers on the desk and cut a gash in my left palm with a well-placed box cutter. Bright red blood trickles between my fingers before the pain kicks in.

"Lia is very nice. I met her on the beach."

"She's the one Mom saw?" The droplets get bigger.

"Yes."

"How old is she?"

"Twenty-two," he whispers.

"What? No, that's gross." I hold my hand up and watch blood drip down my wrist.

"One hundred years ago, this would be considered middle age."

"Dad."

"Yes?"

I take a breath. "So, you're living with a girl who's not my mother, and she's twenty-two?" My arm is throbbing. I drop my phone in my lap, push the speaker button, and wrap my palm with paper towels. "Where's the apartment?"

"Bangkok."

"Can you be more specific? Isn't that an enormous city?"

"Do you want to speak to Lia? Here, I put her on."

"No, absolutely not!"

I hear her giggle and squeal, "no, no!"

He takes another drag from his cigarette. "She is too shy. Shut down the restaurant and visit me. Please do not bring the asshole."

This phone call is no longer productive. I'm pissed, injured, and my father is shacked up with a tween.

"Dad, I have to go."

"Why you have to go?"

"I cut my hand. It's bleeding."

"Is it bad? Call the emergency, Katy." He sounds alarmed. Guess I should feel grateful. Or should I? I wish I understood my family's new rules.

"It's fine. Send me your address, okay?" The makeshift bandage is turning dark red.

"Yes. Promise you come to see me?"

"I'll consider it," I tell him, though I have no intention of ever setting foot in Bangkok. My stomach churns, pellets of Cap'n Crunch push up insistently at my esophagus.

"We speak again next week?"

"Sure. Call me back, Dad. I want to talk to you about something else."

"What is it?"

"Nothing. Not important." I wind a second layer of paper towels around my hand.

Dead air. He always knows when I'm lying.

"Did the asshole do something?" he asks.

I wait a beat before answering. "No. It's about you and Mom and Jesse."

The line is quiet again, but for a deep inhalation of that fucking cancer-causing smoke.

"Why did you guys make a will and not say anything to me?"

He coughs. I recognize the familiar hack I grew up listening to.

"Dad?" I bend over and close my eyes. Warm blood dribbles onto the tile floor.

"Everything is fine," he says. "We are only being hell-of-cautious."

"Hell-of-cautious, huh?"

"Yes, this was the plan before we go on our big trip. It's nothing for your worries. Now please get Bandaid and fix sweet hand I make with your mother."

"Ew, Dad, that's disgusting."

"Why? We make you and you are sweet and perfect."

And bleeding to death. "I guess. So a normal will? Not because you or Mom are sick or anything?"

"No. We are not sick. We talk about it soon and then you feel better. Now go fix hand."

"Okay. Love you, Dad."

"Love you too! Bye-bye!" The connection breaks.

I inspect the cut, the broken skin standing at ragged attention. The pain is making me dizzy. I consider crawling to the bathroom, afraid I might pass out if I stand up straight. My right thumb is still sore from smacking Dylan, and now my left hand is ground round.

I calculate the possibility of falling, and the velocity with which I'd hit the floor from one foot, or five. Lower seems better, so I slide out of the chair and slither to the toilet, where with much relief, I throw up several servings of Cap'n Crunch.

CHAPTER 10
BIRDIES BY THE BEACH

I sit crumpled against the bathroom wall. The sour tang of milk and stomach acid lingers on my tongue. The ground behind me looks like the set of a horror movie, with a streak of blood smeared across the old tile floor, more splattered on the sink. I focus on the next thing. Stand up, clean the wound.

I'm running warm water over the cut when someone buzzes at the back door. The noise vibrates in my head, and what was a dull headache blooms into a cacophony of misery that makes me want to flush myself down the toilet.

Lightheaded and unsure I've seen the last of the Cap'n Crunch, I creep toward the back of the kitchen. Jesse's yelling from outside.

"Katy, what the hell? Let me in!"

She looks me up and down as I open the door. "Holy shit, what happened to you?"

"I cut my hand."

She follows me to the bathroom and asks questions while I lean against the wall to keep from toppling over.

"Should we go to the ER?" She steps closer. "Christ, Katy, you smell disgusting. Did you stop bathing?"

I nod and wrap a bandage around my palm. Rosy pink blood seeps through each layer as it goes on. "I need to sit."

Jesse supports me during the slow walk to the dining room. She offers to call 911. Unnecessary, I say, collapsing into a booth. It's just a bit of blood and my skin is naturally this pale. My grandmother was born in Transylvania, and right before everything fades into darkness, I try to show her how sharp my incisors are.

I dream of lying on warm soft sand. The ocean flows around me in an impossible elliptical circle, and seagulls sing in the blue and white speckled sky. I feel at peace, content to lie here for eternity.

My eyes open to Jesse's bored stare, a glass of wine perched on her lips. The dream lingers, teasing me. "How long was I asleep?"

"Almost an hour." She motions to the half-empty bottle on the table.

"How d'you know I wasn't dead?"

"What kind of question is that?"

"I could have been bleeding out."

"You think you're going to bleed out from a tiny cut on your hand?"

"No... I guess not. Thanks for staying and keeping me from possibly dying." I tell her about my dream. She grumbles, says I'm weird and that I should check myself into the nearest mental institution.

"It was just a dream, Jesse."

"It means you feel trapped." She slides off the bench seat and pulls my arm. "Let's get you some food and fresh air."

We drive north on Ocean, Jesse's lead foot getting us expeditiously through Dufferin Beach. She barely avoids hitting a few university students who wander like zombies with their heads tilted toward their phones.

"Fucking morons. Why don't they check before they walk out into the street?" She slams on the brakes. A thin blond girl is dancing on the road, wearing a loin cloth which shouldn't pass for shorts, and a tank top with Badass Bitch printed on it. Jesse rolls down her window and cusses her out. The girl doesn't appear to notice and continues swaying for almost thirty seconds. Finally, she swivels toward our car, gives us the finger, and hops back on the sidewalk.

"I'd only be culling the herd if I took her out." Jesse's white knuckled fingers compress the steering wheel.

We continue on; four paved lanes squeeze down to two. A few more miles, the two lanes narrow again, and we're on the old Ocean Avenue, originally running through a town which is still a blip on the map. On the roadside, old palm trees grow wild and sunshine filters through feathery Spanish Moss draped on the twisted branches of Live Oaks.

Another half-mile north and what's left of the road turns into a large gravel lot. On the far end is Birdies Bar, set on the beach like an old man napping on his front porch. A building constructed like an amateur's patchwork quilt, uneven boards nailed together, old paint on top of older paint, and a tin roof stained by years of salt spray, heat and humidity.

The present owner is Jimmy Dalton Junior, named after his father and grandfather, who started the business when Duff Beach was but a strip of ocean, sand and dirt. Being the only known proprietors, people wonder why the bar isn't called Dalton's. Most figure Birdie was the wife of one of the elder Jimmys and leave it at that.

Rumors have swirled about the Daltons, and whoever Birdie was, looking like cartoon characters, because there is no other explanation for Jimmy's striking features. His large head is shaved smooth, and his obscenely well-muscled upper body stops dead at the waist where long, thin legs leak out of him like cooked spaghetti. His disproportion is unsettling, his gait is similar to a bull riding atop a flamingo. He's a kindhearted giant who runs his establishment with the formality of a backyard barbecue.

We drop our shoes in a bin outside the front door and step over the threshold hidden underneath layers of sand. Jimmy greets us with bear hugs and directs us out back. On the other end of the building, dim lights shroud a pool table and a jukebox playing music loud enough to create sound waves that vibrate under our bare feet. We step onto the deck where the seating is nothing more than an assemblage of rattan chairs and benches with old worn pillows and wooden barrels. We pick a spot with just enough sun to feel the heat and hear the ocean rolling in, fifty feet in front of us.

Menus and wine lists are not available here, and there's no discussing the freshness of the ingredients. You'll have beer, hard liquor, and fried food. If those options aren't satisfactory, you'll leave thirsty and hungry.

Jesse orders a beer. I order a glass of water and a Greyhound made from vodka and freshly squeezed grapefruit. Jimmy delivers the drinks personally and after placing them on a barrel, lowers himself next to me on a bench scarcely big enough for two normal-sized people. The wicker creaks and pops as he turns to me. I try to make room, though only the chair expanding by an extra foot would fix this situation.

"How've you been?" he asks, unaware that his personal bubble has not only infringed upon mine, it has swallowed it whole.

"Good, how about you?"

"What d'you do?" He gingerly picks up my hand, rotates it, pokes at the bandage.

"Cut it at work."

"Blood's coming through." He studies my wound, then gazes down at his size thirteen feet. "Did you and Dylan split up?"

"Why are you asking?"

"Because he's inside. With a girl. He's doing stuff with a girl."

"Oh..." I look at a stone-faced Jesse.

"And he has his hands on her bottom parts."

"What are bottom parts, Jimmy? Her ass?" Jesse asks.

"Yes, that's right. And Flip is with him. He's all upset and trying to get him to leave."

"His name is Quinn, not Flip." I correct him for the hundredth time. "If Dylan wants to hang out with someone else, it's his business. It's not my deal anymore."

"All right, Katy. Are you sad?"

"Not sad, just disappointed. It's better this way."

"And Dylan didn't do that to your hand?"

"No. I promise I did this to myself."

He smiles at me; big teeth match the enormous head. He stands up, shuffles in place before lumbering back to the bar.

"Should we take off?" I ask Jesse when he's out of earshot.

"Hell no. I might have to snap a few pictures of your faithful husband touching someone's bottom parts."

I scoot to the center of the chair to discourage any further guests and begin drinking. Silently, we finish the first round and start on the second, which comes with a large basket of fries and onion rings.

After our third drink, I tell Jesse I'd like to be drunk much more often. I'm relaxed and don't care whose stray parts Dylan is touching. In fact, I hope he finds a bottom he might want to move in with. Jesse's chair is opposite mine, facing the back doorway, and her attention is less on me than what's happening inside. I watch her expression grow more serious and realize whatever she's seeing is about to kill my buzz.

"Shit!" She looks at me like a piano is getting ready to fall on my head.

"Are you following me, bitch?" Dylan slides out of the darkness and skids to a stop in white ankle socks. He stumbles and slurs his words. "You my fuck-in-damn stalker now?"

Frozen in place, the sunshine bakes my shoulders while Dylan's hostility rains down on me. He's more intoxicated than I've ever seen him, red-faced with sweat and alcohol steaming off his overheated body.

Before I can speak, Jimmy is behind Dylan, grabbing his arms and ripping him out of sight. We jump out of our seats and run behind them. My eyes adjust to the darkness as Dylan wiggles away from him and lunges at Quinn. I bump into the wooden edge of the bar, and Jesse stumbles into me right before Dylan's fist slams into Quinn's eye. With the thump of Quinn hitting the ground, Jimmy allows no opportunity for a second round. He lifts Dylan up, feet kicking in the air, carries him to the entrance, and launches him off the top step. Applause and cheers rise around us, the crowd saluting his zero-tolerance policy for poor behavior.

"What in the hell happened?" I ask while Jimmy peels Quinn off the floor.

He's stunned. A dark circle is already forming around his right eye.

"Does he have a concussion?" I ask.

He slaps Quinn on the back, propelling him in my direction. "Nah, he'll be fine. I'm gonna go make sure Dylan finds his way out of the parking lot."

Jesse and I lead a startled Quinn back to our seats. A bag of crushed ice and the fourth round of drinks are delivered by a server. She tells us the drinks are on the house and also how sorry everyone is that my husband turned out to be a dick.

"Put it on your eye." Jesse throws the bag at him. He flinches and catches the ice before it tumbles to the deck.

"Are you okay?" I'm not nearly as bothered by him sitting near me as I was Jimmy.

He nods, and with his free hand, gives me a thumbs-up.

"When did you start hanging out with Dylan again?" I ask and take the first sip of my fourth drink.

Jesse pushes forward in her rattan seat. "And whose ass is he grabbing?"

"A random one, faceless, nameless. He won't remember tomorrow." He moves the bag of ice from one hand to the other.

"I didn't come here with him. He texted me, clearly blasted. I was trying to stop him from doing something stupid."

"Like grab a faceless ass?" She winks at him, and he pushes closer to me.

"Indeed." Quinn squints at Jesse with his good eye.

"How did he know Katy was here?"

"I'm not sure. He may have seen you walking in, or someone told him. It doesn't matter. He went ballistic because he thought you were following him, and said he'd put you in your place for everything you've done."

"I wasn't following him."

"I know." He downs his beer. "I need another one."

"I don't love the sound of that." Jesse stands up with one empty mug in each hand.

"The sound of what?" I ask.

"Putting you in your place," she says, heading inside for refills.

I lean back into the chair, close to Quinn. The heat from his body feels right and wrong all at once, and I wonder if this configuration appears as scandalous as what Dylan was just doing. My thought, though hazy, is confirmed by the displeasure on Jesse's face when she returns.

"Are you kidding me?" She sets the fresh beers down. "Katy, switch seats with me." She pulls me up by my hands, twirls me in a half-circle, and drops me into her chair. Then she shoves Quinn to the far side of the rattan seat and takes my place. "Stay the fuck in your corners."

"I was sitting in a comfortable manner. We weren't having sex, Jess... God, we were just sitting." The harder I try to enunciate, the less I'm able to. The waves crash onto the beach, and the salt in the air is strong enough to taste. "Being drunk is so pleasant."

"Until the next day." Quinn sits up straight. "What did you do to your hand?"

The color of the bandage has deepened to crimson. “I cut it when I was on the phone with my dad.” I sigh. “It hasn’t been a great day.”

“Katy, try to focus,” Jesse interrupts.

My response to her is a loud hiccup.

“Dylan threatened you.”

“He didn’t threaten me. He’s just a very young baby. I will purchase him a playpen.”

They stare at me, then glance at each other.

“Jesse’s right, Katy. It didn’t sound like a passing annoyance.”

“It’s fucking apocalyptic. Want to hear about my mom and dad?”

Quinn and Jesse exchange another look, and I feel left out while being the main attraction.

“We’ll need to do something,” Jesse says.

“Why can’t we talk about my parents? I need a milk shake.”

“Do what? Have him arrested?” Quinn’s cheek is swelling. The bruise is turning the same shade of blue that decorated my arms last week.

“So, they were in Thailand, where it’s so hot people melt all over the place.”

Jesse ignores me. “Not enough cause yet, but we can call the cops. I have friends in the department.”

“Just literally melt, like the Wicked Witch of the North.”

“People don’t literally melt, Katy.” Jesse shakes her head.

“Was it the one from the north?” I ask. “Or was she from the south?”

“West.” Quinn winks at me. Damn, he’s smooth even while injured.

“Really… west?” I repeat, taking another drink. “Anyway, they were on a beach, and there was this girl. A girl who was conveniently located on the same beach.”

“You should stop drinking.” Jesse moves the glass out of my reach.

"Leverage with the cops, huh? How did that happen?" Quinn asks.

"Irrelevant." She fishes a handful of onion rings from the basket and drops them into her mouth.

"Then my parents had a lovely evening. Dinner, and a movie or whatever old parents do. And it was all fabulous until my dad took off and spent the night with the girl from the beach."

"He what, now?" Jesse asks.

"And my mom busted him out, so she went to Paris."

"Your dad fooled around on your mom?"

"Yes, Judge Tanner."

"Don't call me that. She left him?"

"Yes... Jesse the not judge," I say, then stuff fries into my mouth.

"And your dad is not in Paris?"

"He is not. He's shacked up with some chick named Lima."

"Lima?" Quinn asks.

"Yeah, Lima, like the bean-shaped country in South America."

"Your folks split up and your dad's living with another woman?" Quinn moves the ice pack again.

"She's not a woman, she's a toddler."

"Gross," he mumbles.

"Totally what I said. And Mom's in Paris with my uncle, and Dad's renting an apartment in Bangkok. He wants me to visit."

"You're not going, are you?" He leans forward, out of the shade. The sun highlights the gold in his hair, enhancing what nature or a salon already gave him.

"No, she's not going anywhere. Jesus, Katy, why didn't you tell me this before?"

"It's whatever, Jess."

"It's not whatever at all. Your parents are out of the country doing God-knows-what and your husband is threatening you. How's your mom? Is she pissed? Is she upset?"

"She's going to the opera."

"What?" they ask in unison.

"It's a long story."

"Do we need to hear it?" Jesse tucks her hair behind her ears.

"About the opera? God no, they're all so long and boring. Someone sings, someone screws the wrong person, and then everyone dies." I look for my drink. It's missing, or I finished it. I can't remember.

"I'm sorry about your parents, Katy, but where does that leave you now?" Quinn wipes away melted ice dripping down his arm. "Spending a quiet evening with Dylan?"

"It's been peaceful since I beat the crap out of him. He might not be there."

"Or he will. Either way, I don't want you near him." Jesse signals for our tab. "We can drive by. If he's there... great, we won't have to worry about him being somewhere else."

"And where will I be?"

"With me," Jesse states this as fact, and I'm too wasted to argue.

I exhale and hiccup again. "And the police thing?"

Quinn glances at me, pulls out a twenty for the bill, and hands it to Jesse.

I push cash in her direction, she waves it off. "You feed me enough, and we'll get the law involved tomorrow. Christ, Katy, it's all so weird."

I smile. My parents are in their own opera now. Perhaps they'll kill each other too.

"I don't feel very good," I announce, visualizing the grease and booze sloshing in my stomach.

With the bill paid, we find Jimmy, thank him, and apologize for the trouble. He says from now on, Birdie's is a "Dylan-free-zone", and hands us a fresh bag of ice. Quinn walks us out and makes some noise about tagging along. Jesse shuts him down but offers to touch base with him in the morning.

The gravel pops like muffled gunfire under the wheels as we head out of the lot. I ask Jesse, "Think he'll be okay driving after getting punched in the head?"

"He's not the one I'm worried about."

I stare out the window, watching the landscape race by. When I was a kid, my parents told me the car wasn't moving, the road underneath us was. No wonder I was always throwing up. We drive back under the canopy of trees. The sky glows red as the sunlight bleeds away.

My car is at the restaurant, so we decide to leave it as a decoy. If Dylan comes looking for me, the car will be all he finds. Jesse rolls by the house. Dylan's motorcycle is parked diagonally in our small driveway.

Was he too drunk to park his bike in a straight line, or is this a passive-aggressive hint that no wife shall pass? The lights are off. He must be facedown, drooling on the bed.

"I'm going to need some new furniture," I tell Jesse before we speed off to her townhouse.

CHAPTER 11
MISS FUBSY & DAN

Jesse's voice carries in any space she's in, living room, courtroom, or in this case, kitchen. "Cover your ears or suffer," she bellows.

She's not a morning person, and she doesn't sport a sunny disposition or optimistic outlook for the promise of a new day. This is her only warning before hitting *pulverize* on the coffee grinder. I shove my head under the pillow and wait for the noise to stop.

"Want some?" She stands over me five minutes later with two cups of dark roast.

I accept it, mindful of my bandaged hand. "Thanks. Who are these?" I ask, pointing to the cartoon squirrels decorating the cup.

She smiles. "Remember my niece up in Buffalo?"

"Of course. Trudy, cutest baby ever."

"Not a baby anymore. She's a toddler mimicking my stupid-as-shit sister who swears like a fucking sailor."

"Oh no." I try to keep a straight face. Does she even get the irony?

"Trudy started saying fuck you and damn it to the kids in her preschool class."

"That sucks." I turn the cup in my hand.

"My brother-in-law came up with this squirrel family to fix it. The dude is Dan, and the girl squirrel is Miss Fubsy. He's a graphic artist, so he made up a whole cartoon."

"Fubsy and Dan? Seriously?"

"Dan straight. Trudy's potty-mouth is all cleaned up." She smiles. "My sister's too."

"How'd they get the pictures on the cups?" I ask, studying Miss Fubsy's short pink dress. She and Dan look so happy. But are they, or is Dan pissed off about spending his life hunting nuts? And is Miss Fubsy truly satisfied with her furry rodent-man, or is she wearing that slutty get up because she's on the prowl for someone whose tail isn't his biggest appendage?

"Hey," I say, noticing Jesse's outfit. "Why are you all dressed up?"

"Filing your papers today so we can get Dylan served and expedite the temporary hearing."

"Oh hell. Do I have to be there?"

"No."

"Am I almost divorced?"

Her eyes narrow. "You're aware it's more complicated than filing a document?"

I am not aware, which is why I hired a lawyer. The coffee burns my tongue; the pain doesn't faze me; the damage gives me a lisp. "Tho then whath going to happen?"

She stares at me like she has so often before, perhaps wondering why or how we became friends. "Dylan gets served. No telling how it'll go. He might handle it like a man, or he'll get drunk, and trash your house. At some point, he'll probably lawyer up. The court will set a date for the first hearing, where the judge will ask questions you'll find intrusive and inappropriate. Hopefully, he'll grant you temporary possession of your property."

She sets a neat pile of legal papers in front of me; my name in bold print: Katalin Ildiko Judit Decker *v.* Dylan Marcus Decker. My stomach lurches. This is real. I'm getting a divorce.

"When will he get served?" I place Miss Fubsy and Dan on the table.

"Couple days."

"Uh-huh."

"This is what you want, right? You want to leave your husband?"

"Uh-huh."

"Say yes, Katy."

"Think I'm gonna throw up."

"Please tell me this is what you want, or I'm going to have to kill you."

"Yes. This is what I want."

"It's all good, Kiss. People get divorced every day and nothing traumatic happens. They go on with their lives, all that happy ever-after horseshit." She scoots away from me. "What's with all the puking? You weren't like this in college."

"Can I leave your townhouse?"

"Of course," she says.

"Can I take a shower?" I pull the light blanket around my shoulders.

"Please do." She keeps talking and pointing to the stack of papers.

I look at Miss Fubsy. Her teeny squirrel butt is peeking out from under her dress.

Jesse watches me watch the rodent. "Are you listening or zoning out to that weird place in your head?"

"I don't have any weird plathe, place, in my head."

"We both know that's not true, Kiss. Your eyes glaze over, and you stop blinking."

"I'm blinking." I bat my eyelashes. "See? Not glazing over anything."

"You were staring at the squirrel."

"Because she's a thlut. Slut. She's probably fooling around on Dan."

"She would never fool around on Dan."

"What if he isn't thufficient?"

"Are you talking about a cartoon penis?" She takes a loud, deliberate slurp from her coffee, then tells me to get myself together because we're expecting a call from the police.

I push myself off the sofa and march away with the blanket draped over my shoulders. It slides to the floor, gets tangled between my feet, and I lurch into the wall. She's still laughing as I scurry out of sight.

• • • • •

Quinn is in the kitchen, cornered by Jesse when I emerge from the bathroom. She's offering him an orange vodka slushy.

"It's eight-thirty, Jess. Shouldn't the ice go on his eye instead?"

He slides around her and looks me over. "What's with the clothes?"

"They're Jesse's. I wasn't planning for a sleepover." I tug on oversized jeans and cross my arms over the white shirt. The pant legs would engulf my feet had I not rolled them up and the sleeves come down to my fingertips.

"Cool," he says and pours himself a coffee.

We settle in the living room among the mess that builds up between Jesse's weekly maid service. I sit where I slept, covering up with the pillow so Quinn will stop gawking at my ill-fitted getup.

"Tasty brew," he says.

"Fresh ground beans!" Jesse yells from the kitchen.

His cup has Dan the squirrel on it, who wears only the top half of his tuxedo.

"Cute cups, aren't they?" I ask, looking at my toes, the carpet, the legs of the table. Anything but him.

"I guess." He stares at the image of Dan on his tree branch.

Quinn's still hot, even with the ring around his eye. I'm flustered and have no clue what to say or how to behave. This is seventh grade all over again.

Jesse stomps back into the room, shoves me over on the couch, and sits down.

"I'm putting her on speaker now, Sheriff Madigan." She drops the phone down between us. "We're ready."

"Katy, you there?" The sheriff's deep voice echoes in the room.

"Yes sir, I'm right here."

"Can you tell me what happened?"

"Um," I stammer. I suck under pressure, and a cop asking questions is pressure.

"Ya'll still on the line?" he asks.

"Yes! Still here. I guess my husband might have threatened me."

Jesse slaps my shoulder and rolls her eyes.

"Tanner says he also knocked someone out. This was at Birdies, right?"

"Yes, sir."

"What got everyone riled up?"

"Oh...well, I told Jesse I wanted a divorce a couple of weeks ago, so she's filing all the paperwork. I think it's almost done. Dylan doesn't know yet, so things have been tense." Between words, I chew on the skin around my pinkie.

"Your husband's Dylan Decker? The guy who keeps losing jobs?"

"You've heard about him?"

"Gossip, small town. Keep talking."

"So, my parents are traveling, and that's a mess."

Jesse whispers not to bring them into it.

"They all right? Your folks are fine people for newcomers. They sure can whip up some good Hungaria food."

I press my lips together. I can't stand it when people say "Hungaria". It's Hungary, and we are Hungarian, which in no way means we're hungry. Also, they've been American citizens for almost twenty-five years, so they're not *new* either. I scowl at Miss Fubsy. Jesse nudges my foot, trying to get me back on point.

"No, I meant I'm the mess. They're fine. So, we went for a drink, and Quinn was there because Dylan was drunk, and he was trying to get him to leave. Then Quinn got punched instead, and Dylan yelled at me, and Jimmy threw him out. Not in that order. I mean, kind of like that. There's more, but it would make it confusing."

Madigan's sigh comes through loud and clear. "No idea what you're trying to say. Put Tanner on."

Jesse launches into lawyer mode, reciting only what he needs to know. She tells him about my looming divorce, the increasing animosity, and recounts what happened at the bar with clarity I will never possess.

"So, Decker's acting an ass and got violent?"

"Quinn Healy is here too. He can answer himself." Jesse pushes the phone in his direction.

"Morning, sir." Quinn leans in. "I'd like to clarify that he didn't knock me out. He knocked me down."

Another loud sigh from the phone. "And you heard him threaten Katy as well?"

"Yes, sir."

"Did he frighten you, Katy?"

"Oh no, not so much. I think, though, it's not entirely impossible that he could be somewhat dangerous."

"Which one is it?" the sheriff asks.

"Which one is what?"

He clears his throat of the irritation that is me. "Not sure you have enough for a restraining order, Tanner."

"We don't," she agrees.

"I'll make sure everyone's made aware," he says. "We'll keep an eye on him. Call me if something comes up."

"We surely will. Thanks for your help, Sheriff."

"It's no problem. And Katy, if you have any trouble with your husband, call me directly. Tanner, give her my number."

• • • • •

Half an hour later, Jesse heads to court, and I hitch a ride in Quinn's truck.

"Is this chair buckled all the way in? Isn't that a thing with these cars, like the seats fly right the fuck out if you forget to attach them?" I wiggle back and forth, remembering a friend in high school whose boyfriend took her for a joy ride in his truck without checking. She wasn't injured when she became airborne with an automobile seat attached to her ass. The boyfriend became single.

"Don't you trust me?" Quinn asks. "Is it because you're from Hungaria?"

"I'm serious." I watch him change gears, his left leg moving up and down with the clutch as he navigates out of the neighborhood. It feels so wrong to be here. I touch my forehead to check if the Scarlet A has burned into my skin.

"Why didn't you tell me about the divorce?" he asks, gliding into fourth gear.

"I didn't want to bother you with it. Dylan has no clue, so don't say anything."

"You think I would?"

"No," I tell him, looking at the palm trees lining the road.

"What can I do to help?"

"I don't need help. Jesse's taking care of it."

"Obstinate much?"

"What? I'm fine. We'll go to court, work out a couple things, and be on our merry way. It's like Jesse says, people get divorced all the time. No big deal."

"You think it'll be that simple?"

"Sure."

We drive in silence, past rows of orange trees and the ornate road sign welcoming us to downtown Dufferin Beach. I climb out of the truck in the drop off lane in front of Dr. Jonas's office.

Quinn lowers his sunglasses. "Are you mad I showed up this morning?"

"No. But why did you?"

His smile is creamy smooth. "I wanted to check on you. I guess I'm feeling protective."

"Oh. That's not..." I step away from the curb. "Um. Okay then. Thanks for the ride."

Smooth smiles make me want to sprint in the other direction. And what in the hell did I just say? He drives off while I scold myself for being unable to take compliments or acknowledge anything warm, emotional, or tingly.

CHAPTER 12
TIC TAC

The waiting room isn't empty today. A thin man with hollowed-out cheeks sits in a chair by the front door, twitching, sniffling, aggressively itching his left elbow. I diagnose him with alcoholism or a meth habit. Would it be wrong to ask why he's agitated? I sit down, wondering what his teeth or a slice of his liver might look like.

"Are you ready?" Dr. Jonas's voice startles me. She glances at the fidgety man without acknowledgment. He must not be her patient, and I forget him by the time we reach her office.

In no mood to talk, I feel the same nagging in my gut I had as a kid when Mom made me tidy my room before the cleaning lady showed up. At the time, I thought she was nuts. Now I have a similar urge to secure the valuables inside my brain before my shrink tries to wash away all the good stuff.

"How's your week been?" She stares at me, too close, too direct, pushing on the fragile skin of my personal bubble. Why must I suffer this face-to-face bullshit? Why can't I do therapy anonymously, remotely, or with a paper bag over my head?

"What happened to your hand, Katy?"

"Got distracted at work. A lot's gone on, pretty much all of it bad." I recount the week's events and promise my freshly wrapped hand is not a Dylan-related injury. He's still unemployed, beating up on friends and grabbing the asses of women who are not his wife. She asks few questions while I tell her we contacted the police about Dylan's drunken threat, and that I'm staying with Jesse. I search for something else to say about my husband but can find nothing. He already seems like my past, even if he is still lurking in my life.

Dr. Jonas isn't as ready to move forward and asks about Dylan's role within my family, his inability to remain employed, and the friction it causes.

His career path is a pattern, easy to describe. He's attractive, well-spoken, and confident, so he can get a job anywhere. The cycle begins at his first interview, where he establishes himself as the golden boy. Grateful and courteous, brilliant rays of sunshine exude from his very soul while he puts every ounce of energy into his work. Time passes, the luster wears off, and he's set the bar so high that the fall is inevitably more dramatic. Unable to keep up, he becomes resentful about the expectations he created. His anger grows, and before too long, he quits or gets fired, leaving a smoldering pile of goodwill in his wake. The stories are all the same, only the names of his employers differ. Dr. Jonas listens silently while I describe the details of companies and people Dylan has plowed through.

"You've put a lot of thought into his behavior."

"He goes through three or four jobs a year. It's not hard to pin down the methodology."

"How does he get along with your parents?"

Can I say my dad refers to him as "the asshole" and my mother winces each time he opens his mouth?

"They're not fond of him," I reply.

"Openly?"

"At first they tried to like him. Now they nod and smile."

"I imagine it creates some tension."

"You'd have to throw hard for his ego to feel injury." I flash back to him scurrying over the bed like a palmetto bug.

"No, I mean, does it cause tension between you and your parents?"

This line of questioning sucks. Also, some orange Tic Tacs would be delicious right now. I bet a couple are swimming around the bottom of my bag.

She continues. "Even if Dylan is unaware, the three of you are still forced to participate."

I stare at her, trying to find a way out of these questions. I can't though because I am forcing my dreadful relationship down my family's throat. Is this good therapy? Isn't the list of things I fuck up and feel bad about supposed to be getting smaller?

"It never occurred to me before. I've been putting my family through hell. God, I'm a horrible person."

"Why are you jumping straight to that, Katy? You're not a bad person. This isn't about blame, it's about resolution."

"I'm dragging my parents into my shitty life. I'm dragging everyone in, even Jesse. How is it not my fault?"

"Taking blame isn't an uncommon reaction, though it is a waste of your energy. A better direction would be to welcome the positive changes you're ready to make."

I grunt. A positive outlook? SO not in my wheelhouse.

"Can we discuss Dylan?" she asks.

"Sure."

"Have you been able to depend on him?"

"Kind of the opposite."

Dr. Jonas moves on to a second sheet of paper. She scribbles my name on the top.

"I know he'll always disappoint me. Pathetic, right?"

"No. I am sorry to hear it though."

She leans toward me again, my bubble in mortal danger of her insistent jagged edges.

"Who do you count on?"

I blink away the pressure of tears. "My dad."

"You're very close."

"Yeah."

"How do you feel about him being away from home?"

"Fine at first. I was happy they left. It was a chance to be an adult without any strings attached."

"What changed?"

"He fooled around on my mom."

"That hurt you?" she asks.

"What happened in Thailand has nothing to do with me."

"It changes your dynamic with them, which makes it about you."

"Turnabout, right? They watch me screw things up. Now it's their turn? Could I have infected them with the stupid shit I do?"

"That's not how things work. When will your father be returning home?"

"He's staying in Thailand."

"For how long?"

"No clue."

"Okay." She crosses her legs, uncrosses them; razor-sharp knees pivot up and down. Is this an inappropriate time to rifle through my purse? How long before a Tic Tac goes bad?

I try to focus. "It sucks, him hanging out in another country. This isn't my call, though. I'm not a child. I can survive alone."

She nods. "And your mom?"

"She's not coming home either." I fill her in on our conversation, and my dad's weird call from Bangkok. Their life-altering pronouncements without so much as a warning shot.

"A lot to take in," she says.

"At least we know where she is, and that she's safe. Dad's off the map with some girl named Lima."

"Lima?" Her eyebrows furrow.

"Yes...no. I'm not sure what her name is." I rub my fingers over the rough weave of the couch.

"Let's try not to get off track, Katy."

"I live off track. Isn't that why I'm here?"

She nods again, working to keep me on point. "Did you address your concerns with your father?"

"Kind of."

"How did that feel?"

I glance at my bandaged hand. "It felt bad."

"Because he's not coming home yet?"

"I guess. Is he allowed to disappear, walk out on his family?"

She remains silent.

"What's wrong with me?" I ask.

"Nothing's wrong with you. You're doing the best you can."

"Then my best doesn't seem so good. This started when I married Dylan."

"Are you sure?"

"You're implying that I married him because something was already messed up?"

"There's nothing messed up with you, Katy. Some of your choices turned out badly. Now you have an opportunity to examine the reasons."

"Dylan might be a by-product of something else?"

"Possibly." She peeks at the clock behind me.

"This is annoying," I huff.

"What is?"

"I invite bad things into my life for no reason. Why would I do that?"

"A fair question, and it doesn't need to be a mysterious thing or a life-changing event. You've got no memory of trauma, so it may be a thread, a recurring theme altering how you process things."

"That's too open-ended, too vague."

"I have no simple answer, and no way of handing you a preformed theory about life."

"Why not? Isn't it your job to fix me?"

"I can't fix what you can't see," she says, pulling her sleeves up on her bony arms.

"So, therapy is a game of twenty questions?"

She smiles. "What I'd like you to think of are the choices and decisions you've made without assigning blame to them. The past is what you learn from because there's nothing there you can go back and fix."

"That's deep." I look down at my phone. Fifty minutes have flown by.

"This is a process. The results aren't immediate. It sounds cliché, but it took you a while to get to this point, so it's going to take time to make changes."

"That's not very satisfying for someone who has no patience."

"You may be more patient than you realize, Katy. Give it some thought, and we'll pick this up next week."

We finish the session by confirming my safety plan and wishing each other a happy Thanksgiving while I dig through my purse for Tic Tacs. She hands me a new appointment card and I exit her office more agitated than when I arrived.

CHAPTER 13
A MAN IN THE FAMILY

The nervous man from the waiting room is gone, and so am I, out the front door and into the rare, crisp fall air. There is nowhere to go. The restaurant is closed today, my house is off-limits, and my parents are out of town.

Fifteen minutes later, I'm in an empty field adjacent to the small private aviation airport. My dad often brought me here before I got married. We'd talk about life, work and school while the planes came and went. It was our noisy, dusty place to hide from the rush of our lives. Today, I'm hiding on my own from the damage of therapy.

I park facing the runway and sit on the hood of the car. The airport is a half-mile north, beyond a row of metal fences meant to keep trespassers off the property. I watch the jets lift-off; their landing gear is still down as they fly overhead, and the sound of the engines vibrates in my ears.

The wind blows across my face, the sunshine warms my skin. I'm anonymous out here. Not Katy Decker or Katy Kiss, not a wife or daughter or therapy patient. I'm just cells thrown together; organic chemistry doing its thing, pumping blood, and firing neurons.

I watch and listen to the planes for almost half an hour before my cell phone rings. The number is familiar, and so is the voice shouting "bonjour!" It's my Aunt Josephine from Paris. My heart skips a beat, wondering if something's happened to my mom.

"Bonjour Josephine, ca'va?"

"Qui est-ce?" she asks.

"It's Katy. You called me."

"Katy?"

"From Florida." Mom was right about her dementia. How has she already forgotten my name?

"Merde! So sorry, how are you, ma chérie?"

"Good, thanks. How are you?"

"Bien, merci beaucoup. And how is Dylan?" Her pronunciation of his name is Dee-lawn, nasally, and romantic.

"He's well. Why did you call? Is everything okay?"

"Oui, all is good. When will you visit?"

"Je ne sais pas." I say.

"Did you call for your Maman? I get her now."

I slide off the car. A jet flies overhead.

"Katy?" My mom picks up the phone and asks what's going on. "Mi van?"

"Nothing. Josephine called me. Are you okay?"

"Now do you see she is losing her minds?"

"I guess. Not the nicest way of putting it though."

"There is not a nice way of living with it. Márton is beside of himself with her."

"How can it happen so fast? What's he going to do?" I climb into the driver's seat. Another aircraft glides in my direction. In thirty seconds, I won't hear anything she's saying.

"I told you, he is beside of himself. Well, God help him, at least he stays with her."

I shut the door, hoping to drown out the roar. "What's that supposed to mean?"

"The meaning is obvious. What is this terrible noise?"

"Traffic."

"I see. So, what is happening in America?"

"Nothing."

"Nothing is happening, very nice."

"Have you spoken to Dad?"

"No." Her tone is clipped.

"So, there is some stuff going on here... I guess."

She sighs over the phone. I can feel her annoyance from across the ocean. Another jet lifts off. I tell her to hold on and use the time to gather myself.

"I'm getting a divorce." I spit the words out quickly.

"From Dylan?"

I squeeze my eyes shut. "Who else would I divorce, Mom?"

"It was just a question."

"Fine. Yes, I'm divorcing Dylan."

"Why?"

"Because we have a miserably unhappy marriage."

"Are you sure? Does he accept this?"

"Accept what?" I ask, rolling down my window. "It's not a proposal."

"But what does he say about it?"

"He doesn't know yet."

"Explain to me. Because your father and I are not together, does not mean you should leave your husband, too."

My mouth drops open. No words come out. Just hot air, confusion, anger.

She continues before I can respond. "So now we do not have even one man in this family?"

"Are you kidding? You want me to stay with Dylan so we can be socially acceptable?"

"Do not insult me, Katy."

"Then don't insult me. This isn't about you."

"Should I come home?" she asks with the same icy voice I last heard in high school when she caught me in my bedroom with a box of fine wine and an unacceptable suitor.

"No, I'm all right. Jesse's helping me and I started seeing a therapist."

"A what?"

"A psychologist. Her name is Dr. Jonas."

"Why do you need to see this person?"

I swat at a fly. "Jesse told me to. It helps to talk to someone."

"You don't need the psychologist. You talk to me."

"Uh-huh," I mumble. So, more conversations like this one? No wonder I'm fucking crazy.

"Does your father know?"

"About Dylan? No, I haven't said anything."

"He is too busy having the sex with the girl."

"Yuck, Mom. Please don't say things like that to me."

"Why not? If I charge you by the hours, then you will speak to me?"

The fly lands on my bag. Bet it's after my damn Tic Tacs.

"Katy?"

"Yes?"

"Why don't you answer me?"

"Because you're not being fair. Let's chat about your parents' sex life."

A long, loaded silence fills the airwaves. "When will this divorce happen?"

"Not sure. Jesse says it takes a while."

"Jesse?"

"Yeah."

"How is she?" she pauses. "Is she still? You know…"

"Bisexual?"

"I don't understand this thing, Katy."

"I get that, but your confusion doesn't nullify its existence."

"So modern of you. And you are the friends again?"

"We're working on it."

"Maybe the psychologist will help with this too," she snaps.

"Mom..."

"Yes?"

"Nothing, never mind."

"Good, I will call you next week or you can call me if you need me. Yes?"

"Sure."

"Fine," she snaps, slamming down the receiver so hard it hurts my ear.

"Uh-huh, it is fucking fine," I say to the fly.

A dark blue airplane lands, bumps up and down a few times as the wheels meet the runway. So much for positive thoughts. I'll opt for bitchy and unreasonable while examining the reasons my mom can walk out on my dad, yet I'm not allowed the same option. Once I figure that out, I'll re-assess my behavior.

CHAPTER 14
I HATE EVERYTHING

The next few days drag by. My nerves are frayed and I'm being "ugly," as people around here say. Part of the blame lies in the daily tub of espresso I consume. Part is sleep deprivation because who the hell can sleep after drinking that much coffee? I'm sick of wearing Jesse's clothes, and sick of being a guest when my house is a few miles away. I dread going to work, and I'm pissed at my parents for forcing the drudgery of their lives down my throat. Russ, Melissa, and Diana tiptoe around me, watching and ducking as small objects go airborne.

The routines my mom and dad established now feel tedious. How do they live like this? Make the food, serve it, clean it up. Do it over again. When did I buy into their flour-flinging, onion-chopping version of the American dream?

Thursday morning I'm glaring at an ancient soup pot when Russ timidly requests that I start on the Zserbo; one of the most famous pastries from Hungary, and the most requested dessert in the restaurant. Dad claims his mother's recipe is perfection. Mom says hers is better. After years of debate about content and technique, the recipe has melded into something both take credit for. Mom bakes to the sound of Annie Lennox with sugar swirling in the air. Dad listens to Pavarotti. He bellows, off-key, gesticulating and conducting a phantom orchestra. For the last few months, I've alternated their music, not wanting to offend the Pastry Gods. Today, in what the psychological community might call childish rebellion, I tune into the university station and find some noise that would make Kurt Cobain turn in his grave. It sounds awful, like a thousand monkeys having sex.

I toss flour into the electric mixer, pull a chunk of butter from the fridge, and cut it into small pieces. Bit by bit, I drop them in and watch it all spin, slowly adding ice water until the dough holds together in an off-white ball. I knead it, wrap it in plastic, and hurl it into the refrigerator.

I don't recall being this angry when I left Dr. Jonas's office. Annoyed, yes, even sorry I kept getting distracted by my cravings for candy. But I don't remember feeling this way, at least not until the fight with my mother.

Moving far away from everyone, I grab the bin of onions and start dicing. Deep in thought, I neglect to don my onion cutting gear, ski goggles, rubber gloves and a plastic shower cap. My eyes well up as the ingredients splash into a cast-iron pan with oil, spicy Hungarian wax peppers, and enough paprika to turn everything dark red. My fat teardrops drip into the mixture, and I wonder if the customers will notice the stew is too salty. The hot oil sizzles and bubbles. My stomach turns. I can't do it. I heave the pot over the garbage can and dump out the contents.

What did my shrink do to my head, and why does she get to dictate what matters or which parts of my existence are relevant? Perhaps I enjoy the irrelevant details and endless confusion.

Russ creeps by me with a stack of dishes. He stares at the ground; he might even be holding his breath. I'm such a bitch. What if I take responsibility for the stupid situations I get myself into?

Diana shatters a wine glass on the ground. Russ cuts his finger trying to pick it up. Screw it. I don't have the energy to evolve this week.

I start on the stew again, this time without the tears, and grab a cleaver to cut cubes of bloody pink beef. The pressure of the knife presses into my bandaged hand. The skin opens under the gauze and tape. There's nothing for it. This is my job, chopping bits of food and cooking them up, all so I can put them on a plate on a table and smile when someone says this is the best meal from "Hungaria" they've ever had. Fucking shit, why couldn't I be from Ohio?

The rest of the day reinforces my anger. I stare into the bowl of flour, the starter for the dumplings. I add eggs, water and a pinch of salt. The goopy mess sticks to my fingers.

Did I go to college so I could peel paste off my hands? I hate eggs and raw meat and cooking utensils. I hate my mother and father. I hate Dr. Jonas. She's pointy and judgmental. This all sucks, and I hate everything.

CHAPTER 15
MAKING GOOD CHOICES

Friday morning, I wake up to lightning and thunder. Torrents of rain pelt the roof of Jesse's townhouse. The aroma of coffee and burned Pop-Tarts fill the damp air. The blinds are open, yet the room is dark and cold, heavy with my ill will.

Jesse catches on, even with my face hidden under a blanket.

"Notice how I picked a plain mug for you this morning?" She sets a gray cup on the coffee table. "You dissed the rodents, now you get nothing."

I grumble and sit up. I'd forgotten all about Miss Fubsy and her sinning ways.

"What's up with the bitch-face, Katy?"

"Sorry. I'm in a bad mood. Did you submit the paperwork to the court?" I eye her strawberry Pop-Tarts. "Can I have one?"

"Yeah, go ahead. Papers are filed. Dylan will get served in the next few days."

"Why didn't you tell me yesterday?"

She stares at me, the big brain behind the stern face calculating a response. "Nothing to tell until we hear from him or his attorney, if he hires one."

"Not what I asked."

"Noted," she says, finishing her coffee.

"Whatever. I'm not a lawyer."

"Thank God." She winks at me. "I'm off. Keep a low profile, go to work, come back here. Let's keep you locked down in case Dylan goes ape shit."

I nod as my gatekeeper leaves the building.

• • • • •

After a long shower and deep contemplation of Jesse's recommendation, I decide this entire situation is a pile of horseshit. Outside, the storm is clearing up. For sure a good omen that I'm getting ready to do the right thing.

The rain stops by the time I pull into my driveway and the sun is doing its best to squeeze through the gray clouds. I've been wearing Jesse's clothes for over a week, rolled up jeans hanging off my hips, and t-shirts two sizes too big. I'm tired of the look. It's my house and I'm going in.

Dylan's motorcycle is parked dead-center. I circle around to get to the front door. My stomach contracts, my brain ignores the warning. I unlock it and step inside. He's sprawled on the loveseat like he's been expecting me. His long legs are spread apart, and his mouth stretches in a sleazy smile.

"Hello." He sounds like a voice-over from a porn flick.

The house is a pigsty, clothes on the ground, empty food containers and bottles of booze cover every surface. I smell stale beer, cigarettes, weed, and everything else he hasn't flushed down the toilet. The house is desecrated.

"Lots to clean up, now that you're home." He scratches his unshaven face.

"What?" I ask, overwhelmed by the scene.

"Let's skip the drama. You took off, now you're back."

"I'm not…back," I mumble, and step over a crumpled ball of paper towels. The china cabinet is collecting dust. The pieces inside, my great-great-grandmother's silver candlesticks, a crystal fruit bowl given to my mom at her wedding, are untouched.

Everything of value in this house is part of my history, and I have become the absent caretaker.

From under the kitchen sink, I take out a watering can, fill it up, and hope my African violets will survive the next few weeks. Mom snuck the cuttings for these plants into the country when my great-aunt died in Montreal. They were her pride and joy, and I baby them as she did years ago. The basil has not survived and hangs limp over the rim of the pot. The sink is full of dishes, with remnants of food rotting in a climate which has no tolerance for procrastination.

"How was Quinn?" He's behind me before I finish watering the last plant, his muscular body generating waves of heat that wrap around my neck and flow to my shoulders. I flatten myself against the sink. He pushes closer.

"Was he good?"

My fingers tighten along the smooth edge of the counter, and I focus on a bottle of lemon Lysol. I don't want him to touch me; I don't want to hear his voice. Outside the window, a bumblebee circles the rose bush. It hovers, deciding which flower looks juiciest, and settles inside a bloom. Its weight pushes the fragile pink petals downward.

"Is he better than me?" His hands squeeze my waist.

"Holy crap." I flinch and push him away. "Stop it!"

He leers, licks his lips. "Come on, it's been weeks." He laughs. "Well, weeks since I've had you."

"Are you kidding me?"

"And you're not the most creative, Katy, compared to the others. But what the hell, how about you give me a blow job to show your remorse?"

A spasm of laughter bursts out of me.

"Something caught in your throat?" he asks, laughing, fumbling with his zipper.

What was I thinking showing up here? The sanctimonious phrase, *are you making good decisions*, pops into my head. We all know if someone asks, the answer every single time, is "fuck no, I'm not making good decisions."

He tugs on my right hand, then wraps his fingers around my head trying to guide me to him. I twist out of his reach.

"You need to stop, Dylan. Stop talking."

He smirks. "No chit-chat. Works for me."

"There's no working anything here." I take a step back.

"What, you want to do it in the shower?"

"God, no." I stare at him, wondering how I could have married such a creep.

"Cat got your tongue? I got something for your tongue." He smiles, points at his crotch.

I inch away from him. He grabs at my wrist.

"What happened to your hand?" His fingers tighten on the bandage. "That's going to have to come off before you grab on there, princess, because that raggedy thing is for sure going to rub me the wrong way."

He pulls the metal clips off, and it unravels. Blood oozes from the cut. Dylan backs up in surprise.

"Kinky. I can work with it." He unzips his jeans, lets them drop. I take the opportunity to move to the front of the house.

Forget picking up my clothes. This is insanity. I take a last look around as a pang of guilt washes over me for leaving my home, unguarded, in the hands of this piece of human waste. I rush outside, hoping Dylan won't catch up. It takes no more than a quick glance over my shoulder to know he won't. He's become incapacitated by the jeans around his ankles and the anticipation of an imminent blow job.

"Cunt!" he yells from the door while I jump into the car. With fresh blood leaking from my hand, I use my knees to steer, and drive away from my house in a panic. The rain begins again. A deafening crack of thunder rattles the windows and I realize the only thing getting blown today is my mind.

CHAPTER 16
I'VE DONE A BAD THING

So much blood again, swirling in the white sink like melted candy cane. I catch Russ's reflection in the mirror. The tip of his tongue squeezes out between his teeth.

"Can you get me a new bandage?"

"What did you do?" He reaches over my head to pull the first aid kit off the wall. "Why won't it stop bleeding?"

"Don't know." Warm water rushes over my hand, dulling the pain. He dries the wound, wraps my palm with clean gauze, and helps me to the office.

"Have some water." He kneels in front of me with a glass. "Let me help."

"I can hold it." I push him away, my hand brushing against his long, curly hair. Most days it's tied up in a bun, but today the tight gold ringlets hang down to his shoulders. He sits back on his heels, watching water dribble down my chin.

"Thanks," I say, returning the glass.

"What happened to you?"

"It's complicated."

"I'm covered in your blood Katy. You owe me an explanation."

"Dylan wanted a blow job."

"Every guy wants a blow job. Did you bite the damn thing off?"

I giggle despite the pain and show him my teeth. "Not me. Though someone else will one day."

Over his shoulder, I see Jesse stepping into the office. She cuts her eyes at me, her lips squash together in a thin line.

"Really?" she asks, dropping her purse to the floor with a thud.

I take a deep breath. "Yup, here we go."

"Are you fucking stupid, woman?"

Russ turns to her. "He wanted a blow job!"

"So it's true, you went home?"

"I think she broke his thing." He leans forward with his hands over his groin. Imaginary pain spreads across his face.

"I didn't break anything, and I promise this is all my blood." I hold my throbbing hand up. "Why are you here?"

"You have nosy neighbors. One of them called the police and reported a domestic altercation."

"Oh, my..."

"Sweet old lady saw you running out, bleeding, and told them you might have murdered your husband."

"Murdered? Did she not see Dylan standing at the front door with his jeans around his ankles?"

"She's a hundred fucking years old, Katy. She got all excited because this is the most interesting thing that's going to happen to her until the moment she dies."

I wheel the chair backwards, trying to create space between me and the dragon lady.

"Don't roll away, Kiss."

"Don't yell at me, Tanner."

"Why did you do it?"

"I needed clothes."

Her cheeks flush dark pink. "You needed clothes?"

"I was wrong, and it won't happen again. If it makes you happy, I swiftly realized the error of my ways."

She asks Russ to leave the room. He looks nervous and assures me he's two hops away in case I need him.

"You went to the house for clothes?"

"Yes, I told you. I wanted my own stuff. He's an asshole, Jess. He told me to clean up and have sex with him."

"How unexpected."

"Think I'm going to need a cleaning service. The place is a war zone."

"Yeah...but the clothes," she taunts.

"And he accused me of sleeping with Quinn. Though sleeping was not the word he used."

She stomps in small circles, mumbling and swearing. By her third lap around the room, I lose patience and begin checking email. My dad's message is the first to catch my eye.

Katy, the following is my new address in Bangkok. I hope you are doing okay. Now I want you to visit me in Thailand. This will be good for you to meet Lia and some other people who you might find interesting. I think you should do this. Leave the asshole at home. How is your hand? Did you need the stitches?

I miss you very much. Love, Apuka.

The address reads like gibberish, with some words over twenty letters long and a place called Bankoknoi, Bangkok. It's a fine offer. Not one I'll be considering.

"What is it?" Jesse stops and looks over my shoulder.

"From my dad."

"Is he okay?"

"He wants me to go there and meet the lima bean."

"You'll have to tell him you're busy picking out new outfits."

"I said I was sorry. I wasn't thinking."

"You weren't," she says. "And it's wearing me out."

"I'm feeling it too, so back off."

"That's it? Your big comeback?"

"No." I close my dad's email. A wave of loneliness washes over me. I could use his support right now, a hand to keep me upright against the tide heading my way.

"Then help me understand." She sits down, the chair groans as she rolls closer to me. "Because I'm tired of saving you. You have all these great things in your life, parents who love you, a home, a business." She shakes her head. "Your health, right?"

"Yeah," I mutter.

"No webbed toes or an extra head growing off your perfectly normal shoulders. And you're smart. So, what keeps happening in your brain?"

"I don't know."

"Excellent."

"Are you firing me?" I ask.

She sighs. "No."

"I won't do anything else dumb."

"I don't believe you anymore. I wish I did, Katy. Truly."

Her words sting, and though I've earned it, I'm in no mood to be the receptacle of her criticism.

"I'll stay at my parents' place until we go to court. They have an alarm..." I trail off. Nothing I say will improve the situation.

"Good idea. I'll call Sheriff Madigan and update him."

She knows me better than anyone, and her disappointment hurts. I do this to myself, invite all the wrong, and dismiss anything right. She leaves without another word, quietly closing the office door behind her.

Russ knocks a few minutes later. I tell him I'm fine and try to focus on work. There are over a hundred emails in the inbox, most of them spam or requests from suppliers. Mom has sent a message asking how I am, and that she hopes things are better between Dylan and me. She says France is disgusting in November and how annoying it is that the waiters never refill her coffee. "I am becoming such an American," she writes. "Josephine's mind continues to get lost," so she'll be staying on to attend the family disaster.

At the end of the message, she asks if I've heard from "the ridiculous man," and to write back soon. And by the way, can I search the internet for information about being senile in a foreign country.

I answer the emails and check my phone. It's 11:50 a.m., the Friday before Thanksgiving. Time to make an executive decision.

CHAPTER 17
DEAD AUNT GERTIE

Russ tapes a sheet of white copy paper to the front door of the restaurant. "Closed for the Holiday. Happy Thanksgiving Duff Beach!"

"What am I going to do for an entire week?" he asks.

"Hang out with your family."

"Mom won't let me drink in her house."

"Go outside, walk on the beach. Play some board games." I wiggle the knob, the water is off, the gas is off, the alarm is on. "We deserve a break and I need a minute to get my head right."

He fumbles with his car keys. "Dylan got you all riled up, didn't he? Are you leaving town?"

"Not going anywhere, not doing anything. I'm just tired. Tell me you haven't noticed how much of a pain I am lately?"

"No, I noticed. You've been acting wonky. But what about me?"

I recognize the panic in his voice. Being cut loose means down time, empty space he'll want to fill by drinking or getting high. Just because he can't tame the addiction, doesn't mean he's not terrified of it.

"I'll make you a deal, Russ. We'll do Thanksgiving if it's too hard at your mom's. How about we cook up a big ass turkey and watch a bunch of horror movies?"

"Are you saying that to be sweet, or scared I'll get stupid?"

"Yes, and yes. Don't worry, I've got you." I give him a hug and kiss his cheek.

By noon, I'd driven three blocks past my house on Ocean Avenue and pulled into the driveway of my parents' brick A-frame. The architecture fits in with the other homes in the area, but for the ridiculous eco-lawn my parents put in when I started college. The deep green spiky Bermuda grass was replaced by a xeriscape collection of rocks and pebbles that stand out in a bad way.

I enter through the carport, walk through the hallway, and drop my bag in the kitchen. Stale air creeps above me, stirred by ceiling fans set on low. The house feels like a tomb. It reeks of nothingness, of someone's last breath.

It's a morbid assessment. I am, however, in a house where two marriages are dying. I shake off the thought and walk to the screened porch, or what we call the Florida Room. Mom and Dad added it when I was in middle school, the first big reward for their hard work. A few years later, they installed AC with a massive dehumidifier. Another few years went by, and they upgraded the kitchen, then the bathrooms.

The last major addition was for my dad. A twenty-five-foot sailboat bobbing in the canal behind the house. The lower half of the hull is baby-blue, the top half and the deck are crisp white with a blue side stripe interrupted on each side by a picture of a seagull in flight. Standing upright is the mast, held in place by thick braided lines, ready for the sails to be raised. It's his prized possession, named after my grandmother's famous and oft repeated mispronunciation: the *Happily*.

Dad taught me to sail with tough love and condensed instructions. He'd assign a task I was unprepared to complete, then tell me one wrong move would cause him to tumble into the churning sea and drown. After a few close calls, I became adequately seaworthy. For now, *Happily* is my responsibility, and I walk down the gentle slope of the backyard to the dock, step on board and pull on the lines in a half-ass attempt to verify that everything is as it should be.

Back inside, I open the windows and wander into my old bedroom. Taking up half the space is my double bed, covered by a blanket decorated with tiny pink rose blossoms. Teddy, one of the two remaining stuffed animals from my childhood, is propped on a pillow. His coat is so worn, we'd sown new fabric across his chubby body several times over. His yellow eyes protrude from the sockets, one tilting this way, the other that. Sandrine is even creepier, a doll with eyes that follow you no matter which way her face turns. She's also needed a few new outfits over the years. Her latest look is a pink crochet dress with a green ribbon pulled across her waist. My uncle gave me these gifts the day I was born, and they slept next to me all the way through elementary school.

The rest of the room has built-in white cabinets. High school and college awards cover the surfaces, stacks of books I read as a kid, and several framed pictures of me looking awkward, posed, and miserable. I keep telling my parents to repurpose the space, but they always come back with the same response. "It's for the babies, Katy. Your babies... are you pregnant yet?"

I lie on my bed, Teddy and Sandrine tucked close to me, and remember a day back in high school when I found a Daddy Long Legs hiding in a pile of dirty clothes. I flinch, recounting the details. The spider running off in fear for its little spider life, and my mother screaming bloody murder in such an unnatural pitch that Dad almost had a heart attack galloping to our rescue. Smiling, I drift off.

I wake up feeling stiff, groggy, out of sorts. My bear is smashed up against the wall. "Sorry," I mumble and slide him away from such an uncomfortable spot. What would Dr. Jonas think if she heard me speak to a frumpy old stuffed animal? I reach for Sandrine. She's fallen to the floor. "Poor baby." I scoop her off the ground. "You're always the one falling." I fluff the artificial blond hair and straighten her dress. "Good thing you're not real." I stare into her green marble eyes. "Nothing hurts you."

The tears come then, unexpectedly, a flood spilling down my cheeks. I hear myself wail while my brain multi-tasks, casts judgment on my emotions. *On a scale of one to ten, Katy, your melodrama gets a three.* What's wrong with me? Do people sob while casually wondering about other things? I should be tested. Dr. Jonas can pronounce me scattered, with brain waves resembling a Picasso. What if there's a file somewhere with numbers or letters explaining why I have the attention span of a hamster? Crying sucks, especially when I don't understand why it's happening. I wipe under my eyes and dab my fallen tears from Sandrine's hard plastic face.

By early evening, I've recovered from the mysterious outburst. The late November breeze has chased off the musty air, and I've made enough of a mess to fool myself into feeling at home. Things are looking up. It's going to be a week of reparation for me. A week to heal whatever the hell keeps tripping me up. Dr. Jonas was right when she said the past can't be fixed. This is my chance to stop the clock and take stock in what's ahead instead of what's behind me.

The sun is setting, and I lounge by the pool watching the boat bump up against the dock. High tide is bringing the water in, and with it, heavy salty air. In a few hours, it will all reverse, and the water will recede. When I was a kid, I thought the tide was the planet breathing, a big round Earth inhaling, exhaling. I wish for that time back, not caring about anything except catching fireflies or waiting for the dolphins to do their nightly water dance.

The gate opens by the driveway. I assume it's Russ, already wasted six hours into his vacation.

"You didn't answer the front door," Quinn says, walking in my direction. "What's with all the sharp rocks?" He moves carefully. The yard is treacherous, a deterrent for anyone who has feet.

"My parents are preparing for Armageddon. They want the house to look like ground zero, so the mobs won't bother them."

"Weird." He sits down in the chair next to mine. "Saw the sign at The Point and spoke to Jesse."

"How was that?" I try not to stare as the sun picks up the golden highlights in his hair.

"She's scary. How are you not more damaged?"

"After all the years with Dylan, you think Jesse's the scary one?"

He nods and glances at the boat. "What does *Happily* signify?"

"Long story. My grandma was always telling me to have a happy life, but her English was terrible, so it came out as a happily life."

His head moves ever so slightly in acknowledgment.

"Why are you here, Quinn?"

"Because you're alone."

"So what?"

"It's a bad idea." He stands up and starts toward the house. "Show me around."

I follow him to the screen door, trying to recall if I put deodorant on.

He moves through the rooms, describing each like a realtor. "And here we have the weird-ass kitchen. Small and badly designed. Who does this, how old is this house?"

"Don't know. Old. They've made updates, but the footprint is probably original."

"Straight out of the seventies." He keeps moving. "And this living room is inviting, if you enjoy being surrounded by dead Aunt Gertrude's hundred-year-old furniture."

"I have no dead Aunt Gertrude, and it's not a hundred years old."

"Yes, it is." He turns and walks into my room. "I saw Gert's ass-print on the cushion. And this..." He trails off, bending over to inspect the framed pictures. "You are not photogenic."

"They were taken under duress."

He studies my bed. "These are cute. Your old stuffies? Why is the bear two-toned?"

"He's old."

"How old?"

"As old as me. The bear has a gold chain hidden inside him."

He lifts Teddy up gently. "That's cool." He looks up at me. "Don't worry, I won't hurt him. You would never open him up though, to see if the chain is really there?"

"Not a chance." I'd cut my foot off before disfiguring my teddy bear.

"I wouldn't either." He goes back to the Florida room. "Show me the boat."

"It's late, we're not taking it out."

He leans against the door, staring at me with his arms crossed.

"No," I repeat more for myself than him. He's tall and pretty, and probably great in bed.

"What are you thinking, Katy?"

"Huh?" Glad my thoughts aren't streaming across my forehead like ticker tape.

"You went away for a second; didn't seem like it was about sailing."

"It wasn't," I say. This statement is accurate.

He backtracks to the kitchen. "How can someone who owns a restaurant have a kitchen the size of a dollhouse in their home? Got any beer?"

"Don't think so," I tell him. We're not German, we're fucking Hungarian, and we drink lousy Hungarian wine and sweet, delicious brandy.

"You have no beer," he says after checking the fridge.

"Oh." I shrug. No kidding.

"What's this?" He picks up a bottle of red wine on the counter. "Bulls Blood? Hell of a way to market a product."

"I have something better," I tell him.

"Aunt Gertie's schnapps?"

"No, this ain't nothing Aunt Gertie ever drank." I pull open the pantry door to reveal several bottles of brandy. No two look alike, and no two flavors taste the same.

"The stash." He sorts through them, trying to read the labels. "How do you pronounce this?"

"Palinka. Like Pa, sort of like the sound you make when you stick your tongue out for the doctor."

"Pa."

"Not bad. Li, like long e and ka, short a. Pa-lin-ka."

He repeats it several times, each attempt better than the last, then pronounces himself an honorary Hungarian.

• • • • •

Just after sunset, Quinn, me, and Russ, who did last only six hours without drinking, head to the dock and climb aboard *Happily*. We bring brandy, plastic cups, a sleeve of Ritz crackers and a jar of pickles.

I offer them libation with Mom's voice in my head, scolding my hostessing prowess. Drinks in a cup, a container of condiments? No plates, no napkins, no other snacks? Was I raised by wolves?

We do substantial damage to each bottle of cherry, pear and elderberry liquor, while arguing the merits of monogamy. Russ is all for it, but only as it applies to others. I've given up on it, having tried it unsuccessfully, and Quinn has yet to experience what it truly means.

Russ asks us how many people we've slept with.

"I'm not a teenager, I don't keep count." Quinn is first to respond. "How many women have you been with?"

"Ninety-seven," Russ answers without hesitation. "Eleven are regulars."

If it were light out, he'd see the horror on my face. "What the fuck? Do you ever get checked for STDs?"

He holds up his drink. "Sure Katy-Bell, all the time, because that's what's going to kill me. How many guys have you been with?"

"This isn't my fight. Adding up women is a man thing."

"Over twenty?" He winks at me.

"Twenty? Absolutely not. More than two, less than ten. More than three, okay, more than four."

Quinn coughs, tries not to laugh.

"Don't judge me." I sit up straight. "I clean up fine; I can look like a normal human."

"I'm sure you can."

"With the right clothes." I add.

"Like these?" He tugs on my sleeve. "Still from Jesse's closet, I assume?"

I pull back, remembering how this day started, going to my house, Dylan.

"My bad, Katy. I know you haven't been home in a while. That was a low blow."

Russ snorts, "You've got no idea, dude."

"Did I miss something?" he asks.

"I thought you talked to Jesse before you came over here."

"I did."

"She didn't say why she's pissed at me?"

"I didn't get the impression she was. She said you wanted to stay here for a couple of days. What happened?"

"Nothing productive. Want some?" I offer him half of a sour pickle.

He puts a hand up. "No thanks."

The water laps against the hull, and the lights from the homes on either side of the canal twinkle in the darkness. In our silence, the frogs and crickets and the mosquitoes speak up. Their flutters and whistles blend into a twilight symphony, broken by the deep rumble of a familiar engine, the custom tires crushing the loose pebbles of the driveway.

I whisper, "shit." Quinn scoots a few inches away from me on the bench seat.

Dylan opens the gate, struts to the deck. His grin drips with condescension.

"Who-oh-who could be hanging out at Mom and Dad's house when they're out of the country?" His right foot taps the wooden planks. "What do we have here? My wife holed up with two guys under the stars?"

"Go to hell, Dylan. We're just having a couple drinks." My elbow bumps into the pickle jar. This must be what a reality show feels like.

"First you come by the house and offer yourself up, next thing you're here, doing what exactly?"

"Are you delusional? You think I came by this morning to fool around with you?"

He swipes at a mosquito. "Well, it obviously wasn't to pick up around the house."

Russ whispers I should have bitten it off.

"What do you want, Dylan?"

"I told you, honeybun, I saw all the cars and wondered why you were having a party without moi?" He poses with hands motioning to his face. "This is so much better than I could have imagined. I feel so..." he puts his index finger to his lips. "Entertained. Thank you for that." He looks each of us over, then backs away. "I'm out. Y'all have fun with whatever this whole thing is. This nautical threesome."

"No, thank YOU!" I yell as he walks away.

I slump over and pick at the bandage on my hand. "That probably wasn't the best way to handle him."

Quinn nods, says I'm right, and Russ puts his arm around my shoulder. The buzz kill is palpable, and by the time the fourth mosquito has taken a bite out of me, I call it a night. Nobody argues, and we unceremoniously disembark the party-boat and head indoors.

I find bread in the freezer, and unopened jars of peanut butter and grape jelly in the pantry. I prepare three sandwiches, cut them in half, and place them on a tray. The guys are laid out in front of the TV in my parents' bedroom, Russ on the floor, and Quinn on the queen-size bed.

"Why is the only TV in the house in here?" Quinn helps himself to a pb&j. "Why isn't it in the living room?"

"Because they entertain there. And entertaining is done in a formal space, not a family space."

"I don't get it," he says, pealing crust off the bread.

"Not sure I do either." I shrug. "It's about being proper. Like, old European proper."

"I think they watch porn on it," Russ mutters, channel surfs.

"Stop it," I smack his arm and slide onto the covers near Quinn. Russ turns up the volume on a Friend's rerun. This isn't inappropriate at all. Being on a bed with a guy who isn't my husband, late at night, after many drinks. I stare at the screen, distracted, as usual.

Attraction is chemical, physical, electrical. I bet there's a gaggle of pheromones colliding in the air above us. Microscopic electrical sparks, making everything hotter. Making me sweat. I put my head down and stare at Quinn. Even his profile is perfect.

He catches me ogling him, winks, and nudges my shoulder. This is terrible. Why should I be subject to this test of willpower? He turns away, acting like the whole nudge and wink didn't happen. My right foot cramps up, and I feel more intoxicated now than I did an hour ago.

"You okay, Katy?" Russ asks. "You keep sighing. I can hear it down here."

His voice pulls me back to reality, out from the wet, heaving gutter I'm sliding into. "Yeah, I'm just sleepy." I lay my head on the edge of the bed and fall asleep with the boys laughing in the background.

CHAPTER 18
GIANT SUPERBALL

"Katy." Quinn nudges me. "Wake up, your phone is ringing."

"Uh-huh. It'll go to voicemail."

I fall back asleep.

• • • • •

It's almost noon when I wake up the next time. Sunshine pours through the window, and I feel like a drill is pushing through my temples. Quinn is sleeping, Russ is gone. I walk around the house searching for him, though it's obvious he's left the building. No surprise, his powers of hangover recuperation far exceed mine.

I brush my teeth, splash water on my face, and return to the bedroom. Quinn is still tucked under the light bedspread. I should walk away, take a cold shower, slam my hand into a door and watch more blood gush out of me. He might as well be a bowl of M&Ms. Shiny outside, soft and sweet inside. I wonder if Quinn melts on your tongue.

Ignoring the sirens, the bells, the obvious complications, I snuggle back under the blanket, and hope he wakes up. I toss and turn a few times, crack my knuckles, and move the sheets around. He snores, his head half-buried under a pillow.

Finally, he stirs, opens his eyes, and smiles. I'm suddenly fifteen, self-conscious, and certain I'm about to get diabetes from this specific bowl of candy. Going for the power move, I pretend not to care and begin rolling away. He catches my shoulder and kisses me. His fingers draw slow circles in my palms.

"Am I hurting you?" he asks, tracing over the bandage, then moving to my wrists, my elbows, down my back. Time flows in slow motion, one thing, then the next. After years of grinning and bearing sex with Dylan, I'm finally able to participate in something honest between two people, instead of being the host to someone's parasitic demands.

Without discussion, we fall asleep again, his arms encircling me.

The next time I wake up, he's on his side, swiping at images on his cell phone.

"What time is it?" I ask.

"Five-thirty."

It's getting dark outside and losing an entire day is discombobulating. "Why didn't you wake me up?"

"I tried. Your phone keeps ringing."

"Where did I leave it?" I search for it in the pile of pillows, then find it under the bed.

No messages, no texts, no nothing. I assure him they're robocalls.

"Yeah, that's probably all it is," he says. "So, I'm heading down to Miami. I told my folks I'd go home for Thanksgiving."

"You could have taken off earlier. I would have been fine."

He puts his phone on the bed and sits up. "I didn't want to blow out of here after what happened."

Right. The thing that happened. Sex, broken marriage vows, adultery. Instead of guilt, though, I feel ecstatic, liberated. The universe is now in order, blissful, and bouncing like a neon Superball because I *did it* with Quinn.

"I'm not having second thoughts," I tell him. "You might be... I mean, I hope you're not."

"Not even close. Do you want to come with me... to Miami?" It's a half-ass request, sweet, a bit forced.

"I can't leave Russ alone. Thanks for asking, though."

"Are you sure?" he asks.

"Yeah, of course." I wink. Or try to. Both my eyes slap-shut at the same time, then open wide. The right one twitches. He asks if something's wrong. Am I having a seizure? I say no and try to brush it off. The moment has evaporated, my bliss has been short-lived, and my neon Superball has turned into a cherry bomb.

CHAPTER 19
THE CALL

Quinn leaves at half past seven. From the living room window, I watch him drive away in the glow of moonlight.

The blush of the day fades, and I conjure excuses. My husband, by any measure, is an abysmal, unfaithful, disrespectful man. I deserve happiness. We didn't hurt anyone by sleeping together, and his friendship with Dylan was already on the outs. Quinn and I have been circling the drain of attraction for months. Or a couple of weeks.

And since we're talking about the drain, did we toss ourselves into it by fooling around? And is it now clogged and ready to spew up my punishment? I hadn't even noticed how attractive he was until Jesse went off about him the first night she was at The Point.

My head hurts. I'm tired of thinking, tired of being bewildered by the normal things that happen in a life.

I set about in a perfunctory manner to tidy the house. Rinsing the dishes, and checking the boat for bottles, wrappers or signs of the previous night's festivities. My last chore is to move the wet sheets from the washer to the dryer.

"What the hell?" I say under my breath.

I pull out my mom's light blue flannel nightgown and several of my dad's work shirts.

"Three months work of wrinkles." I glance behind me, embarrassed for sounding like a fabric softener commercial.

I fold the nightgown, take it to my parents' bedroom, and drop it in Mom's dresser drawer. The shirts need to be ironed, or at least hung up. I pull open their closet door and fish for hangers in a crowded row of clothes dating back to the eighties. On Dad's side, there's a jumble of them with the dry-cleaning labels still attached. They're intertwined, and not easily pulled off the rack.

"Come on, you fuckers." I twist and tug until the hangars tumble to the floor along with all the clothes alongside them.

I groan. This is a bigger mess than I started off with. Should I leave this crap here? Would they know? They totally would, so I drop to my knees to retrieve the pile of pants and sweaters. Leaning toward the back wall, my hand hits a hard surface. I squint into the darkness and pull apart the clothes to get a better look.

It's a briefcase, pushed snugly into the crevices of my parents' closet.

"What, and who are you?" I whisper to the inanimate object. Is it hidden, or shoved into an empty spot because there's so little storage in the house? "Come to mama", I say, dragging it toward me.

The dark brown leather is scratched and worn along the edges. It's monogrammed with the initials MRK. Miklos Robert Kiss. My grandfather. I trace my fingers over the small metal combination lock between the handles.

I pick up the case and gently shake it. The heavy contents shift. What's in here? Mementos from our past, financial documents, the will? I turn the numbers on the combination and stop on Dad's birthday, Mom's, mine, my grandmother's. Nothing, I'm locked out. I sit and stare at it for a while. It's probably not a big deal. I sigh, slide it back into its corner, and decide my parents have lots of explaining to do when they get home.

By midnight, boredom and exhaustion sends me to bed with the confidence that I'll sleep well into Saturday morning. I nod off easily, but wake up a few hours later feeling restless, pulse racing, my shirt drenched in sweat. I throw the sheets off and watch the shadows drift across the room. It's 4:47 a.m.

After a glass of water, I get back to sleep and dream I'm standing in the center of a cluster of people. No one's face is identifiable, yet everyone is familiar. A section of the group parts, leaving a long open aisle. My father, some distance away, walks haltingly in my direction. When he reaches me, the circle closes behind him. He stands in front of me, motionless, staring.

I have no memory of him with this type of expression. He has no pants on and I'm shocked he would be out and about this way. I ask him, "What the hell are you doing?"

He gazes at me, then turns away. The aisle reopens, and he walks back through the circle of people, never having said a word. I wait for an explanation from the faceless crowd, but they too, are silent. I hear a strange sound. Is he returning to explain everything? The noise persists, pulling me from the dream. My cell phone is ringing in the kitchen.

By the time I reach it, the call's gone to voicemail. The screen is lit, blinding in the night's darkness. No caller ID, no message. "That's fucking great." I shiver, scramble back to bed, and drop the phone on the carpet.

It rings again before I can drift off.

The caller sounds young, panicky, out of breath. I ask her name and tell her to slow down.

"This Lia. I need tell you. Father heart muscle die!"

She's frantic, yapping in a mixture of Thai and broken English. I understand a few of the words: beach, drive, muscle. I try to stop her. "Lia, Lia!" I yell to get her attention.

"Yes, this Lia in Bangkok."

"Tell me what happened."

"His heart muscle die, I take him to doctor," she sobs.

"What do you mean, die? Is he in a hospital?"

"Yes, he there now."

"Is he okay?" I ask, trying to stretch the time, not wanting to hear the words.

"Don't understand this?"

"Is he alive?" I blurt out.

"I get doctor speak to you." The line goes quiet, and I wait for the blow of someone telling me my father is dead ten thousand miles away from home.

"Hello." A soft male voice comes on. "Is this Katy, daughter of Robert?"

"Yes, this is Katy."

"My name is Dr. Orapan. I am helping to your father."

"Okay."

The doctor clears his throat. "He has the heart attack."

"What?" I kick the blanket off, watch it tumble to the floor.

"He is in bad condition. I would like for you to give me permission to do procedure."

"He's alive? My dad's alive?"

"Yes, but very sick."

"How sick? What are you going to do to him?"

"I want to check for artery. Block of the artery. Do you understand?"

"Yes, I think so." Now I'm cold, shivering. I lean over the edge of the bed and drag the cover over my legs.

"I like to do this procedure soon as possible."

"How long has he been there?"

"He come in Thursday night."

I glance at the clock. It's almost 6:00 a.m. here, and Thailand is twelve hours ahead. "He's been there a day, and this is the first time I'm hearing about it?"

"No, Khun Lia try call before. In beginning, Mr. Robert said he call you when he feels good. He arrive here and tell us he has heart problem."

"He walked in on his own?" I ask.

"Yes, when heart attack begin. He tells me he talk to daughter Katy after I explaining to him what is wrong."

"So, why isn't he the one calling me? Can you put him on the phone?"

"After I examine, problem get worse. We have to use machine to help breathe. He cannot talk now."

"You didn't know he was having a heart attack?"

"We see when it get bad. Then we help him and that take long."

My cheeks are burning, I'm sweating, the blanket comes off again. "You're saying he got there, and it got worse. Is he awake?"

"Awake?"

"Is he conscious?" I ask.

"Yes, sometime, no sometime. This is why I must make the examine. Can you give me the permission to do this?"

"Doesn't my mom need to do that?"

"Mr. Robert is married?"

"Yes, of course he's married," I say, realizing the girl, Lia, brought him in.

"Then, please, let me speak to wife of Robert."

"She's in France, in Paris, but we can come to you. Can you wait? Is that okay?"

"Can you come in fast time?"

"Yes. A day or so."

"You must hurry." He tells me the name and number of the hospital. I promise to stay in contact with him and give consent to perform surgery if it becomes necessary.

CHAPTER 20
BABY DON'T LEAVE ME

By late morning, I've booked two overpriced tickets to Bangkok. I'll fly from Tampa International directly to Charles De Gaulle, pick up my mother, and go on to Thailand. Reserving the flights is painless, calling my mom...not so much. After a five-minute negotiation with Josephine, we agree I'm the American daughter of her new live-in maid. She tells me I can speak to her for a moment, as lunch has been served.

"I will kill her soon, Katy. At night, I think of how to do this. I do not care anymore; she makes me into the crazy person."

Her tirade is not to be interrupted while she considers how to murder my aunt. Poison, a fall in the metro, perhaps a goose down pillow.

I'm forced to stop her much the same way I did Lia hours earlier. I yell MOM three times before she shuts up. Crying and sucking in air, I give her the news.

"Oh my God, oh my God!" she sobs. I spare her the details, and she spares me the questions.

I give her the flight information and email the itinerary to my uncle. "Be at the airport by one tomorrow, okay? Then we'll go to Bangkok together."

She agrees, still sobbing uncontrollably as I end the call.

• • • • •

Jesse can't be mad at me for going home this time. I need clothes, my passport, a phone charger. It's early, so the possibility of getting in and out without rousing Dylan from his networking, ass-grabbing stupor is high.

The door is unlocked. The irritation of a stranger needing only to turn the knob to help themselves to my possessions floods my brain long enough to forget that my dad is lying in a hospital bed.

Dylan is snoring softly, hugging the blanket. This is the guy I fell for, the unguarded sweet person existing only in a sleep-state. A flicker of regret sweeps through me, thinking about last night, about Quinn. How much of this is on me, or my overwhelming family? Did he come into this marriage well-intentioned, wanting to love and honor? I can't remember how it all changed so dramatically, and what does it matter, since all that's left are the dregs of the relationship getting pumped through the business end of a meat grinder.

I tiptoe into the closet to find my backpack. Is it warm in Thailand? It's tropical and my mom said something about people melting, though she could have been talking about ice cream. What's appropriate hospital attire? Does it depend on the severity of the illness? I grab jeans, shirts and some tanks. My extra charger is in the suitcase, next to an adapter and some euros. My passport is in my bedside drawer. I hold my breath and pull the handle. Cheap particle board scrapes against the old metal hinges.

"Hey, babe." Dylan yawns, smiles.

A small space in my heart warms like the Grinch at Christmas. "I didn't want to wake you." I pull again. It's so loud. "Sorry!"

"It's fine." He stretches and props himself up on his right side. "What are you doing?"

I stop to consider how much I should say. "Dad's sick. I have to go out of town." It's not like the gossip won't be circulating by the end of the day.

"Need any help?"

He must still be half-asleep. Fully alert, Dylan has no compassion for my family.

"No. Mom's coming with me."

"Bummer, Katy. Your dad's going to be fine. Guess you don't know how long you'll be gone?"

"No."

"Gonna miss you," he says, laying his big hand on mine.

"Uh-huh." I stare down at our hands, placed on top of each other like the day we were married. "I... um. I'll be back soon."

His dark pupils dilate like magnets inside his blue eyes. "Give us a kiss goodbye."

Unable to help myself, I let him kiss me. He's gentle at first, then his grip tightens on my wrist.

"Stop it." I push his hand away.

He laughs, gets up, and shoves me aside. "You're so fucking easy."

I stand motionless by the side of the bed. "What?"

"You owe me a blowjob, dumbass. I was trying to collect." He grins, then disappears into the kitchen.

The coffee I've been pouring down my throat for the last three hours sloshes into my esophagus. I cover my mouth; afraid I might throw up. This relationship has officially slid off the scale, landed in a bucket of shit, and drowned a horrible, meaningless death. I scurry out of the house with my passport between my teeth and a mess of rumpled clothes protruding from the partially zipped backpack.

"Counting the days until you get home, honey pie." he mocks from the front door. "Oh baby, don't leave me!"

CHAPTER 21
TRAVEL

It takes a while to stop crying. By the time I merge onto I-75 heading north to Tampa, the tears have dried. They're replaced by rage and graphic thoughts about blowing Dylan's head off with a hunting rifle. Which head to shoot first, the one on his shoulders or the one between his legs? It's a quick decision. I'd start at the bottom and work my way up. Then he'll have his fucking blowjob.

At eleven, I'm just north of Sarasota, remembering the times I've been this way with my dad. My eyes fill with tears again. Past the Fruitville Road exit, my phone rings. It's Jesse.

"Dylan's getting served today."

"Uh-huh."

"You need to watch your back."

I nod.

"Are you nodding, Katy?"

"Yeah," I say, driving past the signs for Bradenton and Ellenton. "Jesse?"

"What?"

"My dad had a heart attack."

Silence.

"Are you there, Jess?"

"Yeah." The coldness in her voice dissipates.

"He's alive. I'm on my way to Thailand."

"Right now? Let me come with you."

"I'm picking Mom up in Paris."

"Crap, Katy, I love your dad."

"I know."

"Where are you?"

"A couple of miles from the Sunshine Skyway. I'm flying out of Tampa at three-fifteen."

I tell her what I can about his situation, what the doctor said, and how I got the call. She asks questions I have no answers to. Will he be okay? When can he come home?

I reach I-275, heading east to the bridge. The giant yellow cables loom in the distance. It's a beautiful piece of work connecting Manatee County to St. Pete in Pinellas County. I love driving over it and watching the boats float far underneath, near the remnants of the original bridge destroyed by a cargo ship in 1980.

"I'll take care of court. Don't worry about anything." Jesse keeps talking while I glance down at the people fishing off the old pier. "What can I do to help?"

"I'm not sure. We'll figure it out. I've got the hospital's address and the doctor's cell number."

"Good girl," she says.

Good girl? I touch my lips, thinking of Quinn. If only she knew.

• • • • •

Seconds after landing in Paris, everyone is on their phone. I'm no exception. My stomach turns over. Five missed calls from Dylan. No voicemail on any of them. Guess he got served. I text Jesse about the calls and ask her to contact Russ. I text Russ and tell him to talk to Jesse. The last is to my mom, asking if she's at the airport yet. I listen to a message from the doctor in Thailand informing me that Robert is in stable condition.

I head to the gate after buying an espresso. My phone chirps. Mom is checking in.

Our next flight departs from a different terminal. The waiting area is stuffy and full of people who look like they've been on the road for days. The bathroom is clean, though too dark to see much of anything. I stare into the mirror and figure the lights are faint by design. My hair is a mess and there are circles under my hazel eyes. There's nothing for it. The next flight is longer than the last one. Perhaps it'll be dark in Thailand too.

An hour later, my mother is nowhere to be found. Her message says she's in the security area, detained for extra questioning about explosives and bad intentions. By the time she arrives, we're almost ready to board. She's pissed and out of breath, pulling her carry-on luggage behind her like a toy car on a string.

"I have been violated," she hisses, kissing me on both cheeks. "Where do these people think the bomb will fit under my clothes?"

She's thinner than the last time I saw her a few months ago, but as always, nicely put together. Her brown hair is styled in a neat bob, her makeup is appropriately light, and the tailored dress hugs her petite frame perfectly. She shoves her suitcase at me and scurries to the restroom.

We're boarding when she returns, and she joins me at the end of the long line.

"Got your passport?" I ask her.

She holds it up for inspection. "Good?"

I smile, and she moves closer to hug me. "Your father. I am so angry."

"Yup." I say, with every intention of avoiding this subject. "Can we talk about something else?"

"Like your marriage?" She frowns and looks around. In Hungarian, she asks if any of the people in line are terrorists.

"Really, terrorism is where you go?" I take a few steps forward. "And we're not talking about Dylan either."

"You said to talk about something else. I think the one with the curly hair." She tilts her head toward a teenager deep down in his cell phone.

"Half our family has curly hair, Mom. If that's the test, we better get ready for a cavity check."

"I do not understand what this means." She squints at the boy. "He's too young to be the terror man? He is nervous, I think."

The kid seems bored, not at all anxious. I tell her to find a better suspect.

• • • • •

A quick jolt underneath the plane and the tug pushes us back. We roll, turn, then another bump and thump as the aircraft is released. Crew members welcome us onboard and tell us what to expect on this flight. Ten hours, lunch, dinner, 784 movies, then a light breakfast before we arrive at Suvarnabhumi Airport in Bangkok.

"This is a fucking cattle-car," I mumble. "These seats suck."

Mom gazes out the window as the ground slips away below us.

"You can see the Eiffel Tower. Look at the smog." Her voice is flat, monotone. "Did you speak to him before?"

"Him? Do you mean Dad? And before what?"

"In the last few weeks, before this happened."

"I spoke to him once."

"What did he say?" she asks.

"About what?"

"Oh Katy, are you going to make me pull the straws for every bit of information?"

"You mean pull teeth."

"What is the matter with your teeth?" She squeezes my jaw. "Does something hurt?"

I push her back. Having lived in the U.S. for almost thirty years, she needs me to correct her weird English the same way I need her fingers in my mouth.

"They're fine, Mom. Get your hand out of my face."

"Okay." She shrugs. "Tell me about your stupid father."

"I don't remember too much. He said he rented an apartment, and I should go see him. He asked about you and seemed happy you weren't completely freaking out."

"I see."

"It wasn't the most comfortable conversation. I cut my hand halfway through." I show her my palm.

"Let me look." She inspects the fresh bandage. "Did you need the stitches?"

"No, it's fine."

"And the girl? Did he speak of the girl? Was she there?"

"I don't know."

"Do not lie to your mother."

"I'm not lying."

"Was she there?"

I grumble. "Yeah. He tried putting her on the phone with me, which was ridiculous. She giggled, and I never spoke to her."

"Giggled?" Her face contorts into a sneer. "You were going to speak to her?"

"Hell no. It never got that far. My hand was bleeding, so I had to get off the phone."

"Okay," she replies.

"That's it? You're done with the inquisition?"

"Yes, this is all. Thank you for telling me."

"You're welcome," I say suspiciously. The seatbelt light blinks off.

"Now tell me about poor Dylan."

"Poor? Wow. When did you switch teams?"

She shakes her head. “Does he know yet, how you have decided to ruin the marriage?”

I search for the drink cart. If this is the theme for the next ten hours, I’m going to need a vat of cocktails.

“You have not given it enough time, Katy. You are asking too much of him. A man needs the wife to make him feel important.”

“No. Nu-uh. This isn’t 1950. I don’t fucking owe him anything.”

“What is this vulgar language?” she snaps. “We are the good Hungarian family. We do not speak this way.”

“I do when you say crazy things. He’s abusive. Doesn’t that bother you?”

She turns and puts her hand on mine. “He hit you?”

“No, but he’s verbally and emotionally abusive.”

“And so what?” She pulls her hand away. “Bad things are spoken in every marriage. Why are you so sensitive?”

Turbulence jostles the aircraft. The seatbelt sign pops back on. A pleasant voice announces the beverage service will have to wait, and because Katy is too sensitive, she’ll wait the longest.

“Dad’s never spoken to you the way Dylan talks to me. I’m not getting a divorce because I’m too delicate, Mom. I’m getting one because I don’t want to be miserable for the rest of my life.”

She folds her hands on her lap and closes her eyes. “We are done discussing this.”

• • • • •

Over dinner, we agree to disagree about Dylan. She tells me about Josephine and how quickly her memory is deteriorating. We catch up on home, her friends and the restaurant; everything except her husband and my divorce.

After the trays are collected, I nod off to the hum of the engines and dream about Quinn skipping through the restaurant with an old brown brief case tucked under his arm.

• • • • •

"Katy, it's time to wake up. You are too thin, like the skeleton!"

I rub my eyes. "You woke me up because I'm too thin?"

"Yes."

"Fabulous. Can I go back to sleep now, Mom?"

"Yes."

"Thanks," I say, and pull the blanket over my shoulders.

"Are you asleep? What will we do with your stupid father?"

"He's not stupid."

"It is not proper, what he has done to our family." She yanks a magazine from the seat pocket and mindlessly flips the pages.

"Whatever he's done, getting worked up about him isn't productive."

"Why not?" she asks.

"Because it steers you off course and makes you avoid stuff."

"What is this stuff?"

"Fear, anger, anxiety. Avoidance doesn't do anything to get all that crap out of your system."

"You do this avoiding too. Sleeping instead of speaking to me."

"Tree." I point at her. "Apple." I point at myself. "Where do you think I learned all my bad habits?"

"This is very nice." She slams the magazine shut. "You have never used these words before. I think the psychiatrist has washed your brain."

"She's a psychologist, not a psychiatrist."

"Does this terrible woman make you take the pills?"

"Her name is Dr. Jonas."

"I will not say her name. Is this her idea, to leave your husband?"

"No! Good God. Nobody told me to leave Dylan. She hasn't washed my brain and I'm not taking any pills."

She dismisses me, puts on headphones, and studies the travel information on the screen in front of her.

When I wake up again, she's poking my arm, asking if I want breakfast. Pulling my seat tray down, she instructs the flight attendant to leave the meal. "Thank you. Do you see how thin she is?" She looks the young woman over and points at her name plate. "Holy must have the husband who loves her. She is not thin. She has the good meat on her bones, yes?"

"Excuse me?" Holy asks, dropping the tray. "My husband loves who? And my name is Holly, not Holy."

"This is what I have said, Holy. Now tell my daughter it is better to have the good thick hips to keep the man satisfied. She does not want to eat, so now her husband leaves her."

"My hips are thick?" She lowers her hands to her thighs.

I yank the blanket off my shoulders and sit up. "No, ma'am. I'm so sorry. Please don't listen to my mother."

It's too late. Her lips tremble, and her face is full-on fluorescent pink.

"I am not sorry, Holy. You are a beautiful woman and will make the good mother with many of the healthy pigg-e-letts. This is how it should be. Now, bring me coffee, please."

Holly's eyes well up. A co-worker rushes over to console her. She retreats, not to be seen in our section for the duration of the trip. We get cold coffee.

"Eat," Mom says, reorganizing the food on her tray.

"You have to apologize to that woman, Mom."

"Why?"

"You told her she was fat and made her cry."

"I did nothing of the kind. She is plumb. Men prefer this."

"Plump... never mind. Also, you've never been heavy a day in your life. Does the piglet rule not apply to you?"

"I was plumb also when I married your father. Then I have very beautiful baby." She reaches over and squeezes my cheek. "Now you are the skeleton and Dylan is looking to somewhere else."

"So, you can be thin, but I can't? Aren't you ignoring one gigantic fact?"

"What is this fact, Katy?"

I stare at her. How far can I go before she slaps me?

"What fact?" she asks.

"Dad... staying in Bangkok?"

"This is not your business. You are too young to understand how marriage works."

"Am I really? Maybe you could explain it to me some day."

Her nose wrinkles from the coffee. She's mysterious to me. One minute loving and kind, the next minute harsh, ripping the scab off a fresh wound.

"When you are older," she says. "Eat. You will not like the food in Thailand."

"Why not?"

"There is fish in everything."

"Oh," I say. Years ago, I loved fish without realizing I was eating fish. Then, one day, Dad peeled open a can of sardines in front of me, displaying their cramped bodies, side by side, in an oily brine. I threw up, forever swearing off the slimy things washing up on the beach and rotting under the hot Florida sun.

"This is not good either." She points at a strip of bacon. "No fish at least."

I squeeze ketchup on the eggs and force them down with a flattened croissant.

"We need a plan, Mom. I've got the number to the American Embassy and the address to the hospital, so we can at least get there."

"A plan for what?" she asks, inspecting something between the prongs of her fork.

"What are you doing?"

"It's dirty," she says.

"Wow." I push my food away.

"Yes, Katy, have you ever seen anything like this from our dishes? Disgusting. I will ask Holy for a new one."

"I don't think Holly's in the mood to help out. And I'm not talking about the fork. I'm talking about having our shit together when we land."

"What plan do we need? We go there and they tell us something. He might already be dead."

"Why would you say that Mom?" I can't think about this right now, or ever, if possible. My dad will be fine. He should just shake it off or eat a banana. It's what they gave my grandmother in Montreal when she had heart palpitations. A touch of potassium, a glass of water for hydration. This is a misunderstanding, a crack in the language barrier. Who could expect a Thai doctor to understand English with a Hungarian accent?

The crew passes up and down the aisle, collecting garbage, food and drinks. We begin our descent. I can feel the altitude change in my eardrums.

My mom pulls out her purse, and from it, a powder compact, lipstick and a light blue brush she's had since I was a kid. "You cannot be seen like this. We fix your hair now."

"No thanks."

"Why not?" She dives at me. "Here, I will do it."

"Mom!" I lean away as she lodges the bristles into my hair. "Stop it!"

She's relentless, so I give up, and sit in timeout while my mother tends to me. A few passengers gawk at us. Yeah, yeah, we're that family.

Next, she comes at me with lipstick. "You need color."

"I'm not putting that on."

She rolls her eyes and relaxes back into her seat. "You are very pale."

"I enjoy being pale."

"Dylan would like if you are using the lipstick, I am sure. You do not put the makeup on, you do not care how you look."

"I care. Sometimes. And I'm the one leaving him. Maybe I don't care for the way he looks."

She sighs, smoothing the wrinkles in her dress.

The plane descends under the cloud cover, and I get my first view of Bangkok. It's enormous. A river snakes through flat terrain filled with roads, cultivated land and buildings from massive industrial areas to rows of houses to high-rises. The colors change from bright green fields, some submerged under water to urban stretches of gray.

The tires bump on the tarmac. I glance at my mother with her freshly brushed hair and powdered face. She appears perfect, but the expression in her eyes says she's barely holding it together.

The passengers stir. Some stand before we reach the gate. We're scolded over the intercom to remain seated until the cabin door is open.

"Mom." I nudge her. "Are you ready?"

"No." She stares out the window.

We step into the aisle with the herd of travelers, and file past the reception line of exhausted crew, less Holly, welcoming us to Bangkok.

CHAPTER 22
ARRIVAL IN THE MELTING PLACE

It takes almost an hour to pump us through customs and into the arrivals area. Passengers are milling about, searching for a familiar face, or arranging transportation to their next destination. I turn my phone on. Four more calls from Dylan. This time with four voicemails. I turn the phone off.

"We need some Thai money and a car service or cab," I tell my mom and look for a foreign exchange kiosk. "What the hell is the currency here?"

"Baht," she answers, holding up a fat coin pouch. "It will be enough for now."

"And a ride. Got any leads on that?"

She pulls out her cell phone and texts with her index finger. "I have this also under control."

"How do you have this also under control?"

"Ethan. Do you remember him?"

"No," I say." Is he someone I've met?"

"Yes, the son of family friends. Your father's. We visited them when you were a little girl."

"What's their connection to him?"

"Ethan's mother is Hungarian. The parents...the families, were close."

"Do you mean the group Dad talks about when he's had too much to drink? The ones who spent summers on Lake Balaton?"

She gazes at me. "Yes. You do not remember the boy?"

"I got nothing. Why are you staring at me? What does this have to do with getting a cab?"

She shrugs. "Ethan lives here. I called his mother before we left, and he is able to pick us up."

"Why didn't you tell me before?"

"I was waiting for her to send me the texting message."

"So, he's here at the airport?"

"Yes. Do you see?" She shows me her phone.

"How do we recognize him?"

She turns in a circle, studying the faces hurrying by. "I think it will not be a problem."

"How old is he?"

"Five or six years older than you."

It doesn't take long to notice him moving toward us through the crowd. A giant compared to the clump of people around him. By American standards, he's just another tall white boy with short, light brown hair and day-old peach fuzz.

"Mrs. Kiss?"

"Yes, Ethan." She embraces him. "Thank you so much for this."

He smiles at me. "Katy?"

"Hi." Do I hug him, shake his hand? Time goes by and it becomes awkward. I'm sure we'll laugh about it later.

Mom touches his cheek. "You are so grown up. When we saw you last, you were hiding behind your mother. Now you are a man."

"Oh my God, Mom. Don't embarrass him."

She ignores me. "You are so like her with the beautiful green eyes. How is she?"

"Doing well. Not too pleased about me being this far away from home. How was your flight? Long, isn't it?"

"Yes, very terrible," she says.

I shuffle my feet. Time's a-wasting chit chatting about the good old times. "These are all our bags, so we're ready to get out of here."

He nods and asks us to follow him.

"I have the address," I say.

"I know where he is." He takes Mom's bag. "I can carry it for you."

We walk through double doors leading to a parking garage. A wall of heat and humidity hits me in the face. "What the fuck is this? A microwave?"

"Katy!" Mom glares at me. I return with a shy smile and apologize.

The cars are small, the spaces tight. We slither into the seats of a gold Honda sedan.

"You better buckle in," Ethan says. "This isn't like driving in the States."

"Okay," I mumble, having been recently reprimanded.

Sunshine fills my eyes, along with an onslaught of vehicles going in every imaginable direction. At each stoplight, motorcycles and mopeds funnel into the empty spaces between the cars and trucks, piling deeper until the light turns green.

"How is everyone not dead?" I ask, watching the road race outside my window.

"There are a lot of accidents." He checks over his shoulder before changing lanes.

"I bet. Let me find the name of the hospital." I inspect my notes.

"I've got it, Katy. I took him in."

"You took him in where?"

"To the hospital." He glances into the rearview mirror.

"What?" I turn to my mom.

She drops her eyes into her lap as we push through the traffic. Out my window, there's a small motorcycle with a man driving, and a woman sitting side-saddle behind him. She holds on to him with her right arm. With her left, she reads a book, oblivious to the surrounding madness.

"Holy shit!" I cringe as they buzz by.

"At least there's only two people on there." He shifts gears, barely avoiding an orange tuk-tuk which has moved into our lane without warning.

"This is bumper cars. And how is it you took my dad anywhere? Why would he call you?"

"We live in the same building." He looks at me, then back at the road. "He told you he rented a condo, right?"

"Yeah. Why do I feel like I'm missing something?"

"He contacted me when he got to Thailand. I mean when he and your mom got here."

"Did you know that?" I ask her.

"Yes, he did mention that he would call Ethan."

"And then what?" I cover my eyes as a fruit truck merges beside us.

"He said he wanted to stay on for a while and asked about places for rent." He peeks at the rearview again. "My building is full of expats, so I set it up for him."

"And you're aware my dad's shacked up with a teenager?"

He clears his throat. "I am."

"Katy, this is not Ethan's fault. Please do not be rude to the boy."

"Sorry." I grumble.

"No worries, it's Bangkok."

"Not feeling it yet. What's the attraction?"

He stops talking, concentrates on the drive. "It's like Vegas, but much, much worse." He turns to me. "You don't look so different from what I remember."

"Which is probably when I was three years old, because that's the last time we met," I say, glancing at my t-shirt, crumpled jeans, and tennis shoes. I hear Quinn's voice in my head from the other night, making fun of my clothes and my mother begging me to put makeup on. A pattern is developing here. A not-so-subtle message for me to stop acting like the kid who fell off the monkey bars.

"Ethan, do not make her excited about how she is looking."

"Mom."

She rolls her eyes. "Now please tell us what happened to my husband."

"It was pretty quick. He said he didn't feel well a couple of days ago and complained about being nauseous. We figured he'd eaten something bad the night before."

"What did he eat?" Mom asks.

"It wasn't food, Mother, it was his heart."

"Right," Ethan says. "He couldn't get comfortable, he was coughing, his skin was pale."

Mom gasps, swears in Hungarian.

"Do you know what I do for a living?" he asks.

"No."

"I'm a pilot for an air ambulance company and fly people in cardiac arrest, among other things. I recognized the signs, so we brought him to the E.D."

"We?" Mom asks from the back. "What is this E.D?"

"Emergency Department. Uh...Lia came with us."

Mom sputters more nastiness in Hungarian about how she'll explain this to the family.

"We're here," Ethan announces, pulling up to the building. It may have been white the day it was painted; now it's old, stained with pollution and the sweat of everyone who's ever walked by. Bundled power lines are strung erratically on poles, over the streets, attached to exterior walls, and the windows are clouded with dirt.

"This is where you brought Robert?"

"It's a decent facility, a bit rough on the outside."

Inside, the smell of antiseptic, sickness and food engulfs me the same way the hot air did when we stepped out of the airport. In a hallway buzzing with fluorescent lights, I brace myself against the wall to keep from sliding to the ground. My mom tries to help. I shake her off. I'm fine, I'd just rather be anywhere else. Ethan tells me to breathe. I tell him to shut up and my mother tells me to apologize for the seven-hundredth time.

We ride the elevator up to the cardiac care unit. This floor is more modern, and the staff is dressed in crisp white uniforms. They are shorter than us, with darker complexions and calm, friendly faces. They nod at Ethan and smile at my mother and me.

"Take a minute before you see him," he says. "You need to be ready."

We're not ready. In fact, we're the poster children for anything but. Mom grabs my arm to steady herself as it becomes clear how ill-prepared we are for the reality of what's about to come.

CHAPTER 23
A BLOCK OF THE ARTERIES

How can a room with no movement, no color or light be so overwhelming? My eyes scan the dreary white walls, a small window flanked by a drooping curtain, the bed.

My dad, smaller than I remember, is sprouting tubes, springing above and below his blanket, attached to machines on either side.

He coughs, smiles weakly, and reaches his hands toward us.

"It's dark in here." Ethan taps a yellowed switch near the door. The room brightens, the hum of electricity permeates the small space.

The pink in my mom's cheeks fades to a ghostly white. "What have you done?" She goes to her husband's side.

I follow her, taken aback by how much older he appears. His wavy hair is flattened across his forehead. The tubes are everywhere, hindering his movements, carrying liquid. Sustaining him, draining him.

He squeezes my hand and motions for me to kiss his cheek. It's not without effort, and the shame of wanting to recoil after touching him. His skin is dry, stretched over bulging blue veins. He's withered, with a vacant expression in his eyes I could never have prepared for. The machines click and tick, making a rhythmic whooshing sound. Another wave of nausea washes over me while my brain tries to reconcile this person with the giant I grew up with.

I whisper my greeting to him, as though his illness precludes anything but low, comforting tones. His gray beard is scruffy, his lips are chapped. He is a distortion of his former self.

"Did you just arrive?" he asks.

"Yes, dear," Mom says, trying to keep herself together with Herculean effort.

"Katy, do you remember Ethan?"

"Not really, Dad."

"He remembers you."

I flash a fake smile. "Great. Can we talk about you, though? How do we get you home?"

"I am not sure. We have to ask." He turns toward his wife. Their eyes lock.

Does grave illness trump infidelity? Awkward silence hovers in the air. If this were me, and my husband of almost thirty years had so tactlessly misbehaved, a serious conversation would be in order.

"Let's go find the doctor." I motion Ethan to the door.

A man in a white lab coat greets us before we can leave. Barely five feet tall, with shiny black hair framing his face, he puts his hands together and bows. Ethan bows to him in similar fashion, nods for me to follow suit.

"Are you Katy, daughter of Robert?" I recognize Dr. Orapan's voice.

"Yes." I bow self-consciously.

"I am Robert's doctor."

I back up to allow him in. "Mom? This is Dr. Orapan. My mother, Andrea Kiss."

"Doctor." Her eyes narrow. She's weighing, judging, measuring.

He greets my father, who offers a limp wave.

"Did you recently arrive to hospital?" he asks.

"Yes. Thank you for taking care of my dad. Can you tell us what happened?"

"Please come outside to lobby and I give information about his condition."

"No," Mom says. "I am not leaving this room."

He responds without anger or impatience. "Very well. Robert is having many assistance to his health. We observe how heart beats and gets the oxygen. You see this tube into his nose." He touches his nose for effect. "And the liquid, to maintain electrolytes." His sentences sound like questions, with the inflection on the last word.

"I give him the sedative and make less pain. Do you understand this?"

Ethan says yes and nods at me.

"When you called me in Florida, you said he had a heart attack."

"Correct. I would now like to do coronary angiogram."

"To check if there's a blockage in his arteries?" I ask.

"Yes."

"What if there is one? Will you have to do open-heart surgery? How does it work? Do you put him on one of those by-pass machines? Will you have to stop his heart?"

He holds his hands up to me. "You are speaking very fast. Can slow down?"

Ethan repeats my questions in a mix of Thai and English. After several minutes of polite discussion, Dr. Orapan addresses us again.

"We get result of test and discuss with Mr. Robert about this. I say with definite, if artery are not good, he need surgery to live. I have discussed this information with him before you are getting to hospital."

My mother inhales sharply. "To live? He could die if he does not have it?"

"His status is serious. I feel strongly for you to let us help him. You speak to Mr. Robert about plan. Please ask for nurse to call me when you are ready to make decision."

Mom thanks him. As soon as he steps away, she slumps into a chair covered in bright orange fabric with smiley face raindrops. I think of Dr. Jonas's office, her non-committal beige couch, and the stupid plastic fern. So many ways to decorate. So many ways to be traumatized.

She turns to my dad. "Do we have choices in this matter?"

"Is this a safe hospital?" I ask. "How do we even know if Dr. Orapan is qualified?"

"Katy, stop it." She admonishes me. "Ethan, what is your opinion?"

"If it helps, I had my appendix taken out here and survived. The doc's English is good, and we bring a lot of people in from our flights."

"It doesn't help me." I say, distracted by the sound of the blood pressure cuff inflating around Dad's bruised skin.

What I wouldn't give for him to sit up, demand a cute nurse, and a pack of cigarettes. Instead, he's fallen asleep with his head slumped forward. My Mom rushes to him, pushing his shoulders back on the pillow.

"Let me help." Ethan hurries to his side. "I get this is a lot to take in, but he's been pretty happy in Bangkok the past few weeks."

I stand in the middle of the room, feeling useless. "How the hell do you know when my dad's happy?"

"Do not speak to the boy like this." Mom scowls at me. "Let them do the angiogram. When we hear the results, we will decide what is next."

CHAPTER 24
BACHELOR PAD

Afternoon in Bangkok is burning hot and humid. The wet air wraps around everyone and everything, ingesting the smells, getting heavier and harder to breathe in. Millions of people live here, and the ones who aren't committing suicide by driving, walk along the crowded sidewalks or sit on doorsteps and plastic stools watching the others go by.

We leave the hospital wanting to change clothes, take a shower, and figure out where to sleep. Ethan tells us his condo is nearby, and however distasteful the thought, is talking us into staying in the unit my dad rented.

His building is the familiar shade of worn white, underneath a film of murky brown mold. We walk up a flight of stairs and enter through a massive mahogany door. The lobby is a different world, cooled by air conditioning, wood-paneled walls, beautiful carpets, leather sofas and a manned reception desk.

"Savadika." A young man dressed in a dark suit smiles and bows.

My mother and Ethan return the bow. I stare at him, and he grins at me expectantly.

"Do it." Ethan taps my elbow.

"No," I whisper to him.

"You're being disrespectful."

"Shit." I throw my hands together and bend over.

The doorman's smile broadens, as if I'd given him a gift, or a puppy.

"What floor?" I ask, getting into the elevator.

"Eight."

"How much is the cost to live here?" Mom runs her fingers along the polished metal handrail.

He clears his throat, shrugs, doesn't answer.

"This way." He directs us through a long hallway.

"The girl is not here?" she asks before he opens the door.

"No, of course not."

"Where is she?" I ask.

Ethan turns the key. "Not here."

Mom walks in first, her face set in an angry frown. She drops her bag deliberately on the floor in front of a black leather couch.

"Who knows what has happened on this furniture." She steps past a matching chair, a flat-screen TV, and a glass table with shiny chrome legs in the center of the living room.

Beyond is a compact kitchen with an island made of dark wood and marble, running parallel to a counter on the back wall. The sink holds a few dirty dishes, and next to the fridge, there's a bag of instant coffee, fruit that looks like it's from Mars, and a box of wafers. Mom is right behind me, breathing hard. Her chin bumps against my shoulder.

We check the contents of the refrigerator, as if we might find some clue about how this all happened; how my dad ended up in a hospital in Thailand, and the two of us prowling through his den of iniquity. All we find is an oddly shaped container of milk, a loaf of rye bread, and some orange marmalade. I close the door and turn to see tears on my mom's cheeks.

She takes my hand, mainly to steady the shaking in hers. "He lived here, in this place, without me. This is shameful, Katy, I am very angry." She slouches, wiping the wetness from her face.

I follow her into the bedroom. Here too, the furniture is all leather and chrome. The words "bachelor pad," spring into my mind while I explore. She pushes her finger into the soft mattress of the waterbed. It pushes back, gurgling.

"A waterbed. What is in his brain?" She shakes her head, opens a mirrored closet door.

We find shirts and pants I recognize from home. A plastic hook holds the red and blue checked bathrobe he wears every Sunday while reading the paper and drinking his morning coffee.

My heart is heavy, and my thoughts are out of place. Mom drops down, sinking into the waterbed.

"Ethan?" Her voice is soft.

"Yes?" He rushes into the room as if he were waiting for his cue outside.

"Are these sheets clean? Was the girl on these sheets?"

"No, ma'am! I had the cleaners take everything out and bring in new bedding."

"You are a good boy." She smiles at him. "I would like to rest a little." Irritation clouds her face while she navigates the bed's tiny tidal waves. She sighs, her head sinks into the pillow, her breathing slows. She's out cold within a minute.

"I don't think she's ever fallen asleep that fast," I tell Ethan.

"She's got a lot to process and flying ten hours doesn't help." He pushes the closet door shut. "Let's go hang out at my condo or get a bite to eat."

• • • • •

"She's in here," Ethan says, opening the door to his apartment.

He's talking about the lima bean, suddenly here, sitting on a couch, talking on her phone.

She's slender, dressed in mini shorts and a tank top, with long straight dark hair. I hear the same melodic sounding words coming out of her I did a few weeks ago when I tried to leave a message for my dad.

"Lia." Ethan calls her name while pushing his keys into his pocket.

She's startled, drops the cell phone, and jumps up. In a sweet voice, she says, "Savadika," and smiles for us. Meeting her in person brings the reality of my dad's behavior into focus. She's an actual person, and I'm not sure I can be civil with the woman-child who's ripped my family apart.

He mouths, "sorry," to me, and bows to her, hands barely together.

"Do it." He nudges me in the side.

"Do what?"

"Bow."

"Come on. Do I have to?"

His hard stare reminds me of the way I described myself to Dr. Jonas. I'm being difficult, stubborn, for no reason at all. People here bow and I'm blowing it out of proportion, turning something ordinary into something stressful.

"Fuck me..." I bend ever so slightly, hands not touching, not smiling.

Lia approaches us. She's barefoot, her toenails are painted with glossy purple polish.

"I Lia," she squeaks, and similar to the doctor, makes everything sound like a question.

Her skin is perfect, her dark eyes are enormous. She's beautiful and so young.

"I'm Katy. Whatever, this is ridiculous." I glare at Ethan. "Is she yours now?"

"Are you serious?"

"She's in your apartment."

"No, she's not mine, she isn't property. I moved her in here when I found out you and your mom were coming. I didn't want them to meet."

"How proactive of you."

"I thought it was pretty damn decent of me."

"So, you have a different one?" I look at Lia.

"No." His tone is clipped. I'm crossing the line, stomping on it, spitting on it.

"Her English isn't great, right? I talked to her on the phone back home."

"Ask her yourself."

"Do you understand any English, Lia?"

"Yes, little bit."

"Where do you live?"

"You pretty. You daddy say to me, Katy pretty."

"Thanks, Lia. Where do you live?"

"I live with Rob-ee." She smiles, moving seductively in my direction. This shit might work with my dad, but I'm getting more pissed off.

"Robby? Are we fucking serious right now?"

Ethan shrugs and shoves his hands into his pockets.

She turns to him, producing the same inviting smile. He grins, dark pupils expand in his bright eyes. Are all men this easy?

I ask, "where did you live before, Lia?"

"Before?" She pulls her long nails through her hair.

"Before you lived with Robert, where did you live?"

"With sister."

"She lives in Bangkok?"

"Yes, in Bangkok."

"Perhaps you can go back to your sister." I watch her facial expression for any change.

"Fewer words," Ethan whispers to me. "And drop the attitude. Her English is a hell of a lot better than your Thai."

"Lay off, dude. I have my own shit-show going on at home. I didn't ask to be involved in this one."

He shakes his head, and I low-key want to punch him.

"Fine, I'll try to behave." I turn to Lia again. "Lia has to go and live with sister."

"But I live with Rob-ee."

"Robert has a wife. She's here."

"Rob-ee wife come back to Bangkok?" Her eyelashes flutter.

"Yes, she's here," I tell her. "You'll need to leave."

"He say he stay here with me."

"He lied." I deliver the blow, then look away. Being a bitch to this girl doesn't feel nearly as satisfying as I hoped it would.

"Lie?" Her smile fades.

Ethan steps in. "Robert is sick. Family here to help him."

"Family?" She backs up. "Okay."

"Nice job," he mutters to me, then follows her to the far end of the room.

I lean against the door, watching him communicate with her in Thai. She nods, he nods. They're deep in conversation, so I turn my phone on again. It's the middle of the night in Dufferin Beach, but Dylan is still leaving messages.

Voicemail 1: "You bitch. Pick up."

Voicemail 2: "Your Dad's not even sick is he? You're just fucking hiding from me. Where are you really? Orlando, Miami? Come face me, cunt."

Voicemail 3: "Pick up. Come face me, bitch."

Voicemail 4: "I said pick up! Fucking little Hungarian princess."

I wince. Text Jesse about the calls. Turn the phone off.

Ethan pulls out his wallet and extracts several colorful bills. Lia bows deeply after he hands them to her.

He returns to me, pulling the front door open and motioning me out.

"Are you kicking me out?" I ask, stepping into the hallway.

"We're kicking her out, but we're going to get you some food. You look a bit shaky."

We walk around the side of the building to a courtyard filled with people and vendors with carts and portable barbecues. Some have glass cases filled with sliced pineapple, watermelon, cantaloupe and other fruit I don't recognize. Others are selling chickens, their heads not so cleanly removed, feathers still clinging to their yellow skin. The smells, heavy, spicy, and wonderful, make it easy to block out angry Dylan.

Dogs amble near us, all in various forms of decay. None of them are healthy, there are no shiny coats or wagging tails.

"What's happening to these animals?" I ask.

"They live out here. Nobody owns them, lots of people feed them. Sometimes they get hit by cars, eventually, they lie down and die."

"What a disgusting way to treat an animal."

"People suck, don't they? And some people treat other humans just as badly."

I stop walking. Why do I need to defend myself to a stranger about another stranger who is having an affair with my father? He doesn't notice my absence until he's almost twenty feet ahead of me. He stops, turns, and we stare each other down, locked in an argument neither of us asked for. I give in first, focusing on the uneven cement under my feet as I catch up to him.

"I'm sorry. Though hearing me apologize must be getting old by now."

He stays quiet, then puts his hand softly on my shoulder and turns me to a bank of carts.

"This is your dad's favorite place. He loves street food."

The aromas tickle my nose and make my stomach growl for nourishment.

He orders in Thai, which is poor enough to cause both confusion and amusement. The vendors smile and hand us a tray of fruit and two large bowls of noodle soup.

"Let's find somewhere to sit," he says.

The scene resembles an outdoor food court without the high-tech decorations or air conditioning. It doesn't take long to find a table, and we sit down to our first meal together.

Some flavors I recognize, chili, lime, peanuts. The rest I can't identify. I slurp the broth and hope like hell there's no fish heads or exotic insects floating in my bowl.

We finish the soup without conversation. I move on to the watermelon, which tastes stronger than anything I've had before, like the flavor of ten melons siphoned and injected into one single piece.

"Is this stuff laced with ecstasy?"

He smiles. "Goddamn weird, isn't it?"

I groan, eating until the food disappears.

We gather up the dishes and return them to the vendors. Ethan bows to them in thanks, then looks at me.

"Hell." I bow, embarrassed by this new form of greeting. They bow in return, and after some pointing and choppy conversation, we walk away with a to-go bag of food.

"For my mom?" I ask, walking back to the condo.

"Yes."

"Nice of you."

"I'm a nice guy."

"Why? You don't really know us." I stop at another cart and push my hand through a wicker basket filled with wrapped candied fruit.

"Why am I nice to you?" he asks.

"Uh-huh," I say, poking at the candy.

"You'd rather I be a dick?"

I drop the candies. Something in his tone sounds familiar. "Have I met you somewhere before? Like, recently?"

"Is that your best line?"

"I'm married. I have no line."

"Everyone has a line, Katy."

"Not me. I'm off the market in an emotionally perplexed sort of way."

"Why am I not surprised to hear that? And no, I think it's been years since we've seen each other."

Reaching the front of the condo, Ethan sits down on a short cement wall close to the stairs.

"What are you doing? Why aren't we going in?"

"Let's talk about Lia," he says.

"She's leaving, who cares?"

"There are thousands of girls like her in this city."

"I don't live in this city."

"You're here now, have some respect for it." His cheeks glow pink with emotion.

"Why? I'm already pissed and just a tiny bit conflicted about my dad using a woman for sex. Hearing the details will not make me more sympathetic."

"How about expanding your horizons?"

"Fine. Talk." I kick at the concrete with my foot.

"She doesn't want to sell herself."

"Then she shouldn't."

"You think she's not aware of that? She's got no other source of income, and poverty here is different from the States. In Thailand, people are dirt-poor, living in ways you can't imagine. Kids are sold, to whoever, for whatever. Services are exchanged for money."

"You're saying girls get sold for sex? By their families?"

"I'm saying girls *and* boys are sold for sex by their families."

"Boys do this too?" I ask.

He sounds annoyed. "Did you grow up with your head in the sand?"

I think of the beach at home. "Actually..."

He rolls his eyes. "They sell their kids. Not because they don't love them, but because there's a different mindset here. One most of us can't understand. If Lia doesn't make money, she'll end up on the streets."

"Won't her family take her in?"

"No."

"That's not fair. Can she get a job doing something else?"

"She's barely had any schooling. She didn't choose this. How far would you get in America with a third-grade education?"

I nod, shuffle my feet.

"Don't unload your American standards on this country or the people. The rules you grew up with don't apply here. Do you think she wants to have sex with a sixty-five-year-old man?"

I shake my head, wondering how my dad would react if I sold myself for money.

"She does it, or she rots out on the street like the dogs you were feeling sorry for."

"So, she's not some horrible bitch. I get it. Why tell me all of this?"

His eyes follow a couple walking past us, then focus back on me. "Because I acted like you when I got here. I was judging by my standards, without understanding that most people in the world don't have the same comforts and opportunities Americans do."

"I'll try. But forgiveness isn't so simple from where I'm standing."

"Agreed, her methods aren't great. Her situation is crap, and that's not her fault."

"And it's not that my dad wasn't a willing participant." I start up the tall concrete steps.

"True, but he didn't come here to meet a girl and hurt his family."

"Yet he has. It's done and we all have to deal with it."

Inside, we bow to the doorman, who smiles and returns the gesture. "Bloody hell," I whisper. "What the fuck with this bowing deal?"

We let ourselves back into my dad's condo, and for a split-second, I search for him on the couch or in the kitchen. My reality shifts again, in a bad way, like a slap across the face.

In the bedroom, my mother is spastically rifling through the closet.

"We brought you food, Mom."

"Okay," she murmurs. We watch her trying to retrieve something mysterious, something she won't find if she stays a hundred years. She turns to us, looking defeated, tears dripping from her cheeks again.

"We have to go back to the hospital now." She walks past us into the kitchen.

"Please eat." I say, sliding the bag in front of her. "Ethan was nice enough to bring you soup."

"I can't." The expression in her eyes is enough to make me wince. She doesn't enjoy being told what to do, especially by her daughter. When is the day in an adult's life when the tables turn, and the child becomes the parent? This might be that day for us, and it feels about as natural as ripping a fingernail off. Silently she spoons up the soup, her skin taking on color as she finishes the entire bowl.

"Now can we go?" She glares at me and drops her dish into the sink.

CHAPTER 25
#WTF

Another friendly exchange with the doorman and we're outside, wading through the wet Thai evening. People crowd into the streets and more vendors set up to feed them. Ethan tells us it's less expensive to buy street food than to cook at home, so every night the sidewalks become centers for social gatherings.

The hospital is equally crowded, the air conditioning cools to a comfortable eighty degrees, and the smells are thick, like meat stew gone over.

Dad's awake, his face taking on a tinge of color when he sees us. "You fly halfway around the world to visit only for a few minutes?"

"We got some food and Mom needed to lie down."

"Where did this lying down happen?" he asks.

"At your place. Everything's been cleaned out." I catch a glimpse of Ethan's frown and immediately regret my choice of words.

"We will not talk about this now," Mom says, sitting on the bed, carefully easing Dad's tubes out of her way, while telling him about Josephine, her dementia, her refusal to bathe or wear a bra.

She turns and points at me. "Please kill me if I get like this, Katy. If my mind goes, run me over with the car."

"Which car?"

"How does this matter to me? A big one, so it happens quickly."

I shake my head. This is the perfect example of picking your battles.

"Where is the doctor?" she asks, gently adjusting the pale-yellow blankets.

Ethan offers to find him, perhaps wanting to escape the madness of my family.

"Shouldn't we try to act more normal in front of the new guy?" I ask after he leaves.

"We are not normal? Did your psychologist say this to you?" She taps my dad's hand. "Your daughter thinks she is crazy now."

"Nobody's talking about being crazy, Mom. She doesn't tell me what to think or say. But honestly…"

"Yes?" Her eyes narrow, locked and loaded. "Honestly, what, Katalin?"

I groan.

"You are seeing a psychologist?" Dad asks. "Why can't she speak to you, Andrea?"

She shakes her head. In a hot second, locked and loaded transforms into *I told you so.*

"What are you doing with this psychologist? Is it because of the asshole?"

"No. It's fine. It's not a big thing."

"What do you discuss with this stranger?" He gets the words out, then coughs.

He sips water, most of which trickles down his chin between the racking spasms. The sound is awful, coming from the congestion deep inside his lungs.

"Tell me!" he demands, wheezing.

I inhale, terrified he's about to pass out. I'd hand over a lung if it would get him home faster. No way I'm telling him about the divorce. The extra stress might be more than he can take.

"I was worried about running The Point alone when you guys left. It was work stuff. That's it. Not a big deal."

His eyebrow slides up, exchanging a look with his wife. I don't expect him to buy my explanation, but this is all he gets until he's healthy enough to hear the truth.

"So, not to change the subject," I say. "Why is Ethan hanging around? What's his deal?"

"What deal does he need?" Dad asks. "He is friend of the family. We are Hungarian, so it is important to keep to these connectors."

"Connections," I correct. "He seems overly invested."

Before the conversation continues, Ethan returns with Dr. Orapan, and a chubby middle-aged woman dressed in light green scrubs which hug her broad midsection. He turns to me and mouths "bloody hell," the universal code for bowing. We bend over for the twentieth time today. It seems dangerous, all this tilting toward each other, all this potential for concussed skulls.

They approach my dad, check the monitors and the paperwork on his chart, then inject a clear liquid into his IV.

"Mrs. Kiss, this is Dr. Thawan. She is radiologist. Unfortunately, her English is not so good as mine." His smile is genuine. "She give him low dose of sedative now. This is helping to calm. We will take Robert into operating room soon, and the procedure will take one to two hours."

My mother takes her husband's hand. "And you both have done this before?"

"Yes, many times. You may stay here if it is comfort for you, or we have waiting lounge outside."

Mom's shoulders stiffen. "We will stay here."

"Very well, I speak to you again after we finish."

She returns to fussing over my dad, smoothing his hair, and touching his face. He smiles at me, signaling it's going to be okay.

"You are not off the hooks," Dad says. "I want to know about this talking to the psychologist."

Two young men come into the room. They pull cords and stack bags of IV fluid on his blanket. In less than a minute, they unlock the wheels of his bed and push it to the door. He waves at us, and we reassure him we'll be here when he wakes up.

"Now we wait." Mom sits down with her purse perched on her knees.

I ask Ethan for the time.

"Eight-thirty." He rubs the back of his neck and puffs out air.

I chew on my nails for seven hours and ask him again.

"Eight-thirty-three. Don't you have a phone?"

"Why so salty?" I ask and pull it out of my pocket. Five more voicemails from Dylan. Nothing but heavy breathing, followed by one word. "Cunt." Each message is exactly the same. Fuck. I married a psycho-killer. I text Jesse again, close my eyes and try not to panic.

A few minutes later I check the glowing blue Facebook icon. The thought of posting something like *please pray for my person*, is laughable. *Hi y'all, I'm in Bangkok cuz my dad's heart exploded while he was hanging with a tweeny-bopper. # WTF*

A text from Dylan pops up; a short video of a woman's head bobbing up and down in a man's crotch. It's a tight shot. Nothing is left to the imagination. There are three missed messages from people who don't hate me. Russ, Quinn, and the last one from Jesse.

CALL ME NOW!

I glance at my mom. I don't want to leave this room until they wheel my dad in, healthy and ready to get on a plane to the Sunshine State. Jesse sends another message. Same words, followed by an angry face emoji and a fireball.

"I'm going to the lobby," I announce.

Ethan nods. My mother dismisses me with a mechanical wave.

It's hotter on the main floor. The smells are syrupy, nauseating.

"Hello from Thailand."

"What the hell, Katy? What's happening? You've been gone almost two days and all I've learned is that your husband can cuss and breathe hard."

"Time's all fucked-up here. I'm calling you from the future."

"So funny, Marty McFly. How's your dad?"

"We're not sure yet. They just wheeled him off for an angiogram."

"He doesn't know you're there?"

"He does. We talked to him, but he's sedated." I flatten myself against a wall. A young man pushes a moaning woman past me in a wheelchair.

"What the fuck is that?" Jesse asks.

"I'm in the hospital. I believe that is the sound of labor."

She snorts. "Reproduction. Disgusting. So, what happens after the angiogram?"

"Depends on the results. Ethan says the staff here is competent."

"What's an Ethan?"

I explain in my typically disorganized manner, causing more confusion than clarity. She grumbles. I change the subject.

"Have you heard anything from Dylan? Should I be worried about those texts?"

"No, he's just blowing off steam. I'd worry more if there was no reaction at all. He's already lawyered-up with a guy from Fort Myers. They're making the usual noise."

"What does making noise mean?"

She burps. "Sorry. Too much pop. It means asking for a valuation of the house and a couple other things. Nothing to freak-out over."

"Why does he need to find out how much the house is worth? What are the other things?"

"Just things. It's what everyone does, Katy, part of the game."

"I don't like this game," I say, and get out of the way again. The moaning woman is wheeled by me a second time.

"You're paying me to like it for you. Next up is the temporary hearing."

"What happens if I'm not there?"

"It's not even scheduled yet. Either way, I'll handle it."

"Won't it look bad?"

"In a normal town, yes. In Dufferin Beach, it's a non-issue. Almost everyone knows your family."

A young child steps in front of me, stops, and gazes up at my face. Her features are delicate. Tiny mouth, button nose and a pink sleeveless dress with white ruffled straps.

"Jesse, I have to get off the phone. A tiny person is staring at me."

"You can't say that shit anymore. What does it want?"

The girl smiles, lets out a stream of squeaky, unintelligible words.

"It's not an 'it', she's an actual little girl. I think she's three or four."

She continues talking and reaches her pudgy hands up to me.

"She wants something."

"Why? Tell her to go away!"

The toddler chatters. "Listen to her, Jess, she sounds like the Chipmunks!" I lower the phone to her. She laughs, jumps up and down; clearly unburdened by the rules of adulthood. "Oh my gosh, she's so cute."

"Why are you so easily distracted, Kiss? Call me when you have an update."

"Yes, Ma'am," I tell her and hang up.

"Hi munchkin person. Do you want to see my phone?" She gets more excited as I lower it to her. I sit on the ground, and she crouches in front of me, babbling and pointing.

"This is a cell phone."

She giggles.

"Cell phone. Phone," I repeat.

She studies me as I sound out the *f*.

"Phone?" she whispers.

I laugh and clap. "Yes, so cool!" She claps too and repeats the word over and over.

"You are brilliant, Peanut," I say, tears forming in my eyes. She stops laughing, her face suddenly serious. She puts one hand on mine, and with the other, wipes away the water on my cheeks.

"Thank you."

She smiles again, then jumps when a shrill voice breaks the calm. A nurse stomps toward us, yelling in Thai. The toddler leaps to her feet and runs out of the lobby.

"Why are you screaming at her?"

"She not good!" she yells.

"How is she not good? She's a kid."

"She take your phone. Mother outside tell her what to do."

"What the hell?" I mumble, searching for her through the window. Usually, I'm nervous around kids. They're mysterious, breakable and their hair often has food stuck to it. This one is different. I want to scoop her up and take her home.

I text Jesse about what happened and walk back to my dad's room. Mom is still planted in her chair like an armed guard. Ethan is sitting cross legged on the floor.

"Do small children steal things here?" I crouch next to him.

"What did you do now?"

"I didn't do anything. The cutest kid I've ever seen might have been trying to run off with my phone."

"It's possible." He rests his head against the wall. "Another unfortunate consequence of poverty."

"Start 'em young? First theft, then, you know, the other?"

He looks tired, irritated. "Yeah, the poor ones. Does casting judgment on them make you feel better?"

"It makes me feel like crap, actually, so now you're the one judging. She was so sweet. I wanted to take her with me."

My mom tells us to quiet down.

"She has parents, Katy. They love their kids but do unappetizing things by Western standards." He yawns. "Sorry about what I said. To be honest, I did some judging when I got here, too."

"I earned it. I'm tired, out of place, and being a bitch."

"How are the things at home?" Mom asks. "You have told Dylan that you are here safely?"

"I have not. But thanks for having his back."

We give each other the stink eye for ten seconds, then the silent treatment.

An hour later, we're still waiting, and in unison, twist toward the door at any sign of activity outside. I spend the time stalking Ethan on Facebook and Instagram. His mom tags him with baby pictures on every birthday. His friends post selfies with the mountains or baseball and football fields as backdrops; and all have similar captions. Miss you, dude, here's a picture of us getting wasted. Wish you were here.

I scroll back to high school and find a mess of typical prom pictures. Ethan with a date, her corsage, a line of the guys in their tuxedos, a line of the girls in their fancy dresses. The most recent post is a video from the cockpit window as he lands in Phuket. He flies over the beach and the rocky islands jutting out of the aqua blue water. The beauty is surreal, it allows me to forget I'm sitting on the stained linoleum of a hospital floor.

Three hours after they wheeled my dad off, they return him on his fancy rolling bed. He's out cold, his skin sallow. In a moment of panic, I think he's dead. He's ghostly white, unnaturally still, and smells like freshman year chemistry lab.

"Is he okay?" I yell at the men. They're spooked by me, which is ironic because I'm not the one pushing the dead guy around.

Dr. Orapan arrives shortly after Dad is reattached to his tether of medically necessary equipment.

"We have the success and see positive news."

"What did you find?" Mom turns to him.

"Mr. Robert has blockage, but not so bad as we first think."

"And you are able to fix this?" she asks, straightening her clothes.

"We can do smaller procedure. He does not require the open-heart surgery."

"And the heart attack?"

"Yes, Mrs. Robert, this still happen. The damage is not so bad. We do the angioplasty. This means we blow up the ..." He cups his hands together and looks at Ethan.

"Balloon," Ethan offers.

"Yes, balloon, and place stent into artery for the better blood flow."

He explains the procedure, the timing and the plan. Dad stirs and opens his eyes.

Dr. Orapan advises us to let the patient rest and leaves the room.

"Did I live? Did they kill me?"

"Nope, Dad. You're all good!"

"I feel like shit." His words are slurred as he reaches for Ethan. "You are still here?"

He steps closer to the bed, bends forward, and takes his hand. Before he can straighten back up, a thin necklace with a small heart-shaped charm drops from his collared shirt.

Dad takes hold of the charm, studies it, smiles. "It's very nice."

"Thanks. My mom gave it to me when I was a kid."

"Yes?"

"Yeah, she said I'm not allowed to take it off." He tucks it back into his shirt.

We spend a few minutes chatting, but my dad is fading, and so am I. The adrenaline keeping me alert for the last few days is wearing off after hearing his improved prognosis. We leave with a sense of optimism. An hour later I drop onto the waterbed next to my mom, and as she did earlier in the day, fall asleep before my head hits the pillow.

CHAPTER 26
GUY-IN-VAN

The jet lag coma is real. My eyelids are glued shut. Mom's yelling at me, shaking my shoulders, but the fog won't dissipate. She quits for a few minutes, then grabs a pillow and lobs it at me. This time I wake up, unsure of where I am.

"Why are you abusing me?"

She tells me to get out of bed and take a shower. I'm not here on vacation.

I sit on the edge of the mattress, trying to find my bearings.

"What did you bring to wear?" she asks. "Let me see."

"No, Mom. Stop it."

"Why?"

"I'm awake. Don't go through my stuff."

"Why?" She unzips my backpack.

"I dunno. Please leave it."

"What do you have in here? Do you have the drugs?"

"Yes, I do, you caught me. I snuck in five kilos of heroin and I'm meeting some dude named Guy-in-Van later tonight to make the trade." I drag my bag away from her, throw it open, and rummage through the clothes I flung in a few days earlier.

"Fine," she says, stomping out of the room.

"It's perfectly safe. I just need to get my hands on a gun or machete... a bat." She's still listening. I can tell from the force of the dishes hitting the kitchen counter.

• • • • •

It's early when we arrive at the hospital. A janitor mops the entryway. We bow to him, and he does the same; slightly dropping his head in acknowledgment. What is the protocol? A walk by gets you a slight dip, face-to-face requires the deep dive?

We check-in on my dad, who has better color, and is complaining about the sludge he's being fed. After an hour of coaxing him to eat, we promise to bring street food for lunch, if the doctor allows it. Mom sits at his bedside, spoon-feeding the sludge and telling him about France. He nods and curses at the colorless pile of overcooked vegetables on his plate.

"How is the asshole?" He pushes the spoon away.

I glance at Ethan. "Do you know who the asshole is?"

"Yes, he knows," Dad says. "You should get rid of him."

"I should?"

"You can do better. You should have married a Hungarian man."

My mom slams the spoon down. "She is a married woman. She does not need to do better."

"Thanks," I tell her and sigh.

"Of course," she says, and pokes at a bowl of Jello.

I turn back to Ethan. "What did he tell you about Dylan?"

"He calls him asshole. How much more information do I need?"

"Fair enough."

"He is not so terrible," Mom says. "I think he is not getting this type of attention a man needs. If you are not taking care of him, he will be in the unhappy mood."

"The boy can shove his moods up the horse's ass, Andrea. Why do you defend him and not our daughter?" A sharp cough erupts from him. Bits of fluorescent green gelatin fly out of his mouth.

Mom swats him gently on his back. "See what we have done to your father? We will not discuss your big ideas now."

He tries to catch his breath. "What ideas? What is happening?"

"Nothing's happening, Dad. Everything's great."

She tells him to rest and again turns the conversation to family gossip. For a while, I listen to the stories about France, the same ones I heard on the flight over. The repetition makes me groggy, so I settle into the creepy raindrop chair and take a nap.

• • • • •

"Katy!" I hear my mom's voice and it occurs to me that she hasn't woken me up in years. Now we're two for two, and I'm reminded of another reason I hated living at home.

"Uh-huh."

"You are vimpering in your sleep like you are sad." She surveys her surroundings. "Guess this is not the surprise, is it?"

"I'm fine." I push out of the chair. "Whimper, Mom, not vimper."

She shrugs.

I look out the window. The sunshine is waning.

"What time is it?"

"Four."

"In the afternoon?"

"Yes."

"Shit! Why didn't you get me up?" I ask, hurrying to my dad's side. "How are you doing?"

"I'm in a hospital eating the disgusting foods. I can't use the big boy toilet and have to piss into a tube. Other than this..."

"This is all so miserable. I could have helped if someone had gotten me up."

Nobody answers. Why should they? I was tired. I fell asleep.

"So, what's happening? Has the doctor been in?"

"He has," Ethan says. "He wants to do the next procedure tomorrow morning."

"The angioplasty? And we're on board with this?"

Dad tries to sit up. The tubes don't leave him any leeway.

"Why not?" He pulls angrily on the neckline of his hospital gown.

"Shouldn't we talk to your physician at home?"

"We have left a message," Mom says.

"And?"

"And nothing. It is the holiday week. The office is closed."

"Ethan was nice enough to call." Dad pats him on his hand.

"I could have done it."

"You were asleep, dear," Mom points out.

"Passive-aggressive much, Mom?"

"Did your psychiatrist tell you to say this to me?"

"She did, actually. She implanted a microchip inside my brain at the first appointment."

Her lips push together. The familiar shadow of dismay spreads across her face.

"That's right, she's got me on fucking remote control."

"And she tells you to speak to your mother this way? Does she also give you the idea to get the divorce?"

The room gets quiet. We lock eyes.

"Just perfect, Mom."

Ethan quietly watches the volley between us.

"Divorce?" my dad asks. "Really, Katy?"

"She is ridiculous. Robi, tell your daughter she is making the terrible mistake."

"Leave him out of it, Mom. It's my decision, not his. Definitely not yours, especially right now, so back the hell off."

She glares at me through narrowed eyes. This isn't the day to evaluate her performance as a wife. Not that there will be a time. Ever.

"What does this mean, right now?" Her voice is low, slow, controlled.

"Girls." Ethan steps between us. "Maybe not here."

"Seriously?" I snap at him. "Stay out of this."

"Please," Dad says. "This is not the time." He looks at his wife sheepishly, then blinks, like his eyeballs have been singed.

"Wow, this is insane." I back away from them and turn to the door. I need some air, even if it's the convection oven outside rather than the bullshit wafting in here. In the elevator, I pull out my phone and text Jesse.

I want to go home.

It's almost 4:30 p.m. in Thailand, twelve hours earlier in Florida. No way she's up.

Not into the Ethan dude. He talks into everything.

I wait for a response. Not expecting her to be awake is different than hoping she is.

He had the f'ing gall to tell me to stop fighting with my mom. I hate him.

My screen glows in the darkened hallways. Wouldn't I have done the same thing had the tables been turned?

Call me if you have time. This place bites.

I walk through the lobby and out the front door. The area is busier than yesterday, though I can't remember what time or order anything has happened since we've been here. When did we arrive? When did I eat dinner with Ethan? I'm not even sure how long I've been gone from Florida. It feels like weeks.

The buildings outside are uniform, moldy, with colorful posters and lettering in their windows. It would help to walk off my anger, but I can't read the signs and would rather not get lost in this big city. Instead of going for a stroll, I sit down on a cement bench to consider my current predicament. I tap my feet, sigh, inhale, exhale; wait for some mystical being to imbue wisdom upon me.

After twenty minutes of tapping and sighing, wisdom is not forthcoming. What if I walk back inside and roll with it? I'll thank Ethan for trampling over my family's boundaries and kiss my mother on the cheek for delivering such focused maternal instruction. It's all good. The medical decisions are made, the consent forms are signed. I'm here to support my dad and will acquiesce to the status quo.

They're huddled together, whispering, when I get back to the room. Some fake concern about my tiny traumatic exit would be cool. Should I clear my throat, shout out a friendly "Hello!" or shamefully shuffle in with my tail tucked between my legs?

I can't decide, so I stare until they notice me. So pathetic, these three; like all the cats that ate all the canaries.

"What's going on?" I move closer to them.

Mom turns away. Dad blurts out, "Nothing!"

"Okay. Excellent answer," I say under my breath.

Can I tape this exchange and give it to Dr. Jonas as evidence of who and what has made me so fucking weird?

"So..." I trail off. "Guess we can't bring you any food if surgery is in the morning?"

They shake their heads, mumbling, "uh-huh," and "good point."

"Can you spend some time with me, Katy?" Dad asks, pulling on the tubes popping out of his gown.

"Sure."

"Come talk with me."

Mom whispers to Ethan and they leave the room. Dad pats the bed, motioning for me to sit near him. Still pale, he shows no evidence of having lived in Florida for almost thirty years. There are deep wells under his eyes, and everything about him smells antiseptic and stale.

"I know," he says. "I stink like the science laba-ra-tory."

"It's not so bad."

"I smell it too." He wrinkles his nose.

"It's this face." I motion to myself. "It always gives me away."

He nods. "Professional poker, then, is not for you."

"Probably not."

He shifts again. Urine slides through a tube by his left leg. The blood pressure cuff inflates around his bruised arm, then beeps, measures, and deflates.

"I'm sorry, Dad."

He grins. "For which of the excitements?"

"I'm sorry you're here."

"I am also. It is my fault."

"And I could have avoided the blowup with Mom."

"Are you really divorcing Dylan?"

I nod. "I feel awful about you guys going all out on the wedding. Such a waste, in hindsight."

"Not waste. How do they say in America? It is the waking up call."

"That's one way of looking at it." I run my finger over the worn thread of the blanket.

He watches me. "Is this hand you cut? Show me."

"It's almost healed."

"You did not need the stitches?" He inspects my hand and playfully wiggles my fingers.

"Nope."

"Good." He takes a deep, raspy breath. "Can I tell you my best day?"

"What's your best day, Dad?"

"Day you are born makes me happy man. But day after when I take you home from hospital. This is better than any other."

"Why?"

"This first day, the hospital still responsible for you. They take you here and there for the tests and take footprint and make us follow around like duck-a-lings in the line. When we bring you home, you become our daughter. My little girl. Nobody telling us what to do, and I know my heart, in here." He taps his chest. "Is not just for me on this day. It is for our perfect new child."

I suck in air and dab my eyes. "Why are you trying to make me cry?"

He chuckles. "It is important for you to know. Now go get the divorce."

"You're not mad?"

"I am very proud. But it is not my decision if you stay or go."

"Oh, I'm going for sure."

"Then good enough for me."

"You're not going to try to shame me out of it like Mom?"

"Your mother has her ideas." He pats my hand. "I trust you."

"Why? I married a moron."

"Because you have learned something."

I scoot up on the bed, for a minute reminded of Dr. Jonas's extra puffy couch. "I learned there's a laser beam on the top of my head signaling safe harbor for wayward losers."

He tousles my hair. "I see no laser here and you do not owe me the explanations. You owe it only to yourself."

"You think I'm doing the right thing?"

He rolls his eyes. "Look, you run into the wall one time like idiot, yes?"

"No need to rub it in, Dad."

"You run into same wall second time, also this being the idiot."

"Guilty as charged, though the idiot thing stings."

"So what? It sting, you learn." He clears his throat. "This is thing, Katy. If you keep running into wall, you probably always an idiot. No hope for you, too bad. But you are not running into this wall again, are you? It is good news. You are not idiot anymore. This is what the learning is. Stupid part of brain conversions into genius."

"Converts into."

"Yes, converts, professor lady. Mondd jobban Magyarul és én jobban mondom Angolul."

"Why do I have to speak Hungarian better than you speak English? You're the one lecturing."

He chuckles.

"Fine, I get your point, Dad. I still don't feel so smart."

"You remember how hard your mother and I work for the restaurant, to make it the success? To find this American dream everybody talks about?"

"Yeah, I do. You worked your asses off."

"Then we take all this work and give to you."

"Uh-huh."

"This isn't a mistake. We do this because we have the big faith in you." His hazel eyes twinkle. "As your grandmother says, we want the happily for you." He rushes to the end of the sentence, then tears up.

"Really?"

"Katy," he says, sweeping the curls from my face. "You know this answer."

"I guess."

"No need for the guess. This is the fact. Now tell me about work because I do not want to do more crying. It will upset your mother."

He confesses to checking the business account a few times per week and reading our online reviews. The longer I'm with him, the more hopeful I become about finding my new normal when the divorce with Dylan is finalized. Once my parents get back, things will fall into place. I'll keep going to my angular shrink, even see Quinn again. I smile. The mystical wisdom I was waiting for outside is this guy, my dad, sitting here next to me.

"What do you think of Ethan?" he asks.

"He seems nice. What do you think of Ethan?"

"I also think he seems nice." He chokes out another cough, wipes a few droplets of spit from his lips and reaches for a cup of tepid water.

Before I can say another word, the doctor arrives with a small team of people. They bow to us.

My dad can't stand or bend, instead he shakes his hands like the Pope does from the Vatican balcony.

I try not to laugh.

"These are my students, Mr. Robert. Do you mind if they learn of your medical history?"

"Yes. It's fine." He continues waving to the crowd of young people surrounding him.

Still giggling, I give him a quick kiss on his cheek and excuse myself.

• • • • •

I find my mom and Ethan tearfully hugging each other in a small waiting area.

"What's wrong?" I ask. "Did something happen?"

They wipe their faces. "No, nothing," Mom says.

"That's a lot of nothing. Why are you crying?" I turn from one to the other. They stare at the ground, mumbling about what an emotional time it's been.

Their thinly veiled denial feels absurd.

"Can we talk about it?" I ask, channeling my inner shrink. I should read a book about mental health. Maybe I'll go to school and become a therapist. Or not. Probably not.

My mother shuffles away, saying she'll be fine.

"What happened, Ethan? Did she say something to you?"

"No." He peers over my shoulder.

"Is it about my dad?"

"No, Katy, he's doing great. I think we're just all exhausted."

He hurries out of the waiting room. I snort and send another text to Jesse about how much the interloper sucks. The rest of the evening is spent with my dad, running out for street food, and finally retreating to his condo for the night. I've pulled away, trying only to talk to him, and ignoring everyone else. If they don't want to include me in their play date, I have no interest in being their third wheel.

CHAPTER 27
THE ADVANCE OF IT TEAM

Early the next morning, my mother and I are having a quiet breakfast. We speak to each other like strangers on a bus. She's not giving up any information about yesterday's private sobfest, and I'm still feeling the sting of being left out of the loop.

I check my messages. One missed call from Dylan. "Good morning sunshine. Had me some fun last night with a sweet woman. The bed springs, holy shit girl, they're plum wore out."

Beautiful. Now I'm going to have to fumigate my house.

Ethan knocks on the door and tells us he has to fly today. He seems tired, deflated, addressing my mom in the same detached way she's been with me. Is there something going on between the two of them? Something unappetizing, a weird mommy complex he's playing out? Or is this her attempt at payback for her husband's affair with a teenybopper? Either option makes my skin crawl. One parental misdeed should not beget another.

"You can find your way to the hospital?" he asks.

"I think so," I tell him. "Straight on the road with the food carts, then left on the main avenue for two blocks."

"Perfect. And don't feed the elephant in the abandoned field. You can give some cash to the old lady who hangs out with him. I should be back by eight tonight."

I smile. When do you ever get this type of warning in the States? "I won't feed the elephant." I promise. "Happy flying."

"Thanks," he says with a wave. "Gotta go save lives."

• • • • •

The walk is becoming familiar, the sights, even some faces. The same dogs are sleeping in their corners, and the vendors bow in greeting as we pass.

The doctor is speaking to my dad when we arrive. He's administering a sedative and explaining the procedure to him.

"Mr. Robert, we are almost ready. I give you time with family." He bows and leaves the room.

"Don't let them kill me." Dad says, clutching our hands. "You understand the instructions."

"We will not speak of this!" Mom launches into a rant about a family like ours ending up in a place like this. She begins her tirade in English, then shifts into Hungarian with a flurry of French cuss words.

I interrupt her. "What instructions? What are you talking about?"

They're suddenly tight-lipped.

"You should see your faces right now. Can you look any more cryptic?"

Their silence is deafening. I sigh knowing I've just collected more evidence to submit to the court of family dysfunction.

"Yes," Dad says. "I will be fine. I love you both very much, for the records, if these are my last words. Also, Katy, remember what we talk about. You get rid of the asshole. I die a happy man."

"Robi!" Mom shakes a finger at him.

His eyes glaze over.

The same two men who wheeled him away yesterday return, disconnect him from the tubes and machines and roll him toward the door. We stay by his side until they move him into the hallway, but he's already out cold.

We expect the wait to be three to four hours, so I turn to my phone for distraction. I scan a few messages from Jesse and Quinn. One more from Dylan. *CUNT. BET UR BUMMED YOU DONT GET MORE DYLAN.* I snort, wondering why calling me a cunt would, in any way possible, make me want more Dylan.

I go back to Quinn's text. He's concerned about my dad and offers to help at the restaurant. I conjure his image, the chocolate brown eyes, his lean muscular body, and the drunken night we spent together. He's fucking yummy, so I spend an inordinate amount of time composing a response which lies somewhere between *thanks for checking in*, and *please sir, can I have some more?*

I listen to the voicemails from relatives and friends asking for updates.

"Did you call Grandma?"

"Yes," Mom says from the creepy smiley face chair.

"Do you need me to call anyone else?"

"No."

"Okay." I gaze at her. She's clearly anxious, too proud to show weakness.

"Why do you stare at me, Katy?"

"I dunno." I mumble and pick at the scab on my palm.

Two hours later, she asks if we should get food. I tell her I'm not hungry. She nods and says she's not either.

Three hours go by, and we're both pacing the hallway, separately, in opposite directions.

Three and a half hours later, a nurse delivers a message in broken English. The patient is out of surgery.

Four hours later, we stand like palace guards at the door, while the orderlies roll my dad in. He looks worse this time, less human, more of a lumpy growth entwined by tubes and rumpled sheets. His face is swollen and shriveled all at once, a balloon losing air.

Cold sweat drips down my back, and I wonder if he'll ever recover from the trauma his body is going through.

Dr. Orapan appears after the orderlies leave. He smiles and adjusts the stethoscope around his neck.

"The operation goes well. Mr. Robert now needs to rest."

"When will he wake up?" Mom asks.

"Soon."

"And you have repaired the damage in his heart?"

"We did best to repair, yes."

"When can we take my husband home?"

"Few days, if he is recovering correctly."

"When can I take him to Florida?"

"If recovering well, then travel allowed in next one week or two."

Her hands shake as she bows to thank him.

He turns to me. "Are you having any questions?"

"Is there anything we can do? Also, why is he so pale?"

"Pale?"

"Colorless. Kind of gray."

The doctor smiles. "Ah, yes. It is because the surgery is always hard on body. Color will return in short time."

"Okay, I guess that's it. Thank you." I bow before I remember how much I hate bowing.

• • • • •

The waiting game begins again. With my dad ensconced in the bed, and nurses coming to check on him, we can only idly stand by with no useful purpose. I lean against a wall. Mom hovers, watching him breathe.

"Is he okay?" I whisper.

"I don't know." She looks at me. "Katy?"

"Yeah?"

"Nothing, I forgot."

"What is it?"

"It's nothing, I told you. I don't remember."

We remain silent for another half hour before he stirs. He coughs, eyes pop open, and he tries to sit up. A monitor beeps.

"Water?" He touches his lips.

"Yes, dear." Mom delivers with lightning speed.

Dr. Orapan arrives a few minutes later. "I see he is awake?" He smiles and peeks under my dad's gown, gently putting a hand on his thigh. "We make incision here too. Leg feels correct temperature with no swelling. Procedure is success for you. Mr. Robert, how is pain now?"

"Not bad," he says with more strength in his voice.

The doctor seems pleased, scribbles on a paper chart, then excuses himself.

"He sounded reasonably positive, right?" I ask my parents.

"Yes, this is twice they did not kill me."

"Stop saying that, Dad! You can come home soon."

"I would like this." He turns to his wife. "If I am allowed there?"

She drops her hands to her waist. "I already said we will discuss this later. Katy, we need ice."

"Ice?"

"Yes, ice."

"You think this hospital has ice?"

"Katy."

I shrug and step away from my dad's side. It takes forty-five minutes to find ice, ten minutes to ask for it, and ten more for someone to deposit it into a small cup. By the time I return to my parents, it's melted into a pool of water.

I present it to my mother. "Here's your ice."

She looks down at the cup, then up at me. "Thank you."

"Sorry," I tell my dad.

"Don't worry, I didn't need it."

"Then why did I have to chase it down for an hour?"

They eye each other.

"What? What's going on?"

Mom turns to me. "I have spoken to your father about this, and we think you should go back to Florida."

I look from one to the other. "Go back when?"

"Later today or tomorrow." She swirls the cup of *not ice*.

"Oh," I mutter. Her edict feels like acid pouring into my stomach.

"Katy," Dad says. "You will be my advance of it team."

"What the hell does that mean?"

"It means for you to open the house with the fresh air and talk with my doctor. I need to see him soon after I arrive. And the restaurant. You cannot be away for so long."

"Are you both serious right now?"

"Your mother needs you to shop for the groceries."

"You want me to leave Thailand today, so I can buy rye bread and coffee in Florida?"

"We have to eat, Katy. Imagine how tired and hungry your father will be after the travelings in his condition." They nod in unison. "And have Miss Lisa clean."

"And we need the ride from the airport," Dad adds.

"This is stupid. Why are you sending me away?"

"Do not be ridiculous," Mom says. "We are only asking you to get the house ready."

"Fine," I tell them, recognizing that this battle is lost. It's not like I'm itching to stay in Thailand, anyway. I let them suffer a little longer, marveling at the list of reasons they produce to convince me to hie my ass on home. All manner of undesirable things may be growing in the water pipes, the vents or the carpet after their long absence. And what about the ants, spiders and cockroaches the size of small aircraft? And what if the car has been similarly infested? So much for me to handle. After fifteen minutes, I agree to their terms and begin taking mental notes as the sole participant of the "advance of it team."

CHAPTER 28
WINDOW AND AISLE

By nine o'clock that night, the runway is sliding away from me again, along with the billion twinkling lights of Bangkok. The wheels retract into the belly of the third aircraft I've been on in the same number of days. My parents, with fake smiles plastered across their faces, shoved me on my way like I was part of the zombie apocalypse. It was hurtful, confusing, and now I have a good twenty-five hours of travel to mull over why they so desperately needed to be rid of me.

I contemplate their dismissal as we climb into the clouds. The big aircraft hasn't reached cruising altitude when I fall asleep next to a young man watching Anime on his laptop.

He's still at it when I wake up. He studies my face for a moment, then with no acknowledgment, turns back to his hot Asian cartoon.

"Beautiful," I mumble to myself as his indifference washes over me; one final rejection stinging only as an addendum to an already stellar day.

• • • • •

The second flight, from Frankfurt to Tampa, is more crowded, and my last minute reservation has secured the shittiest seat assignment possible, between two large German men. They're clearly acquainted and perhaps thought taking the window and aisle would improve their chances of an open space between them.

They're polite, and I'm willing to act invisible for the next ten hours if it guarantees they'll leave me alone.

"Are you German?" Man in the window seat asks.

Fuckety-fuck. "No. American."

"We are going to Tampa Bay."

I slump in my seat. Nobody from Tampa says Tampa Bay, only an outsider or the Weather Channel would use this vernacular. No homegrown Floridian would say it, not even someone from Georgia or Alabama. I glow with superiority, then move on to feeling petty, judgmental, shallow. And guilty. Just like Dr. Jonas said that first day of therapy. I wonder if she was on to something.

"To a scientific conference." Man in the aisle seat informs me.

"That's interesting," I say, fishing through my pockets for earbuds.

"Have you enjoyed our beautiful country?" Window asks.

"I was in Thailand."

"Thailand? Quite enjoyable."

"Is it?"

They grin at each other.

"Would you like to sit together? I can switch places."

"No-no, this is fine," Aisle says. "The beach areas are first class."

"I'm sure they are."

"You were not there for pleasure, then?"

"No."

"Business?"

"No."

Aisle says something to Window. Their body language and my limited knowledge of German communicate their dissatisfaction regarding my unfriendly demeanor. Any other day I'd be a better sport, pleased to chit-chat about Florida's best vacation spots, bars and beaches. Not today, though. I can't be the in-flight entertainment.

The rest of our journey is long. Turbulence keeps me from sleeping. Aisle spills two cocktails on himself, Window tramples over me once per hour to avoid blood clots or stroking-out. By the time we begin our descent into Tampa, I super want to kill them both.

• • • • •

The international arrivals process is slow and squashes the excitement of newly landed passengers. I'm released from the security area forty minutes after landing. In theory, I'm confused and depressed. In actuality, it feels damn good to walk out into the chilly evening air.

I had called Jesse while I waited for my connecting flight in Frankfurt. Her response was a mix of "what the fuck happened?" and a caution to stay at my folks' house because Dylan has not yet moved out of ours. I've got no fight with her directive, and no energy to deal with my not-so-beloved. In a happy jet lagged trance, I head south across the Howard Franklin Bridge toward St. Pete, Sarasota, and then home to Dufferin Beach.

It's past midnight when I pull into the driveway. The crickets chirp and the mist rolls in off the water. It's all so familiar, and delicious. I linger outside to absorb the feeling of early morning Florida.

Less than a week ago, I'd left the house in a rush to Thailand. Now, stepping inside, the evidence of my hasty departure surrounds me. Though I did my best to tidy up that last night, the empty bottles from the boat party with Russ and Quinn are still evident. My bed is unmade, and a pink towel lies limp on the bathroom floor. If my mom saw this mess, she'd rip my head clean off, then lecture my torso about the impropriety of an untidy home. I suppose it is better that I'm getting back before them.

CHAPTER 29
QUICK TURN JET LAG

The phone buzzing wakes me up the next morning. I turn my head; my body is reluctant to follow. All the traveling and heavy sleeping has left me stiff from neck to toe.

I sweep my finger across the screen of my cell. A voicemail from my mother-unit, one from Ethan. I'm in no mood to speak to either of them.

Dylan's sent a text. It contains only a GIF of SpongeBob, saying I'm a loser.

I slide to the ground, then pull myself up by hanging on the side of the dresser.

Trying not to bend, I walk to the kitchen and stare into the pantry. "Nope, not happening." I hobble back to my room.

The second time I'm woken by the doorbell. I roll off the bed and end up on the floor again, flat on my stomach, arms pinned under my chest. My movement is limited to lurching onto my side and watching the dust bunnies skitter under the desk.

"Katy?"

"Hi, Jess. Figured it was you."

"Welcome home. Is this a new workout, or are you facedown on the ground for the hell of it?"

"I'm stuck."

"In so many ways." She hauls me up by my waist and drops me on the bed. "And did you message me last night when you landed like I asked?"

"Yes, I did."

"Liar," she says flatly.

"Then no, I did not."

She shakes her head. "Making coffee."

Three cups later, I'm still hazy and feel confident the jet lag hasn't entirely had its way with me. We sit out by the pool, where I tell her about my dad, the meeting with Lia, and Ethan's insistent participation in my family melodrama.

"So, he works there as a pilot? Is he American?"

"Yeah. I stalked his Facebook and Instagram. Everything's from Colorado."

"And your parents know his family?"

"I guess. His mom's Hungarian."

"So, a family friend. It's not weird he's hanging out. Maybe his folks told him he has to help."

"Possible," I say, pulling my knees close to my chest.

"Your mom would make you do the same thing."

"Yeah, she would."

"What if she's trying to set you up with him?"

"I'm a married woman."

"She's being proactive and saving you from yourself. Is he cute?"

"Why does it matter? You hate men."

"Incorrect. I enjoy them."

"For one thing, Jesse. Then you hate them."

"Right. What's the issue?"

This debate started in a dorm almost eight years ago. "It's an existential blunder to use people for sex and then want to murder them."

"The existential gods are cool with it." She smirks. "What does he look like?"

"You're not going there. You know the rule about Hungarian men."

"Yeah, I do. Your mom taught me."

I watch a lizard scurry along the pool deck. "They go into a revolving door behind you."

She finishes the sentence for me. "And come out in front of you."

"Yup," I say, sliding down in the lawn chair. Seventy degrees never felt this good. "God, I'm so sleepy. I can handle normal jet lag, but not the quick turn version."

"No kidding. You came and went in five days." She pulls out a cigarette.

"I thought you were quitting?"

"Why the fuck would I do that?" She blows smoke in my face.

I wave away the gray cloud. "What's going on with Dylan?"

"He was served with papers last week. Now we wait for a court date."

"Did he respond?"

She chuckles. "Yeah, he did."

"Want to share?"

"Let me read it to you." She scrolls through her texts. "Here it is. 'Jesse you can fucking blow me. I'm not leaving the house, I'm keeping it.'" She snorts, smiles. "You hooked up with a real prince."

"Indeed. Is there more?"

"Why yes there is." She looks back down. "'My lawyers gonna jack ya'll up so you better learn to swallow.'"

"Holy shit, Jess. I'm sorry."

"Why? As an officer of the court, I have preserved this communication as required by law. Well, not by law exactly. But I'm holding on to it."

"To use as evidence?"

"Depends. It's golden if I can. If it doesn't come into play, nothing's lost." She inhales, blows out a perfect smoke ring.

"I shouldn't have married him. Why didn't you put me in a cage?"

"So you could run back to him when we let you out? Acceptance is the first step to recovery, and you were down deep in denial. Am I wrong?"

"No," I say, remembering the headaches, the warning signs. Denial only scratched the surface of all that's ailed me.

We watch the late afternoon sun dip over the Western horizon. The tide rises in the canal, the boat nudges the dock, and the lines clink against the mast with each incoming wave. My eyelids weigh a thousand pounds.

"Did you text back?" The exhaustion is like being drugged. I'm not sure I've said the words out loud.

"No, absolutely not."

The ocean sloshes against the sea wall, bubbles, recedes. The seagulls glide over our heads, chit-chatting in the dusk.

"What time is it?" I ask.

She looks at her phone. "Six."

"Christ. It's so early."

"Go lie down. I'll clean up and lock the door on my way out."

"I can do it."

"It's two coffee cups, Katy."

"You're so nice to me. Thank you. I'll call you when I wake up."

She pulls me out of the chair. "Try not to fall again, or I'm buying you an old lady alert necklace."

Walking straight is an effort. In my room, I drop into bed, check my phone. One more message from my mom. Perhaps she shouldn't have sent me home so damn fast if communication was such a priority. I toss it aside and tuck myself under the blanket.

Barely awake, I hear Jesse in the distance. She possesses neither the grace nor agility to be quiet. She's talking to someone as I slide into sleep.

CHAPTER 30
THE BAD THING

Some moments in life stick with you. Events, minutes, seconds, grabbing hold, preying on your emotions, eating up your sanity. They stay near the surface, triggered again and again by a word, a smell, a sound or an image.

My moment, *this* moment, will refuse to properly file itself away. Jesse kneeling beside me. Tears streaming down her cheeks.

"Katy!"

"What?"

"It's your dad. Something happened to him."

I pull the sheet over my head.

She leans over me. The words come out in slow motion. "I'm so sorry, sweetie." She takes my hands, holds them tight. "He died."

"Fuck," is my only response. Then from the shock or jet lag, I roll over, my brain shuts down.

• • • • •

Hours later, I wake up. Jesse's sleeping on the floor next to me, covered by a light blanket. For a few seconds that stretch out in time, I wonder why she's here. Then I remember what she said, the alarm on her face and red-rimmed eyes.

I cry, gulp air. My arms and chest ache, my stomach contracts. I am raw emotion, puking up grief.

"I'm here. I'm with you." Jesse's by my side, saying the words over and over.

The sobbing slows down only because I'm hyperventilating. I lie down, shaking. My lungs burning.

"When?"

"I don't know, Katy. You need to call your mom."

"How? How did it happen?"

"They wouldn't give me any details."

She calms me down as I cycle from fits of bawling to deep sleep throughout the night.

Early in the morning, I crawl out of bed with a horrendous headache, swollen eyes, and the residue of salty tears on my face. Jesse's asleep next to me. My phone is by her pillow. I can't look at it. Can't touch it. Not yet.

I tiptoe around her and walk outside; not stopping, hardly thinking until I climb on the boat, sit down, and dangle my bare feet over the bow.

I watch the sunrise cloak everything in cherry-red light. The water shimmers, tiny bubbles surface from the minnows swimming below. How ironic for this new day to be so beautiful in the face of such an emotional assault. Nobody knows what I do. They'll get up, eat breakfast, go to work, feel happiness. How inconceivable that everyone isn't slumped over, as I am, in the darkness.

"Katy-Bell." Russ jumps onboard, gingerly walking to the nose. "Jesse called me last night. It all sounds like crazy talk."

"God, I wish it was." I take a deep breath. "My ribs hurt."

"You're on a bad trip, darlin'. Tell me what I can do."

"Not a fucking clue," I say, watching the pink glow fade with the rising sun.

Inside, Jesse is making breakfast. "Russ brought us coffee and Cool Whip and Pop-Tarts." She rips the foil off the packet and drops them into the toaster. "Wild Berry."

I hug them, begin sobbing again, apologize, try to breathe, get the hiccups.

Someone makes a joke. We laugh.

Jesse says, "call your mother."

"I will."

"Soon, Katy. I have no idea who I spoke to. Maybe a doctor. He was hard to understand."

She piles whipped cream on my coffee. It brings back the memory of Dad saying he'd only need espresso, cigarettes, some bread and butter if he were ever stuck on a deserted island.

Russ hands me a Poptart and I go to my room, stare at the phone. I push it with my toes, finally, pick it up like it's on fire. I press "MomUnit" on my contact list, press end. My head is spinning, a whale is rolling across my chest. The fourth time, I let it ring through.

She answers immediately, her voice is hoarse. "No, I cannot." I hear the phone being moved around.

"Katy, it's Ethan."

"Hi."

"It happened so fast."

"When?"

"Early yesterday morning. He was fine, sitting up, eating, joking with everyone."

"Okay." I picture Dad, sitting, eating, joking.

"And then it was like he fell asleep."

I inhale, blow out. "Uh-huh."

"They said it was a blood clot."

I have no words. Water leaks down my cheeks. I lick my lips, then wipe the wetness away with the back of my hand.

"Katy, are you there?"

"Yeah."

"It might have been from lying down for so long or because of the surgery. It was fast."

"Fast? Okay. So, he died quickly?"

Ethan sounds shaky. I ask if he's all right.

His turn to be silent. Dead air hangs between us.

"Was my mom there?"

"Yeah. She was sitting on the bed. They were talking."

"How is she?"

"Bad. She goes from screaming at everyone to silence. I think she's in shock."

"Doesn't sound great. So, he just died without any warning, no fucking anything?"

"I'm sorry, Katy."

"Okay."

"I don't understand why they sent you home."

"Yeah." I don't either, but now I'll never see my father alive again. "I'm flying out."

"You don't have to. I think your mom is leaving tomorrow."

"What about his...what about my dad?"

"She wants me to handle everything."

"Handle... she's coming home without him?"

"She's going to Paris. She doesn't want to go to Florida yet."

I grunt, then decide she's probably making the right decision.

"I'll bring your dad to you. Let me do that much."

"I can't talk about this anymore."

"Of course. I'll make sure your mom catches her flight."

"Okay, thanks." I hang up without waiting for his reply. I never want to hear his voice again.

CHAPTER 31
LAST TIME I WAS HERE

I cry for days, stare off into space for hours. The restaurant has a sign on the door, a brief message about my dad. Patrons and friends drop off flowers, balloons, and interestingly, casseroles. My mother is hiding in Paris, and I try my best to tackle the onslaught of calls and sympathetic wishes. Jesse and Russ remain nearby, and each night one of them stays over at the house. In the narrow corners of time when I'm not consumed by sadness or anger, I feel indescribably grateful for them.

During a particularly bad moment, Jesse suggests I go see the shrink. I agree, call her, then cancel an hour before the appointment. My justification, as usual, is well thought out. I went to therapy only to pacify my divorce attorney, not because I needed it. She forced me, and I participated within the limited scope of understanding why I married a dickhead. Never was there a plan for further behavioral intervention, or discussion of why my dad would leave the country, die, and gut me like the fucking grouper on ice at the grocery store.

Every day, almost every hour, I play a game of *last time I was here*. Last time I drove by the beach, my father was alive. Last time I did a load of laundry or ran into Target, he was alive. The last time every single thing happened in my life, he was breathing, thinking, being my father.

Jesse catches on about my canceled appointment, then forces me to make and keep the next available session. Which is now.

Dr. Jonas takes my hand. "Katy, I'm so sorry."

"Thanks." Last time I was in this office Dad was alive.

"Tell me how you're doing." She settles into her seat.

"Not so good."

"I wish I could say something, anything, to help. What are you feeling?"

I stare at the thermostat on her wall. "It's as if I've been hit in the stomach with a sledgehammer. And not hit, like you know, in the wrong place at the wrong time, but with intent. It feels violent."

She takes notes without looking away from me.

"I don't want to be here...in your office."

"I'm aware," she says with a half-smile.

"It's obvious, huh?"

"I am getting to know you, Katy."

"Makes sense, but I feel bad about it."

"No need. You scheduled the visit. It's good enough for me."

"Do I have to tell you how it happened?" I notice the tissues on her coffee table. I hate them more now than that first morning I was here. Their presence is presumptuous, front-loading a predetermined outcome of if-then. If you sit on this couch, then you will become a weepy, uncontrollable mess.

"No, you don't have to share how he passed."

I stare into her small dark eyes. "He didn't pass anywhere. He's just dead."

She presses her lips together. Her pen hangs over the yellow pad of paper.

"Dead. Wow." I inhale, feel the familiar pressure in my eyes, the waterworks ramping up again. "Only, Dad would say vow, because he can't always pronounce the letter w and it comes out as v. So, he'd say 'I'm dead. Vow!'"

I hear his voice in my head and begin sobbing, unable to stop for the remainder of the hour. My only victory is in ignoring the tissues, though I may lose the battle, because it's Jesse's shirt I keep wiping my drippy nose on. It's disgusting, stubborn; yet a minor win against the damage of my metaphorical sledgehammer. Dr. Jonas remains patient, and we agree to meet again tomorrow.

CHAPTER 32
THE KATY SANDWICH

A new day, a different shirt with clean sleeves.

Eudora pulls a fresh sheet from her yellow pad. "How are you doing?"

"Fine."

"That's how you're feeling?"

"Sure. I feel fine."

"Okay, Katy. Tell me what you've done today."

"Is that therapeutic?"

She shrugs. "It's progress."

I look at the goddamn box of tissues, then back at her. "I signed some legal documents for Jesse. My father has a will and I'm supposed to do something with it."

I push down my anger. Before Dad died, everyone wanted to hide the will from me. Now the tables are turned. Jesse keeps bringing it up and I keep putting her off.

"I don't want to see it. I don't want to think about it."

"You may be the executor, Katy. You'll need to read it."

"And I will. Just not now." I tuck my hair behind my ears. "I also signed more papers for the divorce."

"I wasn't aware you were moving ahead with that so soon after..."

"No reason to wait." I bite my lip. "Then I paid some bills at the restaurant. I'm making Russ the manager."

"Russ?"

"He's worked there for a long time. I need the help, and he knows his way around as well as me."

"Excellent. You're delegating, giving yourself a break."

"I guess. I went to Target and bought some clothes. Then I had lunch."

"Lunch is good."

"Do you want to know what I ate?"

"I do," she says.

"I had a Katy Sandwich."

"What's a Katy Sandwich?"

"It's toasted rye bread, cream cheese, really good bologni, and red bell peppers."

She sits back in her chair, takes a long swig from her bottled water. "There's no such thing as really good bologni."

I laugh for the first time since the bad day. Dr. Jonas giggles.

"Well, it still sounds okay," she says.

"I get it, it's weird. You can use salami instead."

"Then it wouldn't be a Katy Sandwich."

"Not according to my dad. He says it has to be pure. I mean, he used to say that." I turn away from her. The tears start again. "God, I'm so sick of crying."

She smiles, the expression softens the rigid angles of her face.

"Do you want to talk about Dylan?" she asks.

I use the bottom of my shirt to dry my cheeks. "Doesn't matter."

"Have you had any contact with him since you've been home?"

"He sends a couple texts each day."

I chew on my left thumbnail. This morning he sent a video of a lion pulling the intestines out of a goat. Dr. Jonas doesn't need these details. "And Jesse's gotten a few choice messages from him. She chatted with his lawyer, some sleazebag from Ft. Myers."

"And you're feeling good about separating?"

"Nothing feels good right now. Leaving Dylan feels right. Feels sort of powerful, actually."

"I'm pleased to hear that." She jots down notes. Maybe the recipe for the Katy Sandwich.

"On the other hand, I'm having these weird dreams."

"Can you describe them?"

I scoot back on the couch. "It started a couple of nights ago. I was walking through this old house, not a scary house, maybe old-fashioned. And the rooms were small, all in a straight line, and I was going from one room into the next. Then I got to this bigger room, a library and my dad was sitting in this stuffy chair like that old British man from the skits on SNL. The PBS skits with the guy who introduces the films."

"Do you mean Alistair Cooke?"

"Yeah, that's the one. SNL had some funny stuff with him."

"He was an actual person, Katy."

"Are you sure? I thought it was a character they made up."

"Google him. He was on *Masterpiece Theatre*."

"Never heard of it."

She rolls her eyes. "You're too young to remember. Let's go on with your dream."

"Okay. So, there he is, sitting like the Alistair dude, smiling like everything was great. But I knew he was dead, and I started hyperventilating, totally freaking out. He was asking me why I was crying, and I kept asking why he didn't understand what was happening. Then he realized." I clear my throat. "You know." I stop talking, afraid I'll lose it.

"Take a minute and focus on your breathing."

I breathe in, count to three. Breathe out. "And he was sad, and he put his face into his hands. And I was sobbing because I had so many questions. Then he disappeared..."

"The dream is a coping mechanism, Katy."

"Does coping have to be so damn painful?" I scrape the cuticles off my ragged nails.

"It's a part of healing, and healing is personal. There is no preparation for loss, and no way to predict how you'll feel on any given day."

"That's too bad. I wish I could blink and go back ten years."

Her head tilts down. "I know. But you'll have to work through the emotions, or they'll work through you."

"That sounds terrifying."

"It's not terrifying, Katy. I won't sugarcoat the process. It's appropriate to feel a lot of confusion and heartache right now."

"I don't think I'm ever going to feel normal again."

"I'm not a big fan of the word, 'normal.' Everything you're going through is expected, especially this early. It's going to be bumpy. Painful. But you're doing better than you think."

CHAPTER 33
FIVE-SECOND RULE

I return to work on the two-week anniversary of my father's death. The day is a partial success because, for once, I've gotten through it without crying. It also feels like a failure. Last night, I was excited about getting back to my routine. A few hours in, everything seems boring in the same old ways. Old ways which remind me that running this restaurant is not what I want to do with my life. Hunched over a hot stove, mopping floors, hauling twenty-pound bags of flour. It's what my parents wanted to do, more likely what they needed to do. I don't though, and the tether holding me in place has been vaporized.

I stay at The Point well past closing, after the staff has gone for the night. There's little advantage in rushing home because it's still not my house. I'm tired of sleeping in my childhood bed, tired of being surrounded by the reminders and memories of a mother and father who have disappeared.

I settle into the office with a bowl of chicken soup and search online for *fun jobs*. By midnight, I'm over it, unimpressed with the internet's suggestions. I don't want to work in a circus or be a private detective. Hollywood stunt double. No. Art school. I can barely draw a stick figure. Nurse. No. Phlebotomist. What the fuck even is that? The web doesn't know me very well, and while

I gather my things to head home, I decide to un-decide. Walking away from the only job I've ever had will sort itself out. Just not tonight.

• • • • •

When I get to my parents' house, Jesse is in the kitchen, staring at the oven.

"I could have brought you food," I tell her.

"I wanted pizza." She puts her hands on her hips. "How was your first day?"

"Uneventful."

"Good. Quinn dropped by."

"Uh-huh."

"Have you seen him since you've been home?"

I drop my bag on a chair and kick off my tennis shoes. "No. We've texted a few times. I think he's trying to steer clear of all the doom. Do you know what he wanted?"

"To talk to you about something." She pulls the pizza off the rack and slides it on the counter. "He didn't stay long. Want some?"

"I've already had second dinner."

She blows on the pie and tries to pull it apart with her hands. "Damn it!" Her arms flail in the air. She's impatient, willing to burn her fingers. She tears the crust. It rips, cheese, and pepperoni slide off and land on the floor. "Fucking bitch!" She picks the toppings up and stacks them back on the misshapen piece. "Five-second rule."

"I don't know, Jess. Doesn't it depend on how clean the tile is?"

"No."

"And how gluey the food is?"

"No." She takes a bite. "Have you heard from your boyfriend in Thailand?"

"Give it a rest. He's some dude who had front row seats to the worst few days of my life. Better seats than I had, as it turns out. I don't want to think about him."

"Thou doth protest too much."

"Jesse, seriously. Drop it."

"Yeah, okay. Have you spoken to him?"

"Oh my God. Yes, I have. If I tell you, will you let me be?"

She holds out her hand. "Pinkie promise."

"A pinkie promise from a lawyer? Will it be contractually binding?"

"Fair point. Tell me what Ethan said."

"He's working with the U.S. Embassy in Bangkok to get the paperwork together. Then he can bring my dad..."

I hold up my hand and inhale. "Need a minute."

"Did Eudora teach you the breathing thing?"

"Eudora? What a wild name. Yeah, she gave me some tips."

"Does it help?"

"Am I a big fucking blubbering mess right now?"

"No."

"Then it helps."

She nods, chews her food.

"I FedExed him a copy of Dad's birth certificate and citizenship papers. Then he'll get some documents permitting him to transport him, his remains."

"Sounds complicated. How long will it take?"

"Dunno."

"How's your mom?"

I grunt. "Same thing each day. She talks like everything is normal for a couple minutes, then starts crying and hangs up."

"Maybe she needs some Dr. Jonas in her life." She takes another bite, cheese drips over the side again, but she catches it in time.

I pick up my shoes and walk toward my room. "When all of hell freezes over."

She laughs, stuffs an olive into her mouth and tells me to sleep well.

• • • • •

"Coffee!" Jesse yells, her voice carrying to the shower. By the time I'm dressed and have made my way into the kitchen, a large cup is waiting for me near the sink.

"Will you marry me after I divorce Dylan?" I pour cream in.

"Because I make dark roast? Aren't you setting the bar pretty low?"

"My bar is off. It's broken. I have no bar."

She shakes her head. "No kidding."

"Whatever," I tell her. My phone vibrates. A text from Quinn lights up the screen.

"Who is it?"

"Quinn. He wants to see me."

"See you where? Can't he see you at the restaurant?"

I hope she can't read my mind. "It's not a thing, Jess."

"Better not be. You recently proposed to your attorney."

"He wouldn't care." I say and return Quinn's text.

She pours more coffee into her cup. "I need you to read the will, Katy. It's more than just instructions."

"Uh-huh." I pop bread into the toaster.

"It's been two weeks. If you don't do it yourself, I'll sit on you and force it down your throat."

"I don't doubt it."

She grins. "How are you doing otherwise? I haven't seen you cry in twenty-four hours."

"I feel better. Not great. Not happy. Do you hear those birds outside making a racket around six-thirty in the morning?"

"Yeah, the ones singing *birdie, birdie*?"

"Yup. I smiled when I heard them this morning. Figure that's a positive sign."

Jesse nods. "Progress?"

"I suppose. I'm not sure how this works, but I feel okay right at this moment."

CHAPTER 34
ICE CREAM

The lunch rush is busy, and the dining room chatter is loud enough to make communication between the staff and our customers difficult. The crowd is great for business, and it's likely driven by nosy Dufferin Beach residents searching for gossip about my parents. At half past two, I take a break to meet Quinn.

We agreed on an ice cream parlor a few blocks from work. It's mid-December, the place is almost empty. I order a scoop of Choco-Toffee-Yum & Crunch, find a table on the back patio and think about what Jesse said last night. This isn't a *date,* date, because I wouldn't be in a dirty t-shirt, smelling like a deep fryer and raw onions. No, this is only a quick check-in after my trip to Thailand.

I wait for Quinn and imagine what our future might be like. What would my family say about my skipping to Man B so quickly after ditching Man A? What would Dad say? And my grandmother? My only surviving grandparent, in her late eighties; modern, cheeky, and full of hellfire.

I shiver from the ice cream and daydream about the night we spent together. Shiver some more, not attributable to a frozen dessert.

Thirty minutes later, he opens the glass door. I catch sight of my big grin in the reflection of the window. I am so stupid.

And unprepared for the detached body language and the terse greeting. He sits down and stares at me. No smile, no hug, no warmth. He starts with "so," all of it combining to create the universal beginning to nothing good. Ever.

His flat expression gives him away before he speaks. He could have sat down, remained silent for ten seconds, gotten up, and left.

"So, I think we made a mistake," he says.

"What do you mean?"

"I mean, about us having sex. I don't want you to get the wrong idea."

"What does the wrong idea consist of?"

"Um, you getting attached, I guess?" He glances at the white plastic tabletop. "I just wanted to see if you'd be into it."

"If I'd be into it? Are you fucking kidding me?"

"You're not really my type. You knew that going in."

I push away the bowl. Choco-Toffee was yummy on the way down. Now it might come back up.

"It wasn't love or anything, Katy. You get it, right?"

I study his chiseled cheekbones, perfect lips, and the longest lashes I've ever seen. "I am starting to. Good for you on lowering yourself to Dylan's level. Nice work."

"Yeah..." He trails off. "I'm heading out of town for a while. Sorry about your dad." He stands up, tells me he'll see me around and walks away.

CHAPTER 35
BE THE SLINKY

I'm in no mood for my appointment with Dr. Jonas; not up for another hour of soul-searching or finding some inner fucking peace. I'm distracted and embarrassed for not having a better response to Quinn's declaration than becoming a deer in headlights. Katy-on-the-spot, I am not. Had he given me time, I would have declared his weasel move "well played" and asked if he'd gotten a new hole punched in his extra shiny man card. Instead, my day-long streak without crying crumbled the second he left the ice cream parlor. Returning to The Point was a true walk-of-shame; a flashing billboard announcing how I'd done it again. Picked badly. Picked a person who would maliciously inflict pain.

I consider confessing about Quinn, then decide it's too fresh to share. If Jesse finds out, she'll punch me. And anyone else...it could get to Dylan, who would use it against me, even though Florida courts have no interest in who screws who before a marriage is dissolved.

In Dr. Jonas's office, I make myself *not* comfortable on the couch by digging my heels into the thin carpet and pushing back on the cushions like I'm about to hit the first big drop on Space Mountain.

"So, you seem tense, Katy."

I laugh out loud. She must have gotten the memo from Quinn to stare at me disdainfully and start the session with the word *so*. Therapy is such an intrusion. Can't she snap her fingers and transform me from a suicidal squirrel on the side of a highway to someone purposeful or evolved?

"What's so funny?" she asks.

"Nothing at all."

She raises an eyebrow. "Have you had more unpleasant dreams?"

"A few, not like that first one."

She writes something down. Her sharp knuckles bulge through thin skin as she moves the pen.

"How are you doing otherwise?"

"Not great. Closer to terrible."

My phone vibrates. The message is from Jesse. *Temp hearing set! FRIDAY.* She follows up with a GIF of a baby whacking itself across the cheek. I snort and try not to crack up.

"Is there a problem?" Dr. Jonas leans forward and my file slides off her lap. She squeaks and yells "shit!" before the papers float to the ground.

"Apologies," she says. "I don't make a habit of cursing in session."

"No worries. It's nice to know you're human."

She collects my notes. "Do I come across as other-worldly?"

"No, well, you're a doctor."

"Which means I've spent a lot of time in school and owe money to a loan company somewhere in Michigan."

"Oh."

"Exciting stuff, right?"

I nod, unable to provide an appropriate response to her disclosure. "Jesse texted me. The first hearing is scheduled."

"Big news. What are your thoughts?"

"I'm ready to get on with it. Hopefully, the judge will kick Dylan out of the house."

"You still haven't been home?"

"At my place? No."

"And no contact with him?"

"Just texts. Some vile shit about my parents and how I'll be homeless once he's done with me. Yesterday, he sent two pictures."

"What kind of pictures?" she asks.

"Memes. One was of a funeral and the other of some dude winning the lottery."

"Oh Katy, I'm so sorry. Do you show them to Jesse?"

"Yeah. I forward everything to her, but I'm not allowed to respond to him."

"What would you say if you could?"

"I've got no clue what I'd say. Who gives a shit?"

"I do. Getting a clue is why you're in therapy."

"Isn't my life the clue? Marrying Dylan?" I inhale and focus on unclenching my jaw. "Why are you pushing my buttons?"

"Because the world will always push your buttons. Learn how to cope, so not all the buttons lead to shut down."

"How do I do that?"

"By being mindful, gathering yourself. You're in fight-or-flight right now and it's not productive."

"That's horror movie stuff, getting chased by some misunderstood monster with a machete. Or you know, gazelles, lions and tigers. And bears."

"Oh my," she says, straight-faced. "Those are good examples, but it's triggered by emotional danger too. I notice you're sweating, beating my sofa to death with your hands, and there are little blue sparks coming out of your eyeballs."

I turn my hands over. My palms are pretty pink with a patch of purple where the cut is healing.

"Do you see it?" She leans closer to me.

"Yeah."

"You should learn about the limbic system. I can give you some information about it."

"Never heard of it."

"They're a set of brain structures. The hippocampus and amygdala, regulating physiological and psychological reactions, emotions, even hormones. They trigger, or more scientifically, regulate each other." She keeps talking, but much like my first day of therapy, I lose focus, get sleepy, fantasize about raspberry danish. I'm brought back to the session after she sneezes. "Excuse me. Fascinating stuff, isn't it? I don't want to lecture."

"Ship might have already sailed."

She smiles. "It's one experience, or type of input, controlling or triggering another. The most obvious flight-or-fight response. Fear triggering a reaction, a quick movement, an adrenaline rush. Avoidance, nausea, rapid heartbeat, an anxiety attack when someone senses chronic pain intensifying or coming on. A migraine, for instance."

"Sounds terrible. Two hits for the price of one."

"Essentially, yes. And then there's our Katy."

"I'm today's limbic poster child?"

"You win the prize. What was your trigger a few minutes ago?"

I rub my hands together. Danish. Raspberry or cheese... "Dylan?"

"Exactly. The blue sparks, even the rigid way you were sitting. That's the limbic system at work."

"Sounds super not fun."

"You can control it. Recognize the triggers and learn to manage your reactions."

"I need to do the breathing thing?"

"It's a bit more complicated and learning those specific skills takes time. For now, practice being in the moment. Slow down, listen to your heartbeat."

"Okay."

"Do you feel it?"

"Yeah, my heart's beating."

"I want you to relax into the seat. Imagine collapsing into it."

"Like melting?" I ask.

"Be a puddle."

I wish she hadn't said *puddle*. It reminds me of ice cream, which reminds me of Quinn, which reminds me how stupid I am.

"You're agitated," she says. "What's happening?"

"Nothing. I thought of something funny."

"That's not the face of humor, Katy. Something made you tense up."

"No, I'm fine. Can we keep going?"

She gazes at me. No words, only her shrink death glare.

"It's really okay," I say. "Work stuff popped into my head." *Not.*

"If you say so."

"Can I imagine I'm a slinky instead of a puddle?"

"Yes. Now relax, close your eyes, be conscious of your breathing. I'm going to stop talking. Be the slinky."

We sit quietly. A slinky might not be the best visual. It's literally a spring-loaded toy.

"How are you doing, Katy?"

"I'm not sure."

"That's okay. Let's keep trying. Breathe. Think of a place where you feel calm and safe."

"I don't do calm that well."

"Then imagine a place you feel safe."

"I don't feel like I'm in danger."

"Work with me a little. How about a place you go to relax?"

"The beach?"

"Yes. Picture yourself there and tell me what you're feeling?"

"I feel stupid."

"Give it time. Let your guard down."

"Fine." I close my eyes and sink into the cushion. "The sun feels warm. And the breeze is whipping up the sand, hitting my arm. No, hold on, that's some idiot shaking their towel out next to me."

"Happy place, Katy. Not piss-you-off-place. Assume everyone's following proper beach etiquette."

"Okay, no sandstorm. I hear the seagulls and the waves. I can't smell the water. Is that bad?"

"You're not being graded. Try to enjoy that wonderful beach."

I drop my shoulders and inhale. "I smell sunscreen, coconut, and can feel the texture of the sand on my fingers."

"Beautiful."

"I'm doing it right?"

"Yes, you're doing great. Now return to where you started. And no worry or pressure. What are you saying to, or asking of Dylan?"

I take my time and focus. "I'd ask why he picked me?"

"Okay."

"Actually no, that's crap. *Why me* is victimy."

"What does victimy mean?"

"It means poor pathetic Katy has no power to control anything. It's a cop-out, an excuse to let things happen to me. Can I open my eyes? This is getting weird."

"Of course. So, you're talking about giving someone else your power?"

"I think so. Why would I allow someone to take everything from me? Not even Dylan, specifically, but anyone?"

"Identifying the onset of a behavior can be tricky; as is learning how to change the resulting patterns."

"This is too complicated. If we're all the same when we're born, why do some people take while others get taken from? Is it an ego thing?"

"Well, first of all Katy, we're not all the same when we're born. That would discount nature versus nurture. We have built-in personalities from the get-go."

"I guess."

"Then there's development. How you're raised, life experience, wealth, poverty, race, religion. We learn along the way. Good things or bad, war, crime, addiction. Those variables mixed with genetics makes us all unique. Beautifully unique."

"So, life is churning out some people with big egos. And then me."

She taps her notepad with a pen. "You're fixating on the concept of ego. It's not the same thing as entitlement or narcissism or even overcompensation for low self-esteem. There is a space where humility and healthy expectations can coexist."

"That space is mysterious to me." I watch her pen drum up and down.

"Maybe some therapy would help with that." She smiles, crosses her thin ankles. I cringe, half expecting to hear her fragile bones splinter like walnut shells.

"What's wrong, Katy?"

"Nothing!" I blurt out. Holy crap, her tiny sharp bones freak me out.

She tilts her head and I'm reminded how complicated this therapy thing is. What does her head-twisty-bendy-thing signify? What does my cringy face mean? I'm so exhausted.

"All right," she says. "Let's work on figuring out that mysterious space. I have some ideas about the patterns in your life."

"Patterns?" I repeat the word and think of Nick. Nickety-Nick. My lovely boy from college who was too good to be true. If Dr. Jonas wants a pattern, I've got one. The more I fell for him, the more I ignored him. The more I ignored him, the more he ignored me. And so on, until my soul was crushed like a beer can thrust into the forehead of a wasted varsity lacrosse player. In the end, I got rid of him because it was better than him getting rid of me.

"Who's Nick?" Dr. Jonas asks.

"What?"

"You said Nick."

"No, I didn't."

"I promise, Katy, you did. Is he the same person you told me about last month?"

"I said his name out loud?"

"Yes, out loud."

"I don't know why I'd do that. Ask Jesse about him. They were friends."

"I'd rather ask you." She tears off a new sheet of paper. Guess I'm *extra* today.

"We were all in college together."

"How was that?" she asks.

"Always interesting. Jess and Nick bonded like siblings. They were close. Both smart, both used sarcasm to stamp out their emotions."

"Where did you fit in?"

"Nick and I didn't have any sibling vibe going on if you get what I mean. And I was the sweet one, the sugar to their vinegar. You may have noticed Jess isn't warm and fuzzy."

"She's very professional."

"She's very something," I say. "In any case, the three of us were a unit for a long time. Honestly, we didn't make much sense if you were looking from the outside."

"I'd like to..." The end of session chirp from the laptop interrupts her sentence. "We'll come back to this. I have a client waiting." She stands up. "We are not done with Nick."

"Nick isn't relevant." *Stop lying, Katy.* "Or I guess maybe he is."

My shrink lady smiles. "It's why we'll be circling back. Good luck with the hearing. Call me if you need anything before or after court, okay?"

I nod, and after confirming our next appointment, she sends me away with more questions than answers, and a brain full of the boy I ditched because nature versus nurture has done nothing but leave me Nickless.

CHAPTER 36
CANDY MAN

After leaving Dr. Jonas's office, I drive to the grocery store for junk food, raspberry danish and extra strength ibuprofen. My head hurts, my jaw aches all because it's hard work wading through a lifetime of fumbled decisions. Like Nick, and where he is now or if he ever thinks about me. And how long his blond hair is these days, and if he still has the same tattered old wallet I would fish out of his jeans just to mess with him. And how that always ended because I wasn't really fishing for his wallet.

At the ten items or less line, I wait behind an older man, setting his food on the conveyor belt, deliberately positioning them in the order he wants them bagged. Meat, cheese, fruit, assorted cookies, a loaf of French bread. I count sixteen items. That's fine, it's all fine. He's probably someone's fun grandpa, and I'm not going to stress because he's mathematically challenged.

"Now, what treat should I purchase?" he asks nobody, index finger to his chin. The checkout process comes to a hard stop.

I sigh, cross my arms. Getting more than ten items is forgivable, but I'll be damned if I'm waiting for him to window-shop for a candy bar.

He turns to me. He's got the typical bronzed Florida image. Too much sun, not enough time left for skin cancer to win the race against his advanced age. The only feature which sets him apart is a large birthmark in the shape of a spoon on his wrinkled right cheek.

"What do you think, young lady?"

"I dunno."

"Don't you have an opinion?"

I survey the options. "Snickers."

"Disgusting, pedestrian."

"Sir, can you pick one?" Also, he's wrong. Snickers are perfect and delicious.

He looks me up and down. "Which one, though, is the correct one?"

"The one you pick quickly."

"Which would that be?"

"Tobler." I say, glancing at the triangular container.

"No, I don't like the Swiss. They won't choose a side."

"How ironic," I say. This ain't anyone's nice grandpa. "Almond Joy?"

He considers this. "No."

"Why not?"

His eyes dart from candy to candy. "They're shaped unpleasantly."

I glance at the cashier who's lit his aisle beacon requesting assistance. Biting down on my lip, I imagine grabbing the old man by the scruff of his neck and shoving him into the display shelf. My headache is getting worse, and blood is going to spurt out of my eyes if this situation doesn't resolve promptly.

"Can you please pick, sir? You have sixteen items in the ten or less lane, and now you're making us wait while you analyze the chocolate."

"You've counted my groceries?" He studies his bags, which are more than ready for removal from the belt.

A manager appears and timidly asks Mean Grandpa if there's a problem.

"No problem." He frowns at me, then gingerly picks out a Hershey bar. "See how easy that was? Perchance you can learn something from this."

I rub my jaw. I've learned that he's a sunbaked bastard with a misplaced superiority complex.

Once he's out the door, the manager apologizes, bags my food, and tells me they're on the house.

I thank him and head outside, scanning the parking lot to see if Mr. Birthmark is still in the vicinity or aiming his vehicle in my direction. He seems to have gone, so I get into my car and begin texting my dad about my troubles. On the third letter, the familiar wave of misery washes over me. I delete the characters and replace them with *come back, this is stupid*, and hit send. The message lingers, never to be delivered, read, or responded to. Tears roll down my cheeks as the first few drops of a cold December rain splash on my windshield.

CHAPTER 37
BUSTED

It's the day before the temporary hearing, and Jesse has requested I come to her office to prepare for court.

"Are you ready?" she asks when she sees me peek in from the doorway.

"No," I tell her, tiptoeing around the mess of files under my feet. "Why can't you clean these up? Aren't these confidential client records?"

"Do not move them out of place and grab yours, the two red ones." She points to a spot next to my left foot.

"They're almost all red. Are we playing Twister?"

"What's Twister?"

"Did you not have a childhood, Jessica?"

"I experienced formative years, during which I learned how much the world sucks." She takes the files from me and begins paging through a small notepad. "Sit down."

"Thanks," I say. "So, what's our plan?"

She slides a packet of documents across her desk. "Read it."

I lean forward. "That's the will? The thing you all lied to me about."

She grumbles. "Technically."

"What does that mean?" I poke it with my index finger like it's a hot iron. On a yellow post-it note is my dad's neat handwriting. *To my Katy:*

"Oh hell," I whisper, and begin crying. Again. "I can't yet, Jess. Please don't make me."

"I knew this would happen." She groans, picks up a roll of paper towels from the floor and offers me a single sheet.

"One sheet is all I get?" I ask, blowing my nose.

"Yup." She tosses the roll back to the ground.

"What's in it?"

"What's in it? Obviously the fucking key to interdimensional travel. Or... perhaps, instructions about when and what and how." She pulls it to her side of the desk and flips through the pages. "And how much."

"Oh."

She inhales, holds it, and exhales. If this exercise has calmed her down, it's not showing anywhere on her face. "Take it with you and read it when you're ready. Then we'll handle the rest." She slides it to me. "There's also another document..."

"No!" I interrupt her and cover my ears. "Don't want to talk about it yet. I swear I'll read it. I'll take it with me."

"That's progress, at least. Put it into that old school bag of yours."

My backpack is propped up against my knee. It's tattered, well-loved and easily has room to store this specific stick of dynamite. I glance at her. "In here?"

She doesn't answer. In fact, she's back to shuffling a different set of papers.

I flip it over so I can't see his writing, and gently drop it into my bag.

"Done," I announce, and wipe my nose with what's left of the paper towel.

"Congratulations. Hold on a second," she says, still focusing on the other file. "How've you been otherwise? Sorry I couldn't keep staying over at your place. I missed my bed."

"I'm okay, Jess, and no, I get it. You've gone way above and beyond."

"Thanks. Are you sleeping?" She staples two papers together.

"Yeah."

"Are you having dreams about your dad?"

"Yeah, why?"

"Just curious. Are you still seeing Eudora?"

"I told you I was."

"Are you eating?"

"Yeah, I'm eating." I sniffle. "Are you my mother now?"

"No. Are you keeping your parents' house clean?"

"Not particularly."

"Excellent." She taps her pencil on a plastic folder. "Did you fuck Quinn?"

"What?"

"It's a simple question. Did you screw your husband's best friend?"

"No!" I fixate on my feet, cross, and uncross my legs, wipe nonexistent crumbs off my jeans.

"Katy."

"What?" How can news travel this fast?

"Are you going to do that in court? Sputter and stare at the ground while your cheeks turn bright pink?"

I need a minute to think. I've got to stop doing so many stupid things. It's exhausting trying to keep the lies straight. "Okay. Fine, I maybe spent the night with Quinn. But Russ was with us."

She laughs, snorts the way the devil would right before setting you ablaze. "So, Russ was there too? How reassuring."

"That came out wrong. You're taking it out of context."

"Decide what you mean before you open your mouth. Stop and reflect for a change. Or how about if you stick to yes or no responses?"

"I can probably do that."

"Okay, let's try again. Katy, did you fuck Quinn?"

I twist in the chair. "I can't imagine a judge would use such foul language."

"Uh-huh. Did you fucking have sexual relations with Quinn?"

She's so angry. I begin to giggle despite her expression. The giggles mutate into uncontrolled sobbing that feels like a seizure.

"What's happening?" Jesse's voice is distant, alarmed. "Are you having a breakdown?"

"No!" I drop my head into my hands, searching for the stupid happy beach Dr. Jonas forced down my throat. I hate my brain. I hate it for being a superhighway with no speed limit and no rest stops.

"You're freaking me out, Katy. Should I pat you on the back, or rub your elbows or something?" She's standing, leaning toward me over the desk.

"No, I'm working it out." I look at her. "Why would you rub my elbows?"

"How the hell would I know?"

I sit up straight, wipe the tears off my face. "I think your reaction is calming me down."

"I'm not the one losing it," she says, sitting back down and throwing another paper towel at me. "You are."

"You said you were too."

"Well, who wouldn't? You should have your own YouTube channel."

"Wow, so rude." I dab my eyes and squash my hair into place. "How did you find out about Quinn? He's an asshole, just like Dylan. I should have done it your way and killed him right after."

"Doesn't matter how I found out. I needed to hear it from you. Can I ask why?"

"Not if you're holding me to one-word answers."

Her shoulder blades tense, her fingers grip the sides of her chair. "Tell me why."

"I was lonely. He's attractive. He was nice to me."

"You're an idiot, Katy Kiss."

"For wanting to feel something good? You're the one who swooned over him and went on about how he liked me."

She purses her lips. "Okay, a point for you. I could have kept my mouth shut."

"Is this going to come up tomorrow? You said the temp hearing was a formality."

"No, I didn't. This shit about Quinn is why I wanted to see you today. I wanted both of us to be prepared."

"Does Dylan know?"

"Yeah, but he's not well behaved either, and Florida is a no-fault state."

"Then who cares what we've done?"

"Appearances matter, and the judge has a reputation for being rough. I need you pulled together. Let me do the talking, answer with a yes or no. And no anxiety attacks or whatever just happened here."

"Yes or no, only. I thought you knew all the judges."

"My go-to is out on maternity leave. Don't forget to say your honor."

"Yes or no, your honor."

"And don't have that look on your face. Go get some Botox."

"I don't have a look on my face."

"You always have a look on your face, Kiss."

"Not always."

She sighs. "Smoke some pot, take some downers."

"I'm not into pot. It makes me weird."

She stifles a laugh. "You think pot's the thing that makes you weird?" She leans back in her chair and crosses her hands behind her head. "I have Xanax. I want you to take one before court."

"Are you sure? What if I fall asleep?"

"You won't, you'll be relaxed."

"What if I get addicted?"

"You're already addicted to ripping your life apart. Drugs might be a nice counterbalance. And put decent clothes on. Something you'd wear to a job interview."

She pulls a bottle of pills from her desk drawer and throws them at me. "Take it thirty minutes before court."

"Got it."

"It's not rocket science, Katy."

"I understand. Why do you have a prescription for Xanax?"

She slaps my folders shut and drops them on the ground. "Because you're not the only shit-show in this town."

CHAPTER 38
ACCOUNTING

I head to work with Xanax in my pocket and my father's last will and testament burning a hole in my backpack. Do I have time for a quick walk down by the water? I could take the pharmaceuticals for a test drive. To see what it feels like. To forget.

I reach Ocean Avenue, across from the public entrance to the beach, and the answer to my question is that I'll freeze to death before the Xanax kicks in. It's mid-December, and winter has come to the South. Forty degrees and windy; blizzard conditions. I know it's not, but really it is.

When it gets this cold, the water turns steel gray and churns under angry miniature whitecaps, trying their hardest to be big boy waves. On Florida's west coast the foamy swells are the most weather drama we get unless there's a hurricane brewing.

I decide on a quick stroll. Frostbite or hypothermia won't have time to set in, but it's enough to reinforce the calming bullshit Dr. Jonas keeps shoving down my throat.

With my feet dug into the sand, I close my eyes and listen to the ocean heave itself onto the shore and inhale the chilly air. I need a mental compartment for this feeling, a pressure gauge alerting me I've sucked in the serenity required to carry on.

It's four when I return to The Point. Russ is moving from one food station to the other with purpose. His hair is tied up in a neat ponytail, and there's a healthy blush of color on his cheeks I haven't seen in years. He is two weeks clean, and almost everything about him has improved.

He hugs me with a firm grip, and even more impressive, no scent of alcohol on his breath.

"Wow, Russ, you're a superstar."

"Steppin' up darlin'. Two weeks, two days. Someone should have told me being clean would be so groovy."

"I've been telling you since high school."

He winks. "Those five years are dicey in my memory."

"Uh-huh." I head to the office. "What's going on? What do you need help with?"

"I'm good out here, but we might have bounced a check."

"The bank would have called me."

"No, they wouldn't. We gave them my number when your dad… you know."

"Had a heart attack and died?" I say these words with as much emotion as stating I'd run out of dental floss. I've repeated them over and over, explained how and why a thousand times. It's only when I hover that I fall apart.

On the laptop screen, the light green and white journal entries show a balance of almost fourteen hundred dollars. The most current entry date is late last month when I closed up shop for the entire week of Thanksgiving.

He points to it. "Too much input for this scrambled old brain."

"It's a ledger. Accurate as the person recording the transactions, and I haven't posted in a while."

"So, it's true?" His voice rises an octave.

"Hold on." I change screens and log into our bank portal.

"What does it say?" he asks. "Is there money? Are we broke?" He backs away and begins pacing in the tiny office.

"Until mid-November, everything was fine. Cash and credit cards were posting into our account the same as always."

"And then what?" he asks. "Did I mess something up?"

I study the activity. Deposits are usually split down the middle between two types of payments. Our older customers prefer paying with paper currency, anyone younger than sixty pays with a credit card. Over the holidays, revenue from cash is higher because the college kids are away on winter break.

"Why are our Monday cash deposits so low?" I ask. "They're all the receipts from the weekend."

Russ frets, bites the tips of his nails.

I move the cursor through the transactions. "The deposits are half as much as they should be."

"Can't this shit wait until I've been sober a little longer?" He turns away, dramatically leaning against the wall, feet kicking the sideboard.

I keep scrolling through the account activity. "Cards are processing. The cash is fucked-up."

"Jesus Christ," he squeals. "We're gonna be out of business."

"Please stop making out with the wall, Russ."

"No, I can't. I'm trying to stay grounded."

I shrug. His coping skills were a lot better when he smoked pot and drank a liter of scotch each day.

"Fine, let me know when you find the ground. I'd prefer not to talk to your back."

He pivots and leans on the door frame. It reminds me of when Dylan was here, informing me he'd lost another job. They look similar. Same height, blond hair and blue eyes. In every other way, they represent good and evil perched on the far ends of the cosmic soul-o-meter.

"Come sit with me, Russ."

He rolls the extra office chair over to the desk and with a straight back he grips the armrests like he's about to get launched on a rocket. "I'm ready."

I turn to the monitor. “Let’s walk through this. In November, all hell rained down on us, well, on me. I’ve been a no-show, mentally and physically, and something in our process has fallen through.”

“Sure as shit, baby,” he says.

“Everything else is functioning perfectly. The lights are on, the bills are paid, we haven’t poisoned our customers.”

“But the money.”

“Russ, you jumped into my shoes without a hiccup. You saved this place.”

“I did?”

“Nobody else could have pulled it off.”

He gives me an *aw shucks* grin.

“So,” I continue. “We’re left to figure out one component. The messed up deposits.”

“You sound like a damn professor,” he says.

Is he giving me a compliment or an insult? When he was high, he was easier to read. His facial expressions, his entire body, would drift like an amorphous blob of jelly. With sobriety, the lines of his face have become more severe, increasingly willing to commit to their full emotional expression. The result is like meeting a new person, and I’m having a hard time putting his comment into context. Am I the good professor, or is he about to drop my class?

I focus on the data again. “Let’s think about this. We’ve always done cash payments the same way. Count it after we close, make out the deposit slip, and shove it into the safe.”

“I added an extra step,” he says.

“Which is what?” I ask him. “All you have to do is get it to the bank first thing every Monday and Thursday morning.”

“I made copies of the deposit slip the night before to have a record.”

“No other changes?”

He shakes his head. "No. I take it to the ATM by eleven. It gives me the receipt and I staple it to the paperwork." He opens a desk drawer and pulls out a green file. "It all goes in here."

"When did you get so organized, Russ?"

"I wanted proof."

"You don't need proof. I trust you." The papers and original receipts are stapled to each dated 8 x 11 copy. "This is a great idea, though."

"For real?"

"Yeah." I search the numbers for clues. Something from the printed deposit tickets catches my eye. "What in the hell?"

"What?" he asks, leaning closer.

I go through the pile of deposits again. "The Monday slips don't match your totals."

"I count cash three times. You're telling me I'm adding wrong only on those days?"

"Look at this," I say.

He leans over the numbers. "What the fuck?"

I stare at the totals. My cheeks burn, the echo of my heartbeat rings in my ears.

"What, Katy? Your face just got red as a cherry, darlin'."

I open a new tab on the screen. "Pretend you're not seeing this."

He crosses his heart. "Yeah, yeah. I see nothing."

"I'm not joking," I tell him, then type in the username into a different portal. *Dilpikelsbig*.

"Is that your account?" he asks.

I slouch my shoulders and turn to him. "Would I ever use the name big pickle?"

He shrugs. "Ain't no tellin' anything in this town."

"It's not mine." I punch in the password. *Bite.d@.pical2*. The welcome screen pops up, and we access Dylan's bank account. The one he had when we got married and insisted on keeping for his *guy* expenses.

"Why do you have his password?"

"He got drunk and gave it to me. Didn't remember the next day, and I didn't remind him."

He giggles. "But you did."

"It's bite the pickle. Not hard to retain."

"Oh shit darlin', your man is dumb as fuck."

"He's not my man," I say, reading through his activity. "And he is dumb. Check this out. Every Monday there's a deposit into his account. And if you add his numbers to ours, they equal your totals to the penny. Either he's stupid or too full of himself to think we'd figure it out."

"He's jackin' your cash, Katy."

"We made it easy for him. He's got a key, and he has the combination to the safe."

"And he knows we leave the money in there Saturday night." He rolls the chair sideways and giggles.

I navigate to the portal's user settings. What if Quinn's involved? What if they've been setting me up? I think about the Xanax and the will. It's too much information crushing my brain. I take a breath, hoping to cleanse the clutter. With my index finger, I backspace over Dylan's password and peek at Russ.

"Do it," he says.

"Think I will." I lick my lips and change the first five letters of his password. "The days of messing with Katy Kiss are over."

CHAPTER 39
A BEHEADING

Friday morning. Outside it's dark and cold. Rain hammers the roof of the house. The windows rattle with each crack of thunder, and I like it. I want the weather gods to channel my wrath; I want them pissed off.

Dylan took something that didn't belong to him, and in doing so, secured a special place in my soul where forgiveness becomes laughable, ironic. Not an option. The thunder gets closer. Maybe he hears it too, wondering if payment is coming due for stealing from my family. For canceling out the few decent memories left of our relationship.

I gaze into the mirror, and a crazy person looks back. My ponytail has traveled during the night. What started in a normal location on my head is now a projectile jutting upward from the side. I'm the Little Tea Pot with only a spout, and the handle's run off in fear of what's about to pour out. My extra-large t-shirt hangs down to my knees, there's a coffee stain across my chest. One sock on, the other, I don't know, haven't seen it in days.

"Get your shit together, Katy." I lean on the counter and begin crying.

My phone buzzes. It's Jesse checking on me. *You up?*

Yeah.

Take the Xanax.

I drop the cell by the sink and walk into my bedroom. The bottle is still in my jean's pocket from yesterday, the same jeans I've been wearing all week. I take a pill with some coffee that was fresh a couple of days ago and head back to the bathroom. She leaves another message.

Take it before you leave the house.

What? oops... I took one already.

She texts an angry emoji.

Whaaaat? I respond.

They don't last that long, dumbass.

I'm not sure what to tell her. I'll just take a second one when I get to court.

While drying my hair, I decide Xanax is the best thing ever. This is the calmest I've been in months, or ever. I put on a smidge of makeup. Smidge is a silly word. I search my mom's closet for a respectable outfit. She has suits, dresses, and what I believe people with proper jobs call trousers.

I'm taller than she is by about four inches, so the trousers won't do. What an awesome word. I have to say trousers in court, work it into the conversation. I unzip a plastic garment bag and find the dusty rose, tea-length dress Mom wore to my wedding. Oh yeah, this is the perfect ironic attire for a legal confrontation. Except Dylan wouldn't remember, so it would be ironic only to me.

Another deterrent. Mom's a size four. I am not. Also, what's with this wild-ass flower brooch hanging from it? It's pretty, I suppose, old-fashioned, and the pin is sharp enough to take out an eyeball. This fucker belongs in the china cabinet, not near human skin. I zip the bag up and find a dark gray skirt with a white blouse and black purse from the shelf. Good to go.

With thirty minutes left, I grab some water and head out the door. In the driveway, I realize I've forgotten my phone, and my bag, and I'm barefoot. I huff, giggle, and run to the house. My phone's still in the bathroom. I pick it up and see the last text from Jesse. Oh, yeah, I need to take the next Xanax. So I do.

The parking lot at the courthouse has plenty of room, especially in the employee section. I'm for sure employed.

She's waiting for me at the door, all professional, Ms. Ann Taylor.

"Hi, Jessica. Very smart trousers."

She gives me the once over. "Oh God, what did you do?"

"What, did I spill coffee on myself?" I brush off the blouse.

"What are you wearing?" She points at the skirt.

"Why? I shaved. What's the problem?" I ask.

"The shirt's way too tight and the skirt is so short. You look like Tinder's morning after spokesperson."

"No, I don't. These are my mom's clothes."

"Katy, your mom is a half foot shorter than you." She bends toward me, tugging the waist downward.

"Stop it, you're gonna pull it off."

"Pull the skirt down and untuck your shirt so you're not flashing your belly."

"No." I back away from her.

"Yes, do it."

"No." I put my hands on my hips.

"Not going in there with you unless you do it."

"Fine." I adjust the skirt on my thighs. "Is this acceptable, your majesty?" I twirl in a circle.

"It'll do," she says, and heads into Dufferin Beach City Hall.

• • • • •

"It's like a giant threw up bubblegum in here," I tell Jesse from the Plaintiff's table in courtroom 1A.

"It's marble. One of these walls costs more than your house."

"I don't like the shade of pink. It's gross. Can I sit down?"

"Go for it." She pulls on her sleeves. "Haven't you been here? Jury duty, parking ticket? You've lived in this town all your life."

"Yes! I love jury duty. Remember the week-long one I had? It was so fun and interesting, then it was so sad and emotional. I was like seventy-four percent conflicted, but the person on trial wasn't. He was evil. We voted for his beheading." I cover my mouth and giggle.

She puts down her pen. "Katy?"

I try to stifle my outburst.

"You took one Xanax?"

"Yes, I took one."

"Because you're acting weird."

"I feel weird, and that might have happened after I took the second one."

Her eyes get freaky big. I can see all the white around all the dark. Pretty sure she's going to head-butt me.

"You said you took one."

"I did take one. You're correct." I flatten my hand against my lips so she won't hear me. "Then I took another."

"Oh, Jesus Christ. What am I gonna do with you? Have you eaten anything today?"

I shrug.

She pulls me out of the courtroom and into a small cafeteria. "Sit down. Do not move."

After what seems like hours, she drops a triangular shaped sandwich in front of me.

"This delicious food is for me?" The bread is pale, nutritionally barren. It is perfectly geometrical, though. Like my shrink.

"Yes, eat, scarf the fucking thing down."

"But it's so pretty. Can I re-gift it to Dr. Jonas?" I glance at her. "You seem super tense. Want Auntie Katy to fix it for you? I got a bottle, and I can tell you it's the shit!"

"Nope, I don't need a pill."

"Whatever. Your loss. I'm eating this food, right?"

"Please." She pulls it out of the plastic carton. "Eat as much as you can, as fast as you can."

I take a bite, stand up, and trail after her out of the cafeteria. This tastes like fish, yet still delicious. Who knew frapped tuna could be so yum? Didn't we come through this hallway before? Are all these people here for my sentencing? I hope the beheaded guy doesn't show up. What if he only brings his head?

"Oh my gosh, look! PURPLE!" I point to a young woman in a knee-length wedding dress. She's a vision. I have to inform her.

I break away from Jesse and rush over to where she's standing. "I love your sash. You know it's purple, don't you?"

Bridal girl seems surprised by this question. I should warn her about my marriage and Dylan and his scheming and lying and debauchery. What a stupid word. It's gonna sound weird if I say it too many times.

"Are you getting married? Is this your dude?"

She and her dude nod. "We're waiting for a justice of the peace."

"Me too!"

"You're getting married?" the groom asks.

I snort. "No, no. I'm being removed from my matrimonial, thingy, situation."

I feel someone grab my arm. "Excuse my friend." Jesse pulls me away from the couple. "She's not getting married, she's being committed. Best of luck."

"No more pit stops, Katy. Walk with me. When we get inside, sit down, and don't make a sound."

"What's the big fat problem?" I ask, taking another bite of my fish shake sandwich. "Mm. Squishy."

"What are you mumbling?" She takes away my food and lobs it into a garbage can. "That's all you get."

"But my squishy food!"

"Katy, stop it." She taps the chair when we reach the table. "Right here, don't move."

"Why are you whispering?" I ask

"Because this is a private conversation. Try to stay quiet, and remember, your answers should be short and sweet."

I smile at her, aware of how weird I'm acting. But pulling it together feels impossible because the part of my brain still functioning is a spectator watching helplessly from some ethereal lockbox. "Yes or no only," I say the words slowly.

She exhales. "Please, for the love of God, don't say anything else."

"Yes or no, only." This chair isn't comfortable. I'm bored. Did I just eat fish? I swivel to my left and see Dylan with some pale looking guy at the table next to ours. Is that the suit he got married in? Where's my wedding dress? Why's he sneering at me? It's fine, I'm going to smile.

"Eat me," Dylan mouths.

I wave, turn away, and tap Jesse on her shoulder.

"What the hell?" she hisses. "Put your tongue in your mouth."

"What?"

"It was popping out of your mouth. What's wrong with you?"

"It was?" I touch my lips. "Are you sure?"

"Yes, Katy, I'm sure. Please act like a sane human being."

"I was."

"No, you weren't. You looked like you were trying to lick your nose."

"Is this better?" I relax my face.

"No. Now your face is the WOW emoji. Stop it."

"How about now?"

She slides her elbow onto the table, resting her chin in her palm. "Kissy-face emoji."

"What am I doing wrong?" I concentrate. Appearing normal is a lot of work. "How about like this?"

She sighs. "Not so much. Just keep your tongue inside your mouth."

"Okay. Hey Jesse, were you informed that Dylan's lawyer is see-through?"

"He's not see-through, Katy. His name is Stan Bottum."

"Stanley Bott-um. Cool. I bet Dylan used the money he stole to hire him."

Her chair scrapes the floor as she pushes back a few inches. "Possible. And it's just Bottum, like, bottom of the barrel."

"When do we bust Dylan out for stealing? I'm ready to read my dad's will now. Do I have time to pee?"

"You're out of time, so hold it and also no, we're not letting on about the money yet." She hands me a pen and a notepad. "If you need to communicate with me, write it down here."

"Don't you have a pencil? I don't like pens. Do you have a Sharpie?"

"I don't have a Sharpie. Stop making noise. It's why I gave you the pen."

"How about a mechanical pencil? I'll totally stop talking if you give me one."

She rubs her temples. "How about a crayon?"

"I hate those, too."

"Who hates crayons? It doesn't matter, Katy. It's time."

I sit up straight, watch her shuffle papers, and glance at Dylan again. He's still staring at me. This time he mouths, "bite me."

I grin and think about his new and improved password. The bailiff enters. Tells us to rise.

The room gets quiet, a door opens and closes, the judge appears. He surveys his courtroom, turns his focus to Dylan, Stan, Jesse, then me. My stomach lurches. I grab the edge of the table, stop breathing. We stare at each other as a smile creeps across his tan, lined face. Oh. Fuck. Me. I can't turn away from the spoon-shaped birthmark on his cheek and the dark eyes buried under the drooping lids. It's the asshole from the grocery store, the candy man, and he's literally about to stand judgment over me.

We're permitted to sit. I drop my head and study the table, then peek at the judge. He's still grinning at me. Guess I'm the candy bar on deck, the one he's about to chew up with his thousand-year-old teeth. They talk around me, muffled buzzing in my ears. Judge Birthmark speaks louder, looks at me, looks away.

I hear Jesse. "Katy, answer him."

I turn from her to Birthmark.

"Young lady, are you with us?"

"Yes, Your Honor."

"And you are." He picks up a document. "Why'd your parents give you so many peculiar names? Perhaps they should have had more children and spread them out better." He chuckles, "pronounce these for me, would you?"

"Katalin Ildiko Judit Decker," I tell him, then peer at Jesse for approval. I need to pee.

"I only understood the surname."

"Katalin is the same as Kathleen in English."

"Kathy. What's this mess of a middle name? Where are you from?"

"I'm from here, Your Honor."

"Don't be smart with me."

Jesse jumps in. "She's a U.S. citizen. She was born in Florida."

He studies her, then me. "Where are your parents from?"

"Her parents are from Hungary," Jesse says. "They've been American citizens for over twenty-five years. Her father died a few weeks ago."

"Did he? You have my condolences. Now tell me about this name."

"It's Ildico." I say slowly.

"Isle-dye-co?"

"No, Your Honor."

"I'm saying it incorrectly?"

"Yes, Your Honor."

"Want to enlighten me?"

I just did, you sun-scorched old man. I smile and pronounce my name one more time.

"Isle-dike-o?" he asks again, grinning.

"No, Your Honor."

"No? I'm still not getting it?"

He's trying to confuse me, and we're only on names. "It's fine. People have trouble pronouncing it correctly."

"We'll have to agree to disagree on your name then, won't we? What about the next one?"

"It's the Hungarian version of Judith." Do I have to agree to disagree with someone mangling my name? I don't think so. Also, was that tuna? My stomach tightens. I push away the image of chewed up fish mixing in with coffee and acid.

He nods and moves on to Dylan.

"Dylan Marcus Decker?"

"Yes, sir."

"You address me as Your Honor in this courtroom."

"Sure thing." He pauses. "Your Honor."

"Mr. Decker, do you require a quick lesson on how to conduct yourself here?"

"No, I don't think so."

The judge studies him the bad way. The way ending with a poke from the big syringe. "Let's keep going."

He speaks to Jesse and pale Stanley Bottum, discussing things I don't understand but probably should care about.

"Mrs. Decker, you've been working hard?" The Honorable Birthmark asks me.

"Yes, Your Honor." What a fucking stupid question.

"Your husband says you were on vacation in Thailand and left him in charge of everything."

"Vacation?"

"Stay calm," Jesse whispers.

"My dad died in Thailand. I wouldn't consider it a vacation."

"Mr. Decker says it was," he pushes.

I try to focus. "Mr. Decker is wrong. My father was in the hospital. Then he died."

Birthmark grunts.

"If you don't believe me, I can bring his ashes as soon as they're repatriated. I also have documentation from the U.S. Embassy in Bangkok. His death certificate and report of the death of a U.S. citizen abroad." I take a breath. That all sounded reasonable. Do I smile now, or puke? I want the dead fish out of my stomach.

Jesse tells me to shut up.

Mr. Bottum interjects. He tells Birthmark that Dylan had to keep up the house and pay the bills, so the court should allow him to stay. My father's death is irrelevant.

"Your Honor," Jesse says. "I'd like counsel to expand on how a parent's death is irrelevant."

"I would too, Ms. Tanner." Birthmark locks on Stanley. "Care to explain?"

Stanley apologizes and says he was out of line. Fucker, I'm gonna punch his translucent face when we get out of here.

"I think we can all agree that Isle-dye-co was not on vacation. Ms. Tanner, your client wants her husband to leave the marital home. If he's been paying the bills and maintaining the property, I see no reason to grant her request."

"He doesn't pay any bills, Your Honor," she says, standing up.

"You say he's lying to the court?"

"We can provide proof of every expense related to the home paid by my client. Mr. Decker has made few, if any, contributions during their marriage. I've also provided two depositions stating the house is currently not being maintained at an acceptable level."

"I see the documents here, Ms. Tanner. The word hazmat caught my eye."

"Mine as well." She sits down.

"Hazmat? What?"

Jesse grabs my arm and tells me to be quiet.

Stanley Bott-um argues with Jesse about the depositions and filings. I focus on the city seal hanging behind the judge, and the stenographer who periodically comes up for air. What did he do to my house? Doesn't hazmat mean things are glowing or radioactive?

"Let's talk about money," the judge addresses us. "There's a joint account?"

Stan says Dylan should get it all because he's currently unemployed.

"Your client should get money because he's got no job?" Judge Birthmark asks.

Stan confirms that this is so. Birthmark watches him squirm.

Jesse interrupts. "We have no objection to letting Mr. Decker have the funds in the shared account as a good faith gesture. We hope one day he'll find work or someone else willing to support him." She scribbles "follow my lead," on my pad of paper.

I draw a stick figure on a toilet seat. She ignores me.

I write "you suck." She eyes the paper and takes my pen away.

"And how much money is in the joint account, Counselor?"

Jesse nudges my arm.

"This morning the balance was $3208," I tell the court. "And thirty-seven cents. And there's a charge from Dufferin Liquors for $23.12, which hasn't cleared."

"You like things to be exact, don't you Isle-ko?" Birthmark asks. "You like to follow the rules?"

Fucking bag of bones. "Yes, Your Honor." I'm gonna throw forty unpleasantly shaped candy bars into his grave.

"You okay handing over this account to Mr. Decker?"

"I am."

"Noted." He whispers something to his clerk. "Who originally paid for the home?"

Jesse is on her feet. "My client's parents provided the down payment, and Mrs. Decker pays the mortgage."

"Mr. Decker?" The judge focuses on Dylan.

He sits up. "Yes, sir."

Birthmark sighs. "Do you agree with Ms. Tanner's assessment of the finances?"

"Yes, sir. But I've put a lot of sweat labor into the house. Katy may bring home the bacon, but she can't cook it up." He chuckles.

Jesse responds. "My client owns and operates a popular restaurant in Dufferin Beach. She can cook bacon. And for the sake of enlightenment, can Mr. Decker describe what type of sweat," she gazes at Dylan, "equity he's supplied?"

"Mr. Decker?" the judge asks.

"Yes?" Dylan flashes an angry look at Stan Bottum. Stan Bottum shrugs.

"I painted," he offers.

Jesse shakes her head. "No, Mr. Decker. You went to The Keys on the weekend Katy and her parents painted the exterior of the house."

"I did the kitchen," he says.

"Mrs. Decker painted the kitchen with her father."

"I helped."

"You watched The Daytona 500 from the couch," she shoots at him.

Dylan frowns at The Honorable Birthmark. "She can't prove that."

"Ms. Tanner, can you prove he watched cars drive in circles while your client painted?"

"I can indeed. We have video he took using a selfie stick to record himself sitting on the couch, drinking beer, and commenting about how great it was to be the king while his wife and her father worked in the background."

Dylan's mouth opens and closes. No words come out.

"Selfie stick?" The judge again leans close to the clerk for an explanation of something he'd understand had he not been born before The Mayflower hit ground at Plymouth Rock.

While they discuss technology, I steal my pen from Jesse and add an oversized unhappy face to my toilet stick figure.

"What's your problem?" she asks.

"You fed me mutilated fish guts. My house is radioactive, and I feel sick."

"No, I didn't. I thought you had to pee."

The urge to puke is superseding the needs of my bladder. I can hold it in. I'm not sure I can hold it down. "Why would you feed me tuna?"

"Wasn't tuna." She looks around to make sure nobody is listening. "It was chicken salad."

I stare at my lawyer. She's trained to manipulate the truth, and I, over several years of married bliss to Dylan, have been trained to accept such manipulations. She returns my stare without so much as batting an eye.

"It looked like tuna," I tell her.

"Does thinking it was poultry make you feel better?"

"Possibly…unless you're lying. Are you lying?"

"I would never lie to you. It was chicken. You're gonna be fine."

"It didn't smell like it."

"Katy. Stop."

"I hate you. You gave me whipped fish."

She winks at me. "Chicken."

The judge clears the cobwebs from his throat and taps the microphone. "Are we all still here?"

He receives a round of "Yes, Your Honor."

"Mr. Decker, can you provide any proof regarding the improvements you've made?"

"I can't think of any this minute," Dylan answers, grimacing at his lawyer.

"Let's move on then. I see no mention of offspring and Isle-Ko isn't currently pregnant?"

Jesse tells him he is correct.

"Alimony?" He smiles at Mr. Bottum.

He takes his cue and asks for $1000 per month.

Birthmark grunts again. "Mr. Decker, can you stand up for me?"

Dylan looks from his lawyer to me. After shaking his head, he stands up.

"Can you take three steps to your right, then three steps to the left?"

He does as he's asked.

"Can you put your arms out to the side?"

"Yes."

"Tell me what fifty and twenty-five add up to?"

Dylan is still standing, jaw tight, eyebrows furrowed. "Why do you want to know?"

"Can you answer the question?"

"Seventy-five."

"Excellent. Sit down."

He sits, leans toward Pale Stanley to confer.

"Isle-Ko, can you think of any reason to pay your husband $1000 per month?"

For a split-second I consider how the old Katy would have given in; been nice and sweet and miserable. Screw that. Old Katy is what landed me here. I smile at him. "No, Your Honor. Absolutely not."

"Counsel? Is there some mysterious reason your client can't find a job?"

Pasty Stan says Dylan can probably find a job.

"Anything else to cover?" Birthmark asks.

Everyone agrees that there is nothing else.

The judge whispers to the stenographer who glances at Dylan.

"Very good. Let's put these rules down until the two of you can come to a final agreement." He looks directly at me. "Isle-Ko, you're like a deer in headlights. You're making me nervous." His off-center smile is like my grandfathers. It makes me hate him even more because I'm starting to like him.

"Sorry, Your Honor," I tell him. I can't help my face, it's just here on the front of my head.

Birthmark addresses Dylan and Stanley. "Mr. Decker is ordered to vacate the marital home by end-of-day, tomorrow. I don't care where you go, young man. Get out of the house. Mrs. Decker will have sole use of the home for now. Mr. Decker shall pay to have the home cleaned before he vacates."

Stanley Bottum interjects; the judge tells him to stop speaking.

"Mr. Decker, the joint bank account is yours. Mrs. Decker is not to withdraw funds or make deposits into this account."

Everyone nods.

"Mr. Decker, there will be no alimony at this time. Get a job."

Dylan makes no movement to acknowledge him.

"Did you hear me, son? Answer the court, or I'll hold you in contempt. I'm tired to death of your attitude and can tell you I wouldn't have been nearly as patient had you belonged to me."

He scowls. "I heard you."

"Isle-Ko." His beady eyes lock on me. "Again, my condolences for your loss. I'm sure your father was a good man. May this day's results bring you some manner of relief on your journey." He taps his gavel lightly and announces that court is adjourned.

The bailiff orders us to stand as The Honorable Birthmark takes his leave. I stare straight ahead, trying to keep it together.

Why did he need to mention my dad and eulogize a man he's never met?

Jesse squeezes my hand. I blink and hold my breath while the impact of his loss rolls over me one more time. No manner of judicial relief will repair the ache in my heart. So far this journey sucks, and the universe can blow itself for constantly reminding me it took away the best person I've ever known.

• • • • •

Ten minutes later Jesse ushers me out of the building, asking if I'm okay to drive because she has a few more details to handle.

"Shoot me a text when you get home," she says.

I hug her. "Thanks for getting my house back."

"I just took out the garbage. And all things considered, you did a pretty good job in there. I'm proud of you."

I nod and step out into a day that's become gloomier, rainier, colder. The jacket I grabbed this morning isn't meant for a downpour, and I get soaked in no time flat. I trudge through the public lot twice before remembering where the car is.

My old Toyota is parked surprisingly well beside a sleek pearl-gray Audi. In the downpour, I search for my keys, find them, fumble them, and helplessly watch them drop into a puddle between the two cars. I squat down, legs constricted by my mom's tight skirt, lose my balance, and topple over, landing with no grace at all, ass in the water, and one shoe under a stranger's car.

"Damn it!" I yell into the storm. Mud coats me as I stretch under the car to retrieve the shoe. In the time it takes to climb up from the narrow space, my stomach revolts and I throw up half a tuna sandwich on the passenger side window of the Audi.

Then it gets quiet. The rain and wind stop, fish slide down the expensive paint job. I notice the facility gate has a large camera pointing in my direction.

"I'm so sorry!" I yell at the lens and wipe down the car with my hands. The smell of tuna wafts into my nose, thunder breaks the silence, and the rain starts again. I improve my aim for the second round, throwing up whatever is left directly on the pavement, freeing the fish bits into the temporary stream flowing through the lot of the Dufferin Beach courthouse.

CHAPTER 40
GIFT

Ethan arrives the evening after the day I have little recollection of. A day I took drugs, went to court, returned home on a river of mud, and poured myself into bed.

The sun shines brilliantly from a deep blue sky and the crisp temperature is a welcome reprieve from the usual… lukewarm, hot, and blast furnace.

The Point is packed with a line out to the sidewalk by noon. Dufferin Beach locals have come out to feed on equal portions of gossip and good Hungarian grub.

When the workday is over, I set the alarm at the restaurant, and for the first time in almost a month, head to my own home. It's exciting to use my big girl key to unlock the door to my big girl house. I'm grateful to have had somewhere to hide out, but my parents' place has become a chain around my neck connected to a four-walled time warp haunted by my life's memories.

"Figured you wouldn't wait until tomorrow."

I'm not surprised to hear Jesse behind me. I thought she might show up when I didn't answer her text about staying away one more night.

"It's my damn house, Jess. I'm fine, go home. Come over in the morning and I'll make you breakfast."

She walks in with me. "You're on for breakfast, but I'm here now, so might as well check it out."

We take a few steps inside, survey the area, and take a few more steps into the kitchen.

I sniff the air. "Smells okay."

"They had to deep clean." She moves past me into the bedroom.

The cheap bed, both nightstands and the dresser are gone. All that remains is the forty-year-old Persian rug donated by my family when we got married.

"What a dumbass," I say, poking my head into the bathroom. "He took the plywood furniture and left a carpet worth $3000."

"He wasn't supposed to take anything." She looks over her shoulder toward the kitchen.

"I hated his shit. I'm glad it's gone. What are you looking at?"

"I brought you a gift," she says.

"An early Christmas present? Is it a truckload of chocolate?"

"I only buy chocolate for myself."

"Is it Henry Cavill or Chris Hemsworth?" I ask.

"Would you take Jude Law with a bow?"

"I wouldn't reject him. You can skip the ribbon if you bring a superhero."

She laughs. "Would you take no decoration and a completely different person?"

"Would you?"

"I'd give it all up for Gal Gadot." She returns to the front of the house and opens the door. "Here's what I brought you."

My gift is Ethan. He grins and raises his arm in an understated wave. "Hey, Katy."

Before I can say a word, he steps inside and hugs me.

My reaction is stiff-armed, hands poking out behind him.

"You're a shitty hugger, kid," he says.

"No, I'm not. I just don't like you that much."

He nods, glances at Jesse.

"When did you get here and why didn't you tell me you were coming?"

"Flew into Miami this morning, rented a car, drove for a while."

"How did you find Jess?"

"Your mom gave me her number. Guess she thought you'd take it better if I showed up among friends."

"Of course she did." I look at Jesse. "Does it seem like my parents put a lot of effort into creating a buffer between me and reality?"

"No kidding," she says, sitting down on the couch. "They swaddled you in bubble wrap."

I flip her off and look at Ethan. "You could have called me. The bubble wrap has come off and I'm still here."

"I didn't want to make your mom angry." He smiles, and I notice his hair is longer than it was in Bangkok, with thick dark blond waves, and he seems more substantial in a heavy cable-knit sweater and white button-down shirt underneath.

"She's not a simple woman to navigate. But you're here now, in Dufferin Beach." I stand with my arms crossed.

"I am. I'm here in Dufferin Beach."

"With my dad?"

"Yes."

"Where?" I ask, half expecting my father to stroll in after such an informal question. Did he bring Dad? Sure thing. He just needs a minute to get undead and reconstitute out in the driveway.

Ethan clears his throat. "In the car."

"How is he...contained?" I brush away Dad's image, standing in my living room. Big shit-eating grin, happy as hell to see his bubble-wrapped kid.

"In an urn which is in a container."

"Is it large?"

"Not really."

"Is it medium?" I ask.

"How do you define medium?"

I blink. "Somewhere between large and small."

"I'd be comfortable describing it somewhere between large and small."

"Is it pretty?"

"Are you asking about the urn or the container, Katy?"

"Um. The one he's most directly in."

"The urn is tasteful. The container was for travel."

"I don't think I want to see it yet."

He rubs his chin. "That's not coming through at all."

"Whatever. Do you have a place to stay?"

"He can crash at my townhouse." Jesse winks at me.

"You're staying here," I say, not wanting him to be a victim of her death by sex decree. "You must be tired after all the travel."

"Thanks, I'm wiped out."

"Actually, can you bring him in?"

"Yeah, of course." He dips his hands into his pockets. "You sure?"

"Yes, sure. Don't think he'd want to be stranded in a stranger's car."

His eyebrows move up, lips push together into a frown before he walks outside.

"Wow," Jesse says. "Calling him a stranger is pretty damn cold."

"It just came out of my mouth. How do I take it back?"

"By apologizing. Ever heard of it?"

I sit down with her. She's right. I will apologize, and it will feel good.

She rubs my shoulders as we wait for Ethan to return. When he does, he moves slowly, like he's carrying a bomb instead of an off-white bucket.

"Is that a garbage can?" I jump up. "Is my father in a garbage can?"

"This is what they gave me, Katy. The urn's inside."

He hands me the remains of Robert Kiss. The moment is surreal. He was a person a minute ago, with skin and bones and eyes that twinkled like he'd figured out how the universe popped into existence. Now all that's left is dust in a bucket. I hold it close, cradling my arms around it, and feel an unexpected surge of happiness. My dad has come home.

CHAPTER 41
FAT GOLD HEART

The morning sun pours into the windows, warming my face and waking me from my first night home. I sit up on the couch, stretch, and wait for the usual tug of dread to envelop me. I tap my fingers, wiggle my toes. It doesn't come. My optimism is alive and well. I smile, imagining how productive I'd be without dragging through a daily list of what if and then what, and the corresponding guilt of every mistake I'd ever made.

I'm so excited I want to text my favorite behavioral health provider. It's the weekend, though, and my appointment isn't until Monday. I could call her, but reporting happiness is probably not the best use of her emergency number.

I tiptoe into the bedroom where Ethan is curled up on an air mattress, with his right hand tucked under his face. The sunlight reflects off the chain I remember him wearing in Bangkok. I hold my breath and lean over to get a better look at the heart-shaped pendant. It's small in dimension with rounded edges, a fat droplet of pure gold. I squint at the inscription. III 16.

What the hell? Three-sixteen. Is it a bible verse, a symbol, a date? I back away, grab some clothes, and lock myself in the bathroom. Could III be the third month? Sixteen. March 16th, a day like any other. Except it's not. It's my dad's birthday. Trillions of people are born on March 16th, so what are the chances? I lay the phone on the toilet tank and step into the steaming hot shower.

• • • • •

Ethan wakes up two hours later. I've spent the morning hand washing every dish I own and putting out Christmas decorations. I'm contemplating my dad's bucket when he walks into the kitchen.

"How did you sleep?" I ask.

"Good. Great, actually. I'd forgotten how nice the fresh air is."

"You're here at the right time. I keep the windows open most of the year, but it's usually a hot breeze blowing in."

He slides his finger across a chubby ceramic Santa on the end table. "Interesting," he says, and continues to stroll around the room. He stops again in front of the pictures near the window. "Is this the infamous Dylan?"

"The one and only."

"Good-looking guy. Your mom said he was charming."

"Charming? Okay. That's all she had to say?"

He chuckles. "Not exactly."

"What else?" I offer him a cup of coffee.

"No way, I'm not getting between the two of you."

"Tell me or I'll take the coffee back."

"I'll spit into it." He moves the cup close to his lips.

"Hard bargain. I don't want a stranger spitting into my fine china." I grin, hoping he'll get the joke. "I'm sorry for what I said last night. It wasn't right."

"No worries. We are strangers." He takes a sip. "She said you could have molded him into something better if you'd had more patience."

"That's rich coming from her."

"Not getting in the middle of it. She's not the type of person I want to cross."

"My father did, and see what happened to him?"

"Grotesquely unfair, Katy."

"Grotesquely? Wow, I feel very told."

"It's what came to mind." He leans against the counter. "He died of a blood clot. Not karma or guilt or payback."

"And now he's in a bucket." I touch the side of the container holding the remnants of my dad. An entire human, erased, poof, gone.

"Even more grotesque." He sips the coffee.

"I'll give you that, though you could have used a different word. When's your birthday?"

"How about offensive? Appalling?"

"Better. When's your birthday?" I ask again.

"February. Why?"

"No reason. How about your mom's birthday?"

"July 4th."

"And your dad's?"

"January, I think."

"You think? You don't know when your dad's birthday is?"

He shrugs. "Why are you asking?"

I take a step closer to him. "The heart on your necklace."

"What about it?" He reaches up and clutches it with his hand.

"What does the symbol on it signify?"

"When did you get close enough to see the symbol?"

"When you were sleeping."

"Personal boundaries aren't your thing, are they?"

"My house, my bedroom. And the light was shining on the heart, it was... calling to me."

"Calling to you. Sure." He smiles.

"I won't do it again. Just tell me what's up with the necklace."

"It's complicated, and part of why I asked to bring your dad home myself."

"Uh-huh." I chew on my nail while he fidgets with the little heart.

"Okay, Katy. Can you stay calm if I tell you something strange?"

"Not when you say it like that. I don't want to hear any freaky shit about you. I just need an explanation about the charm."

"I'm working on it," he says. "This is all new to me as well."

"What's new? Haven't you been wearing it for years?"

"Only because my mom insisted."

"She makes you wear some chain, but it doesn't occur to you to ask questions?"

"She said it was my guardian angel. And I did ask a few times, but she'd get so rattled I let it go and figured she'd eventually come clean."

"Didn't her reaction make you more curious? You're wearing the damn thing around your neck."

"I keep it on to pacify her. And it's not a symbol, it's a date. March 16th."

I stare at him. My universe wobbles a few inches this way and that.

"It's someone's birthday," he says, putting his cup down.

"It's a lot of people's birthday, Ethan, so what? My dad was born on March 16th."

"All true."

"Is it his necklace?"

He rubs his hands together, visibly nervous. "Yes."

"Why do you have his necklace?" I don't really need to ask. The wobble goes full tilt, falls over, splinters everything I know.

"You're swaying." He grabs my arms.

"Are you serious?" I ask, pushing him away. "It's his chain?"

"He gave it to my mom the day I was born."

I scan his face and find all the familiar pieces. The shape of his eyes, the curl in his hair. Everything about him comes into focus.

"He wasn't just my dad, was he?"

"No," he says softly.

"You're my brother?"

He nods.

"My brother. I have a brother."

"Do you want me to leave?" he asks.

The question takes me by surprise. "Why would I want you to leave?"

"You look angry. Sort of like you want to hit me."

I touch my ice-cold cheeks. "I'm freaked out, not mad."

"I'm sorry."

"Why are you sorry, Ethan?"

"Because it's a hell of a curveball."

"Are you sure about this? Who told you?"

"Your dad did."

"*Our* dad did. God, that sounds crazy." I sit down on a barstool.

"Yeah, it does. It was the day at the hospital you walked in on your mom and me and got all huffy because we were upset."

"Is that why they sent me home?"

"They were nervous about how you'd take it. I don't remember too many details."

"He said those words? He's your father and you're his son?"

"Yes." He sits beside me.

"And what did my mom do? Did she flip out?"

"I don't think so."

"That would be something you'd notice. She must know."

"Honestly, her reaction was the last thing I was watching for. I don't have any memory of her getting too excited."

"Wow. Okay. What about your parents? Does your mom know?"

He looks sideways at me, one eyebrow raised like Dad used to do, like I do. "Who my father is?"

"That's not what I meant. Did you tell her what happened?"

"I called her right after. She told me everything."

"And your, um... person you thought was your father?"

"He's out of the picture," he says, finishing his coffee. "Which suddenly makes a lot more sense."

"Why?"

"Because he wasn't my biological father. And he was malicious, controlling. They split when I was pretty young."

"That must have sucked. Do you ever see him?"

I'm unable to turn away from his face, searching for a trace of my dad, a sliver of his spirit or energy.

"No, not in years," he answers. "Why are you staring at me?"

"I'm looking for my dad. Weird, right?"

He laughs. "No, I was doing the same thing last night."

"You were?"

"Yeah. But I didn't have enough time with him to recognize what to look for."

"No, I guess you didn't, which sucks. How old are you?"

"I'll be thirty-three in February. You?"

"Twenty-seven in May."

We stop talking long enough to refill our coffees. Long enough for Jesse to plow through the door with groceries and two unlit cigarettes hanging from her lips.

She drops the bags to the floor and spits the cigarettes into her hand. "Thought you'd be more excited by the delivery. Why the tense faces?"

"You are not smoking in my house, Jess. That's not gonna be a thing."

"It'll be a thing later when you're not watching. So what's with the faces?"

"You didn't tell her yesterday?" I ask Ethan.

"Tell me what?"

"No." He peeks into the bags. "Did you bring American food?"

"Eggs, waffles, bacon. American enough? What am I missing? Spill it or I'm going to assume the worst." She looks at us. "And my mind's low down and dirty."

"Ew," I say. "Please don't. Ethan, you want to do it?"

"Sure," he says, pulling out groceries. "Holy shit, I missed this stuff." He tears into a pack of sliced cheese. "Katy's dad gave me some important information in Thailand. I think it's fair to call it life-changing."

"Juicy gossip? Spill it." Jesse pulls a cup from the cabinet.

"Robert Kiss is, was, my father. Katy's my half-sister." He unwraps a slice and shoves it into his mouth.

Her eyes go wide. "Excuse me? She's what now?"

"My mom, who lives in Denver, and Katy's dad..."

"Who lives in this bucket." I extend my arms, presenting his ashes like a game show hostess.

"Shut the fuck up, Katy. Let the man talk."

Ethan's face scrunches up. "You two have a peculiar relationship. And yeah, they had a thing."

"When did they have this thing?"

"About thirty-three years ago."

"And you're the product of this thing?" Jesse asks.

He nods.

"Did it happen before Katy's parents were together?"

"Yes. Years before."

"Babies having babies." I shake my head. "So no wedding bells?"

"No. It was a scandal. Two kids from good families having sex, getting pregnant." He stops and looks at me. "And she was the one who'd be showing the evidence, so she got sent away, far away."

"Sent away from Hungary?"

"To Colorado. They had a friend who knew my dad. Or the person I thought was my dad. He agreed to take her."

"Take her?" I ask. "Are you kidding? Like she's a trade-in?"

"Her words. She married him, about three months pregnant."

"That's crappy," Jesse says. "Is he nice?"

"My dad? No."

"What's his deal?" She pours herself coffee.

"He's shitty. He forced her to name me Ethan."

"Diabolical," I say.

"Why?" Jesse asks. "What's wrong with your name?"

He looks at her. "Ever hear a Hungarian pronounce *th*?"

"Oh shit. I used to make fun of Katy's parents for that."

"Remember how pissed off they'd get?" I ask. "Imagine having to name your kid Ethan, knowing how hard it'll be to say correctly. So, what does she say? Eten?

"Yes. Ee-ten. A custom-made reminder he was doing her a favor. I hated the fucker." He glances out the kitchen window. "I could never understand why he was so hostile or why my mom put up with it. At least in front of him."

"And behind him?"

"My middle names are Robert Thomas. She called me Tommy, Hungarian style."

"With a long o. Tomeee." I grin.

"You got it."

"Sounds like they're not together anymore." Jesse dumps sugar into the mug.

"No, he left. Probably found someone else to abuse."

"Does your mom hate us?"

"Not at all." He frowns and picks up a glittery red ornament from the counter and rolls it between his hands. "Katy, can I ask why you decorate for Christmas?"

"Is this a trick question? We always decorate."

"You and Dylan?"

"Me and my family. Why are you so mystified?"

He puts the ornament down, slowly, taking his time.

"Oh boy," Jesse mutters. "I had a feeling."

"What does that mean, Jess?" I turn to Ethan. "What do you do for Christmas?"

"We don't," he sputters. "I mean… we don't decorate for Christmas because we're Jewish."

I shrug, wondering why he's making such a production out of this. "Oh. Do you put sparkly blue stuff up for Hanukkah? Is that done? Why are you both looking at me like that?"

Jesse turns her face down, ogles her coffee.

"Katy." He squashes his bottom lip with his fingers, searching for words. "I'm Jewish because my mother and father are Jewish."

"Uh-huh," I mumble.

"Both my parents. Both my biological parents."

He stops talking then. For hours it seems. The silence is crushing. Sweat trickles down my back as another bombshell makes a direct hit in the uninformed mind of Katy Kiss. It's bad enough Mom and Dad neglected to tell me about my older brother. Now my entire background is a lie too?

"But." I twist my fingers in my hair. It's a handful; thick, wavy, and unruly. Of course, it is. So is my *surprise* brother's, and my mom's and Dad's. It all makes perfect sense, so naturally it got right by me.

The wise-ass expression on Jesse's face melts away. "You get it, right?"

"I might be strange, Jess, but I'm not stupid. I assume Mom's Jewish too?"

Ethan nods. "Everyone, on every side, in every way possible."

"Okay. Well. There it is then." The wheels turn in my head. The dots I so love to throw into disarray force their way into connection. All the war stories told in hushed tones. Years and years of keeping me *safe*. "I might need a second to process all of this, a new brother, and um… the Jewish thing."

"They never said anything at all?" he asks. "Did you guys go to church?"

"No. I mean, I've been in a church. Never… you know, for official church things, like for praying or asking for restitution, or however that stuff works."

"Restitution?" He tries not to smile. "So, no religion in your life? They don't have a menorah tucked away somewhere, or a mezuzah?"

"That goes on the front door, right?"

"It does."

"Then no. None of that."

He twists the cap off a jug of full pulp orange juice. "No discussion? No stories or documents or paper trail?"

"I have memories of my relatives talking about the war when I was a kid, and my mom would cover my ears."

"Really?"

I nod. "Really. What's up with all their secrets? Why keep everything from our past locked…" I stop short. "Oh my God."

Jesse puts down the package of bacon. "What? Where are you going?"

"I remember something!" I yell and rush out the door.

CHAPTER 42
GOTCHA

I drop to my knees and reach under the clothes hanging in my parents' closet. With my right hand, I fumble around for the old briefcase I'd found before I left for Thailand.

"Gotcha," I say and drag it out onto its side.

Jesse's huffing and puffing behind me. I had a thirty-second head start when I ran out of the house, and more motivation to haul ass the entire three blocks to Mom and Dad's front door.

"What are you doing?" she asks, collapsing on the bed.

"I found this last month and totally forgot about it until just now."

Ethan sits down on the carpet with me and smooths his hand across the initials and worn leather. "Do you have the combination?"

"I don't."

"Who's MRK?"

"My grandfather." I stop and correct myself. "Your grandfather. Miklos Robert Kiss. If there's information about us anywhere, I bet you it's in here."

Jesse is still trying to catch her breath. "Screw it. Blast that thing open with a hammer."

"Absolutely not; this was someone's property." I turn to her. "Also, I have to relock it so I can someday hide my family's entire past from my kids. Since that's what we do."

She smiles. "You're going to break the chain?"

"Somebody should." I swivel back to Ethan. "Your birthday. February what?"

"The first."

"Of what year?"

"Eighty-eight."

I rotate the lock to 02 01 88. Nothing. I move the tiny numbers on the locking mechanisms to every relevant date. My mom's birthday, dad's, mine, anniversaries. It holds tight.

"What was your grandfather's birthday?" Jesse asks over my shoulder.

"No clue. I know my grandmother's." I spin it to April 21st 1935.

"No." I lay the briefcase flat on the ground. "I'll ask Mom, though using Miklos's birthday seems too obvious."

"Or devious," she says.

I push my hair behind my ears. "We need to think outside the box."

Ethan stands up and begins walking around the room. "This place reminds me of my mom's house. Old Persian carpets, books everywhere."

I watch him make a wide circle and remember Quinn wandering around the same way. It was an amazing night, or so I had thought. A chill tickles the back of my neck and shoulders.

"Why are your cheeks so pink, Kiss? Why are you blushing?"

"It's called healthy circulation, Jessica." I shake the thoughts away. Why am I so easily distracted?

"Which side does your dad sleep on?" Ethan asks.

"Next to the sliding door."

"Hm." He picks up one of the framed pictures on the bedside table. "From your wedding, I assume?"

"Yeah," I say, gazing at the photo of my parents walking me down the aisle. Mom is beaming in her dusty rose dress. Her hair is perfect, her smile, dazzling. Dad is in a gray tuxedo, sporting a tight-lipped smirk covering up a whole mess of *why the fuck are we doing this*? I'm in the middle, stiff, my expression frozen in a dazed grin.

"This is great," he says. "It's like you're being marched to the front of a firing squad."

Jesse cackles. "And that was with at least three drinks in her."

Ethan moves to the other side of the bed and studies the only picture on my dad's nightstand. "Baby Katy. Damn, you had a lot of hair from the get-go."

"Guess so." I turn away from the image. It's too soon to be wandering down memory lane.

"Can I see?" Jesse asks him.

"Sure," he says, handing it over.

"Look at the two of you, staring at each other." She studies the picture of me swaddled in a light-yellow baby blanket perched on my dad's knees. He cradles the tiny bundle, his head bent close to my face, and I'm gazing up at him, all chubby cheeks, and big round eyes.

She sighs. "Check it out. Pure love."

I wipe the tears away. I cry now, once a day, four times a day. Then it hits me. "Oh my God," I pick the briefcase up. "I know the combination."

"What is it?" Ethan crouches next to me.

I click the numbers into place. May 30, 1993. 04 30 93. The lock snaps open. "It's the day after I was born. The day they brought me home from the hospital." I swallow the gigantic lump in my throat thinking of that last afternoon with my dad in Thailand. His words about his "best day" ring in my ear.

The case creaks open, the rigid leather stretches like old skin. In my peripheral vision, I see Jesse sliding to the edge of the bed.

"The mysteries of the Kiss family," she whispers.

My fingers drift over the contents. "This is worse than breaking into the Vatican's secret stash."

"That's a yarmulka." Ethan says.

I peek up at him. "No kidding."

"You're the one who thinks you find restitution in church." He grins. "I'm just trying to be helpful."

"That's fair," I say and carefully pick up the black woven cap edged with golden thread. On the top, sewn with the same color filament, is The Star of David. I pass it to him like it's the Dead Sea Scrolls.

Jesse leans closer. "What's under there?"

I push on a soft cloth draped around something with hard edges. My phone vibrates in my pocket as I move the covering off. It's a small menorah, six inches by six inches. I lift it out of the case and trace my fingers over the engraved metal petals, doll size candle holders, and the faded teal paint. "Beautiful," I whisper. The phone buzzes again.

"Damn it," I grunt. The screen is lit up with Dylan's daily inspirational message. I hand it to Jesse.

"I can't deal with him anymore. Just tell me if it's something I should worry about."

She giggles after a few seconds. "I gotta give him points for entertainment value. He must spend hours coming up with this shit."

"Can I see?" Ethan asks.

Jesse looks at me. "Do you mind?"

I nod. "Go for it."

She shows us the screen; a GIF of a hairless Sphynx cat, with wrinkly skin, glaring like a ghoulish, ancient alien. Under it is Dylan's caption: *This gonna be YOU in a few years—nasty old ugly bitch!*

Ethan shakes his head. "Is he allowed to harass her this way?"

"It's not recommended behavior." Jesse tells him.

"I'm so tired of him. He should move on. Life isn't about the piddly shit." I stare at my new brother. "It's so much bigger than revenge."

The phone lights up again.

Jesse reads the message. "Russ is wondering where you are."

"Oh hell. What time is it?"

"Eleven-thirty."

"I'm so late. I gotta run." I pick through a few family photos; people I don't recognize posed like statues with somber, colorless expressions. Under the layer of images there's a pile of letters. No envelopes, only yellowed, heavy stock note paper. The cursive is beautiful, written with considerable care. I check one, then another, before giving them to Ethan. "Do you read Hungarian?"

"Never learned," he says. "Do you?"

"A bit, enough to get by if I recognize the words."

Jesse smirks. "Interesting."

"What?"

"The will. There's a second document your dad wrote with a couple of words in Hungarian. He wouldn't translate for me."

"He left me a letter? It's not just a will? Why didn't you lead with that, Jess?"

She shrugs. "I tried. You said you weren't ready, so I didn't push."

"That's the day you don't push me?" I huff, but deep down, I know it's been my responsibility all along. "Guess it's time then." I begin repacking all the treasures. My eye catches on something. "Holy crap."

"What?" Ethan asks.

"The dates." I leaf through a few of the letters. "These are from Miklos to his dad, Bela, in 1944." I turn from him to Jesse. "These were written when the Nazis marched into Hungary."

CHAPTER 43
THE PLAN

I do finally make it into work, though I have no memory of cooking, or chopping or slinging dough. Russ and Melissa ask if I'm okay because I keep staring off into space. But it's not space I'm staring into. It's the emotion churning in my head about a past that's been kept from me, and how different my life would be had I known who I was and where I'd come from.

After closing, Jesse arrives with Ethan. Diana, Russ, and Melissa are eating at the bar. I introduce him the way Mom would: A family friend, nothing to see here. Blah blah, lies, fairy tales, reputations on the line, total horseshit.

Diana gives him the stink eye, asks how long he's staying, then excuses herself. Melissa gets flustered, drops food on her shoes, apologizes, and scurries away. Russ shakes Ethan's hand, says, "good to meet you, brother. Love to hang out, but I've got a lady waiting."

After locking all the doors, I bring wine and a bottled water to a booth.

"You're not drinking?" Jesse helps herself to the wine.

"No way." I unscrew the cap on the water. "I'm still getting over the Xanax."

"Xanax?" Ethan asks. "Why are you taking downers? And why did Russ call me brother?" He holds out a glass for Jesse to fill.

"I didn't tell him anything. He's just affectionate. And the Xanax was Jesse's doing. She drugged me before my temporary hearing."

"No one forced two down your throat."

Ethan smiles. "Not the recommended dose, Katy. Did you get stupid or pass out?"

"She was entertaining." Jesse swooshes the wine. "Wish someone had taped it."

"There might be a video of me throwing up in the parking lot. Probably on the judge's car."

"What the hell were you doing near his car?" she asks.

"I was a bit turned around. What did you guys do today?"

"I got the tour," Ethan says.

Jesse slides out of the booth. "Anything still edible in the back?"

"Go forage. You know where everything is."

She walks behind Ethan, points to him, gives me two thumbs-up.

"It's a cool town, isn't it?" I ask, trying to ignore her.

He nods. "Yeah — don't you feel like you're on vacation all the time?"

I show him my fingers. They've turned into raisins; waterlogged and wrinkled after scrubbing pots and mopping the floor. "Do these seem like any vacation you've been on?"

"Okay, maybe not a full-time paradise. Your parents' house gives me the weirdest feeling. It's decorated like my mom's place. Post-war remnants of Hungary. The paintings, the colors, the carpets all over the place."

"I have...I had a friend who said everything there was courtesy of our dead relatives." I shall not say Quinn's name. Not out loud, at least.

"Your friend had it right."

"We're not on good terms anymore." I take a swig of ice-cold water.

"You're not talking about Dylan, are you?"

"No."

"Want to tell me about it? I'm your big brother now. I can beat him up."

"It was my fault."

Jesse returns with a tray of cheese, desserts, and left-over bread. "How'd I do?"

I inspect the arrangement. "Nice work. Need a job?"

The smile on her lip's twists into a sneer. "Imagine me waiting tables. I'd send half your customers home in tears and stick knives into the rest of 'em." She drops onto the seat and pushes a fistful of sharp cheddar into her mouth. "How are you feeling now that you're an Israelite?"

"Seriously, Jess? That didn't take long."

"What? I've been holding it in all day."

I shake my head. "I'm confused. I got a new sibling and new culture all in the span of an hour. If I could take it all in, I'd be completely overwhelmed."

"You never suspected anything?" Ethan asks. "About the Jewish thing?"

"No. Nobody ever said a word. We celebrate the normal holidays." I stop short. "Christian holidays. Though now that I think about it, it's not like we went to church on Christmas or Easter, or whenever Christ does his thing."

He places his glass on the table. "Wow, Katy. When Christ does his thing? Do you mean when he was born or was crucified?"

"I dunno. I guess. And Easter, when all that Passover stuff happens." I stare as my brother's eyes get big and I wonder what I've done wrong this time. "What?"

"You think Easter and Passover are the same holiday?"

"They're both in March or April so I just assumed. I never did Sunday school or church. No, take that back. I went to Sunday school with a friend once, but the mean lady said I didn't get to have a snack with all the other kids because I wasn't one of them."

"Ouch," Jesse whispers. "Damage."

"Indeed." I study Ethan. "How into it are you? Are you… like a devout guy? Orthodox?"

His facial features crinkle into a look of concentration. "That would be a great gaming handle. Devout guy. No, I'm not Orthodox, I'm not even very religious. I'm just aware and respectful of our past."

"Aware is a step ahead of me."

We sit silently while Ethan tries a pastry, finishes it, moves on to a second one. Jesse eats with the gusto of a kid who just got home from school.

"I'll be having a chat with my mom." I finally say. "About so many things."

They both nod. Nobody would argue against this. More silence, more food.

"So, what's the plan, kids?" Jesse tears a piece of bread apart.

"The plan for what?" I ask.

"Aside from these new developments, you didn't think the temp hearing was the end, did you? You're not divorced, nothing's finalized. Dylan's not done making demands yet, and I have a very real need to body-slam the fucker."

"Is this why you were asking me so many questions during the day?" Ethan picks cheese off the tray. "If I can stay in town, and where I'm going after this?"

"Perhaps. If you're willing to be bait, we can make some waves."

"Ethan isn't bait, Jess. He's my brother. He's not a chess piece." I notice the shocked expressions on their faces. "Sorry. Not sure where that came from."

"I don't mind, Katy. Whatever your plan is, I'm in, and staying as long as you want me to." He glances at Jesse. "Or until January 15th, when I start back at work."

"Are you sure? What about your mom? Doesn't she want you in Colorado?"

"She does. For now, she's relieved I'm in the States and not buzzing around Southeast Asia."

"What were you doing there?" Jesse asks. "I feel like you told me. Magical winged doctor?"

"Flying for an air ambulance company."

"Why there?"

"I needed flight hours, and this was a great way to pile them on. The pay is excellent. Living in Thailand is cheap."

"You're going back to Bangkok?" I ask and pick up a stray roasted hazelnut.

"No, my contract is up. I'll be flying private charter in Denver."

"My dad loved planes. Our dad. Damn it, I'll eventually get it right. He'd take me to the airfield out here to watch them take off and land."

"Really? Can you show me?" He smiles, and I see Dad's smile. Holy shit, it's eerie to see my father's face suddenly appear in front of me.

"Okay then," Jesse interrupts. "We're getting sidetracked. And your flying is fascinating, but we need a plan. Actually, I already have it worked out."

Ethan and I look at each other, then turn our attention to Jesse and the plan.

Part One, according to Jessica Tanner. Don't tell anyone Ethan is your brother. Be seen in public together, often. Say he's an old friend. No reason to mention anything about Bangkok. Be clear he's hanging out with you at the marital home. Don't give your staff any details, let them gossip. It'll add fuel to the fire.

Part Two: Keep quiet about Dylan stealing money from the business. The locks have been changed; passwords updated. Don't talk about any of it, no sharing, no complaining. We're going to play stupid during pre-trial discussions or negotiations. For a minute...

Part Three: It's time for Katy to read the will.

Part Four: On a need-to-know basis. And we don't need-to-know.

CHAPTER 44
GIANTS

I can't wait any longer. The newly forming adult in me accepts the responsibility of reading the will. The old me, stubborn and avoidant, is kicking and screaming. I walk to my parents' house with my backpack flung over my shoulder. The morning sun, still faint on the eastern horizon, is hiding behind a layer of ruffled clouds.

Jesse offered to go over the documents with me, but I wanted the first shot at them. I need to be alone with my dad and the very last things he wished for.

On the walnut dining room table, I arrange the papers, side by side, edges lined up evenly and equidistant. Busy work. So far, so good. These are just typed words. Names, dates, legalese. I make it through two paragraphs in great shape.

I am the co-executor, along with my mother. Logical. Not emotional at all.

The house is left to Andrea Kiss, a clause addresses the right of survivorship, the bank accounts and the 2005 Volvo. I learned how to drive in this car the same way I learned how to sail *Happily*. By fear of imminent death. Dad shrieking for me to stay in my lane from the passenger seat, swearing, promising God he'd never take his spatially challenged daughter on the highway again.

My eyes well up; all the lessons with him. Breathe. I read on. Mom is the beneficiary of an insurance policy and the IRA. She's given permission to dispose of his personal possessions as she sees fit. Tax instructions – blah, blah, blah. A short paragraph pertaining to Dylan that makes me smile. I'm doing great. I can get through this.

Page two. I now own fifty percent of The Point. My poor dad worked for years to make a successful business, then skipped right past retirement to death. I dig my ragged nails into my palm and wince. The cut is healed, but the fresh new skin is still sensitive. Oh God, Mom and I have to work together. Just the two of us. No buffer to stop our mutually assured destruction. I force myself to keep reading. Details about the business account. No reason to get weepy. I drum on the dark tabletop.

Page two and one-third. The boat, *Happily*, goes to me. All expected. I'm great, perfectly fine. Ignore the sniffling and wet cheeks and soggy sleeves.

Page two and a half. Katalin Ildico Judit Decker (Kiss) is requested to read the personal letter from the deceased. Oh hell. How can my father be deceased?

The letter is in an envelope addressed in his handwriting. Draga Katika. My dearest Katy. I run my fingers over the words. Some are in English, some in Hungarian. Shouldn't humankind have gotten better at dying and losing and grief by now? We send helicopters to Mars and splice DNA. Why can't we figure out how to say goodbye without falling to pieces?

I take a deep breath and begin.

Sweetheart,

I woke up this morning and think I have to make this letter for you. At first, I believe, no problem, I can write easily. Then I begin, and it is very difficult. Well, you will see.

These things we want to say to you many times before. Never feels like good time. This is my fault. I am planning on coming home from vacation and tell you everything - but never sure, right?

You will have many questions. Your mother and grandmother can be the big help. Do not be angry with them.

Elso Dolog: First thing. *You have the half-brother. This boy has different mother. I am the father. His name is Ethan Sindall, and he is living in Colorado. He is nice boy, older than you. I have met his mother before Andrea. Go find him. He does not know either, but now it is time. I leave a bank account for him I opened when he was a baby. Make this good thing, Katy. Not the tragédia.*

Második: Second. *Mi zsidók vagyunk.* We are Jewish. *We suffer at the hand of everyone. Everyone likes to beat up on the Jews. Now is better times, maybe? We don't tell you for many reasons. You can learn more from briefcase in the back of my closet. There you will find many informations. Remember. The Jewish people fight. We always fight, and we survive.*

Combination is day after your birthday. Why? Because day after you are born is my favorite day. You are the daughter I always wishing for. This enough already for any man, any father. Please, go have the happy life. The Happily *life. If this bad thing is happening to me, (you understand this means I am being dead now) – I try to visit from the outer space where the dead people flies around. I love you very much, Katika. I am hoping I am not dead, even as I write this, and then everything will be explained when we are home from our travels.*

I walk out back. *Happily* is bobbing, as usual, in the canal. I haven't taken her out since my parents have been away. Not since Dad died. But I can't. Not yet. If his best day was bringing me home from the hospital, then his second best would have been tying *Happily* up to the dock for the first time. I imagine him, smiling, rudder in hand, skimming over the waves. I turn away, not ready to create new memories while the old ones are still tearing me apart.

My heart thumps in my chest. Did Dad realize what was happening in the end? Dr. Orapan promised his death was "quick," but I'm not buying the company line used to comfort the living. My mind wanders to the darkest places about my father feeling fear in his last moments, or terrible loneliness or shock. I flinch, trying to rid myself of the images.

Whatever he did or felt is out of my control. I hope he went quickly, but hope doesn't apply to things past. It applies to the now, to the future. My options are to come to terms with his loss or be wrecked by it. Dad was a giant in my eyes, and I won't let his life go to waste. I stand up straight and square my shoulders. Getting wrecked is off the table. After all, I grew up with a superhero in my corner.

CHAPTER 45
DOMINO

My eyes are still red and puffy when I walk into Dr. Jonas's office. Nothing like a morning of misery to get you ready for the trauma of therapy. I have plenty to discuss. The results of the temporary hearing, my brother, my new Jewishness. The letter.

"Not very festive in here," I say, sliding onto the sofa. On the coffee table, there's a round wicker basket with a faded red bow. Propped inside is an emaciated plastic Christmas tree with three miniature ornaments. I poke at the needles, wondering if I'm cut off from decorating or celebrating Christmas from now on.

"Well, I'm Jewish," she says, watching me fuss with the miserable Christmas twig. "So that's all I've got. Are you okay, Katy? Have you been crying?"

"I'm all right. And you are? What the hell, is everyone Jewish?"

"Excuse me?" She gives me the much-deserved side-eye.

"Never mind," I sputter. "I don't remember seeing all those games last time I was here."

She glances over her shoulder at the stack of boxes behind her. "I use them for play therapy with my younger clients. The dominoes are for my husband." She turns back to me. "Are you sure you're okay?"

I nod. "You're married?"

"You sound shocked." She reaches for the set of dominoes and places them next to the sad Christmas tree.

I bite my lip, twirl a clump of hair between my fingers and assure her I'm not at all shocked. The woman is a stick bug, and the idea of her in close proximity to another person is vexing. Unless her husband is also a stick bug; and stick bugs need love too. I drop my hair and cover my mouth. What if opposites attract? What if he's a roly-poly? Pleasantly round. I snort.

"Do you need a tissue?" she asks.

"No." I focus on the leather case holding the dominoes.

"Open it. Take them for a test run." She readies her pen atop a new sheet of yellow lined paper.

"Really? I haven't played in years."

"Go ahead." She pushes the box closer to me. "How are things going?"

"Pretty good." I raise the top. The tiles are large, smooth with rounded edges.

"Can you expand on that, Katy?"

"The hearing went okay, and I just read my dad's will. Like an hour ago."

"Ah. That's why." She touches her cheek. "The red eyes."

"There was a letter from him."

"Do you want to talk about it?"

I let out a long sigh and remove a domino from the case. "It's oddly informal. That's him, though, it's his style."

"Mm." She shifts in the chair, fully and professionally empathetic.

"It was written last minute, if I had to guess, because he assumed he had way more minutes left."

"Mm." she mumbles again in a lower octave.

"It was sweet." I nudge my backpack with my foot. The letter is in there, safe and sound. "I'd rather not talk about it yet."

"Whenever you're ready."

"Anyway, the judge made Dylan move out, so I'm back home."

"Congratulations. Good to be there, I assume?"

"Kind of wonderful. Though we had it cleaned because he made a mess."

"A mess?"

"Yeah, biohazard level. We took care of it." I take a second tile out.

She leans toward me; I lean back. I've been coming here a while now. Hasn't she picked up on the fact that my personal bubble is all sorts of extra-large? "Katy, I'm sensing you're rushing through this. Is there something else going on?"

"No."

Jesse instructed me not to discuss Ethan. Does this include my shrink? I want to share my important news. Also, I suck at lying. I tried many times, especially as a teenager, but was often caught and subsequently embarrassed by my actions. I understand dishonesty is bad, immoral and all that crap, but the humiliation of getting busted feels like the greater deterrent.

"There's nothing else?" she asks.

"Okay, there is. You can't tell anyone."

She frowns. "As your therapist, I can't even tell anyone you're my patient without written consent."

"Oh, yeah." I remember all the papers I signed at the beginning of therapy and how they weren't really about jacking my kidney. With my privacy ensured, I tell her about Ethan, how I met him in Thailand and how annoying he was, glomming on to my family, insisting on bringing home my Bucket of Dad.

Dr. Jonas looks stricken. "Bucket of Dad?"

"It's what I call him now. He'd think it was funny."

"Okay." Her face goes blank, no expression, just skin stretched tight around those sharp bones and eye sockets. Poor Mr. Roly-Poly Jonas. I hope he has plenty of pudge to keep from being injured.

"Anyway, yesterday Ethan told me this thing." I put the dominoes down on the table. "He's my half-brother."

"Oh, my goodness, Katy."

"He also told me I'm Jewish."

"Um..." she tilts her head. This time I know it's because she's the confused one.

"What?" I ask.

"I just assumed you were Jewish."

"You did?"

"It seems rather obvious."

I rub my fingers together. "In what way?"

She's flustered. Her mouth opens and closes a few times. "Perhaps in the same way it's obvious that I am."

"It's not obvious to me."

"Well... how about if we take one thing at a time?"

I watch her sidestep after stepping into it.

"Let's discuss your new brother," she says.

"Not sure the information has sunk in yet. So far it's nice, like my dad left me a gift."

"What a lovely thought. How's he taking it?"

"He's happy about it too. It's got to be rough for him to learn one parent wasn't the real thing, and then my dad died... our dad. He said his father was a jerk, so knowing there's no blood relation might be a relief."

"It would be a lot to process. When did he find out?"

"The day before my parents sent me home from Thailand."

"He's had a little time to work through it." She stops talking for a few seconds. "Have you spoken to your mom yet?"

"No. I'll call her later today. I bet she's known all along." My phone buzzes in my pocket. I pull it out and read the text from Dylan. *Hope ur happy, hurd u have a new friend.*

"Everything okay?" Dr. Jonas asks.

"Yup." Right on cue. The Dufferin Beach grapevine is more of a vineyard, with roots everywhere, and stems that move gossip from one end of this town to the other with lightning speed.

"How might that conversation go, Katy?"

"With my mom? I have no clue. I'd like to ask why they kept it from us for so long. I know the adults make the decisions, but we haven't been children in a long time."

"Perhaps they wanted to protect you?"

"From what?"

"Society was different twenty or thirty years ago, Katy. They must have thought it was the right thing to do. You mentioned before that your parents were protective. This would be a legitimate cause."

"Keeping me from my brother and finding out I'm Jewish?"

"Not from him necessarily. Perhaps from the judgment. On both of those fronts, actually."

"The way I act has something to do with this, doesn't it?"

Dr. Jonas tugs on a tiny diamond stud in her right ear. "Things happen for a reason."

"I mean, they were so overprotective and controlling. Do you think my reaction was to run in the opposite direction, or find situations where they couldn't insulate me?"

"Yes. It's possible," she says.

"It didn't work out too well."

"Parenting is an imperfect process. Not every choice is the correct one and being in the moment blurs the lines. They're not all-knowing, Katy, they're just people facing challenges at the same time you are. Each new thing for you is new for them, too. The first time you bring home a boy is their first time. The first time you're hurt, scrape your knee, cry… another first for them. Demanding they always be spot-on isn't realistic."

"I get what you're saying." I pick a domino up in each hand. "Holy shit, what they do is like this game."

"What do you mean?"

"We're in a gigantic line of dominoes. One action creates another. Ethan's mom getting pregnant, the secrecy, my parents' behavior. And that's just one part."

My phone vibrates. More messages from Dylan. I turn it over, screen facedown on the couch. "The other parts might come from how they lived in Hungary."

"Which would have been post-war Europe," she says.

"I remember being in Budapest, walking down the streets, and seeing bullet holes and the marks from artillery shells in the old buildings. All that trauma is still in their collective memory. And what my grandparents went through during World War II? I have so many questions. It's like there's an origin domino embedded with our history, getting passed from generation to generation."

"Embedded with more than just history, Katy. It's embedded with behavior."

"Right," I tell her. "Fear, anxiety, keeping every damn thing a secret. They grew up on the heels of the Nazis, the Hungarian Revolution, the Communists. Their lives were rough. It's no wonder they fled their country."

"They came here to have a better future," she says.

"Which I'm grateful for. Except for the toxic domino they brought along."

"Absolutely."

"They make a life in America, have a kid, and because they've never dealt with their crap, their domino from Hungary topples over on me. No discussion about the past, only this stoic, wildly overprotective attitude with a child who's unknowingly absorbing the full brunt of their decisions without understanding what's happening."

Doctor Jonas scribbles on the yellow pad. "Go on."

I take a breath. "Instead of talking about it, I fill in the gaps and keep the game going. I learn to believe my parents protect and control me because I can't protect myself or handle the reality of their trauma. I'm not smart enough, not able. My self-worth plunges into the toilet."

"And now you've imprinted your own trauma on the domino."

"Exactly. My domino shoves over the next one, shoves hard, because I've got a streak of the Kiss family stubbornness. Then the self-fulfilling prophecy comes true. I can't make a good choice, so watch me make the shittiest one ever."

"Yes," she nods quickly.

"My domino is just piling on." I pick up more game pieces and begin setting them in a row.

"What are you feeling, Katy?"

I glance at her. "Angry. Confused. Oddly enlightened. This all makes my parents sound like terrible people, and they're not. If anything, they cared too much. I could have taken responsibility for myself a while ago. That's not on them, it's on me. Mostly on me."

Her thin lips stretch into a smile.

"Am I right about this?" I ask.

"You're getting there," she says. "You've created a self-reflective loop which provides insight into behavior you find troubling and confusing."

The domino case is empty. I've stacked the tiles in a winding pattern on the table.

"What do I do with all this insight? Yell at my mother for dropping their stupid game at my feet?"

"Would it improve anything?"

"No." I put my finger on the lead tile.

"So, what will you do?"

I push it forward. It taps the second tile, which falls on the third, the fourth, clickety-clack. In the middle of the table, I pull two out from the sequence just before they're tipped over. The cycle stops, and the rest of the dominoes are left standing, unaffected by the turmoil behind them. I turn to my shrink and smile. "I'm gonna stop the game."

CHAPTER 46
LEARJET

I creep into the house after my appointment with Dr. Jonas. Not because I'm afraid to wake an unruly, unemployed husband, but because Ethan is still readjusting to the time zone. We stay up late each night, talking for hours, walking downtown or at the beach, staring out into the darkness between the ocean and the sky.

I warm up the coffee I made earlier and forward Dylan's text about my *new friend* to Jesse.

She responds right away, asking if I've told anyone else about Ethan.

Nobody. Work people and you.

Who's the leak…

Dunno. We haven't been hiding. We've been out and about.

Doesn't matter. Screw him. Plan working, she texts.

Ethan walks into the kitchen as I send off the last message.

"You look better," I tell him, and hand over a cup of coffee.

"Getting there. Do you have time to go to the airport you were telling me about?"

"Yeah, I'd love that."

"And then we're going to the grocery store because I'm eating all your food."

I nod and drop a bagel into the toaster.

"And I'm buying," he adds.

"No, you aren't."

"Yes, I am, Katy."

"This is my house."

"And I'm the guest in your house."

"You're my brother, so no way. When I go to your place, I'm not even bringing my wallet."

He shakes his head. "You're a little weird. Let me help pay."

We stare each other down. He cracks first, his straight face melting into a grin. I smile back, feeling stronger than I have in years.

• • • • •

"Learjet." Ethan points at the small aircraft flying overhead.

"How can you tell?"

"The shape, the nose, the winglets."

I cover my ears. "Is it a good plane?"

"Yeah, it's a great plane. Named after the founder."

"Mr. Lear Jet?"

"Bill Lear. Guess what his daughter's name is."

"How the hell would I know?"

"Guess, Katy."

"No."

He grins. "Shanda."

"Shanda Lear? I don't think so."

"It's true." He watches it land. "Your dad brought you out here a lot?"

"Our dad. Say it."

"Our dad," he says with hesitation.

"See how easy? And yeah, a couple times a year."

"What was he like?"

"You spent time with him in Thailand. What was he like there?"

"Otherwise occupied." He turns around, watching for the next plane to approach.

"Oh, with the girl, the lima bean. Did you ever see her again?"

"No, not after the day you met her," he says.

"Didn't you hang out with him when she wasn't around?"

"I did. He seemed nice, asked me lots of questions. What was I doing with my life, and how long was I staying in Thailand? He talked about you a lot and said you might come out and visit him."

"Might? Wishful thinking until he forced my hand."

"Indeed," he says. "What was he like when he wasn't trying to hold on to a thirty-year-old secret?"

"Stellar," I tell him, kicking the dry grass under my feet. "That doesn't sound very objective. It's messed up to think about him in the past tense. I get he's gone, but I have this irrational expectation that he's still here, and this is all a test. Sounds crazy, right?"

"Not at all. I didn't mean to upset you. We can talk about something else."

"You're not upsetting me. He is. I'm pissed that he's not around anymore. He was good. And I don't mean warm and cuddly. I mean solid at his core. Principled, logical. At least until last month. He was great before. He'd have your back if you needed him, always. And he was smart. He could talk about anything."

"Airplanes?"

"Yeah, definitely airplanes."

"What else?"

"He was funny as hell. He had this low-key, dry humor. And he loved to argue and push everyone to think for themselves. He'd say something horrible or off-the-wall, then wait to see if you'd fight back. There was this time he wanted to hire an assistant to help with the accounting, and he had only two questions for the interview."

Ethan's eyebrows move up. "What were they?"

"Was she planning on having babies in the near future and was she capable of making a decent espresso?"

He laughs. "Holy shit, you can't ask that!"

"No kidding. I lectured him on and off for weeks."

"Did you change his mind?"

I shake my head. "He was never planning on doing it; he was seeing if I'd stand up to him."

"Interesting way to teach a lesson. Funny though." He smiles, then points to a sleek gray aircraft gliding over us. "Gulfstream."

"He left you a bank account." I say after the noise from the engine dies down.

"I heard. Mom told me." He drops his stare to the ground and kicks his feet in the dirt. "Are you upset?"

"No! It makes me love him more to find out he took some responsibility."

His face lightens as he looks up at me. "I feel weird about it. Mom said he sent money every month."

"Sounds about right."

"Pretty generous. Wish I could have gotten to know him better."

"He would have loved having you here, Ethan. He would have dragged you out here all the time."

"Yeah?"

"For sure. He wasn't perfect. He could be impatient and had a major lapse in judgment there at the end. Shit, I sound like a politician. Obviously, something went sideways, and we'll never understand how or why. He was a good guy, and with all the shit I pulled, all the stupid things I did, he always tried to save me. He was there no matter what."

"What stupid things did you do?"

"Almost everything I've done is stupid."

"I doubt that. Is it why you see a therapist?"

"Sort of."

"Do you mind me asking?"

"No. I married an asshole and threw away a prince. We've got a working theory going, but I'm pretty sure it takes more than six weeks of therapy to switch on all the right circuits."

"Who's the prince?"

"Nobody."

"Tell me," he pushes.

"Why?"

"Curiosity?"

I sigh. "Nick." Nickety-Nick.

"What's the story with him?"

"He's just a dude from college." I stop to watch a jet take off in our direction. The nose pulls up, it roars over our heads.

"Up close and personal, man. I love it," he yells, eyes glued to the aircraft. It gains altitude. "So, Nick is some dude, and also the prince? Does he know you're splitting up with Dylan?"

"No."

"Hm."

"What? I've been busy, legally entwined, and recently half-orphaned."

"Half-orphaned is not a thing, Katy."

"Yet here we both are, one parent gone."

I stomp on the dead weeds and smile at the memory of Nick's face. It doesn't matter though, he's out-of-touch, out-of-reach. Probably churning out mini-Nickety Juniors with some fertile, glowing superwoman.

"You're putting a lid on reaching out to him?" he asks.

"I put his lid on three days after graduation."

"And he let you? Was it mutual?"

"I don't remember."

He sighs and turns his face to the sky.

I watch a bright green lizard scurry through the pebbles, and for the first time in years, consider contacting him. What would I say? Dear Nick, how are you? I am fine. No, too formal. Dear Nick, you are the sunlight, and I am covered in sunscreen. Nope, trash. No clue where that even came from. Dearest Nick, you were good, and I was too. I just didn't know, and nobody told me, so I did everything wrong. If you don't hate me, if you're not in the middle of dinner, if you don't have 2.5 children and a Golden Retriever named Rex, if you have even a minute or twenty seconds. Call me.

CHAPTER 47
MUCK

Jesse's sitting in her car, smoking, when we arrive home from the airport and grocery store.

"Got any chocolate? I need some chocolate." She rifles through our bags and finds mini-Yorks. "These will do."

She tears into them, shoves a handful into her mouth, chews, takes more.

"What's happening, Jess? You seem stressed."

She looks at me, unblinking. "Not stressed. Angry. Got any chips?"

Ethan offers her a bag. "Salt and vinegar?"

"Fuck no. A chip should be a chip. Potatoes, salt, oil. If I want vinegar, I'll drink it."

"What's going on with you?" I ask, putting a dozen eggs into the fridge.

"Your husband's a dick. Truly, Katy, what muck did you squeeze him out of?"

She has my attention now. I leave the groceries on the counter and sit down with her. "What did he do?"

She fidgets with a cigarette, tucks it behind her ear. "I figured he'd keep fighting for the house and more money, that was a given. I didn't think he'd go lower."

"What's lower?" I ask.

"He and Mr. Bottum are coming after The Point. They're asserting your family made him work under the radar, under duress, which is why he couldn't get ahead in his career."

"Are you kidding? The only thing he does there is drink beer."

"They're also demanding to see your dad's will." She stops and stares at me. "Which you read this morning, per your text."

"Yes, Judge Tanner, I read it and cried a bunch. Dylan can kiss my ass. Nothing in there is for him, and my family's property isn't any of his business."

"It's not. They're fishing, trying to find a hole."

"He never worked a day for my family; we never asked him, and he never offered."

"He's a lying piece of shit," she says. "You need to tell your mom."

"Her head's going to blow off. She's barely functioning as it is." I stand up and start pacing. "Never let me forget this, either of you. Never let me forget what a low-life Dylan is. If I ever, for any reason, say anything remotely positive about him, slap me across the face and remind me of this day."

CHAPTER 48
THE SKYPING APPLICATION

"Hi, Mom." I try to appear neutral. Normal. Not like I'm planning on murdering my husband in the wee hours of the night.

"How are you, dear? Can you see me? Is the Skyping application working?" She speaks slowly, like she's sedated. Her cheekbones are more prominent under her pale skin, and there are streaks of gray in her dark hair.

"I'm pretty good. And it's just Skype. Are you okay?"

"Just Skype," she repeats.

"How are you doing, Mom?"

"I am sad, of course. So what? You live, you die. These things happen."

"Yeah, but this thing happened to us. Don't we get time to process what we're feeling?"

She shakes her head. "Why do you think so much, Katy? It is terrible, yes, but nobody cares of our troubles."

"I care, Mom."

"Oh, Katy. You are always the sweet little girl." She smiles and wipes the tears from under her eyes.

"Yup," I say, wondering how our relationship will change now that my dad's gone. "Ethan's in town."

"Yes, dear. I know."

"And he told me the news; about him being my brother."

"I thought this would happen."

"Did you know about him?"

She turns away from the camera; the pixels blur her image.

"Stop moving, Mom. You keep going out of focus."

"I'm watching Josephine. We run after her because she tries to escape from the apartment. She thinks I am the maid, and your uncle is the butcher. Every day she tells him to bring her a dead lamb and five pounds of goose liver."

"That's a weird and specific request."

"Yes. The same order, seven days of the week." She pulls a tissue out from her sleeve and blows her nose. "What does it matter. This comes to us all, one of the ways or the other."

"Hopefully not, Mom." I squint at the screen. Her eyes aren't flashing their usual fire, and her sass is on low burn. For the first time in my life, I worry about her.

"And yes," she continues. "I knew about the boy."

"How long have you known?"

She sighs, looking older than she did five minutes ago. "After we married, when I became pregnant with you."

"You've known my entire life? Jesus, didn't it piss you off?"

She shrugs. "It was a different time, dear. He was my husband." She stops, her eyes fill with tears again. Another tissue materializes from her sleeve. "Where was I?"

"He was your husband," I remind her.

"Poor man. We decided it would be best to keep this quiet after the treatments Ethan's mother received in Budapest."

"Poor man? She's the one who got pawned-off like a secondhand lawnmower. Ethan says his dad was a nightmare."

"Your father should have married her, but they were young. Her parents did not think this other man would be this, what you said. The nightmare. It was the big secret between the families, and we had to respect it."

"And keep it from us all this time? All these years?"

"I did not always agree. And I am sorry. I believe now it was a mistake."

"A mistake," I repeat.

That doesn't quite cover it. And why didn't they tell me we're Jewish? Is that also a mistake? My jaw clenches.

"What do you want me to say, Katy? What can I do now to fix this?"

I think of my breakthrough with Dr. Jonas this morning. Being angry with her won't solve anything. But where and when do Ethan and I register our displeasure with this situation? Or do we, and does it matter?

"We'll fix it now, Mom. It must have been rough for you to keep something so stressful to yourself."

"I do not understand." She pats her hair. "You are not angry?"

"It wasn't your fault. You all did what you thought was right. For what it's worth, I like Ethan. I'm glad he's here."

Patches of color brighten her cheeks. "This is good thing. It will be a happy time for you both." Her eyes move to something in front of her.

"What's wrong? Is it Josephine?"

"Yes. She is putting the table salt into the plant. She has killed most of them already. Tell me about the divorce. Is this still happening?"

And we're changing the subject. At least she's not asking if I'm knocked-up. "I need to tell you something."

"Is Dylan angry?"

"Is he..." I stop and take a breath. Where's that beach of serenity when I need it? Let me try to find it. Oh, it's right here where the seagulls have exploded and the sand's turning into glass. "He is upset, Mom. So much so that he thinks he deserves our house and The Point."

She moves her face close to the screen. "He what?"

"And he wants to see Dad's will."

Her eyes narrow into a look of disgust I recognize all too well. "No, tell him no. This is enough. Tell him to be a man and go from here."

"It's not that easy. He's got a lawyer. We can't ask him to go blow himself."

"What language is this? You are from a proper Hungarian family. We do not speak this way."

"Uh-huh." This will be my goal after I'm divorced, after I get over my father's death. To speak better, to behave better. To be proper...or at least adequately proper. "Got it, Mom. He still wants to see the will, and we have to allow it."

She peeks at me over the top of her reading glasses. "Fine. If this is necessary. Have you read your father's will?"

"This morning."

Silence.

"Have you read it, Mom?"

Silence.

"Mother? You've read it, right?"

She huffs out air. "Of course, Katy, I have read the damn thing."

"So you've seen the letter he wrote to me?"

Her head cocks to the left. "What letter?"

My turn to be silent. I should have kept my mouth shut. "Um. It's a poem. I'll show it to you when you get home."

"I see," she mumbles. "I miss you, Katy. Can't you come for Christmas?"

"It's in two days. Why don't you come back to Florida? Don't you miss being here?"

"Very much. I wait and see what we can do with Josephine, then I come back. Please don't worry about Dylan. He is, like your father said, the asshole. Stupid boy. He is nice to look at, Katy, but empty in his head. There is nothing in the will for him. I have to go now. Your aunt is taking all the clothes off again."

"Thanks for the help, Mom, and good luck. I'll call you Christmas day."

She throws a kiss. Her pixels blur one last time with her movement away from the screen.

CHAPTER 49
CHRISTMAS

Christmas Eve comes, and I want it to go. The restaurant is open only for lunch. I send Diana and Melissa home before two. Russ takes off at three. I finish up from there, working slowly, feeling the ghost of my parents all around me. Their voices echo in my head, their images appear and disappear in every corner, as if the building absorbed the memories and emotions of the last twenty-five years. I check over my shoulder, spooked by thoughts of the walls recording our lives, watching until the tape is full, then opening the valve and spewing the information back into the universe; on to me, right now, standing in the walk-in freezer with pink rubber gloves, a mop, and a million fragments from my past slicing through me.

• • • • •

The chime of incoming texts wakes me up Christmas morning. Most are from friends and family wishing me a happy holiday under such sad circumstances. Three are from Dylan, delivering his own brand of glad tidings.

You-a-ho-ho-ho. I'm taking the restaurant - naming it Dill's Pickle. Gonna be the Hooters of Duf Beach. Cunt!

Taking the house, daddys not here to protect u from Dylan.

Dylans gonna c- u in cort- gonna wipe the floor with u.

After a quick shower, I snap a screenshot of the messages and, for the umpteenth time, send them to Jesse.

Joyous greetings from my husband.

She responds: *Don't text back.*

Wasn't planning on it. He can't do that, can he? Take the restaurant?

I don't guarantee results.

I put the phone on silent and shove it into my pocket while Ethan slides a tray of cinnamon buns out of the oven. Our plan is to spend the morning at my parents' house, watering the plants, getting the mail. Picking through the contents of the old briefcase.

"Should we take the food to-go?" I ask, licking frosting off my fingers. "I'll make coffee over there."

"Let's do it." He wraps two pastries into a paper towel. "These are both for me, woman. I don't share the buns." His green eyes twinkle.

"Fine. I'll carry my own." I smile and squeeze past him through the front door. I haven't known my new brother long, but I feel him grinning, even behind my back.

We walk past manicured lawns bedazzled with all manner of Christmas decorations. Blow-up-Santas, reindeer made of wicker, candy canes and lights and wreaths.

The house beside Mom and Dads' is one of my favorites. Each year, they string enough lights to be visible to the International Space Station. Fat Santa is surrounded by Donner, Blitzen, Rudolph and the elves. So many elves. I stop to marvel at the meticulously arranged figures. "What if I want to keep celebrating Christmas?"

He stands beside me. "It's a free country, Katy. Do what you want."

"Really? There's no rule?"

"You're not Orthodox or active in a synagogue. If you love Christmas, then have at it." He takes a few steps forward and turns back to me. "Probably don't hook up with a rabbi."

"Rabbi?" No thought has ever been further from my mind than marrying a religious man. I believe in God, though I don't much care for the way humans, men, repackage and control the rules of the game. Every religion claims the real God, so which one is right? Is he black or white, or turquoise, no gender, every gender? To me, God has always been the collective good on this planet, in the entire universe. I realize this is a simplistic view and an easy rule-out for any rabbi who might consider putting a ring on my agnostic finger.

Inside the house, I brew strong coffee. Ethan unloads an armful of mail on the kitchen counter. I sort through the pile of greeting cards, condolences and bills. I have my parents' checkbook, so I'll pay for the utilities. The rest, Mom will have to deal with once she finds her way home to Florida.

After watering a droopy spider plant, I head into Mom and Dad's bedroom, and for the third time, retrieve the Kiss Family mystery briefcase.

"You open it," I tell Ethan. "Miklos was your grandfather, too."

He grunts and moves the numbers into place. The lock snaps open. "Voila," he says.

"For sure, dude. Let's dig in."

I take out the menorah and yarmulka and set them aside. "I thought menorahs were bigger. This one is so tiny."

Ethan glances at it. "Fun size."

I sort through the pictures again. Some are loose, others stuffed into old envelopes. "Check this one out. It's Dad's mom."

"She seems familiar. Who are the other people?" Ethan asks.

I bring the photo closer to my face. Black and white, formal clothes, stern expressions. "Looks like some type of get together. Oh damn!"

Ethan takes the picture from me. "What?"

I jump off the bed and trot to my mom's side of the closet. "Look at the brooch our grandmother is wearing."

He looks at the picture. "The flower pin on her dress? What about it?"

"It's here. I saw it when I was looking for something to wear to court. Hold on." I unzip the heavy plastic bag holding the dress Mom wore at my wedding and pull the covering back to reveal the brooch pinned to the fabric. "This is that brooch. It's like it traveled through time."

"Wow," he says, looking back and forth from the image to the real thing. "Eerie. I wonder where she got it?"

I run my finger over the delicate flower design. "What if it was handed down to her? She's the youngest one in the picture, so it's possible. We have to find out."

Ethan turns the picture over. "No names or dates. I can upload these; put them on a shared drive so we can do some research."

I sit back down and lift a random sheet of stationery from the pile. "Nice handwriting. Edes Apukam. Dearest Father."

Ethan sits with his back against the headboard while I attempt to translate.

"Don't make fun of me." I clear my throat and slowly begin reading.

Dearest Father,

Mother and I are well. We are warm and safe and have food. Mother says the potatoes are old, but we do not complain. She cries each day. We hear only that you were taken from the factory and have gone to Siberia. We pray this is not true and hope for your safe return.

Before I read another word, Ethan jumps up. "I've heard this story before!"

"Holy shit, you just about gave me a heart attack. What are you talking about?"

"My grandmother talked about this when I was a kid. All these men worked in a textile factory in Budapest and were marched off together by the Nazis. Does it say anything else?"

I turn back to the letter. "Um. They miss him terribly, then he signs off saying they're trying to find some way to get this to him through Laci. Varadi Laci. I don't recognize that name."

He puts his hands into his hair, demonstrating the head exploding emoji. "Yes! Yes! Varadi is Mom's maiden name. Laci would have been one of her uncles. This is how far back our families have been connected. Can I see it?"

"Yeah," I say, and hand the document over.

"Do you mind if I show my mom?"

I nod, and he snaps a picture of the letter.

"Texting it to her," he says.

"You don't think it'll be too upsetting?"

"Don't think so. She's probably just as curious. I remember my grandmother telling us these stories. Funny how a few words can trigger a memory."

We stop talking and stare at his phone. Minutes pass. I fidget with my ponytail. Ethan paces the room.

"She's writing back."

I watch a shadow creep over his face. "What is it, Ethan? What's she saying?"

He types a response, then looks at me. "They never came back. All those men. Mom says your grandmother knows the story better than she does. The entire group, about ten of them, were working when the SS showed up and took them away. No warning, no nothing. Just gone." He drops the phone onto the bed. "Fucking animals."

A chill settles across my shoulders. We learned about the Nazis in school, but it was never personal. It was other people; over there, far away and long ago. Faces in blurry textbook photos and small print sanitizing the stories of families ripped apart, experimented on, put in gas chambers.

He scans the document. "Wish I could read Hungarian."

I sift through more letters. "Dearest Bela. This one's from Katarine to her husband." I close my eyes to concentrate. "So, Bela and Katarine are Miklos's parents, and Miklos is our dad's father."

"Our great-grandparents," he adds. "They would have been in their forties during the war?"

"Seems about right."

"And all friends from way back," he says. "My mom's grandfather, Varadi and Kiss all got taken away together. No wonder our families were so close."

"Even if you weren't my brother, we'd have a pretty serious connection."

He picks up another letter. "I couldn't make this cursive out even if I could read the language."

I lean over for a better view. "Yeah, not even close. It's a bunch of squiggles."

He puts it back down. "This is a lot of information. Where's your grandma?"

"Montreal."

"How old is she?"

"Almost ninety, and still pretty damn feisty. She's always surrounded by her friends, at least the ones who are still alive. Dad calls her the queen of the Hungarian Mafia. Did. Past tense. He did call her the queen. How long am I going to talk about him like he's still here?"

"I'm not sure, Katy. It may take a while."

"Me either. God, all this stuff. This is a project. Like our own personal history lesson."

"Can I help?" he asks.

"Counting on it. It's your history, too." I pull a small, tattered book out of the case. The cover must have originally been beige, faded over the years to a muted white.

"This I can read," he says. "It's in Hebrew."

I watch him mouth the words.

"I've seen this before," he says. "It's the Mourner's Kaddish, the prayer for the dead."

We stare at each other for an instant, then, like we're related, blurt out the exact same words at the exact same time.

"I have an idea!"

CHAPTER 50
NOT-CHRISTMAS

A few hours later, we're back at my house. Ethan's loafing in a cinnamon bun coma and I'm pacing; confused about what a newly Jewish person should do on December 25th. I've sent a whiny text to Jesse, and as usual, she has the perfect response. A trip to Birdies, our favorite beach bar, so we can spend what's left of this day celebrating Jimmy's annual "Not-Christmas-Christmas" party.

We haven't been to Birdies since Dylan punched Quinn and got himself permanently expelled. It's been too long, and I could use a drink and a convenient excuse from pretending today is going to be like any other holiday.

• • • • •

"Where are you taking me?" Ethan buckles himself into the passenger seat of the Toyota.

"Place on the beach called Birdies. It's old Florida, laid back. We're meeting Jesse."

"How far is it?"

"A few miles. You're going to love it."

"Are we staying on Ocean Avenue? I'm trying to learn how to get around."

"Yeah, but it goes farther north than the snowbirds know about."

He leans forward, gazing out the windshield. "Interesting trees."

"Live Oaks, and the fuzz hanging off them is Spanish Moss."

"I can't decide if I like them or if I'm creeped-out."

"The old-timers say they stand guard over the road, and the branches snatch you up if you don't belong." I think about Dylan being snatched up at Birdies. Maybe the legends are true.

"That's ominous," he says, watching the landscape change. Concrete turns into gravel, then sand, and Birdies appears in front of us. "Wow! It's like a hundred-year-old shipwreck washed up on shore."

He gets out of the car, turns in a circle to take it all in. "It's so close to the water. Think the Gulf is trying to reclaim it?"

"Anything's possible." I lead him to the front door and sand covered steps.

"What in the hell?" he blurts out when he sees Jimmy bent over a beer tap.

"Don't stare. You'll meet him in a minute."

He whispers, "Those oak trees had a baby, and it's that guy."

We walk past a few wooden tables to the back porch.

"What took you so long?" Jesse asks.

"You said three. It's three." I sit down beside her. Ethan pulls a chair over.

"I've been here for an hour." She pops a handful of peanuts into her mouth. "I might have scared Jimmy."

"What did you do?" I ask.

She burps. "Asked if I could rub his head."

"Why would you do that? Did you make him cry?"

"Only for the shortest amount of time. Fuck it, I wanted to see if I could get a shine on it. Why's everyone so delicate?"

"Fair question," Ethan says, staring at the Gulf. "Hell of a view."

"How is it fair?" I ask. "He's sensitive about his appearance."

"I would be too if I looked like a cartoon." Jesse waves down a server.

"What-ju-need?" the young man asks. He's tall, attractive, with a man bun neatly twirled atop his head.

She looks him up and down. "They need drinks, and we'll take those fries you've been carrying around."

"Yes, ma'am." He places the food on the ancient whiskey barrel between us and asks if we want some fried turkey. We accept the offer because, of course, we'd love a meal of nothing but fried food. And a beer and a Greyhound with a thick wedge of grapefruit.

"So, Jesse, are you from Florida?" Ethan pops two french fries into his mouth.

She tips her beer, glares at him over the rim, drinks.

"She's from Buffalo." I answer on her behalf.

He nods. "New York?"

"Yup. She's not into the cold and doesn't get along with her family. It's an irritating experience for her."

"You're an irritating experience for me." Jesse stares at me. Burps again.

"Still, you love me, and I'm your bestest, bestest friend."

"Shut the fuck up." She smiles and wipes foam from her top lip.

"That's what I'm talking about." I return her grin.

"What's the problem with your family, Jesse?"

"Imagine an earthquake wrapped in a hurricane wrapped in an ice storm."

"Sounds turbulent," he says. "I'm sorry to hear it."

"Some families become weaponized after a while. Too much damage, too little remorse." Her face softens. "Except for my niece, Trudy. She's a doll-baby."

Ethan grimaces. "Okay, then. What was your weirdest court case?"

"Why?"

"Because I'm trying to change the subject."

She does a quick sweep of the people sitting near us. "Had a client divorce her husband because he said he had DID."

"Multiple personalities?" Ethan asks.

"Yeah. Dissociative Identity Disorder." She glances at me. "It's how I met your shrink."

"Oh," I mumble, then wonder if she believes I have DID.

"No, Katy, I didn't send you to her because I think you have DID."

"Oh." I'm happy she can also read my mind.

She continues. "She wanted out of the marriage because one of his alters gambled, one was an astronaut on his way to Mars, and the third one owned a brothel in West Texas."

"Mars? For real?" Ethan asks.

"No. He was an asshole with a high IQ. He played it pretty well until Eudora tangled him up in the lies."

"What's wrong with people?" he asks, wiping the condensation off his glass.

"The ones coming to me are already fucked-up, so, not the lens you want to look through to judge all humanity. Your turn. What's the weirdest shit you've seen flying?"

"Weird how?"

"Anyone famous?"

"Can't talk about them."

"Rich people? Freak show people?"

"Not lately. Not with air ambulance because nothing's fun there. If you're on with us, things are bad. Private charter's a different story. We had this kid who crumbled up food and threw it all over the cabin."

"Why did he do that?" I ask, fishing the grapefruit out of my drink.

"He wouldn't behave on his home turf, so his parents sent him to a military academy in Kansas. Wasn't his idea of fun, so he took the snacks we had onboard, crushed them into tiny pieces, and spread them everywhere. Even in the lav."

"Perhaps he's related to the DID man." I bite into the fruit. "Did the family pay to clean it up?"

"Of course. Then we had a guy who wanted us to transport his pet dolphin."

I swirl my drink. "Who has a pet dolphin?"

"I had a stuffed whale named Bubbles when I was a kid," he says. "The most interesting passengers are the ones flying in and out of Vegas in the middle of the night. If you want a freak show, look no further."

"A bit worse for the wear on the way home?" Jesse asks.

"A bit." He turns to me. "Your turn."

"We've got nothing..." I say as Jimmy arrives. I jump up to hug him and get a return squeeze strong enough to push the air out of my lungs.

"Happy Not-Christmas, Katy," he says, then looks at Ethan. "Who are you?"

Ethan introduces himself. A friend, staying with Katy. Let the rumor mill fly.

"Where's Flip?" Jimmy asks.

"Quinn, not Flip. There is no Flip. I heard he's out of town."

"I'm sure sorry about your dad, Katy."

"Thanks."

"And about Dylan."

"All good. And even better that you're keeping the doors open today. You saved us from a crappy Christmas at home."

He leans closer to me. "Can I tell you something?"

"Sure, anything."

"I wasn't here for a couple days last week, and Dylan got in."

"It's okay. It's your place."

"No, I don't want him here, but I had some new servers working who didn't know the rules." He motions at Manbun. "Dylan was here with a girl again."

"Same girl?" Jesse sits up. "How do you know? You said you weren't here."

"Different one. And that." He points up at a small camera. "We put a network of them in last month."

"It's all right," I tell him. "He can hang out with anyone he wants."

"But they were doing stuff."

"Fooling around? Not my business anymore."

"No." He pulls out his phone. "Look at this."

"What is it?"

"A video from when he was here." He swipes his fingers on the screen and hands it to me.

I watch the image. My stomach tightens around the fries, the vodka and cinnamon bun I had for breakfast. So much for having a jolly not-Christmas.

I hear Jesse over my shoulder. "What, Katy? You look like you're going to puke."

I hand her the phone.

She glares at Jimmy. "Why didn't you tell us about this right away?"

His tall frame crumbles into itself, his lower lip pooches out. "I just only saw it last night."

"It's not his fault, Jessica. Back off." I grab his hand. "You don't have a bigger screen we can play this on, do you?"

"I sure do," he says, and hurries away.

Fifteen minutes later we're huddled around an iPad, watching the video in disbelief. My husband is cuddling with his new girl. She's sweet, smiling like a boatload of fucking sunshine. Smiling like she never does at work. Not for her customers, not for anyone in the kitchen. They stare at each other, my husband and Diana, my bitch-faced waitress.

"I shouldn't care, but this is some bullshit. I've had a bad feeling about her, like she was watching me, biding her time."

"You were right." Ethan says.

"Doesn't matter," Jesse says. "What matters is what they're doing. Can you make out the documents?"

Ethan leans closer to the screen. "It's a menu."

"This place doesn't have a menu." I squint at the video. "That's mine! It's from The Point! What the fuck are they doing?"

Jesse picks up the iPad and pulls it close to her face. Her eyebrows furrow before she abruptly puts the device on the table and begins laughing.

"What's so funny?" Ethan asks.

"Check out what they're doing now." She grins. "It's a beautiful thing."

We do as she says. Dylan is practicing writing something over and over again. Finally, he seems content, pointing out his work to Diana. She claps and pats him on the shoulder because he's done such a wonderful job. A bang-up job. Too bad it's on tape, too bad we caught him, stupid piece of shit he is, forging Quinn's signature on a document titled "Witness Affidavit."

CHAPTER 51
BUTTERFLY

Dr. Eudora Jonas is wearing a festive sweater with Santa as a therapist talking to the kids on the naughty list. She tells me her husband is Catholic, and he bought it for her as a joke. Any other time I'd appreciate the humor. Not today.

I begin babbling as soon as my ass hits the couch. "Sorry about bugging you right after the holiday. Things are moving too fast and I'm weirding out."

"You're not bugging me, Katy. Tell me what's going on."

"We have a meeting with Dylan and Pale Stanley tomorrow."

"Pale who?"

"Dylan's lawyer. He's cadaverous."

She looks away, possibly trying to conjure the image. "How did Jesse schedule anything before the new year?"

"I have no clue. She said Dufferin Beach is a small town and whatever strings needed pulling were more about the angle than the strength. I didn't have the stomach to ask for details."

"Typical Jesse, isn't it? Okay, let's break it all down. What's on your stress list?"

"Stress list? Like a written inventory?"

"Sure, why not?" She rips a clean sheet of paper from her pad. "Ready."

"Item one." I hold my index finger up. "Dylan's a trash bag. He's evil."

She grins and writes, "husband is a trash bag."

"Are you making fun of me?"

"Only for your choice of words. So, Dylan is bad, he's evil. In all the time you've been with him, have you ever been able to change his behavior?"

I rub my hands together. "No. And he'll be out of my life in a minute, so it doesn't matter."

"Exactly." She crosses the first line off. "Scratch line one. Do you agree?"

"Yup. Item two. Dylan stole money from the restaurant when I was out of town."

She writes, then stops. "This is an item for him to feel stressed about, not you. I assume Jesse has a plan up her sleeve?"

"She has a nuke up there, and we have proof. He's also going after the house and the restaurant. Guess that's number three. And we had to provide a copy of my dad's will. Number four. I lost count. And he's screwing one of my employees. Diana." I stop and slap my hand over my mouth. "Oh shit, am I allowed to say her name?"

Her head bobs up and down. "Yes, you can say her name. Dylan wants the house, the restaurant. Affair with employee and the will."

"Uh-huh."

"And last time you mentioned you'd read the will."

"Yes. Finally."

"Did you and Jesse find anything pertaining to Dylan?"

"It's airtight and then some."

"Excellent. Do you feel comfortable taking it off the list?"

"I guess. What if the judge gives him my house and The Point? What if I'm such a fuckup I lose my parents' business?"

"Stop doubting yourself. What's Jesse saying about these demands?"

"That it's handled and not to worry."

Dr. Jonas pulls on her sweater. Santa's chubby face stretches downward. "Is she giving you any details?"

"Only for Ethan and me to be seen out and about. Not much else."

"She's a wonderful lawyer. Do you have faith in her?"

"A hundred percent. But I'm so anxious I can't think straight."

"Anxiety sucks the air out of the room; out of you. No amount of worry on this end will alter what happens on the other end."

"So, flipping out now won't stop the bad thing from happening?" I lean back, trying to unclench all the muscles in my body.

"It will only exhaust you. Focus on what you can control instead of spinning out over the things you can't. This takes practice too, similar to the other skills you've been learning."

"I can't change what's going to happen in that meeting, can I?"

"Not by worrying, Katy. It'll just zap your energy."

"Zapping seems bad."

She shrugs. "Shall we talk about Diana? You're certain she's seeing Dylan?"

"Yeah. I had a gut feeling. Of course, I ignored it."

"An unpleasant situation," she says.

"It for sure took me off guard. It's not like I didn't want him to bother someone else anyway, and she might be enough of a bitch to keep him in check. So let them go at it?"

"Perhaps they deserve each other." She draws a line through Diana's name. "What have you learned about listening to those gut feelings?"

"To trust myself. Also, gut is a weird word when you say it over and over."

Her thin eyebrows move up. "Good example of picking your battles."

"You don't find gut to be a strange word?"

"I haven't considered it. Even if I had, I wouldn't spend energy demanding Webster strike it from the lexicon."

"Point taken. I can let the gut thing go."

"See how well you're doing? What's Jesse's opinion about the house?"

"She said there's nothing Dylan can do legally. He has no right to it."

"Sounds like you're in the stronger position, Katy."

"Uh-huh." I imagine packing up boxes and handing the keys over. My fingers curl at the thought of him gloating. At least until I rip out a handful of blond hair and kick him in the balls. I notice Dr. Jonas waiting for my response. "True. It'll be okay, and if not, I'll deal with it."

"Absolutely," she says. "What about the restaurant?"

"That's what scares me most. Losing it after the lifetime of work my parents put into it."

"It doesn't seem likely. And if the worst should happen, you would survive."

"It's conceivable. I would not die instantly."

She looks at the paper. "Two items on your list. Your home and the business."

"He's going to ask for money." I glance at my phone. "And he's gone radio silent since the day after Christmas."

"Was he contacting you a lot before?"

"Yup. Daily texts since I got home from Thailand."

"Okay. We'll put the money on here. The silence is likely coming from his attorney reining him in. We're at three items." She adds another line and hands me the paper. "Anything else?"

"No. We covered everything. It doesn't look so bad all written out."

"More manageable?" she asks.

"Yes, oddly."

"And Jesse's your lawyer. So, the pissed off tiger is on your side."

"Thank God."

"How is it going with your brother?"

"Good. He asked me about Nick."

"Nick?" She grins. "The friend from college you avoid talking about."

"Yes."

"Want to chat about him?"

"Not yet."

"We'll leave him as a possibility, then?" She tugs on her bright red sleeves and crosses her arms like she's sitting in the frozen tundra rather than southwest Florida.

"Nick might have potential," I say.

"I'm proud of you, Katy."

"You are?"

She shuffles the papers in my file. "You're doing great."

"Really?"

"Your ability to consider the possibilities and put things into perspective is the key to keeping your anxiety under control." She puts her notepad down on the coffee table. "It's… well, imagine what a butterfly experiences the first time it climbs out of its cocoon and sails up into the air. How clarifying and beautiful it must be, soaring in the sky, through the trees. Literally, getting out of the darkness, out of the thick of it into a clear view."

"Uh-huh," I mutter. Receiving compliments isn't my strong suit. Her imagery is charming, but now I can't unsee my enormous Katy head on the body of a winged bug.

She continues. "I believe the gift of seeing the big picture requires an understanding of our separate pieces, all our history, our experiences. We don't earn our wings until we put those bits in order."

"It's an odd story, Dr. Jonas. And lovely."

"Thank you." She straightens her narrow shoulders. "Perhaps a bit unusual. Trust me, you are rising up to that clear view, Katy, and closer than ever to being a butterfly."

CHAPTER 52
GUARANTEED RESULTS

This is it. This time without sedatives, with a new brother at my side, and high hopes that no puking will occur on or near a stranger's car. I park, clear-headed, in the visitor lot of the Dufferin Beach courthouse.

Jesse is waiting inside, and ushers us to a room on the second floor.

She sizes me up. "Thanks for dressing appropriately this time."

"Found a cool pantsuit in Mom's closet, but Ethan put the kibosh on it."

"Circa 1980," he says. "Shoulder pads and all."

"I appreciate one of you having some fashion sense. Are you ready to rumble?"

"You said all I had to do was follow your lead."

"Still the case. Don't speak unless spoken to, don't lie. I know you're nervous."

"My whole damn life is on the chopping block."

"I own all the knives, Kiss, every last one of them."

I rub my hands together. It's fine, it's all fine.

"We're meeting in room 102. I want you," she points at Ethan, "to stay here until I text you. Then haul ass downstairs and do what the message says. Did you bring the papers?"

"Good to go." He holds up an envelope.

"What papers? What's she talking about?"

"Just some documents," he says. "Don't worry, Katy. Your lawyer's a land-shark."

Jesse stands and smiles. "That's the nicest thing anyone's ever said to me. Let's hit it."

• • • • •

"Why's the cop staring at us?" I ask her as we approach room 102.

"Need-to-know, and you don't." She shakes his hand.

"Katy, this is Pete."

"Hi, Officer Pete. Am I being arrested?"

The solid, square-faced man answers. He looks like a refrigerator. "Not unless you've done something stupid."

I drop my eyes to the ground. I wouldn't be here had I never done anything stupid. "Want to fill me in on why he's here?" I ask her.

"No. Let's head inside. I like to be first."

"You're really not going to tell me?"

"I'm really not. We're over there, facing the door." She gives me a not-so-gentle shove to the far side of the room. "And keep this folder closed in front of you."

"What's in here? Is it bad?"

"Don't open it. Glance at it randomly, with purpose."

"What the hell, Jessica?"

"Do you trust me?" She drops two accordion files onto the tabletop.

"Yes."

"Then stop asking questions."

I slouch in the chair and watch her organize documents. Why can she open her folder if I can't open mine? I run my hand over the top of it.

"Don't," she says, not turning her head.

A few minutes later, a woman comes in carrying a large purse, an aluminum case and a cup of coffee.

"Hey Ms. Tanner. Another day in paradise, huh?"

"You got it. Thanks for doing this on such short notice."

"No worries." She removes a plastic cone-shaped air freshener from her bag. "It smells like wet laundry in here." She twists the bottom, a puff of artificial pine scent spews out, fake paper flames dance from the top. "We'll cover it with some Christmas."

Jesse pats my arm. "Katy, this is Celestine. She's our stenographer."

"Nice to meet you, Celestine. Are you going to take down everything we say?"

"Yes, I am."

"Do people ever yell and scream and act psycho?"

She chuckles. "I've heard it all."

"Must be weird." I watch the paper flame gyrate with a second puff of scented air.

"Not for me to judge. I sit here quietly and pretend to be a robot."

"Isn't that hard?"

"It was at first, but I've been doing this for years. I can get through anything now." She adjusts her necklace. "You've got a brilliant lawyer here. I love listening to her speak to a jury."

"Yeah, I do. She's the best."

Stan Bottum, aka the bloodless ectomorph, and Dylan arrive ten minutes later. Stan's face is set in a frown. He leans across the table, shakes Jesse's hand; ignores me.

Dylan looks tired. Sun bleached hair out of place, his white shirt unironed. He settles at the head of the conference table, the king waiting for the presentation of the stuffed pig.

The stenographer glances at him, then at me.

"No," Stanley says to him. "You can't be there." He pulls out the chair next to him.

"Why? I'm comfortable here."

"Please sit by me, Mr. Decker."

We listen to them negotiate. I try not to giggle or puke or scream.

Dylan glares at me while he relocates. "Time to bend over, Wifey. Going down, down, down."

Stan prepares. His pen rolls away, documents flutter to the floor. He swears under his breath.

"Down so low," Dylan whispers in a way that's not quiet at all.

Skinny Stan hisses at him to stop speaking. Jesse stares at them. I reconsider my moratorium on Xanax.

"Are we ready?" Celestine asks with hands perched above the small keyboard.

Jesse tips her head in acknowledgment. Stanley huffs and puffs. "Yeah, yeah, fine. We'll go first." He continues without asking for permission, drops a pen, swivels in the chair, bends down, groans as he comes up for air. "Our demands are straightforward. I believe you'll find them to be reasonable."

Dylan emits a long, loud burp. Celestine's eyebrows rise toward her hairline. She taps on the keys.

Jesse remains silent. I inhale the aroma of fake pine. The smell of no forest ever will be my temporary, calming beach.

Stan reads from a typed document. "Number one. Defendant, Dylan Decker, demands possession of the marital home. Mrs. Decker, the plaintiff, is to sign a quit claim transferring ownership. Two. Because the plaintiff's family did not allow my client to work outside The Pont.. Pontoon-It, one-third ownership shall be transferred into his name and one-third of monthly gross sales will be deposited into an account of his choosing until the entity is closed. If The Pontoon-It is closed prematurely to avoid payment to my client, the matter will be relitigated. The company books will be audited yearly; Mrs. Decker shall pay for said audits." He eyes his client. His client cackles.

Jesse raises her hand and addresses Celestine. "He's talking about the restaurant. Pont Itt is the name, but everyone calls it The Point." She turns to me, winks; seems pretty calm except for a vein throbbing in her neck.

Stanley continues. "Yes, noted. The Pontoon-It. Number Three. We demand to see Robert Kiss's Last Will and Testament. We believe Mr. Decker is entitled to assets listed therein. Four. Because the husband was coerced into working for the family business, we ask for alimony in the amount of one thousand dollars per month through the year 2030. This request is supported by the fact that Mrs. Decker has had multiple affairs and is currently cohabitating with a man who is not her husband. The emotional damage has caused irreparable harm to my client's ability to support himself." He puts down the document and clears his throat. "And court costs, of course."

"Slam!" Dylan yells out.

"Please, outbursts are not appropriate here," Anemic Stan says, adjusting his glasses.

Celestine's typing slows, her eyes fix on Dylan.

"I assume you have supporting documentation?" Jesse asks.

"Yes, yes, we do." He pushes his jumbled papers an inch forward.

"That's all of them?" She looks at the papers with feigned confusion.

Stan hesitates. "Everything we need is here."

"Excellent." She slides a folder to them. "Copy of Robert Kiss's Last Will and Testament. Notice the highlighted paragraph pertaining to your client."

With heads close together, they inspect my dad's last instructions.

"What's this shit?" Dylan looks at me.

I shrug. "No need to be disrespectful. He was nice enough to mention you by name."

He picks the paper up and reads. "With clear mind, I, Robert M. Kiss, leave no money, no property, no personal possessions, and no further thought to Dylan Decker. That is all. Nothing follows."

"Wow." Jesse taps her fingers together. "I could use a break. Would anyone object to taking five minutes?"

Stanley Bottum does not object. He pops out of his chair and tells his client to walk with him. The stenographer sips her coffee, smiles at me.

"Why did we need a break?" I ask.

"Hold on," she says, sending a text. "I didn't. I'm just having some fun."

"But..."

"But what? His claims aren't true. Dylan's spouting off and his attorney didn't do his homework."

I tap my fingers on my mystery file. "That seems obvious."

She sets her phone down. "You remember me telling you I don't guarantee results?"

"Repeatedly."

She puts her hand on mine. "I was lying. I very much guarantee results. We're going to whip their asses into fucking oblivion."

"You've been setting me up?"

"I have. And it's going to be better than sex." She winks at me and turns her attention to the folders.

"Ready to resume?" Celestine asks after the lawyer and his angry client return.

Jesse gives her a nod. Dylan smirks at me.

Stan eyes the folder I'm not allowed to open, then begins speaking. "Ms. Tanner, will your client be agreeing to our terms?"

"I think we should see some of your supporting evidence first. Doesn't that seem like a good idea?"

"I don't require it," he says, fondling his papers.

"Of course, you don't. Yet I'd be remiss if I didn't take a peep."

Stanley shuffles through his notes.

"Fucking dyke," Dylan mutters to Jesse.

Celestine's eyes grow to the size of bowling balls. She keeps typing.

"Just chit-chat, honey." He smiles at her. "You can leave it out."

"Mr. Decker, as your attorney, I'm asking you to refrain from such derogatory comments." He wipes sweat from his blond eyebrows. "I apologize, Ms. Tanner."

She smiles sweetly. "We don't all evolve at the same pace. Anything on that evidence yet?"

Dylan sneers and flips her off.

"Yes, here's our financial affidavit." He hands us a document similar to a tax form.

Jesse studies it, takes her time, then abruptly begins speaking. "Does your client understand the repercussions of falsifying information with the court?"

"Fuck you!" Dylan snaps.

"Please!" Stanley wrings his hands.

Jesse grins. "Apologies. I didn't want to start a fight."

"My client filled out this document to the best of his ability."

"And you can back these numbers up?" Jesse asks. "You have cleared checks, bank and credit card statements, pay stubs?"

"I don't have any pay stubs." Dylan slams his hand on the table. "I told you, her fucking parents never gave me a dime."

"On the record, Mr. Decker, you're stating that during the marriage you worked only at your wife's business without compensation?"

"Damn straight, you uppity bitch."

Jesse lets the insult hover long enough for Celestine to record it. "Well now, I'm confused. Katy, didn't you tell me your husband has had approximately ten different jobs over the last three years?"

"Yes, I did."

"And he quit, or was terminated from each of those jobs within the first three months of his employment?"

"Correct." I stare at him and feel a rush of relief in erasing him from my life.

Jesse continues. "Did Dylan Decker ever work for the family restaurant, with or without pay?"

I answer. "Absolutely not."

Stan scoffs. "Of course, she'll deny it. But we have proof."

Jesse's mouth stretches into a grin. "Excellent. May we see it?"

"We have a deposition from Diana Johnson." He points at me. "Your employee, Mrs. Decker." He thrusts it in our direction. "Your copy. I'll submit the original to court if your client doesn't agree to our terms."

"Splendid." Jesse takes the paper. "Mind if we read it over?"

"Please."

She sets the document between us and begins reading. "My name is Diana Johnson. I have worked with Dylan Decker at The Point for two years. Katy treats him like so much dirt. I can't even stand watching. Sometimes he cries about it. Her mom and dad are also not nice to him. He says they don't pay him at all. They barely pay me, so I know it's right. I think he should be the new owner of the restaurant. He has ideas about how to make it better, like Hooters. Katy runs around on him, and she is almost always drunk."

Jesse finishes reading and smiles at Dylan in what appears to be genuine emotion. She's scary as fuck and I silently thank God she's on my side.

"Wow," she says. "This deposition is terribly damning."

"Terribly," Stan agrees.

"I'm curious Mr. Bottum, and I hate to repeat myself. Does this witness understand the penalty for perjuring herself before the court?"

"Miss Johnson has selflessly stepped forward as a witness. She works at The Pontoon-It and was brave enough to come forward regarding the mistreatment of a co-worker. She's a fine young woman, Ms. Tanner, with no ulterior motives."

"Other than sex?" Jesse slides a photograph to them. "Mr. Decker's been busy."

Stanley picks it up. His lips move, no words come out.

"Also, a little problematic for your timeline; my client hired Diana Johnson on August 15th of this year. That's four months ago. And I'm not great at math, but four months is less than the two years she's sworn to. We have her I-9 here, employment application, payroll records, all signed and dated. Additionally, Diana has never met Katy's parents. They left the country prior to her application date." She holds up a copy of their itinerary and stamped passport pages.

"I don't understand." Poor Pale Stan is still locked on the photo of Dylan and Diana engaging in non-platonic behavior.

"Was I unclear? I'm asking if you need proof your deposed witness has lied?"

"I'm sure there's been some misunderstanding."

"Might your client's understanding improve if we show him pay stubs from his last seven employers?" She holds up one of the fat folders.

"No need." He reaches his hand toward Diana's deposition. "I'll take it."

She pulls it away. "You said this was our copy."

He grumbles. Dylan appears uncomfortable. Jesse's just getting started.

"What's next?" she asks. "How about the house?"

"Yes. As I said, your client will agree to the quit claim, and vacate the home..."

"Why?" Jesse interrupts before he finishes the sentence.

"Because..." Stan fumbles through more papers. "Mr. Decker has been used, taken advantage of."

"How so?"

"The plaintiff has had relations with men; affairs, one after the other. My client has considerable emotional distress, which has kept him from making a living."

"Is it her affairs or all the forced labor?" Jesse asks.

Stan's blue shirt shows small patches of sweat. "I have another deposition here, one moment." An entire file falls on the floor. He disappears from our view.

Dylan speaks to the stenographer. "She's fucked half the town. Tell that to the judge. She'll screw anyone." He turns to me. "Except her husband. Dylan doesn't get any, does he?"

She stops typing. Her mouth drops open. Really, Celestine? You said you could handle anything.

"Here it is." Stanley tosses the second deposition at us with a flourish. "Mr. Quinn Healy."

Jesse's cheeks are glowing. "May we take a minute to look it over?"

"You may."

She clears her throat theatrically. "Let's see. What do we have here? My name is Quinn Healy, blah, blah, blah. I'm friends with Dylan Decker, blah, blah, blah." She stops reading, makes a weird groaning noise, then continues. "Oh, here's something. Katy is not a good wife. She disrespects her husband, and I've had sex with her so many times I can't even keep count. Every time Dylan leaves his house, she's calling me to hook up. I'm embarrassed for him, and I shouldn't be doing it, but she's willing and easy. Also, she's drunk almost all the time."

I cover the bottom of my face and try not to smile.

"Well, this is something else." Jesse's pupils dilate.

"Yes, intolerable," Stan says. "Imagine what a jury would say."

"Damn straight," Dylan throws in. "We're back in the saddle."

"It would be horrible. You're absolutely correct." Jesse grins, all teeth. Sharper than I remember.

"Look, Ms. Tanner. We want to be fair and we're willing to compromise. Full ownership of the house, spousal support as stated, and a minimal fraction of the revenue. Perhaps an additional $500 per month for ten years. This way we avoid humiliating Mrs. Decker in court. Her family is well known in this town."

"Being humiliated does sound unpleasant. How about if we talk about these first?" She slides five 8 x 10 photos toward them. They're enlarged images from the video Jimmy gave us.

"What is this?" Stan takes the pictures. Dylan's cheeks turn Pepto-Bismol pink.

"This is your client forging a legal document."

"These are photoshopped." He drops them like they're on fire. "We can show they've been manipulated."

"We have the video that created the stills," Jesse says. "And we've contacted Quinn Healy. He has no knowledge of this deposition."

"Bullshit!" Dylan yells. "I watched him write it myself."

Stanley Bottum again asks him to be quiet. Celestine records the drama.

"Shall we call and ask him?" Jesse takes out her phone, fingers hover over the screen. "He's not pleased about the situation and is considering pressing charges."

"No!" Dylan jumps up from his chair. "I'm being set up!"

Stan tells him to sit down and stop speaking. It doesn't work.

Dylan's voice cracks as he yells. "She's manipulating all of you, stupid bitch! She has threesomes and some guy's shacked up with her right now. In Dylan's house!"

I watch his face change, light to shadow. Here comes that third, fourth, and seventh person he warned me about last month. Idiot. I fucking hate him.

"Let's all calm down here," Stan says. "We can reduce our demands further. It seems my client is confused about a few facts, so we'll make do with just the house and spousal support.

However, Mrs. Decker is brazenly disrespecting her marriage vows by cohabitating with another man. We have photographic evidence of our own."

"Of what?" Jesse asks. "Katy walking in and out of her house with a man?"

"Yes, several pictures." He shovels through his pile again.

Jesse watches him for a few seconds, then sends a text, followed by a knock at the door. "Enter," she says, smiling at Mr. Pale Bottum.

Ethan walks into the room, around the table, and sits down beside me.

"This is the man in my pictures!" Stan's arms flail. His phone goes airborne. "The man you're living with sinfully." He turns to his client, who is currently jabbing his index finger toward Ethan.

Jesse nods. "Ethan, please introduce yourself."

"Good afternoon." He looks at Dylan. "I'm Ethan Robert Sindall. I'm named after my father, Robert Kiss. Katy is my sister."

Stanley and Dylan go quiet.

"Next!" Jesse bellows.

Officer Pete opens the door, takes two steps inside with a set of handcuffs conspicuously visible in his left hand. He looks at Dylan, then Jesse. "Ready when you are, Ms. Tanner."

Jesse leans back in her chair. "The officer is here because Mr. Decker stole money from my client's family. Thousands taken from the safe at the restaurant while my client was grieving her father's passing." She sets her elbow on the table, cups her chin in her hand. "It's not a fabulous situation. Felony, forgery. So many f words. Wish I appreciated alliteration far more."

The paper candle flutters, the scent of not pine wafts under my nose.

Attorney Bottum tells his client not to speak. His client is not so good at following directions.

Dylan moves to the corner of the room. “Dylan took what he was owed. Dylan knows about the safe and your dad never changes the combination.”

Stan slams his pen down, mumbles something about doing favors for friends.

Jesse is radiant, flushed, and now I understand why she wants to kill everyone she sleeps with. Nobody can compare to this legal stimulation, this oxytocin delivery vehicle. I hear her sigh right before asking if opposing counsel needs to see Mr. Sindall’s birth certificate.

Dylan is quiet, motionless, his stare fixed on the wall behind me. The husband, soon not to be mine, has checked out.

Stan studies the birth certificate, driver’s license, pilot’s license, then asks for a ten-minute break.

“What’s happening?” I ask after Stan leads Dylan out by the shoulders. “And what’s the deal with Quinn? Did you talk to him?”

“I did.”

“Why didn’t you say anything? He told me to screw myself after I came home from Bangkok. He was a total dick.”

“Not exactly accurate.”

“Which part do I have wrong, Jess?”

“All of it. I told him to do it because you needed to stay out of trouble. You understand what I’m talking about, and you know I’m right. Maybe he’s the real deal. Honestly I don’t give a flying fuck about all the romance shit. The guy did what I asked, so if you want to be pissed, have at it. I was protecting you.”

“I have to think about it,” I tell her, though I don’t. She’s right and I’m wrong. I was all over Quinn and would have only become more consumed and careless had he hung around.

“Want to fire your lawyer?” She pokes my arm with a pen.

“Not today. Possibly next week.”

Stanley Bottum returns to the room alone. Jesse grins, licks her lips. Yeah, she’s frightening. Even Ethan looks nervous.

“We won’t require a copy of the record,” he tells Celestine. “I think we’re done here. At this time, we withdraw our requests and agree to your terms without further litigation. Will you be pressing charges Ms. Tanner?”

“We’re considering it.” She hands him a thick binder. “Here’s our settlement offer. I’d like it signed and delivered to my office by six p.m.”

CHAPTER 53
HI HAPPILY

In the twilight, I set foot on board *Happily*. She's mine, by the decree of my father's last wishes. I shiver in the late December chill and walk to the bow.

"Hi, Happily," I whisper, and sit down at the nose of the sailboat. "Guess it's you and me now."

Along the canal, Christmas lights, strung like colorful spider webs on the neighboring docks, twinkle.

My feet dangle over the still water. I feel strong, focused, gathered down to my core. I miss my dad. He is forever with me.

One more thing. Nickety-Nick.

His phone number hasn't changed. I leave a voicemail. *Hope springs eternal.*

CHAPTER 54
SOME DOORS

One door closes, another one opens. Does life move forward according to our plan, or are we on a random outing, propelled by a bazillion gradations of choice and circumstance?

Tonight, for instance, New Year's Eve, it's my choice to open the doors of the restaurant. Friends and customers gather to say goodbye to my Bucket-o-Dad, now only in his urn, placed on a table, surrounded by pictures and flowers and cards. They wait their turn to write memories into a large leather-bound notebook. The line is tight. People huddle in spontaneous group therapy sessions filled with tears and laughter about a man who was well-loved and highly respected. A man whose goodness was quantifiable by the shimmering imprint he left on the people he met.

I walk through the crowd, offering small plates of food and lots of drinks. I try not to cry but fail miserably with every story, every hug, every utterance of how much he was adored. At midnight, raised bottles and glasses knock together in a toast to his memory.

Then it's January 1st. The restaurant empties, leaving only Jesse, Ethan, and me. I brew a pot of coffee before we all sit down at the table with Dad's urn.

"Are you ready?" Ethan holds the worn book we found in the briefcase.

"Yup," I say. "I practiced."

"You sure you're up for this?" Jesse asks.

I nod, trying to keep the mood light. "You're the one who's about to lose it, Tanner."

"Maybe. Shut up."

Ethan lights a small candle, takes my hand and clears his throat. This was the idea we both had at my parents' house. To honor my dad, both of us reading the Mourner's Kaddish; he in Hebrew and me in English.

He begins.

Yitgadal v'yitkadash sh'mei raba b'alma di-v'ra chirutei, v'yamlich malchutei b'chayeichon uvyomeichon uvchayei d'chol beit yisrael, ba'agala uvizman kariv, v'im'ru: "amen."

Y'hei sh'mei raba m'varach l'alam ul'almei almaya.

Yitbarach v'yishtabach, v'yitpa'ar v'yitromam v'yitnaseh, v'yithadar v'yit'aleh v'yit'halal sh'mei d'kud'sha, b'rich hu, l'eila min-kol-birchata v'shirata, tushb'chata v'nechemata da'amiran b'alma, v'im'ru: "amen."

Y'hei shlama raba min-sh'maya v'chayim aleinu v'al-kol-yisrael, v'im'ru: "amen."

Oseh shalom bimromav, hu ya'aseh shalom aleinu v'al kol-yisrael, v'imru: "amen."

Jesse is weeping by the end, and I'm barely holding it together. Ethan bows his head, signaling that it's my turn. I take a deep breath and my first step into Judaism. In a shaky voice, I recite a prayer for my lost father.

Magnified and sanctified be Your name, O God, throughout the world, which You have created according to Your will. May Your sovereignty be accepted in our own days, in our lives, and in the life of all the House of Israel, speedily and soon, and let us say, Amen. May Your great name be blessed for ever and ever. Exalted and honored, adored and acclaimed be Your name, O Holy One, blessed are You, whose glory transcends all praises, songs, and blessings voiced in the world, and let us say, Amen. Grant abundant peace and life to us and to all Israel, and let us say, Amen. May You who establish peace in the heavens, grant peace to us, to Israel, and to all the earth, and let us say, Amen. May God comfort you among the other mourners of Zion and Jerusalem.

Reading this makes me feel better, and I'm willing to explore this new piece of my life. I have no plan to become, as Ethan mentioned, the wife of a rabbi, but I think there's plenty of space between understanding nothing at all or enough to appreciate who I am and where my family came from. We sit with our thoughts until Jesse blows her nose. She sounds like a French horn. The sound breaks the tension, and we all crack up.

"How're you holding up?" she asks after we collect ourselves.

"Happy it's over. How about you?"

She pours sugar into her coffee. "You did great, Kiss, and I'm glad you took your dad's urn out of the bucket."

"I wasn't going to leave him in there. I just needed a moment."

"To be stubborn." She winks at me.

"I'm not stubborn," I tell her, trying not to smile. Who am I kidding?

Ethan clinks his spoon inside his cup. "Did Katy tell you about all the other papers we found?"

I slide a glass decanter of milk toward him. "Are you changing the subject?"

"A hundred percent."

"She did tell me," Jesse says. "Said there's a fine assortment of family pictures and letters."

Ethan and I exchange looks. I say, "Going to organize it, and ask the moms to decipher some of them. Think we both have a lot, well, almost everything, to learn about our past."

"The moms?" she asks.

"Ethan's and mine. And our grandmother too."

"Grandma in Montreal?"

"Yup," I say. "We want to fly up to see her at some point. Think he should meet his real grandmother."

"Wow. Big plans for you two."

"Big changes in our lives," Ethan says, then slurps the hot coffee.

My phone buzzes. I turn it over, not wanting to deal with whoever's calling this late.

"Hey Jess, what was in the mysterious folder you gave me at the courthouse? The one you wouldn't let me open?"

"Nothing important."

"Bullshit. There were documents in there."

"It was a decoy, a mind game."

"Seriously?"

"Seriously," she repeats. "Three recipes for cornbread and five pages of directions from Duff Beach to an organic egg farm in Texas."

I shake my head. "Damn, Jess, you're devious."

"If I ever need a lawyer." Ethan smiles at her. "Sucks I only saw the tail end of the takedown. Dylan's pretty damn weird. And not in a fun way."

"I tried to tell her before she married him." Jesse pulls out a cigarette.

"You did, and now I see Dr. Jonas for all the required behavioral adjustments." I reach for the cigarette. She tucks it behind her ear. "She'll award me a certificate of completion when we figure out which screw is loose."

She leans her elbows on the table. "I'm willing to shake you upside down until we find it."

"You're very kind. Think I'll keep seeing her, though, because I finally understand my imprudent decisions were mostly based on not wanting to be controlled by controlling parents who were only trying to protect me." I yawn and rub my eyes. "Which is some stupid shit, or what Dr. Jonas calls counterproductive and self-defeating behavior. I'm a good and worthy person who deserves to be around other good and worthy people."

"You've made decent progress for two months of therapy, Katy Kiss."

"Thank you, Jessica."

"For what? You needed a swift kick in the ass. I was more than happy to deliver."

"And you did. I'm grateful for everything. Which doesn't cover it. Not sure which words do, and I'm not good at mushy stuff."

"Mushy stuff." Ethan fidgets with a packet of sugar. "Acceptable only on New Year's Eve."

Jesse rolls her eyes. "So uncomfortable with all this late-night emotion."

"You guys are the bomb," I say. "The best bomb a girl could ask for."

Jesse retrieves the cigarette. "Please stop embarrassing yourself. Do you think we should have announced the long-lost son? Not that word won't get out."

"Think I was hidden more than lost," he says. "No, it would have been too much for one night."

I swirl the coffee in my cup wondering if being hidden more than lost applies to me as well. I take a sip. "I'll start telling everyone about you. Then they'll tell two friends."

"And so on," Jesse says. "How do you feel about being officially divorced?"

"Healthy and weirdly peaceful." My phone buzzes again.

Ethan points at it. "Are you going to check it?"

I shrug. "Later."

"Did you tell your mom what a phenomenal attorney I am?"

"Totally. I led with what a mind-blowing experience it was seeing you in action."

She smiles. "I have a reputation to uphold."

"You certainly do." No shit, it felt like watching porn. I'm surprised she didn't need a drink and a smoke by the time Dylan and his lawyer slithered out of the room.

"And she's cool with her newly divorced daughter?"

"Yup. She got there pretty quickly once she heard his demands."

"Then you're on to the next thing. Are you going to call Quinn?"

"Not right now, Jess."

"Really?"

"I'm feeling gun-shy. Even if he took off on your orders, I can't get that day out of my head. He was so damn cold." I grab at the cigarette again.

She holds it up against her middle finger. "Your life. Your choice. Do what you want."

"So many options. I could take a vacation."

"Why don't you fly back to Denver with me?" Ethan asks. "I have two more weeks before work starts."

"I could meet your mom. Maybe she could tell us her version of the story."

"I think she'd be up for it. She's kept all of this quiet for so long, it's time she has her say."

"And she should. So, Denver? Can you guarantee snow?"

He swipes this way and that on his cell. “Yes, I can do that.”

“Then let’s go,” I say. My phone vibrates again.

“Who keeps calling you?” Jesse grabs it and checks the screen. Her face morphs into a frown, amused and accusatory at the same time. She shows me the caller ID and whispers, “What in the fuckety-fuck?”

Some doors close, some doors open. Some have *happily* written all over them.

THE END

ACKNOWLEDGMENTS

In November 2011, I went to my first meeting of the Atlanta Writers Club, Roswell Critique Group. They welcomed me with a glass of wine (or three) and asked me to read the first five pages of my manuscript. I was terrified. I said, "tell me if this sucks, I can focus on my day job."

They said it didn't suck. But it did need work. Since then, I've been graciously schooled by the kindest, most eloquent people I've ever known. Led by my wonderful friend, and president, George Weinstein, there aren't enough ways to thank you for your wisdom, energy, support and that thing you teach us. *Make it better.*

To the members of AWC, past and present: Chris Negron, Emily Carpenter, Manda Pullen, Kim Conrey, Chuck Storla, Marty Aftewicz, Patrick Scullin, Bill Barbour, Tom Leidy, Jane Turner, Kathy Nichols, April Dilbeck, Fred Whitson, Joe Amley and Lizbeth Jones. I thank you all for the obnoxious fun we have, and the constructive criticism we all need.

The Wild Women Who Write. Team Mom - Kathy Nichols, Kim Conrey, April Dilbeck Lizbeth Jones, and Kat Fieler. What a mighty group of women. I'm honored to be one of you.

To my early beta readers: Gail Weeden, Ann Herring and Lizbeth Jones. I'm so grateful for your time, honesty and enthusiasm. Thank you for giving me the confidence to keep writing.

To Paden Herring. You made my day when you asked if you could read Happily.

To Mason Moreau. Thank you for drawing Happily back to life. She's perfect!

I want to mention Erica Armstrong. Former co-worker, incredible writer, rock star in the world of aviation. Thank you for letting me vent and for being so generous with advice and support. I am so grateful.

To my mom, Susan Lukacs Reich. Thank you for passing down the gift of imagination, and the love of reading and writing. Thank you for listening for hours (and years) while my ideas careened in and out of logical thought. You've been my support and sounding board. This story couldn't have been told without you.

To my brother, Peter. Your advice is the best I've ever gotten. "Take out words." Thank you for listening and looking out for me.

Alex and Mia. Your sweet, funny, feminist, outspoken, brilliant thoughts and ideas are a part of Katy. Her literary DNA matches ours. Thank you, my beautiful girls, for being the spark.

To my husband, Andy Anderson. You've given me support, confidence and room to write. Thank you for being one of the funniest people I've ever known, for the love, patience and all the weird things you say. Lovely words you toss out for me to catch and weave into sentences. Most importantly, thank you for being my big, strong man.

For more information about the author, please visit:
https://www.anderson-author.com/

ABOUT THE AUTHOR

G.A. Anderson is a first-generation Hungarian-Canadian. At age twelve, she became a U.S. citizen and a hybrid of the tight-knit immigrant community in Montreal, Quebec, and the American dream. She graduated from the University of Denver with a degree in Business Administration.

She's worked in commercial travel, private aviation, pharmaceutical instrumentation, and is currently a practice consultant for behavioral health providers.

She is married to one of her best friends from college, has two amazing daughters and many animals rescued from the local shelters.

NOTE FROM THE AUTHOR

Word-of-mouth is crucial for any author to succeed. If you enjoyed *South of Happily*, please leave a review online. Visit the author's website for podcasts on Hungarian word pronunciation and bonus content.

Thanks!
G.A. Anderson

Made in the USA
Thornton, CO
01/17/23 07:37:52

0c4970be-5a59-4881-b569-138828fca5feR01